EAGLE
IN THE
LAND
OF
DRAGONS

EAGLE IN THE LAND OF DRAGONS

PETER GOH

Copyright © 2012 by Peter Goh.

Library of Congress Control Number:		2012904642
ISBN:	Hardcover	978-1-4691-8288-9
	Softcover	978-1-4691-8287-2
	Ebook	978-1-4691-8289-6

All rights reserved. No part of this book may be reproduced or transmitted in any form or by any means, electronic or mechanical, including photocopying, recording, or by any information storage and retrieval system, without permission in writing from the copyright owner.

This is a work of fiction. Names, characters, places and incidents either are the product of the author's imagination or are used fictitiously, and any resemblance to any actual persons, living or dead, events, or locales is entirely coincidental.

To order additional copies of this book, contact:
Xlibris Corporation
1-800-618-969
www.Xlibris.com.au
Orders@Xlibris.com.au
501196

AUTHOR'S BIOGRAPHY

Professor Dr. Peter Goh was awarded the President Scholarship by President Benjamin Shears of Singapore in 1975. He graduated at the top of his Medical Class in 1980 at the University Of Singapore. Subsequently he became Fellow of the Royal College of Surgeons in Edinburgh and Glasgow. He studied Military History in the Army and took courses at Harvard University in Classical Greek and Roman History while he was a Surgical Fellow at Massachussetts General Hospital, Harvard Medical School in Boston. He later became Associate Professor at the National University Hospital in Singapore, Guest Professor at University of Cologne, Germany and is currently Professor of Surgery at Monash University. He was an officer in the Singapore Armed Forces Reserves till 2006 retiring with the rank of Major.

PROLOGUE

Winter 36 BC, New Year, Liqian, Gansu Province, China

    I awake energised this freezing winter morning. I know what I must do. The urge is irrepressible. I have this great motivation to tell a story. The hairs on my head and beard grow daily whiter. I write this for you, my children, because you need to know that the world is immense. In distant lands, there are unimaginable wonders—empires with elegant marble cities, naked savages with red beards, women with golden hair and milky white skin . . .
    The air is crisp and cold. Fresh snow lies like rice porridge on the ground in my courtyard and line the skeletal branches of my cherry trees. A warm fire flickers in a rectangular bronze cauldron next to my writing desk, but the chill penetrates my silk robes like needles. The windows are open, and outside I see shrouds of snow blanketing grey mountains and a clear cobalt sky. It is morning and there is not a whisper in the air.

My name is Li Bi.

    I am prefect of Zhangye prefecture and have built a summer villa in Liqian, a small town in the west of the Han Empire. This villa has been built according to my conception and has all the comforts I used to enjoy in my parents' villa long ago. It was completed only last fall, although I recently commissioned one last addition. I spend much time here when I am not attending to matters of state. I serve the Han emperor, Yuan Di. In truth, I have been in his service for many years. Most of that time was spent in the military. There were interminable petty conflicts with the Xiongnu and the Kangju. These were eventful years. In time, I rose to the rank of Senior General in the Han Army. Recently I retired and was rewarded with a small prefecture.
    Now, at last, I have found peace. I am not used to so much peace. I cannot quite believe the life I have now. My previous life had been a turbulent one filled with war, politics, and conflict. Now for once, I enjoy the life of a

country gentleman with my wife, children, and friends, enjoying the vibrant golden leaves of autumn before they fall. The days crawl along.

I have decided to write a story about a remarkable man from the west, one that should be the subject of the histories of his civilization but, alas, will never even be remembered except in my humble annals.

The story starts on the other side of the world. It is a land so far away it takes many years just to get there. At the far extreme of the world is an empire called Da Qin Guo or Luoma. In their language, the empire is called the Roman Empire. The capital city is Rome which they call the Eternal City and is regarded as the centre of the world. The people are called Romans. They are surrounded by fierce barbarian tribes in every direction at whom they make war upon constantly and conquer if they can. The Romans have the finest soldiers in the world and their generals are second to none.

It started as a small village on the banks of the River Tiber. Here lived salt traders. After 700 years, it grew to a huge empire. Perhaps it is as big an empire as the one we now live. We are in the middle kingdom. The land of the Han people also stretches far and wide from the deserts of Central Asia to the Eastern Ocean.

The hero of my story is Gaius Livius Drusus. He was an officer in the Roman legions. In this story, he will be known as Livy.

I return to the warmth of my study and feel the heat of the bronze brazier, whose burning coals bring comfort to the room. On the walls hang the calligraphy collection which I have accumulated over the years. They include lines by ancient poets and wise sayings of philosophers and military experts.

Among them are quotations from Sun Bin and Wei Liao from the Warring States Period and Jiang Ziya from the Zhou Dynasty.

My favourite is a quotation from Sun Tzu, the renowned Chinese military genius.

"Swift as the wind, silent as the forest, fierce as the fire, immovable as the mountain."

The calligraphy is especially strong and vibrant in this piece. It is done by a famous calligrapher from the capital Chang'an. It is written in the standard Han script called Li Shu.

I sat on the pink silk cushion beside my elegant low rosewood table and unrolled the pristine white silk on which I intend to write my book.

I take a deep breath of the biting air and finish the excellent Pu'er tea which my servants had prepared. Then I take up my brush, smear it with black ink from my ink slab, and begin to write.

CHAPTER 1

Belgica, Summer, 57 BC

Rainwater smashed down from the sky with a vengeance, dissolving the sodden earth into muddy slurry. It was as if the great deluge of ancient legend was beginning once again. Beyond twenty paces all one saw was a sheet of cascading water. To Decurion Lucius Cornelius, it was a blessing from the Gods. Jupiter Optimus Maximus, king of gods, offered them his watery cloak and announced his presence with rolls of thunder. His bolts illuminated the grey skies. The dozen Roman scouts had been shadowing the Belgic host for the last two days, keeping always under cover of the forest, mostly moving at night. The army had flowed over the countryside like lava from a volcano, devouring all in its path. Villages and farms were burnt and pillaged.

Timorix was a Remi. The tribe had joined the Romans in opposition to their own Belgic kinsfolk who were joined in a confederation to expel the invaders. Now he sported the blood-red tunic of the Roman Army. He scampered, splashing though puddles and slithering across the muddy slope to his commander's position. "Something big is happening," he panted.

"What now?" Lucius wiped the water dripping from the rim of his helmet and drenching his five-day stubble.

"A large contingent broke off from the main force about an hour ago. They are moving south and fast," he said loud enough to be heard over the clatter of the torrent.

"What sort of troops?" asked the seasoned veteran with a worried frown. He had campaigned with Pompey in the East and was near retirement.

"Mostly light infantry," Timorix said. "Half-naked young men with spears and swords. I saw some cavalry but not many," He took off his helmet and wiped his face with his scarf.

"They're going after Bibrax," Lucius concluded. "They hope to take it on the run. We have to give warning to Iccius right away."

"Shall we send a rider?" Timorix asked.

"I think we all best make ourselves scarce. Their patrols are thickening, and I think to get back in one piece and enjoy my retirement," Lucius grinned.

"You deserve it, sir," Timorix had been impressed by Lucius's competence over the entire mission. The old man seldom missed a beat. "Any idea where you will settle down, sir?"

"A vineyard in southern Gaul would be my preference. I know a young Gaulish wench or two there who wouldn't mind playing house with me." He grinned.

The small team mounted up and were soon swallowed by the curtain of water from the heavens.

The rain stopped abruptly. There was a strange silence, which made the scouts look around nervously. The smell of wet moss and decaying leaves was in the air, but Lucius could smell something else. It was odious and familiar. He smelt unwashed bodies.

The enemy burst out of the brushwood like demons from Tartarus. Lucius saw naked bodies painted with swirling blue patterns. They flitted around the horsemen like silent ghosts. One appeared to his left. The blow from his axe was taken on Lucius's shield, but the force of the strike nearly knocked him off his horse. Instinct took over. His three-foot long spatha, a heavy cavalry sword, came down hard, cleaving flesh and bone at the angle between neck and shoulder with a succulent crunch. Warm blood shot into the air from a severed artery. Lucius turned right in time to see a naked blond Hercules hurling towards him with a long hunting spear thrust forward.

Lucius willed himself with all his might to parry the blow with his spatha, but his arm just would not obey fast enough. Time decelerated as he watched the broad steel spear blade rip through his chain mail into his abdomen accompanied by a sickening rasping scrape. Strangely, there was no pain as he watched the blade sink in even deeper. He looked up and saw the clear blue eyes of his assailant whose pupils were dilated. There was no hatred in those eyes, only determination.

The barbarian wrenched the spear out with a squelch and a gush of blood. Lucius tasted his own salty blood as he felt himself falling. The sky and the trees swirled madly about. He could see golden beams of sunlight piercing through the leaves. He thudded to a stop, throwing mud and wet leaves into the air. Then the pain came, excruciating and burning, screaming into his consciousness.

He was aware that the battle was over. There were no more sounds of fighting. His Celtic was sparse, but he caught the meaning as his enemies conversed.

"Did we get them all?"

"I count ten, Commander Murato. I think one or two of them got away."

"Get after them. We can't let them reach Bibrax alive."

"Right away, Commander."

The rest was gibberish, and Lucius gave up listening. He started to think of his vineyard in southern Gaul. His vision was playing tricks on him. The forest was becoming a blur. He forced himself to open his eyes and take one last look at the world before he slipped away.

He looked into the face of a goddess. Her golden hair burnt like fire in the sunlight. Her eyes were the blue green of the Middle Sea. Her naked breasts were painted with spiral blue patterns. She had the face of Aphrodite.

"Goddess, are you here to escort me over the Styx?" His eyes were clouding over.

"No, I am here to send you to Elysium," she spoke in Latin with a musical voice. Her slim-bladed dagger was in one hand, ready to slit his throat. She didn't need it. Lucius had died with a strangely peaceful look on his face. She closed his eyes.

Nearby, Murato grabbed a wounded Roman by his hair and proceeded to decapitate him as if he was breaking open a cask of wine. It took three strokes to hack off the head, leaving the neck spraying blood like a fountain, staining the commander's naked torso a hellish crimson.

"What the fuck are you doing over there, Leuce? Finish him and be quick about it. We have to hunt down the bastards right now," Murato yelled. She looked back speechless, taking in his immaculate physique and formidably exposed genitals. Her mouth was open a little. He glared back. His gaze lingered a moment, sweeping over her svelte, stark naked body. Then he turned abruptly and bounded on to the decurion's brown Remi horse and galloped south. He liked the horse immediately. It was strong and responsive with a massive chest and well-muscled legs. Half a dozen naked warriors scrambled on to the Roman horses and hurried after him.

Murato's mind was a muddle of images. He imagined brutally butchering the fleeing scouts, hacking off their limbs one at a time and finally slowly drawing his sword across their exposed throats. The picture flashed to rape. He was pulling Leuce's blonde locks, tilting her head backwards as he pummelled her from the rear with his turgid phallus. The thought made his blood rise.

Iccius, the Prefect of Bibrax, was soaking in a wooden tub. The sturdy oak tub sat on the balcony of his two-story villa amidst the stone huts and thatched roofs of Bibrax. The elevation gave him a panoramic view of the surrounding countryside as Bibrax was a hill fort or *oppidum* in Celtic. Iccius had spent his youth in the Roman province of Transalpine Gaul in the south and was enamoured of Roman ways. He found bathing the most civilized cultural contribution of his new-found allies.

His neck was extended and his eyes were half closed. He was caressed by the light touch of the sun on his face and the rasping sensation of the razor scratching the stubble off his chin. Iccius had decided to discard the Gaulish habit of the moustache and beard for a clean-cut Roman look. The irritation and discomfort of facial hair was just impossible to bear. He was savouring the pleasure of two delectable pale orbs bouncing rhythmically as his topless body slave administered her razor deftly. He looked at her pleasant face through half-open lids. She had a rustic comeliness, somewhat marred by a sharp narrow nose. Her brow was knitted in concentration. By Roman custom, she should have been more fully clothed, but on a beautiful warm day like this, Iccius was content to allow her a reversion to more ancient customs. He noticed that the water was already cooling, but he decided to enjoy his bath just a little longer. The air smelt so pristine after a storm.

The sound of running feet interrupted his thoughts. "Prefect Iccius." He recognised the urgency in the guard commander's voice. "You must come at once. Riders are approaching. They look hostile."

Iccius's eyes shot open. He sprang up from his bath, splashing water about and making his body slave gasp with shock. The serpentine speed of his movements surpassed her expectations, considering his somewhat corpulent figure. She wiped him down and helped him struggle into his tunic. In a flash, he was dashing down the stairs, then away towards the walls with the guard officer.

Timorix felt acutely the arrow in his back. The pain was searing. Every step of the galloping horse heightened the agony as the arrow bounced up and down in his tissues. He broke out of the forest and saw the hill fort about a mile ahead. Half a dozen Gaesatae warriors were in scalding pursuit. Another of his men had also fought free of the ambush and was a mere three horse lengths to the rear, but his horse was exhausted and he was steadily falling behind.

Timorix could do nothing to help the man. They had been comrades for years and had fought many a good fight. He looked round and could see the utter despair in the man's face. He waved to Timorix to leave him behind. The fate of the town hung in the balance. Timorix turned around with drenched eyes and urged his horse to a final sprint. The sturdy stallion responded with a perceptible acceleration.

The lone scout turned to face his pursuers. He whipped his horse to make one last exhausted effort. The animal bounded forward towards the nearest Gaesatae. He was a young, slim man barely out of his teens. The scout parried as the warrior thrust his spear forward, then cleaved the young man across his naked back, half severing his spine. The young Gaesatae screamed in a high-pitched voice and fell backwards.

Murato didn't even slow his horse. The scout had barely time to turn to meet his attack. The first blow from Murato's long Celtic sword was parried, but the scout was so stung by the blow, he dropped his spatha. His arm was numbed by the ferocity of the blow. He turned to flee, but Murato was quicker. The stroke was so fast it was invisible. A detached head flew up in a curved trajectory, and two red fountains of blood spurted upwards from the severed carotid arteries of the decapitated body. The Gaesatae commander didn't even hesitate one moment to resume the pursuit of the remaining scout. The five horsemen were soon closing on the last fugitive.

Iccius was on the rampart of the town's northern wall. "Get the gate open," he snarled. "Fire at the pursuers," he yelled at the crew of the two ballistae positioned next to the gates. "Archers, start shooting as soon as they get in range. Take care not to hit our man." The first ballista thudded and a bolt whizzed over the horsemen. They were a mere ten horse lengths from their quarry. A second bolt whipped away, and this time one of the enemy horses tumbled. A squad of spearmen were exiting the gate on the double to receive the lone scout.

The pursuers had closed to about five horse lengths. Timorix was frantic. The next few moments would bring succour or death. A flight of arrows tore the air above his head. Horses whinnied and men screamed. The line of friendly infantry seemed to fly towards him. In an instant, he was engulfed and safe within their wall of steel and wood.

Iccius saw the remaining enemy warriors turn reluctantly and retreat out of range save one. He wore a winged helmet and was blond as the sun. He had muscles like a bull and handled his horse like a barbarian war God. He reared his horse just short of the spear tips. With his enormous sword, he beat the spears aside, then reached down and snatched one from its owner. Twirling it over his head, he aimed and threw. There was a loud crunch as spear pierced armour. The guard commander fell noiselessly skewered, the spear tip emerging a foot from his rear.

The nude barbarian howled like a wolf. It was a cry of victory. Iccius saw the rider grin at him. Perhaps he had imagined it. In an instant he was flying, his black cloak billowed, clods of earth sprayed from his horse's feet. A few arrows chased the fleeing target, falling short or passing harmlessly overhead.

Iccius ran down from the battlements. Timorix could not endure more. He felt himself slipping off his horse. Steady hands caught him as he fell. A canteen touched his lips, and he sipped the cool water. He closed his eyes a moment and opened them to see the prefect's shaven chin. He gasped and coughed violently as the drink went down his windpipe.

Iccius shook him gently. "Tell us, man. What have you seen?" Iccius's expression was fraught with dread.

"They are coming, thousands of them," Timorix answered in a rasping voice.

Iccius was ashen. He had a mere 5,000 men to defend the town, and only 1,000 were really trained soldiers. "I need numbers, Timorix." He shook the man, causing him to grimace in pain.

"At least 25,000, maybe more, forty or fifty thousand even. I lost count, and they were hidden in the rain," he said.

"How long before they get here?" Iccius said.

"Two, maybe three hours."

Iccius had heard enough. He stood up and scanned the men around, his vision defocused. Images of burning, slaughter, and rape tortured his mind. The confederation regarded them as traitors. They could expect no quarter. Every man, woman, and child would be put to the sword. The town was doomed. He had to decide quickly to run or to fight.

"Sound the alarm. Prepare to defend Bibrax. Every man, woman, and child must fight or die."

Life in Tarraco (Modern Tarragona) 76 BC

Marcus Livius Drusus was a retired senior centurion from one of Pompeii's Spanish legions. He had campaigned for years against the enemies of Rome. First there was Mithradates of Pontus and after that the rebel Sertorius in Spain. After sixteen years, the legion was demobilised and the men given land according to their rank and length of service. Marcus was fortunate to receive a sizable parcel of arable land just outside the Roman city of Tarraco in north-eastern Spain. The land was fecund and the days were mellow.

Marcus was from an agrarian family and turned his holding with military efficiency into a successful olive plantation. He was also able to buy several neighbouring plots which he used for fruit orchards, livestock, and horse breeding. In a short while, he had amassed a small fortune and could build a modest four-room homestead perched on a cliff overlooking the sea on the part of his land nearest the town. He became drinking friends with a neighbouring Celt-Iberian Chieftain named Vasco, who was frequently entertained at the Casa Livius, enjoying the luxury of many a Roman bath or sipping wine on the porch, savouring the sea breezes in the evenings. They were both somewhat addicted to playing dice.

One evening after a few too many goblets of Chian wine imported all the way from Greece, the gaming got to a critical point where the betting got somewhat out of hand. Marcus threw in his prize Iberian stallion to up the stakes, and Vasco, somewhat flushed with spirits, for want of anything better, wagered his daughter. Marcus threw an XI and Vasco, hands shaking, managed a mere IX. He smacked himself hard on the forehead in disbelief. The result was that Marcus won himself a Celt-Iberian wife whom he had never even met.

A week later, Vasco presented his sixteen-year-old daughter, Stena, to Marcus. Marcus went to the meeting with trepidation, which evaporated into admiration at first encounter. Stena was sylphlike, with long brown tresses and graceful legs. She appeared to him a veritable Artemis of the hunt. Her face was decorated with pouty lips and large hazel eyes with long lashes.

And then there was the horse, a steed fit for Alexander himself. The grey Iberian stallion stood sixteen hands. He was elegant, strongly built, and had a massive chest and white stockings. When he pranced before Vasco, the gait was energetic. The portly chieftain with his comical Celtic moustache was all smiles.

Marcus adored Stena even though her Latin was rudimentary. A month later, they were wed at a hybrid Romano-Celt-Iberian wedding, attended by a small audience representing both families and those of Marcus's comrade-in-arms who had settled in the vicinity. The feasting and drinking lasted two days. Most of the guests had to be carried home in litters.

Marcus enlarged the humble house to a modest villa hanging precariously over a cliff, overlooking the deep azure of the Mediterranean Sea. The site had a stupendous view. Below the cliff, the jagged foaming waves battered against the rocks. The house had two unique features. There was a broad balcony overhanging the cliff which allowed al fresco dinner parties in good weather. Inside there was a large pool right in the centre of the house. The rooms of the house were built round this feature, of which Marcus was exceedingly proud. The pool area was part of his private bath complex. The caldarium was the hot bath, the tepidarium was a warm room for massage and oiling, and the largest section was the frigidarium, a large pool filled with cold water. The bather went from one section to another starting from cold to hot and then back again. The whole area was surrounded by mosaics which depicted decadent scenes of nymphs and satyrs. Marcus was inordinately fond of bathing and equipped his private bath with two nubile, young Celtic bath slaves. The long, luxurious bath became his morning ritual. He woke before sunrise, and the bath lasted more than two hours. The two nymphs gave excellent service, which went beyond merely bathing their master who, though already in his fifth decade, maintained his military physique.

A year later, 75 BC, our hero Gaius Livius, later known as Livy, was born. Marcus was delighted that he had a son and celebrated with his friends, offering libations to Jupiter Optimus Maximus, Minerva, and Venus. His mother, Stena, looked after him till the age of six after which he was enrolled in school. The boy had a delicate constitution, but it was apparent early on that his mind was as sharp as the point of a *pilum*. Two years later, Stena had another child, a girl. They named her Livia. She was blonde and grew to be a pretty and effervescent child.

Gaius was interested in all things and wanted to learn about everything. His mind devoured knowledge like a wolf gobbled up sheep. The world was a truly fascinating place for him, full of wonders and magic to be scoffed up ravenously. Early in his life, his father, Marcus, fuelled his imagination. Every evening after dinner, he would plop Gaius down on his knee and transport him to wondrous places encountered in his campaigns with the legions. Some of the stories were true and others, he was now sure, he made up.

Most fascinating were the war stories about Sertorius and his clever guerrilla warriors skirmishing in the hills of Spain against Pompey's mighty legions. He especially enjoyed the detailing of tactics and strategy as each commander tried to outsmart the other. On one side was Pompey—slow, methodical, and relentless, and on the other, Sertorius, who was canny, innovative, and desperate. In the end, Rome's methodical grinding war of attrition had won the day but not before poor Sertorius was unfortunately murdered by someone from his own side.

During the day, the boy attended school with the other boys at the prefect's palace. The prefect of Tarraco had started a school run by a Greek philosopher named Aristarchus from Athens. The school was attended by the sons of the Romans settled in the area and also the children of the richer Celt-Iberians who lived in the town.

The basics were Latin, reading, writing, and arithmetic, but Aristarchus also taught a variety of other subjects to mould the minds of his young charges. He lectured on rhetoric, philosophy, and history. He highlighted military history, filling the hours with rousing stories of battles, campaigns, and the deeds of the great generals of the past. There were Greek wars like the Persian wars and the Peloponnesian wars and Roman conflicts like the Punic Wars and wars of Marius against the German tribes. He detailed the exploits of Scipio Africanus, Hannibal, Leonidas, Alcibiades, Pericles, and many others. In all of these subjects, his best student was the young Gaius Livius.

Aristarchus also taught geography and languages and made sure the children learnt Greek as well as some Celtic, which was the mother tongue of many of the boys. In the teaching of this, he had the help of a Celtic slave, Brocus.

The afternoons were spent in honing of the body. The boys trained interminably in running, jumping, gymnastics, and horse riding.

Marcus was slightly disappointed at his son's inability to excel at the basic infantry skills of sword fighting and *pilum* throwing. The infantry was the backbone of the Roman legion, and Marcus hoped for the young lad to follow in his footsteps. He tried his best to train Gaius in those skills, but despite hours of concentrated effort, the boy remained mediocre. He could barely hurl a *pilum* twenty yards and hit his target only half the time. As for sword fighting, he was slow and clumsy and many a time came home with painful bruises after matches with the local boys who were assigned to be his sparring partners.

His only redeeming quality in the physical arena was the ability to ride like a Scythian. He seemed to be born on horseback. He had a sixth sense about the animal and seemed to be able to read its thoughts. With these advantages, he could outride anyone in the class even when it came to advanced skills like jumping, negotiating slopes, and swimming rivers on horseback.

His father Marcus's interest in the equine ran deep. He bred some of the best horses in Eastern Hispania. The horses were tall, sturdy, and had great stamina with elegant lines. Gaius helped with their breaking and training and could have his pick of the best to ride. Many a memorable evening saw Marcus and Gaius exercising their mounts over the scenic hills around Tarraco bathed by the golden light of the dying sun.

In despair, Marcus decided to try him on another weapon—the bow. On the plantation was a forester named, Xeno, who was a freed man working for Marcus. He was a keen hunter from Crete and an expert in the use of the composite bow.

The composite bow was a fearsome weapon. Xeno was an expert and taught Gaius well. The bow was a composite laminate of horn and sinew. It was re-curved away from the archer. When drawn by an expert, it had a range beyond 300 yards. It was also small enough to fire comfortably from horseback. Gaius took to archery like an eagle takes to the air. He spent all his spare time practising until his fingers bled. Archery became an obsession.

One afternoon, Gaius and Xeno hid in the reeds beside a lake. Several slaves were tasked to stir the ground on one bank as the two hunters waited with arrows nocked. "Don't think over much," Xeno reminded him. "Let your instincts take control. Picture in your mind where you want the arrow to go."

One solitary frightened duck ascended into the air, its wings thrashing frantically. Both Xeno and Gaius raised their bows. The bird accelerated swiftly silhouetted against the silver clouds, its green head feathers glowing emerald in the long rays of the sun. Gaius held his breath and aimed three lengths ahead and two lengths above his prey. He released the bowstring smoothly and watched the missile streak to intercept its target. Gaius heard a thwack and saw Xeno's arrow also streak away just to the left and below his own. He smiled quietly with satisfaction as his arrow struck home, plucking the bird out of the sky. He had never managed to hit a bird in flight before. He turned and saw Xeno nod in satisfaction.

After that day, Gaius and Xeno invariably came home with meat for dinner after their hunting trips. They usually brought back rabbit or duck, but ever so often they would bag a deer or a wild boar. On those occasions, the cook would make a signature dinner, and his father would invite friends over for *cena*.

On that night, Marcus invited the philosopher Aristarchus to join them. Stena had made a sumptuous dinner, which included honey cakes, flat bread, fresh vegetables, and fruits to supplement the roast venison and duck that Gaius and Xeno had harvested in the forest.

The conversation turned to geography and what lay beyond the known world. "So who think you live beyond the lands of the Parthians?" Marcus asked. The men reclined like seals on cushioned divans while the women and children sat on stools or cushions.

"Alexander the great had already gone beyond Persia in his time, so we already know what lies there. Beyond the borders of Parthia is a wild inhospitable land, mainly deserts and mountains. The inhabitants are savage tribes. Alexander and his Macedonians had to fight them for years and still could not subdue them. In the end, he had 2,000 of his officers marry Pashtun women, and he himself had to take one as wife." There was much laughter. "Only then did the war come to an end," Aristarchus said, pausing to sip a fruity Sicilian vintage.

"I guess beyond that lies India," Marcus said. "We know something of those lands from those who chronicle Alexander's exploits like Callisthenes, Ptolemy, and Nearchus. The people have a darker complexion and ride elephants to battle. It's quite an amazing place. The weather is hot, humid, and rainy, and they have lush jungles." He popped a large piece of duck in his mouth and washed his fingers in a silver bowl.

"It seems you know a lot already," Aristarchus said admiringly.

"I read," Marcus said self-confidently. He still had a military bearing, although lately he had grown a visible belly.

"I want to know about the lands beyond that—the Land of Silk, Seres some call it," Gaius interjected excitedly. He could hardly contain himself.

"Hmm, a tall order," Aristarchus said, stroking his black, pointed beard. "No one has ever even been there, so what we know is part myth and part speculation," He gave the boy a genial smile.

"Tell it anyway." Marcus slapped his knee in amusement, always ready for another tall tale.

"They say the people have black hair and eyes and ivory-coloured skin. Their women have complexions like porcelain and are as seductive as the sirens," Aristarchus expounded. His audience were listening wide-eyed in rapt attention. He especially noticed a pretty young slave girl who seemed to be drinking in every word. He remembered her name. It was Aurora. He had often caught her hiding behind a column in the lecture room of the school, listening to the lectures and the discussions. At first he had chased her away, but she kept coming back. At last, Aristarchus gave up and just ignored her presence.

"In the east, I came across a fine product from this land. They make a shiny, smooth cloth called silk. It is highly prized in Rome. The colours are vibrant, and they come decorated with patterns and pictures of flowers, birds, and animals," Marcus added.

"Yes, it seems the products come across the deserts of Parthia and the Parthians, then sell it to us at an exorbitant mark-up," Aristarchus said. "I also hear they have amazing fighting skills. They have developed very sophisticated fighting techniques where their entire body becomes a weapon."

"By Hermes, I will set eyes some day on this wondrous land," Gaius sighed longingly. Marcus and Aristarchus both smiled indulgingly. It was a childish dream.

"I have often wondered how our legions would fare against their armies," Marcus said. "There hasn't been an army yet that can stand up to a rain of Roman *pila*."

"I wouldn't be so confident, Prefect. Roman armies have been slaughtered many times," Aristarchus pointed out.

Marcus didn't look too pleased to be reminded.

"Stop all this ramblings," Stena protested. "My wonderful *cena* is getting cold. Aurora, help our guest."

Gaius tucked into the venison. It was delectable. The meat was juicy and not overcooked. The wonderful aroma of the tarragon and rosemary smothered his senses. Aurora came up playfully and offered him a cup of wine. "Don't worry." She smiled reassuringly. "It's well watered. Your mother said you could have just one tonight."

That night, he lay down to sleep and dreamt of Seres. He saw a land shrouded in mist with peculiar-shaped mountains and buildings with upturned roofs. He imagined tall pagodas and people with dark almond-shaped eyes and fine garments made of silk.

Gaius was twelve years old at that dinner. Aurora had joined the family two years previously. She was an orphan from a fisherman's family, and her uncle had sold her as a household slave to Marcus because they could not feed her. She had been an undernourished waif at the time. Marcus and Stena had been kind to her. They treated her more as a poor niece than as a slave and gave her as a companion to Gaius, who was often lonely and unsupervised. She was his playmate, governess, and big sister all rolled in one, and she kept him company when he wasn't in school or out practicing archery or horse riding. Lately she had blossomed into a rather beautiful adolescent with lustrous brown hair, gazelle legs, and breasts the size of peaches. She was fourteen years old.

Gaius had not yet reached puberty, and they played together innocently. Many lazy afternoons were spent swimming in the sea off the beach just below the cliff where Casa Livius perched. On one such day . . .

The sun had disappeared behind rolling clouds and the sea had turned a light grey. Gaius and Aurora sat on a log in front of the little fisherman's hut where nets were stored. There was a wood fire burning and several good-sized fish were roasting on sticks over the fire, giving off a delectable aroma.

The children had been diving for oysters and had retrieved a sac full to bring home to *cena*. Both of them could swim like fishes and could dive like seals. Gaius had been darting after her in the crystal water as Aurora easily outpaced him. She was effortless and moved through the sea like a mermaid. Later Gaius got lucky with his *pilum*, and the results of his efforts were roasting deliciously.

Both children were totally bare although Gaius had a fine layer of sand over his lower body, having been just helplessly wrestled into the ground by the larger girl. Gaius leant forward to turn the sizable fish, brushing against Aurora's breast. Her nipples reacted, and the girl blushed.

Gaius looked at her intently with a curious expression. "You look different. Your breasts are as big as mother's."

"So, you noticed." She looked flustered. "Well, you haven't remained the same either. Your little worm has transformed into a grotesque snake," she countered aggressively.

Gaius reddened, then rushed at her with a growl. He only reached up to her chin but managed to knock her down. Both children splashed into the shallow surf and wrestled for domination amidst the gentle waves. The battle ended predictably with Aurora sitting on his pelvis as Gaius lay supine. She held his hands against the sand above his head, her breasts hanging just above his face.

"Do you give up?" The smile of victory was on her face. His eyes were wide. They were the most wonderful blue like the sky on a clear day. He kept them open even when a wave washed over, submerging his face.

"Fine." He looked resigned. "I give up. You always win."

"The time will come soon, young master, when you will beat me every time and I will have no choice but to bend to your will." She remembered the interview with his mother, Stena. Her place in the scheme of things had been explained delicately. Once Gaius was of age, he would have the normal needs of a man, and if he wished her to fulfil them, she had to perform as any slave.

Gaius looked at her, incredulous. "Whatever do you mean? You know something. I see it in your eyes."

Aurora saw that he was still a child and had no idea what she was talking about. He was innocent concerning matters of the flesh. One day soon he would become a handsome young man and she would give herself to him, perhaps willingly. Looking at him at that moment, it didn't seem possible. She was aware that her mind and body were ready for sex, but that boy could not yet elicit any desire in her. Aurora made a decision. She would educate him.

She took him by the hand and stroked his hair. "Come, Gaius, let's sit by the fire and talk. I have discovered mysterious and wonderful secrets, and I will share them with you," she said conspiratorially in a low voice.

Gaius smiled with pleasure and followed her willingly. He was always eager to learn.

Aurora sat down on the sand. "Have you ever wondered what takes place behind the curtains when your father takes his long bath every morning?"

Gaius looked back blankly. "I am usually escorted by slaves to school at dawn. You peeked, didn't you? What have you seen? Tell me," he demanded.

Finally Aurora laughed. "Let me turn the fish again before they burn." One side was already brown and crackling invitingly. Aurora gave Gaius a mischievous grin, then, kissed him very deliberately on his lips. Gaius instinctively moved one hand to caress her succulent breast. There was no protest. From that moment, Gaius's education took a carnal turn. The fish were forgotten.

When Gaius was sixteen years, an army recruitment team came into town, and the Prefect invited fit boys of sixteen and seventeen years to enlist in the legions. The enlistment was to last sixteen years. At the end of that time, if the soldier survived he would receive Roman citizenship and land.

Gaius couldn't wait to enlist. The army was his ticket to travel to the lands of his imagination. He had completed his schooling under Aristarchus and had become an accomplished scholar. Now he wanted to join the legions to win military fame and see the world. Little did he know that those travels would take him to terra incognita? He would literally reach the ends of the earth.

The first three months of training were conducted in Tarraco. It consisted of interminable drilling and practice with weapons. The main weapons were the *pilum* and the *gladius*. The *pilum* was a six-foot long javelin with a two-foot long soft steel shank and a wicked pyramidal steel tip. Soldiers also carried a *gladius* which was a short sword made of finely honed Hispanic steel. It had a two-foot long tapered blade and was razor sharp. The new recruits were also made familiar with another important job—digging. They also learnt to cut wood to build palisades and set up defences. The training lasted sixteen hours a day, and the recruits were as drained as galley slaves at the end of each day. The centurions kept up the pace relentlessly and beat anyone who was slow or inept. They constantly carried their vine sticks around and meted out punishment liberally. Gaius who was not as physically fit as most of the rest received his share of blows. He pushed himself hard, and his muscles strengthened rapidly.

In the weekends, the new recruits were allowed home leave for a day. Gaius would come home and just collapse. His mother would see that his tunics were washed and that he was fed. Aurora would always bathe and massage him, soothing away his aches and pains. The two became even closer and confided in each other about all things.

"What great adventures marked your week?" Aurora asked playfully as they soaked in the searing Caldarium.

"We went on a long march with full gear. I walked or ran for the whole day with only a short break for lunch. In the end, we covered twenty-five miles. Every muscle in my body feels like it has been run over by a cart," Gaius groaned.

Aurora turned him around and caressed him sensuously, running her finger lightly over his now sculpted chest and abdomen. "I know how to make everything better." She smiled at him coyly.

Three weeks later, the small contingent from Tarraco graduated from their basic training. They made up about half a cohort—250 men. Fifty of the new soldiers were Roman. The rest were Celtic, Iberian, or Celt-Iberian. They were all Roman legionaries now. They swore allegiance to SPQR—the Senate and People of Rome.

Marcus attended the passing out parade. The prefect had given him an honoured place among the town notaries. The small contingent executed their drill flawlessly, moving fluidly from close formation to open, forming a defensive square, then a circle, and finally going into testudo (tortoise) formation. He was proud to see Gaius lead one of the columns in the march past. The boys looked like legionaries now in chain mail and blood-red tunics. They also wore red cloaks and bronze helmets with red feathers and plumes. Among the spectators were a horde of young women waving enthusiastically from the viewing stands and throwing rose petals as the men paraded smartly through the streets. There were wives, sisters, and girlfriends come to cheer their men. Livy saw Aurora cheering enthusiastically with Stena and Livia craning their necks to catch a view.

That night the governor hosted a large party. The men brought their women. The food was sumptuous and the wine flowed freely. Gaius brought Aurora, who was dressed in a short white tunic of linen, lined with gold. The tunic was off shoulder and had a slit on one side up to her waist. Stena had loaned her some of her best golden necklaces, ear rings, and bracelets. She turned many a head.

That night, the young couple made love urgently and intensely after which they lay naked in each other's arms. "When do you leave?" Aurora, asked running her fingers sensuously across his back. They were alone in the dark deserted *triclinium*, reclining comfortably on one of the soft divans.

"Next week, we march north to Gaul to join Caesar's army," Gaius said, shuddering at the sensation of her touch.

"I guess you won't be back any time soon," Aurora said sadly. "What will happen to me? Will I just become another of your father's bath slave or am I to be sold?" Aurora asked.

"My parents won't do that to you. They are fond of you. They have treated you like one of their own children."

"I am no longer a child. Gaius, I'm nineteen years old," she said.

"I will ask father to free you. You need no longer be a slave," Gaius said.

"What will I do even if I am free?" She said.

"Maybe they can find someone for you to marry," Gaius said. He suddenly realised how cold that sounded. She was lost for words. He realised that they were now more than childhood friends. Aurora had feelings for him. Unfortunately, Gaius was not prepared to return those feelings. He was about to embark on life's adventure.

"I didn't mean that," Gaius retracted. He didn't know how to put it. "As you know, soldiers are not allowed to marry till they have finished their term. Let me work out something with my parents," he said as reassuringly as he could although his heart felt like lead.

The next day, after some consultation, Marcus and Stena drafted a document of manumission for Aurora. She was now no longer a slave. They also found her work as an assistant to Aristarchus in the school. Gaius felt comforted by that development, and Aurora braced herself to endure her loss. She would miss him as flowers miss the spring rain.

A week later, Marcus called him to his study the day before his unit was due to march north. That was the room where Marcus used to receive his clients and to do his accounts. The walls were lined with shelves containing scrolls and tablets. Gaius was dressed in full uniform and looked like a young Achilles.

"Gaius, it was always my hope that you would follow my footsteps into the legions, but now that you are leaving, I suddenly feel pangs of anxiety. I will miss you, Son." Marcus began looking suddenly older and wearier.

"I shall miss you also, Father, and I promise not to take any unnecessary risk," Livy reassured him.

"I wish I could believe you. Young men will risk all for honour and glory. I did myself." Marcus smiled sadly.

Gaius just gave him a silent hug.

"I have some parting gifts for you to help you return alive and to ease your way." He went to his large polished desk. "First of all, this." He took up a shiny set of silvery grey chain mail. "I had it specially made. The rings are made of the finest steel. It is twice as strong but only half the weight. It will cling to your body and wear as comfortably as an overcoat. Even an arrow at close range will not penetrate it."

Gaius examined it. It was remarkably light and flexible. He beamed with pleasure.

"Next, I want you to take this sword. Pompey Magnus himself gave it to me on my retirement. It is not a decorative sword. There are no jewels or precious metals, but the blade is special. It is made of the finest Spanish steel. It will cut through chain mail or scale armour like butter."

Gaius took it and tried a few practice swings. It too was light and handled beautifully. He took off his standard issue *gladius* and buckled on his father's sword and scabbard. He was well pleased to have it.

"Finally, Xeno and I scoured all of Hispania to get you this bow. It is made by a master craftsman. Made in the Eastern fashion with lamina of horn and sinew, it will propel an arrow beyond 300 yards in expert hands. I know you will make good use of this. This doesn't mean, of course, that you should rest easy on your practice with the *pilum*." Marcus smiled.

"Thank you, Father, for these fabulous presents. I don't know how I will ever repay you." Livy was touched to his core.

"There is no need. Just come back alive and perhaps with a centurion's transverse crest on your head," Marcus said.

"I will try my very best, Father," Gaius promised.

"The last gift will be from your mother," Marcus said as Stena and Livia came in.

"My son, you look like Mars himself." Stena beamed. She hugged and kissed him, and Livia did the same. Stena offered him a cloth pouch.

Gaius opened it and found twenty gold Aurei and some fifty more silver Denari. It was a lot of money. "You will need some money. A soldier always does," Stena said.

"Thank you, Mother. This is certainly a useful and generous gift." He had never seen so much money in his life.

"I will not tell you to come home with your shield or on it," Stena said. "For me, it is sufficient that you come home alive. I will pray to my goddesses the *Duillae* every day for you." She had tears in her eyes.

"Oh, Gaius, take care of yourself, and don't be a hero," Livia said.

He kissed his sister fondly. She was nine years old now and becoming pretty.

"Don't worry, my little sister. I want to see you grow into a beautiful young lady with big breast and long legs," He teased.

That night, there was a farewell dinner. It was a warm evening, and the family reclined on their torch-lit balcony served by all the family slaves. Gaius would always remember the delicious roast goose with its crackling crisp skin, which was the highlight of the dinner. It was stuffed with apples and chestnuts. The cook had truly exceeded himself. Aurora sat next to him and hung on to his arm most of the night. She was reluctant to let him go. She looked stunning in a new Greek chiton of very fine and delicate material, which accentuated her fully blossomed figure. Gaius noticed the absence of the iron armband which marked her as a slave. It was replaced by a silver bracelet.

Xeno and Aristarchus were guests and so was the prefect. They talked of the coming war. "Julius Caesar has just finished his term of office as Consul in Rome and has been given Gaul and Illyria as his provinces to govern for five years," the prefect remarked.

"I know the man," Marcus said. "He has lofty aspirations. He will not be satisfied till all of the three parts of Gaul bow to his will. Once again there will be war on a grand scale, and the Roman Army has its work cut out."

"In the name of the Senate and people of Rome will he embark on conquest, but I fear Caesar pursues his own purpose in the matter," the prefect said coldly.

That night, Aurora and Gaius slept together for the last time.

"Don't you think it improper now that you are no longer my slave?" Gaius teased.

"Be silent and make love to me"

They went at it with a vengeance. There is no better aphrodisiac than knowing that there may not be a tomorrow. He left silently before dawn as she slept. She lay deliciously nude, and he imprinted the memory of her thus. There would be no tearful parting.

Gaius joined his father for a bath, an experience neither had ever enjoyed together. Gaius had the chance, at last, to discover the secret pleasures daily indulged by his father with the help of his two Celtic nymphs. Aurora's account was not fabrication.

Two hours later, he was trudging with sixty pounds of gear on his back with 250 other sweaty men heading north for Gaul.

CHAPTER 2

Gallo Belgica, 57 BC

Gaius Livius was now an acting centurion in the Roman Army. He had been promoted after Caesar's campaigns in 56 BC, first against the Helvetians and then the Germans under Ariovistus. As he was somewhat underage for the appointment, he had to be satisfied to be an acting centurion. The promotion came of necessity rather than as reward for valour. His century had lost every officer in battle, and Gaius was the only member who was literate. Nevertheless, he enjoyed the privileges of an officer and had the chance to command and prove himself.

The Romans never enjoyed superiority in cavalry. They had heavy infantry second to none and formidable artillery but their weakness in cavalry put them at a disadvantage in many campaigns. They invariably relied on allied cavalry which were of variable quality.

Proconsul Gaius Julius Caesar who commanded the Roman Army in Gaul decided to start a unit of horse-mounted archers. He had the idea after reading historical accounts of Scythians and Amazons and tales of these units among the Parthians and Armenians from his colleague Gnaeus Pompeius Magnus in Rome.

Such troops were indispensable for reconnaissance and skirmishing, and he decided to train an experimental unit of 100 men in this role. They were special forces, and for want of a better term, he called them "raiders."

The main limiting factor was to find Romans who could both ride and shoot from a bow. After scouring the whole army, he found a young lad from Tarraco, an acting centurion named Gaius Livius. Those who knew him called him Livy.

Caesar summoned him one winter evening. Livy had never met the proconsul personally. He stood awkwardly as Caesar peered at him down his aquiline nose. "They say you ride like a centaur and wield a bow like the legendary Paris of Troy," Caesar began.

"I fear my reputation exceeds me," Livy said. He looked up confidently at his supreme commander.

"The boy has a presence," Caesar thought to himself. "He looks forthright and trustworthy and is not afraid to look me in the eye."

"I have scoured my whole army only to find one of you who has the combination of skills I require. I need a hundred of you. How do you think we should proceed, young man?" Caesar enquired.

"I would look for riders to train on the bow and bowmen to train as riders, Lord Caesar."

"You are astute for one so young. I will chance my confidence in you." He put his stamp on the wax tablet and handed it to Livy. "Here is my commission. With this, you may recruit your men from any unit in my army. How long before my *equites sagitarii* are ready for battle?"

"It will require at least three months to attain respectable competence, Sire," Livy said.

"You will be ready by spring. I will have need of them when the first leaves appear."

After three months of intensive and gruelling training, the special unit made enough progress to be declared operational and was ready to embark on Caesar's campaign of 57 BC, which was the conquest of Gallo Belgica (Belgium). Livy was in command as temporary auxiliary commander. Although the raiders were an army asset, Caesar had attached it for logistic purposes under the Seventh Legion commanded by Publius Licinius Crassus.

It was early summer in 57 BC when Caesar marched his army north of the River Axona (Aisne) and encamped in Remi territory just west of a town called Bibrax. Publius Crassus who was son of the triumvir Marcus Licinius Crassus was a tribune in Caesar's army and had been made acting legate of the Seventh Legion. He was twenty-nine years old. His father was the richest man in Rome and in his younger days was responsible for crushing the terrifying slave revolt led by Spartacus. That day he was suddenly summoned to army headquarters by a messenger from Caesar. He did not know the reason, but he responded with alacrity and came as quickly as he could.

The sun was sinking sullenly into the hills in the west. The horses picked their way unhappily over the sticky muck left after the deluge. Crassus took the broad Via Principalis, which was the road leading to Caesar's command tent. The Roman tents were arrayed in symmetrical military precision. His cavalry escort was left at the gate, and he proceeded with just one centurion and the acting auxiliary cavalry commander, Gaius Livius Drusus, whom he had recently taken on as a personal runner because the lad could ride well and also had a unique skill with the composite bow, which made him a good personal bodyguard.

Caesar's camp was a hive of activity. The legions had arrived at the site some hours ago, and the men were bustling like an army of ants building a wooden palisade, digging defensive trenches and setting up tents. The Roman legionaries after years of perpetual drill at building camps went about their task with quiet, methodical efficiency. The camps were always built in exactly the same layout, and every legionary knew his assigned task by heart.

Crassus's party stopped outside the command tent. It was crimson coloured with silver fixtures and trimmings. The two towering German bodyguards outside the tent looked as ferocious as Cerberus, the guardian to Hades. Happily, they recognized him, saluted and benignly showed the three men inside. In the centre of the tent was a large sturdy wooden campaign table with a map spread on it, made of brown papyrus. Little lead figures dotted the map, representing the position of various units. Red figures were Roman and green were Gaul. Black figures represented the Belgae. There was a sizable cluster of black counters not so far from the Roman camp and another smaller group around the nearby town of Bibrax. The interior of the tent was adorned by a few elegantly crafted chairs and a large camp bed with clean white sheets. A few wooden chests lined one corner and a copper basin of water stood on a metal stand. Bronze braziers provided light and heat.

There were several legates and other senior officers huddled around the map, and the men were speaking in quiet tones. Livy recognized Titus Atius Labienus, Quintus Pedius, Lucius Aurunculieus Cotta, Quintus Titurius Sabinus, and Servius Galba. In the centre was Gaius Julius Caesar, Proconsul.

"Publius, you've come at the right moment." Caesar looked up, his brows knitted together. He gestured the new men to gather around the table. The legates were all in full armour, but Caesar wore only his red military tunic. There were beads of perspiration over his balding scalp.

Crassus and his party gave the military salute and took their places smartly.

Publius Crassus's father was a friend and a strong ally of Caesar in the Senate. He had sponsored Caesar's campaign for Roman Consul, which succeeded. Caesar was Consul in 59 BC and was then given Illyria, Cis Alpine Gaul, and later Transalpine Gaul to govern for five years.

"Danger looms, yet opportunity knocks. A huge Belgic confederation has gathered. They number at least 300,000 men at arms. The main army is perhaps two days' march from us, but they have sent a large force against Bibrax, eight miles east of us. They assault the town as we speak. Moments ago, a messenger came from Iccius, our prefect there imploring our assistance," Caesar began.

"How many do they face?" Publius asked, looking anxious. He was but a junior tribune, but Caesar had made him an acting legate after he saved the day during the last big battle against the Germans under Ariovistus.

"The estimate is about 30,000. I need you to fly swift as the wind to their aid," Caesar said. "We cannot allow Bibrax to fall. The town will be massacred, and this will crush the spirit of our Remi allies. We require them for the coming campaign."

"I will bring my legion to their aid at once, Lord Caesar," Crassus replied.

"Unfortunately, you do not have that luxury. I need all my legions here to meet the main enemy force. You may take two cohorts," Caesar said.

"A thousand men against 30,000, it's a suicide mission!" Livy thought to himself. The expression on Crassus's face was that of disbelief.

Livy had visions of the Spartans at Thermopylae facing the Persian host.

"Don't look so shocked, Publius. You will be surprised by what you can do with two cohorts and a bit of ingenuity," Caesar rebuked him with a smile.

"So this was to be a test," Crassus thought to himself.

"In that case, I will do my best, Lord Caesar," Crassus responded and saluted.

"Labienus, please see what auxiliary troops we can spare. Have them report to acting Legatus Crassus within the hour."

"I'll see to that at once." Labienus bowed.

Battle of Bibrax

The relief force was hastily scratched together.

The Roman force was a mere 3,500 strong—1,000 Cretan archers, two cohorts or Roman heavy infantry of about 900 men total, 500 Balearic slingers, 500 Numidian light infantry, and 500 assorted cavalry. The cavalry comprised 200 Roman cavalry and 300 Remi. The last 100 men were the special force of horse archers fondly known now as Livy's raiders.

Crassus galloped up to Livy and his men with his staff officers in tow. His bronze muscled cuirass gleamed in the dimming sunlight and the wind rustled his crimson plume. "Ave, Gaius." He rode a beautiful grey charger, and his handsome, young face was composed and confident.

"Ave, Commander Crassus." Livy saluted, right hand outstretched, then fist to left shoulder. Crassus examined the young clean-shaven officer. He was only a little above the average height for a legionary. He wore the uniform of a simple cavalryman. His helmet had no plumes and the metal was not polished. Crassus noticed that the young man's chain mail however was not ordinary. He was astride his black charger, Nero. His father had sent it from Spain when he heard that Gaius was now in the cavalry.

"There's not a moment to lose. I put you in charge of all the cavalry. Bring them to Bibrax forthwith and distract the enemy by whatever means from taking the *oppidum* till I can bring up the infantry. Most importantly, distract and draw off their cavalry. Our little force will suffer much if their cavalry catches us in the open," Crassus said.

Livy was as excited as a young eagle spotting its first prey. That was an independent command, which was a rare privilege for someone his age and with his lack of experience. "I'll cut through the forest. It takes somewhat longer, but we may arrive undetected. I am sure they are watching the main road. Nevertheless, we shall be there in just over an hour," he assured the commander.

"I will take the infantry around the town and come in from the east hopefully also to take them by surprise. Once you arrive, send me a rider with the enemy disposition. I want to come in behind their main force so our missile troops can do the most damage," Crassus said.

"Vale Commander, I will see you in Bibrax. A rider will be dispatched to update you on the position before you arrive. By Jupiter, we will give them a nasty surprise before the sunrise."

Publius was a little worried by his over enthusiasm. Should he have chosen a more experienced commander? He decided to let the lad prove himself this day or die trying.

"Move up on them as silent as the forest," Crassus advised. "Let surprise be your ally."

Livy saluted. "For the honour of Rome," he said.

"For Rome," Crassus replied.

Livy met with his sub-commanders at a clearing behind Caesar's camp. The 500-strong cavalry force was commanded by a decurion named Decius. He was an older man of about forty years and a veteran. "So who commands this brave venture?" he asked.

"For the moment, I have command," Livy said. "By order of Acting Legate Crassus."

There was a moment of incredulous silence. Decius raised his right hand in salute and brought his fist to his chest. The movement was slow and deliberate. "We are at your service, Commander." The tone was resigned.

Livius appointed Paulus to lead the small party of ten advance scouts drawn from his raiders. Paulus was transferred from a unit of Roman light cavalry just after the German campaign. He was in his late twenties and hailed from Northern Italy. He was of a somewhat tanned complexion and kept his black hair long to his shoulders. Paulus was an excellent horseman and valuable in a melee as he had formidable skill with his *spatha*.

"Ride ahead at least two miles and make sure we don't bump into anything nasty in the dark. Look out for their cavalry. Stop when you get to the ridge above Bibrax and check out the position of the enemy. Try to locate their main cavalry force. Don't use the main road because they will be looking out for a relief force. If you run into any hostiles, just disengage and report back here. I don't want you to get into a skirmish, understand? Your mission is merely to scout," Livy ordered. His felt his left calf muscles twitch involuntarily from nervousness.

Paulus saluted. "I understand, Centurion." He turned his chestnut Remi steed around and trotted off followed by his ten raiders. Livy noted with satisfaction that each was well supplied with two full quivers of at least thirty shafts each.

Livius turned to Decurion Decius. "Keep your squadron behind my raiders. If we contact the enemy, we will first shower them with arrows while you form up into battle line. As the enemy advance, my raiders will stream to left and right and you will charge down the centre at full gallop and engage. My men will then fall on their flanks."

Decius saluted, thumping his chest. It seemed like a reasonable plan provided the enemy didn't outnumber them by too many. Decius gave the signal, and the whole squadron moved out two abreast. The forest undergrowth was sparse and the hoof beats were muted by mud and fallen leaves.

Livy prayed to Minerva. "Please let us get to Bibrax in time." He could picture in his mind the terrible massacre that would ensue if they were too late.

An hour later, sounds of metal clashing and men screaming and dying filtered through the forest. The raiders dismounted and crept forward expectantly.

A lone raider broke cover and dashed frantically towards them. He was startled as he became aware of a dozen nocked arrows aimed at him. His red tunic identified him as friendly. He looked around, found Livy, and quickly rode up to him. "We were spotted, and Paulus is riding this way with about fifty enemy cavalry behind him."

Livy gave the hand signal to mount and form a double skirmish line. The raiders assumed formation with practiced efficiency, bows at the ready. Almost at once, they heard the sound of hoof beats approaching rapidly in the gloom.

"Pick your targets. Don't hit our own men," one of the decurions called out.

"Fire at my signal," Livy ordered.

Paulus and his men were in full flight, not bothering to engage the enemy with their bows. In an instant, they noticed the line of archers and rode for the gaps. At the same instant, Livy brought down his *spatha* in the direction of the enemy. The thwack of bows and the sound of zipping arrows broke the silence of the forest. Livy drew his bow, aimed, and exhaled partially. He remembered to let his senses take control and released his first shaft. He willed the arrow to its target, and it struck an enemy rider squarely in the chest. The first volley decimated the front ranks of the enemy line. Men screamed and horses tumbled shrieking. Leather and cheap mail armour were punctured with impunity by the high-velocity bolts.

The next volley sent more horses and men crashing to the ground. Then Decius screamed, "Charge!" The heavy cavalry surged forward like hounds from Hades. There were more enemy cavalry than anticipated, maybe about a hundred in total, but they were outnumbered and bewildered. The Roman cavalry swept into their ranks and cut them to pieces. All around were shouts and screams, the clashing of metal, the crunch of spear or sword entering bodies. The raiders galloped after the survivors and decimated them like fleeing chickens.

The skirmish ended abruptly. Livy could hear the cavalrymen calling with anxious disembodied voices to each other in the darkness. Decius's voice was calm as he conducted a role call. Moments later, he cantered up beside Livy. There was blood spattered on his helmet and chain mail, but he wore a satisfied grin.

Decius reported, "About eighty-five Belgic cavalry down with only two of our cavalry wounded. There were no fatalities. Two of Paulus's men are missing. The rest of the raiders are unhurt and accounted for." He took off his helmet and wiped the sweat from his brow.

Livy felt a wave of relief but tried hard not to show it. He kept a cold front. He put on the face of command. The battle was far from over and danger lurked behind every tree. "Very well, Decurion, gather your men and move them forward. Bibrax waits."

There were screams as the Remi went about finishing off the wounded enemy. Livy came across a wounded Belgic cavalryman lying propped up against a tree. His wounds were mortal as he had been run through with a spear. It would have been kinder to put him out of his misery. Livy dismounted and stepped over to him, *spatha* raised. He looked down at the enemy and recognized that he was a boy barely in his mid-teens. The boy was crying and softly mumbling to himself. Livy hesitated. His resolve melted away. In a flash, Paulus stepped up, grabbed the boy by his hair to expose the throat, and slit it with a long dagger. There was a spray of blood. The boy gurgled, rolled up his eyes, and became flaccid.

"Sorry, Commander, missed that one." Paulus smiled and saluted. "Don't trouble yourself, sir. We'll take care of the dirty work. You have more important things to do." Paulus deftly looted a golden torque from the boy's neck and two wrist guards, then, stalked off to finish off the rest of the wounded enemy.

Livy felt deflated. He had flinched and Paulus had witnessed it. The dead boy's eyes were wide open, staring into space with dilated pupils. Livy bent down and closed them reverently. He felt a dull ache inside.

Livy deployed the cavalry just behind the ridge overlooking the town of Bibrax. He then followed Paulus on foot up to the crest with two of his raiders as escorts. The action around the town was illuminated by the brightly lit torches on the embattled walls. Iccius had mobilised the entire citizenry of the town in its defence. There were women among the defenders on the battlements casting stones and pouring hot coals on the assaulting foe. Livy sent off one of the cavalryman with a report to Crassus on the disposition of the enemy.

The town was surrounded on all sides, but the main activity was in the south and east where the major Belgic activity seemed to be concentrated. Battering rams made of massive logs were pounding the gates, and the enemy warriors were throwing stones and javelins at the defenders atop the wood and stone palisade which surrounded the town. The defenders were having an impossible time repelling the tribesmen from the walls, which were being steadily torn apart with axes and bare hands. Nevertheless, they resolutely returned fire with javelins, arrows, and slings and dropped rocks and hot coals on the attackers. At a few points on the wall, the attackers were already atop the walls and slugging it out hand to hand with the defenders, who were on the verge of being overwhelmed.

The attack seemed to be most perilous on the south wall and the east. The other sides seemed to be still holding. Livy remembered that Crassus was coming in from the east, which was the most unexpected direction. The south wall wasn't going to hold for much longer, and Livy quickly decided to hit the enemy at that point.

He told Paulus, "Take the raiders behind the horde below the south wall and shoot at all the attackers trying to climb the wall as well as any warriors wielding a ram or trying to undermine the wall. Pick your targets well. Tell Decius to form a battle line just behind the crest of the ridge and charge over the ridge and down the other side at my command. I want his attack to be as fierce as a raging fire."

"Yes, Centurion." Paulus saluted and ran down the slope to get his horse and round up his men.

Livy followed a few seconds later and retrieved his Black Spanish Charger. He rode over to the trumpeter and told him to follow. "Blow the charge at my signal."

The trumpeter nodded and saluted.

The line of raiders descended from the ridge in battle line unnoticed by the enemy whose attention was focused on taking down the wall or scaling it.

The first shafts zipped with deadly intent into the night. The volley swept the top of the palisade taking down any Belgae who had managed to get to the top. Surprised warriors sprouted deadly shafts out of unprotected backs and fell screaming, splattering their comrades packed under the walls. The next volley was concentrated on the battering ram crews and the sappers trying to undermine the wall. The Belgae were now cognizant that they were being fired at from the rear. There was a roar of rage, and the rear ranks then broke off to charge towards the line of horsemen.

The thin line of mounted archers was now facing several thousand screaming, infuriated Belgic warriors. Livy could see the fear in the faces of his men. The thought of coming face to face with a berserk horde of barbarians churned his stomach. "Keep firing and withdraw slowly," he commanded as calmly as possible, his pulse racing uncontrollably. His men kept their nerve and kept up the fire, taking down scores of the enemy and thinning their ranks.

"Blow the charge," he yelled frantically at the trumpeter. Simultaneously he whirled his sword in the air, the signal for the raiders to move back and split to left and right. Decius and his cavalry came thundering out of the darkness like spectres from Tartarus down the slope, lances levelled. They swept past the raiders and into the charging horde. For a moment, time stood still, then, men and horses collided with a crash like rolling thunder. Bodies flew into the air.

The first ranks were impaled by the lances, and then the cavalrymen drew their heavy *spathas* and started chopping left and right. Heads and limbs were severed, and blood flowed freely.

Livy and his men attacked the flanks, pouring arrows into the mass of seething warriors. The Belgic tribesmen were packed so close together it was hard to miss. Wounded men lay everywhere with arrows protruding from every part of the body. The cavalry charge had lost its impetus, however, and the individual cavalrymen were being surrounded, dragged screaming off their horses, and hacked to death one by one. They were hopelessly outnumbered. The Belgae exacted their revenge with fearsome brutality, stabbing, hacking, and chopping the doomed cavalrymen to shreds.

Livy's arms ached from drawing the bow. "Blow the retreat," he yelled. Crisp trumpet notes pierced the night. The remaining horsemen disengaged and galloped for the ridge. Livy scanned them as they hurried by. At least a third of them were down, most of them the less armoured Remi horsemen.

A fluttering noise to one side signalled danger. Two burly, half-naked warriors burst out of the darkness. A moment of terror gripped Livy as he realised he was alone. Instinct took over as he instantly fired an arrow at point-blank range, impaling one assailant in the eye. The second man thrust at his head with a spear, the blow glancing off the cheek piece of his helmet with a loud clang. Livy felt his whole head explode. For a moment, all the stars in the universe seemed to whirl before his eyes. He fought to stay on Nero, but the horse had swirled to face the spearman, rearing itself up on hind legs. The warrior hesitated, and Livy took the moment to escape, clinging desperately to Nero.

Safe with his men, Livy and his raiders formed a thin skirmish line and covered their retreat with ragged volleys of arrows. His close encounter with death confirmed his dread of close-quarter combat. It was fearfully unpredictable. It also taught him another lesson. To be caught alone in a battlefield was one way to end up quickly dead.

The enraged Belgic warriors pursued, but on foot, they were soon exhausted and returned to regroup. Livy was glad there were no enemy cavalry present. His head still pulsated, and a trickle of blood had seeped from his helmet to draw patterns on one side of his face.

The raiders and cavalry regrouped behind the ridge. Livy remained at the crest with a few raiders who were picking off the enemy who dared pursue. Most of the Belgic horde had returned to the wall to regroup and renew their effort to take the wall. The defenders having been given a brief respite were now raining a torrent of missiles down on them. They had regained the initiative, and the Belgae would have to start all over again. At least the south wall was safe for a while.

At midnight, a messenger arrived from Crassus. The main force had arrived at the east wall and was preparing to engage the enemy. Livy was to take his force to the east side of the town and await instructions.

Crassus had moved his infantry behind the enemy force which were assaulting the east wall. They crept in silence and were yet undetected. The men were arrayed in three lines. The front line comprised the Balearic slingers uniformed in green tunics with leather headbands. The infantry, Roman and Numidian, formed the second line, and the Cretan archers in their broad-brimmed hats formed the third. The slingers and the archers commenced a barrage of missiles whilst the heavy infantry crouched down, hiding behind the slingers.

The mass of bare-breasted, fair-skinned warriors under the east wall was suddenly hit from behind by a shower of arrows and stones. The stones crunched bones and split skulls as they thudded home. Hundreds went down as the volleys came in rapid succession. The commander of the Belgae at the east wall ordered his men to turn around and charge the slingers.

The slingers gave one more volley then turned and ran. The Belgae roared after them like a herd of stampeding bulls only to face a solid line of legionaries who released a storm of *pila* at them at close range. The dark-skinned Numidians in white tunics with bronze helmets threw another volley in short order. The front ranks of the Belgae were mowed down. Those whose shields protected them from the *pila* found the shields suddenly useless as the *pila* could not be extricated. That left them exposed to arrows and slingshots which rained death on their unprotected bodies and faces.

The heavily armoured roman infantry formed a shield wall which was as immovable as a mountain.

The Belgae broke against them like a wave breaking against a rock-strewn shoreline. The charge ground to an abrupt halt as the shrieking half-naked warriors fell to deadly thrusts from hundreds of razor-sharp Roman swords.

That was too much to endure, and the Belgic host broke and started to retreat in disorder. A horn was heard blasting three times. The Belgic commander had called for a general withdrawal. The whole army disengaged and started to withdraw towards the north and west like a swarm of ants.

The legionaries started to give chase, but Crassus called them back, not wanting to lose contact with his men in the night.

Livy was watching from the flank as the Belgae began retreating. No order had come from Crassus to pursue. He noticed that the retreat was far from a rout and that the barbarians were withdrawing in good order. Ordering a charge then would no doubt be met with considerable resistance and multiply his casualties. He called the raiders together.

"Let's hurry them along with some archery! Stay out of javelin range. The rest of the cavalry follow about 200 yards behind and cover us if we have to retreat."

The raiders trotted down the slope towards the rearguard of the retreating army. At about 200 yards, they started to pepper the rearguard with arrow fire. The rearguard turned and formed a shield wall. A few ran forward throwing javelins, but the riders were out of range and the missiles fell short. The arrows were slowly taking a toll, and dozens of warriors were wounded, forcing their comrades to carry them. The pace of the retreat quickened as the Belgae hurried to get away from the tormenting rain of steel.

In a short while, the raiders had run out of arrows, and Livy called off the pursuit. Just at that moment, a messenger rode up. "Message from the commander, you and your men are to withdraw into Bibrax *oppidum* immediately. You are not to engage the enemy further."

"You heard the man. Regroup and head back to the fort," Livy breathed deeply with relief. "I guess we won this round, and we are done for the night. Don't let down your guard. There may be bands of straggler around. Keep sharp." There was new authority in his voice.

The whole troop reacted with alacrity, getting into two abreast formation and started heading back to the *oppidum* at a brisk walk. The eastern sky was showing a faint yellow glow above the hills. Livy felt the exhaustion wash through him as his excitement abated and his heartbeat slowed. The other men also rode silently, too stunned even to talk. Livy saw a new look of respect on their faces. His raiders were now baptised.

As they approached the fort, two men stumbled on foot out of the bushes towards them. Livy recognised them as the two missing raiders. They were both battered and bruised but otherwise unhurt. They had lost their horses in the skirmish in the woods but had managed to hide themselves till daybreak, thus avoiding capture or worse. Two of the raiders pulled them up on their horses to ride double.

The infantry, slingers, archers, and Numidians were bivouacked outside the eastern gate of Bibrax. Fires had been started and everyone seemed to be having breakfast. The men seemed relaxed except for some Remi sentries and lookout parties who were on alert for the return of the enemy.

The messenger led the entire cavalry squadron past the battered iron gate into the town. Much of the town was in chaos. Several buildings had been burnt and were still smouldering. The streets were littered with wounded warriors and soldiers. The women were tending to them as best they could. Piles of corpses, both friendly and enemy, occupied open spaces, laid out in sad rows. The stench of blood, faeces, and putrefying flesh permeated the air. Remi warriors roamed among the enemy wounded, sorting and looting. Those who were salvageable were manacled to be sold as slaves. The less fortunate were dispatched with a quick thrust to the neck. The air was filled with the myriad sounds of crying, moaning, groaning, and the occasionally piercing cry of the executed.

Livy and his men stopped outside an imposing building with a steep roof, a stone base, and high wooden walls. It was the Hall of Warriors and served as a gathering place for the nobles and their retinue. A Remi reception party greeted them, and some long-haired Remi warriors in chain mail took their horses to water while a young blonde Remi girl clothed in a delicate chiton led them into the hall.

Livy took some moments to get used to the poor lighting, then, he smiled. The spacious hall had a high ceiling supported by thick wooden beams and was furnished with a number of large oak tubs filled with water. In each floated a naked man. Some were clearly Romans, cleanly shaven with short cropped hair, and others were Belgic with long locks and shaggy downturned moustaches. Young, statuesque Remi women attended each bather, giving each a vigorous scrub. Some tubs were attended by two attendants, and from one of those, Publius Crassus beckoned, looking cheerful and relaxed.

"Gaius, don't stand there like an imbecile! Come over here. I left you the tub next to me. You, Brigita." He motioned to the younger of the two bath ladies. "Help my friend out of his armour and clothes and get him into the tub. He looks like he crawled out of a sewer." The bath attendant stood up and came over immediately. She was dressed in a short white tunic trimmed with blue. The garment stopped at mid-thigh and was open on the right side to her axilla.

Brigita took him by the hand and sat him on a stool next to his tub and began to undress him, starting first with his helmet and chain mail. As she began to take of his tunic, he began to pay attention to her. Livy could not remember when last he was with a woman. This one was young and blonde with full breasts and curvaceous hips. She had full lips, a pert nose, and big grey eyes. He felt his interest rise as she helped him into the tub. If she had noticed the physical manifestation of his change of mood, she didn't show it. Livy noticed the very slightest hint of a smile. Maybe she did notice after all.

"We saved this wretched town, you realise? They wouldn't have survived another hour. The walls were being overwhelmed even as we fired the first arrows. I think the same was happening on your side of town," Crassus proclaimed as he leant back and enjoyed the back massage administered by the tall brunette. "Yes, that's the right spot. Don't stop," he murmured to the girl.

"You arrived in the nick of time, sire." Livy was enjoying the scrubbing.

"Nevertheless, half of the men in town are dead and another half of the remainder wounded. The town won't stand another attack on its own. That rogue Iccius owes us a great debt." He waved across the room to a clean-shaven middle-aged man in another tub attended by three women.

"Iccius, I presume?" Livy enquired, glancing over.

"The very same. He asked me what he could do for my men and I after the battle, and I said we could do with breakfast and a bath." Publius grinned. "This is the result. I wager you never expected such civilised amenity from such barbaric village. Iccius apparently had spent some time in the Roman provinces and picked up some urban habits, which he had implemented in this town. I must say the women here are of reasonable quality and have rather pleasant manners."

Livy smiled in agreement as his attendant started scrubbing him in some very agreeable areas. He lay back to enjoy her services. He could feel the tension draining from his neck muscles like a taut bowstring slowly being released.

Iccius got out of the bath and sauntered over. "How like you our hospitality, Commander?"

"I am pleasantly impressed, Prefect. Tell me, do we yet know the butcher's bill?" Crassus asked.

"Which prefer you first, the good news or the bad."

Publius frowned. "How did we fare?"

"We lost many men. Four hundred men of Bibrax lie dead and nearly a thousand wounded. Of your forces, there are about forty-five dead and 200 wounded"

"And of the enemy?"

"They lost nearly 3,000 dead, and we found another 1,000 wounded. Most of their wounded were carried away. We also have 2,000 prisoners, which is quite a haul." The prefect smiled with satisfaction.

"Caesar will be pleased because he gets to keep the proceeds from the sale of slaves. At least we get to share out the captured effects from the dead, wounded, and prisoners." Crassus winked at Iccius.

"The women will now serve breakfast, and I think you are best on your way after. That Belgic horde is headed towards the Roman camp, and your chief will need your cavalry before this day is done. Think you can spare me a few men to help bolster our town? I dread to think if a war party will return this way and take another chance at our walls."

"Since you have been so hospitable, I'll leave the Numidians, slingers and the archers with you. I need all the cavalry and the two infantry cohorts. As a further favour for your generosity, I'll leave Centurion Livius here and his band of raiders to scout the enemy's intentions."

"You have my gratitude, Legatus. I now leave you to our young ladies. I think you may take whatever liberties you like with them, and they will be more than willing." There was a twinkle in Iccius's eye and Publius grinned.

"Gaius, when you finally drag yourself out of here, take your raiders and scout to the north and west of the town. See if you can ascertain the enemy's intentions and make sure they don't double back and take the town. Be my eyes and ears. I'll be heading back to the main camp shortly . . .," he paused. "After I thank this beautiful bitch." With that last remark, he reached out, grabbed the tall girl, kissed her roughly, and dragged her into the tub with a big splash.

Livy and Brigita looked at each other in surprise. Livy smiled. "Well, don't you want to come in and join me?" The girl grinned, pulled her tunic over her head, and gingerly swung one leg over and climbed into the tub. The feel of her soft, warm body sent a thrill down Livy's spine. He held her close and kissed her soft, wet, yielding lips. A warm bath with a hot naked girl was just what he needed.

Breakfast was hot and comforting. Flour cakes came with a rich thick stew flavoured with aromatic herbs. The meat in the stew could not be determined, but there was a flavour of bacon. Livy suspected that some of the dead horses from the battle were the main ingredient. It was gratifying to note that the Belgic reputation for culinary skill turned out to be genuine.

Livy felt reenergised and, better still, clean. The bath and frolic did much to boost his spirits, and he was once more eager to rejoin the fray. He gathered his men.

Decius and Paulus were reclining by a robust fire, enjoying steaming hot flour cakes and honey. A few of the younger village girls were serving and enthusiastically engaging them.

"I'm glad to see you gentlemen rested and relaxed," Livy greeted the two officers.

They both got up briskly and saluted smartly. He could see a new respect in their eyes.

"Decius, you take the main cavalry force back to Caesar's camp. I think he will need you if there is going to be a full engagement with the Belgic main force today. Iccius and his crew will look after the wounded. Paulus and the rest of the raiders will scout with me. We'll go see what the barbarians are cooking up for lunch!" He spoke with a new confidence,

The men hurriedly finished their breakfast and bid their new women friends farewell. The women had wet eyes, and the two officers embraced each warmly. Gifts were exchanged—some bread, some bacon, sacs of salt in return for some golden trinket taken from a dead foe.

As Livy was riding past the battered main gate of Bibrax, Brigita dashed impetuously towards his horse. Livy politely dismounted. She fidgeted and blushed.

"I have a small gift for you, something to appease a churning stomach." She produced a small cloth sac, and in it was a freshly baked honey cake. It was still warm, and the lovely aroma made Livy's stomach groan once more.

"That's a lovely parting gift, but I have nothing to return."

"I need only your promise to return. That is all I ask. And take care of yourself."

He gave her a warm hug and kissed her on her lips lightly.

"I am sure we shall meet again. This I do promise." He gave her an extra lingering kiss, tasting her sweet lips and inhaling her fragrant breath.

Reluctantly he turned, swung himself on to the saddle of his horse, Nero, and led it through the gate. The corpses had been cleared away, but the stench and flies remained.

They were wonderful simple people, and Livy was glad to have saved their town and their lives. He was already developing an attachment to that rustic sanctuary.

A short time later, the raiders departed, dividing into two parties. The one led by Livy rode north and Paulus took his party eastwards. Each threw forth half a dozen scouts in front and on the flanks riding in pairs. The weather was balmy, and the countryside looked serene and fertile. The Belgic army had not begun to devastate the land. That would come soon enough.

Livy's thoughts flew home on wings of Pegasus. Familiar faces danced before his eyes—his father luxuriating in his bath with his two sublime slaves, his mother tending roses with effervescent little Livia skipping by her side, Aurora swimming nude on a sun-bleached beach.

The odds were stacked against the Romans. Caesar's eight under strength legions were outnumbered six to one. It was going to be a brutal contest. Would he live to see any of them again? The odds were too long to contemplate. He prayed to Jupiter. At least here was a God who understood man's passions. May he survive that mission and partake of Brigita just once more.

Merv, Parthia: Summer, 37 BC

Chanyu Zhizhi, high king of the Xiongnu, watched grimly from his hilltop headquarters as the town below went up in fire and smoke. He was a tall handsome man in his prime with long black hair and pale grey eyes. They were the eyes of a wolf. The Western Xiongnu had conquered Wusun, Western Dingling, Jiankun (Qïrghïz) and vassalised the Kingdom of Kangguo (Samarkand). The horrors perpetrated by his warriors below were obscured by the conflagration, but blood-curdling screams from rape and massacre floated on the winds.

He had no sympathy for the effeminate Parthians. How could anyone respect people whose generals' wore eye make-up and lip rouge and travelled with a caravan of flute girls, dancers, and prostitutes to battle? They had progressively encroached into the Central Asian plains. The vast Sea of Grass was the preserve of the Xiongnu people. They were the horsemen of the plains. The development of Merv into a fortress was the final insult. It was a convenient staging area for further encroachment. The payback was overdue.

The *chanyu* had another motive for that project. There was something else to be gained. The Parthians were sitting on a treasure. Were they so arrogant in their perceived superiority that they failed to notice that gem in their midst?

The *chanyu* was feeling extremely hot in his full-length lamellar armour. The weight of the suit was becoming unbearable. He motioned to his two squires. They hurried over to help him undress. The battle was already won. There was no further need to put up with the inconvenience of armour protection. One of the squires bowed and offered him a bowl of water.

The *chanyu* reached for the bowl, then checked himself. The young squire looked flustered. The *chanyu* lifted his chin. The beardless youth immediately took a gulp from the bowl, then remained kneeling with the bowl held extended in both hands. The *chanyu* turned nonchalantly away to face the burning town and crossed his arms. The fire in the town had turned it into a furnace. He could see his soldiers leading the captured townsfolk and enemy garrison out of the flames like ants fleeing.

The kneeling squire gasped, then retched. The *chanyu* turned in time to see the youth drop the bowl and foam at the mouth. The boy collapsed sideways, and two heavily armoured bodyguards rushed over. The *chanyu* took hold of the woollen gown of the boy and shook him hard. "Tell me, who ordered you to do this!" he hissed.

The boy rolled up his eyes. There were tears in them. All that he could manage was a gurgle as he drowned in his own secretions. The *chanyu* looked up and let his gaze fall on the second squire. His look was dark with rage. The boy's eyes widened and he cringed in terror.

"I know nothing, Great King. I am not involved," he screamed in terror. Two of the bodyguards had already seized him.

The *chanyu* turned to the guard commander. "Take him away and make him talk."

The commander bowed low. "By your command, Great King," he said. The boy was dragged away, screaming desperately.

The *chanyu* felt both angry and sad. He liked the boy. He had a perfect complexion and his skin was silken smooth. His anus was perfectly formed and had just the right tightness.

A party of heavy *cataphracts* rode up, their horses thundering to a halt amid a cloud of dirt. The men were in full-length lamellar armour which hampered their mobility in no small degree. The ageing leader struggled to dismount, his large curved sword catching momentarily on the saddle. He then immediately came to kneel at the foot of the *chanyu*.

"The town is secured. Everything valuable has been appropriated. All Parthian soldiers are now prisoners and the civilians have been gathered. May I have your instructions as to the disposal of the enemy."

The *chanyu* seemed in deep thought and paced around a few moments. "Kill all the soldiers. Separate out the senior officers and interrogate them under torture. When we have gathered whatever information we can, have them all impaled."

"What of the civilians?" the general asked.

"Kill all the men and all the boys above fifteen seasons or higher than a cart wheel. Keep the rest as slaves. If any look reluctant, kill them as well. Give all the women to our men. Keep the best ten for my personal disposal. Have them delivered to my chief retainer by the evening," the *chanyu* ordered.

The general was dismayed at the harshness of the order but dared not contradict his sovereign. "Your servant," the general said, his forehead touching the ground.

"One other matter, Dagu," the *chanyu* added.

"Yes, High King."

"The slaves whom the Parthians use as labour, did you find any?"

"Yes, My Lord, we captured about a thousand of them," Dagu said.

"Are there any of unusual appearance?"

"Yes, My Lord. They are clearly from a white race, different from the Parthians and the inhabitants from these parts. One of them told me they come from the Far West. There is an empire there with an unpronounceable name."

A smile crept over the face of the *chanyu*. "Dagu, I want you to treat them like honoured guest. Feed them well and get them cleaned up and dressed in the best clothes you liberate from the Parthians. Find their leaders and invite them for dinner tonight. We shall feast together. Plundering the town is of course profitable, but these men are the true prize."

The *chanyu* turned and strode back to his tent. He was already calling for his retainers.

Dagu was perplexed. "Why such special treatment for mere slave labourers? There must be something truly remarkable about those pale specimens." He did not ever know the *chanyu* to be so attentive to mere slaves before. He stroked his beard which had many white strands.

Dagu got up when the *chanyu* was some distance away, struggled to mount his horse, and rode away with his escorts.

The victory feast was held in a huge yak skin tent decorated with bright silk banners. There was a cacophony of noise from drums, trumpets, and reed instruments. Huge platters of roast meat adorned every low table, and the guests sat on large cushions served by an army of servants. The men were dressed in heavy woollen gowns and the women wore fine long silk gowns with elaborate headgear lined with ermine. The Xiongnu lived in a harsh climate where the nights were cold and their dress sense was conservative.

All round the tent, bronze braziers burnt brightly, bringing warmth and light. The aroma of roast meat and incense permeated the cold air.

The *chanyu* ate sparingly from the platter of meat before him. Around him sat several of his concubines and bodyguards. The problem of security weighed heavily on his shoulders. He looked around ever so suspiciously. He had too many enemies. There was his brother *Chanyu* Huhanye who had bowed to the Han. Could he be the one plotting fratricide? Then there was of course the Parthians, who would now want revenge for their razed city. Lastly, there was the Han Chinese. He knew Chen Tang, the deputy commander of the Western Regions, had sent countless agents into Xiongnu lands.

He glanced towards the entrance of the giant yurt. A party of new guests had arrived escorted by Dagu and his men. They were dressed richly in silk gowns. Dagu had brought only two men. Presumably those were the leaders. As they approached very tentatively, the *chanyu* studied both closely. One man was large and fair with blond hair and blue eyes. He had a downturned moustache and a beard which looked like it had just been trimmed that day. Even through his silk gown, it could be discerned that he had a formidable physique.

The second man had dark hair worn long like the *chanyu*. He had week-old stubble and was tanned. He was not as well muscled as the first but looked compact and agile. They came up to the *chanyu* and prostrated themselves, bowing their heads to touch the ground.

"You may arise, gentlemen," the *chanyu* said amiably. "Tonight you are no longer slaves but my guest. Relax and make yourselves comfortable. Partake freely of food and drink and indulge yourself in the women. I am sure your genitalia can do with some exercise after such a long period of deprivation." He smirked.

The two men were allowed to rise and sit to the left of the *chanyu*. They were immediately joined by two maidens each dressed in Xiongnu fashion. Their refined manners and flawless ivory complexion, however, betrayed their Han origins.

"So you are men from Rome? Please introduce yourselves," the *chanyu* began.

"My name is Murato. I am an officer in the Roman Army, but I originally come from Belgica. It's part of the Roman Empire now. My rank is that of Cavalry Prefect of the Gaulish auxiliary cavalry," Murato said.

"I am Aulus Paulus, Prefect of the Roman Legionary Cavalry. I am a Roman from Northern Italy," Paulus said. "We thank the Great King for his kindness and hospitality. To what do we owe this turn of fortune?"

"Are you the only two officers left of your army?" the *chanyu* enquired.

"There are a few other, about a half dozen centurions, another dozen *optios*, a *medicus*, and two cavalry decurions," Murato replied. "We are the two most senior."

"I have heard many tales of your great empire which lies to the Far West of the world. I hear you dominate your part of the world with armies which fight like machines and grind all before them to dust. Yet the effete Parthians manage to crush seven legions with a mere 10,000 cavalry. My own army would have torn them to shreds," the *chanyu* probed.

"Normally 10,000 Parthian cavalry would have been swatted aside like flies," Paulus said. "In this instance, their commander, the Surena, was an exceptional commander. Ours on the other hand was somewhat deficient." Paulus sighed.

The *chanyu* smiled. "You are kind to describe Marcus Licinius Crassus in those terms. He was arrogant and incompetent in my judgement." The *chanyu* sneered. "He more than deserved his fate."

"Orodes the Parthian king used his head as a prop in a theatrical performance. It was indeed an ignoble end," Paulus lamented.

"The fates were not kind to either Surena or Orodes," the *chanyu* said. "Orodes executed Surena out of jealousy, and Orodes was strangled by his own son." The *chanyu* leant back on his cushion and sipped the arak from a golden bowl.

Murato could not restrain himself longer. He took a large piece of meat from the silver platter before him and ate ravenously. "Great King, you spared us for a reason. Pray tell us how we can repay your kindness? We are yours to command," Murato mumbled with his mouth full.

Paulus looked at him disapprovingly. "How can we be of service, Great King?"

The *chanyu* smiled. "How would you like to be soldiers once again?"

Just then one of his retainers interrupted him and whispered in his ear. "Yes, bring me this prize," he commanded with a grin on his face.

Two guards dragged in a raven-haired beauty dressed in sumptuous, embroidered Parthian robes.

"Great One, I present you the Princess Suren of Parthia. I believe she is the sister of The Surena, who defeated the great Roman Consul Crassus many years ago," Baidu the retainer said.

The *chanyu* observed her closely. She was slim and of moderate height. Her skin was light brown and flawlessly smooth. Her eyes were dark brown and fiery with hatred.

"Such a beauty must belong to someone," the *chanyu* observed.

"Her husband was the governor of Merv. Unfortunately as you ordered all officers killed, our men had impaled him before I could intervene. I beg your forgiveness, Great One." Baidu bowed low.

"Can we rescue him?" the *chanyu* asked.

"I am afraid it is too late. His injuries are mortal," Baidu said.

"Have someone put him out of his misery. Give him a quick death," the *chanyu* ordered. One of the guards bowed and exited briskly.

"Bring her closer," the *chanyu* commanded. Suren was dragged close to the Warlord. He noticed her deep cleavage as she knelt on the floor. The guards released her. Without warning, she launched herself at the *chanyu*, claws with long nails aiming for his eyes.

The *chanyu*, always alert for danger, turned his head, and the nails buried themselves in his cheek instead, scouring several long red streaks across his face. The *chanyu* screamed and punched her brutally. She was flung back a short distance, sprawling on to the floor. The guards immediately restrained her and tied her hands behind her back.

The *chanyu* wiped the blood from his face. For a moment, he looked as if he was about to order her immediate execution by impaling. He recovered his composure. "The bitch has spirit," he spat. "We must however punish her for her bad manners."

Princess Suren was stripped naked and tied spread out across a round table. Her mouth was gagged to prevent her from screaming. The table was put on to its side, and she was displayed in the centre of the dining hall like a decorative piece of art. All that night, men came and abused her in every disgusting way short of rape. She struggled violently till she became too exhausted, then just resigned herself to the revolting situation.

The *chanyu* went back to drinking and eating. He turned to Paulus. "I want your men returned to their previous form and level of training. I want them to be Roman soldiers again, not half-starved slave labourers. I will provide the food and the provisions. We have already located your captured arms and armour."

Hope rose again in Paulus's breast. "We are really released from slavery?"

"Of course, I want your men to be the nucleus of my new infantry force. I will build a new army which will be invincible, and we will march east and take for ourselves the rich lands of the Han Empire," the *chanyu* proclaimed confidently.

Paulus could not believe his ears. They were going to be free after so many years of slave labour. His eyes were wet with tears. "I thank you from the bottom of my heart. Of course, I must let my men decide, but I do not think there will be a single man who will say no," he said.

Murato's heart beat with excitement. He looked forward to his old life. He would give anything to be free from slavery and be a soldier again. "May all the Gods bless you, Great One. We will follow you to the gates of the underworld. You will not be disappointed."

"How long do you need to get your men in shape?" the *chanyu* asked.

"The men are half starved and in bad shape. With proper food and training, I think we can have them fit in eight weeks to three months," Paulus estimated.

"I give you two months," the *chanyu* said. "Be ready for battle by the fall."

"As you command, Great One." The two men bowed their heads to the floor.

The *chanyu* gave a satisfied smile. He looked forward to taking the Princess Surena at his leisure. She would make an exciting sex slave.

Liqian, China, Winter, 36 BC

My fingers are numb from wielding the brush. The sun has climbed and the mist has evaporated from the ground. The temperature is warmer now, and I have the urge to remove my outer coat. The smell of roast meat wafts in from the kitchen.

My study room opens on to a large open balcony that provides a panoramic view of the countryside and the distant mountains. In summer, I open the doors and windows to let in the air, but in winter it is usually too cold to do so. Today it is warm enough to brave the elements, so I go forth to enjoy the bracing weather. My humble villa is set on a hill dominating the town of Liqian and the surrounding countryside.

From my vantage, I can see plum and orange orchards and the olive plantation, which I myself started some years ago. The trees are covered with snow, making them sparkle like silver in the sunlight.

I love this land for it reminds me of home, although I don't remember such cold winters and so much snow in my homeland. Still I much prefer the countryside to life in the city.

Two maids have come, no doubt to remind me to take my lunch. They are both small and delicate with creamy complexion and ebony hair tossed into a bun held with silver pins. They bow deeply. "Your Lordship, the honourable Lady Qingling requests your company at lunch."

"Tell the honourable lady to begin and I will join her shortly. What do we have today."

"We have prepared your favourite roast goose with a variety of dumplings and also winter melon soup, Your Lordship," she answered politely in a soft musical voice.

"I will enjoy the air a few moments more. It whets my appetite. You are dismissed."

They bow and leave, their elegant long silk outer garments swishing softly as they shuffle.

I take a few more moments to enjoy the sparkling landscape, listening to the soft whisper of the winter wind. So strange it is that fate has brought me to this place. Yet I now feel as if this is home and I have always lived here. As I exhale, my breath turns to white smoke. I can remember another time when that happened. It was so long ago.

CHAPTER 3

To pull a tiger's teeth, one must ascend the mountain and enter its lair.

Belgica, 57 BC

Livy's patrol entered the forest like two snakes winding its sinuous way round ancient pillars. The raiders were in twin single files, fifty yards apart. Tree trunks stood around like the legs of an army of giants. The verdant green canopy covered sun and sky, producing a twilight gloom.

There was a chill in the forest, and the breath from horses and men showed as silvery grey puffs as they exhaled. An ethereal mist cloaked the ground. Men scanned anxiously fearful of ambush. The thought of half-naked screaming savages bursting forth from the trees filled each man with dread.

Presently, hoof beats sounded distinctly through the gloom. Livy signalled his men to halt, dismount, and seek cover. Bows were readied and arrows nocked ready for release. The men relaxed as recognition dawned. The two forward scouts returned, and Livy showed himself and motioned them over.

The sinewy cavalryman, Falco, came, and Livy drew him behind a sizable tree trunk. "The enemy patrol not 500 yards from here, about twenty horsemen. We can take them, but if only a single man escapes, he will raise the alarm and our discovery is assured."

"Can we not pass them by? Our orders are to locate and discover intent. I intend no major engagement," he emphasised.

"I think their main force is to the north-east of us. If we ride east and then north again, we may come by their rear. As they expect no intrusion from so unexpected a direction, we may find few patrols there."

"Your plan has some merit. Let's ride about three or four miles to the east and then cut due north. We should be able to sneak clear of this patrol if we observe silence. The forest will hide us well enough."

The men mounted and drove their horses east, deeper into the forest. The light grew dimmer still and the trees closed ranks. The smell of rotting leaves was in the air. The men lurked as noiselessly as mice in the vicinity of hungry feline predators.

Sometime after midday, they arrived at the edge of the forest. The trees gradually became sparser, and fifty yards further on, there was bright sunshine. They had ridden more than fifteen miles through the dense forest, and both men and horses were fatigued.

Livy signalled the men to halt, dismounted, and slowly crept to the edge of the forest with two of his men. The sight before their eyes made their stomachs churn. Below them, the enemy army covered the landscape as far as the eye could see, swarming over the surrounding hills like a plague of multicoloured locust. Livy had never even seen so many people in his life and was at a loss as to how to begin counting so vast a host. The three men watched in awed silence. Each was speechless and mortified. How would Caesar's eight legions deal with this vast host?

When the initial shock had abated, Livy began to make an estimation, using the technique of counting grids. He made a rough sketch of the whole host as far as the eye could see. Estimating the size of a block to be about 1,000 warriors, then by drawing a grid and counting the squares, he could estimate the whole. It was a crude method, but at least it gave a number which could be reported to Caesar. Livy stopped counting after 200 squares, and he was aware that more remained hidden.

The army moved as an amorphous mass without recognisable organisation. The different tribes seemed to be roughly grouped together, each with their own wagon train. The cavalry seemed to be in the van and flanks. They did not scout far from the main army, and Livy was sure that his men were yet undetected.

Livy turned to one of his scouts, a Remi named Biorix. "You know the tribes better than I do," he said. "Which tribes display their banners below?"

Biorix was smaller than Livy. He had blond hair in plaits and a downturned moustache like a typical Gaul. He always had a mischievous look which amused Livy. He had been previously a war-band commander of the Remi and could handle a horse. His archery skills were also now formidable after Livy's recent instruction. He and Paulus were Livy's most trusted subordinates and could be counted as friends.

"Nearest to us are the Suessiones. The major contingents which I can see are the Atrebates and the Bellovaci. I also see Menapii, Morini, Nervii, Atuatuci, and Viromandui," Biorix said in Latin with a thick Gallic accent.

Livy wondered how he could tell them apart as the warriors all looked rather alike to him.

"What's that contingent over there at the front? They all seem totally naked."

"Those are Gaesatae," he spat. "They are tribe-less mercenaries who sell their services to anyone. They are scum in my opinion, and their women fuck like animals. They are passed from one man to another. We had to fight them off once when they raided my village. They are savage fighters and fearless warriors who sneer at death."

"I see women among them. Are they warriors too or just camp followers?"

"Apparently the bitches fight as well, side by side with the dogs, as archers and light skirmishers. The main shock troops are usually strong young men though. They fight well because that's all they do besides eating and fucking," Biorix conceded.

Livy turned to his other companion, a tall young lad called Sextus. "Get your horse and then ride as hard as you can to Caesar's camp. Tell him nearly 200,000 Belgae are amassing to attack him and that they are about a day's march away. They have 6,000 to 8,000 horses. I think they will likely camp for the night and then attack in the morning. Go now, swiftly."

The boy scampered off. Livy turned to Biorix. "We observe them till dark to make certain they camp for the night. Once they slumber, we can consider getting back to Caesar's camp and joining the battle on the morrow. Considering the numbers, he will need every man."

"I have an idea." Biorix smiled deviously. He stroked the tip of his moustache. "Maybe we can even the odds a little while they sleep."

"What do you have in mind? We risk being annihilated if they even get a scent of us. I think you have a plan though, so let's hear it."

"Caesar has about 2,000 cavalry at most, about 1,000 if you consider 120 horses per legion for the eight legions, another 1,000 of his army reserve. It will be severely outnumbered tomorrow. Our flanks will be pretty vulnerable. I say we raid the bastards' horse pens tonight and make off with as many horses as we can. The rest we scatter or disable. They will be up all night chasing after their steeds and too tired to give battle in the morning," Biorix said.

"Your plan has merit. It will be dangerous though because if they are alert we will be slaughtered!" Livy cautioned.

Just at that moment, Livy heard a sound and turned to see one of his men running towards him.

"Good news, Commander. Decurion Paulus and his men have rejoined us."

"By Jupiter, that is fortunate. Tell him to come up here at once."

In a few moments, Paulus was lying beside them, gasping at the vast host below covering all the surrounding hills.

"In the name of Apollo, I have never ever seen so many barbarians. That's quite an army. We are in for some serious fighting!" Paulus said.

"So how did you get here?" Livy said.

"We went east as you ordered, but there were heavy enemy patrols in every direction. Finally we had no choice but to head north to try and bypass them, and by chance we picked up your trail, so here we are"

"Thank the gods. Now we can really plan a little nocturnal surprise for our Belgic friends. Let's work out the details over some dinner. I'm famished."

"I can still taste our wonderful breakfast at Bibrax," Biorix reminisced.

"Well, if things go as planned, I will have all of you back there in time for lunch tomorrow." Livy said flippantly. Inside, he was less sure.

"That's bound to raise the spirits of the men!" Paulus agreed.

"I'm counting on it."

The Nocturnal Dance of Death

> Speed is the essence of war. Take advantage of the enemy's unpreparedness; travel by unexpected routes and strike him where he has taken no precautions.
>
> (Sun Tzu)

The Belgae made merry as was their practice before a big battle. The next day, many would be in the underworld, and they seized the opportunity to satiate their worldly appetites perhaps for the last time. They feasted on whatever food remained. Oxen, sheep, and ducks were slaughtered and roasted. The next day, they hoped to loot Caesar's camp. There was much drinking, and the women danced and sang to loud music. Later there would be indiscriminate copulation with the camp followers. Some who could not wait were already entwined amidst the noisy soiree.

The Belgae had posted sentries, but not all were alert. Some felt disappointed at missing out on the festivities. Others had smuggled wine and were already inebriated. The night was dark and the moon covered with clouds. The massive Belgic camp was however lighted with thousands of fires and torches and blazed as bright as a city.

Biorix and his twenty men had started crawling very slowly towards the cavalry encampment as soon as it was completely dark. Most of his men were Remi. A few were ex-horse thieves. The rest had experience in rearing and herding horses, and all could ride bareback. They were armed only with their short swords and a small Remi sickle knife which was ideal for hamstringing horses.

Livy and his squadron hid anxiously in the woods, awaiting the moment to attack. There was no way for Biorix to signal that he was ready, so Livy would have to trust that the two hours he gave for Biorix to get into position were sufficient. Meanwhile, a swarm of starving mosquitoes made a meal over any who exposed skin.

The guards patrolling the stockade for the horses never knew what hit them. They were quietly and violently dispatched. The Remi were expert at that sort of horse raiding. Intertribal raids and horse theft was a cultural pastime among the Belgae and Gauls. The sentries died noiselessly, and their bodies were quickly hidden. Their clothes were swiftly stripped, and the Remi disguised in them, hoping to go unnoticed in the dark. Biorix and his men discovered a stockade which had about 500 horses in it. There were at least 3,000 horses in that camp divided into six stockades. Biorix spread out his men to four of the six stockades.

At midnight, Livy and his eight raiders made their move. Deployed in two ranks, he started walking his horses towards the cavalry encampment. At about 300 yards, the men lighted their arrows which had an oil-soaked cloth tied just behind the metal tip. Any moment, he expected to be discovered and the alarm to sound. He speeded up to a trot, and as yard after yard flew by, he could not believe that things remained still quiet except for the sounds of revelling. The sentries had to be already inebriated or asleep. In the Roman Army, they would have been crucified the next morning. This was not a Roman Army.

He waited till he was 100 yards from the nearest tents, then, released the arrows. The fire arrows were well scattered, and many a tent started to ignite. At fifty yards, a second volley was released, and those penetrated deeper into the camp and fired many more tents.

One or two warriors looking dazed began to notice that something was up. One guard pointed a spear and challenged them in some unknown tongue, and he received an arrow in the chest as a reply.

"Right, men, make every shot count. Shoot everyone that shows himself till you have emptied your first quiver, then regroup," Livy commanded in a loud voice. "Spare the non-combatants if possible."

Chaos reigned. Many a tent burnt furiously, and the raiders grabbed torches wherever they could find them and set alight as many tents as they could. The Belgae were bewildered, running everywhere in disorder, looking for weapons and shouting to each other in confusion.

The raiders amidst them coolly picked their targets and dealt death. In the tumult, the Belgae had trouble telling friend from foe. Arrows seemed to appear from nowhere, and an organised defence became impossible.

Livy spotted a band of leather-clad warriors reaching for their stacked weapons. His first arrow sunk into the side of a spearman, penetrating his leather armour like a needle through cheese. The man dropped his spear to tug at the offending shaft. In one smooth movement, he reached for another arrow, nocked, and fired, this time sinking the missile into the back of a retreating warrior. Both men thus injured would no doubt survive, but Livy was gratified that there would be two less enemies for Caesar to worry about in the battle to come.

A movement to his left registered in his peripheral vision. He swung round to fire but caught a glimpse of a naked thigh and breast. A young woman ran out of a tent, holding her blue tunic in a vain attempt to screen her naked bosom. Livy stopped himself in time to avoid impaling her. A naked black-bearded warrior emerged from the same burning tent after her. Livy released the arrow at him instead as the warrior simultaneously flung a throwing axe at him. The two missiles passed in mid-air. For a moment in time, both men's fate hung in the balance.

In the confusion, Biorix and his men had opened the gates to the horse pens and were stampeding the horses away. Most of the horses were herded south towards the forest and in the direction of Bibrax. The men, riding bareback, herded the animals expertly as they had been doing all their lives. In their past lives, they had been horse thieves.

Biorix and six of his men then opened the gates of the last two horse pens and stampeded the thousand horses through the cavalry camp, crushing many tents and not a few warriors and camp followers. That added even more to the pandemonium. Many fires were started by overturned lamps and tents falling into open fires.

The Belgae were starting to react. A few of the raiders were cornered by warriors on foot wielding spears, pulled of their horses, and butchered mercilessly. Some other cavalrymen found horses and mounted. Livy's men were running out of arrows and remembered not to use their reserves, so they drew their heavy *spathas* and slashed at anyone within reach.

The heavy axe missed Livy's head by the narrowest margin. He could feel its passage as it whirled through the air. The arrow sunk itself into the axe man's thigh, causing him to scream and collapse in pain.

Something made Livy look to one side. At that moment, he saw a blonde naked girl loosen an arrow straight at him. The arrow thumped into his small round cavalry shield, its arrow head protruding through the back of the shield, just missing his arm. He drew his heavy cavalry *spathas* and turned to charge her. He noticed that the girl was strangely beautiful, a naked savage. Her body was covered in blue war paint in swirling patterns. She looked like the Roman goddess, Diana the huntress. He moved quickly before she could ready another arrow. In an instant, he was over her, his sword raised. She had a dagger in her hand, but both realised that the match was uneven. He noticed that she had blue green eyes like a wild animal. She bared her teeth at him, daring him to attack.

Livy decided it would be a waste to kill her. "Run if you want to live!" he said to her in Celtic. She didn't need a second invitation and fled, leaving Livy a brief view of her pert glutei. The opposition was thickening and the counterattack was gaining momentum. Livy decided that an immediate withdrawal was imperative.

"Sound regroup!" he yelled at the signaller beside him. The man took out his horn and blew three long notes. Immediately, the raiders disengaged and retreated. They regrouped just outside the camp. He was glad to see that Biorix and two of his men riding bareback had rejoined him. He threw Biorix his extra bow and a quiver. The other two men also rearmed. "I am happy to see you in one piece, Biorix." He grinned.

"They will have a little surprise back in Bibrax when my men turn up in the morning with more horses than anyone in the town can count," Biorix stated triumphantly.

"I'll see you get your just reward," Livy said. "Are you missing any men?"

"I am not sure. I can't really account for everyone right now in all this confusion," Biorix said.

"I suppose we have to make our count in Bibrax to see how many stragglers return. For now, our task is to cover the retreat of our intrepid horse thieves. Let's ride to the edge of the forest and stop at the tree line. We will form a skirmish line there and delay anyone who tries to follow."

They turned and galloped southwards. Livy looked behind as he rode and saw that a company of enemy cavalry was already forming up. At the edge of the forest, he ordered the men to dismount and form a line. Archers are always more accurate on foot than when mounted.

"Biorix, ride back to Bibrax and warn them that we may be coming in hotly pursued with cavalry on our heels. Warn the commander of the Cretan Archers especially to be ready to give them a warm welcome."

Livy couldn't make out how many horsemen were coming after them, but he was at least comforted that the enemy would be silhouetted against the light from the vast camp while his men would be invisible, hidden in the dark forest.

"Get ready to receive cavalry, men. We release at 250 yards, first at the horses, then aim at the men when they get nearer. Prepare to mount in a hurry and retreat at the sound of the horn. After that, try to keep together and run like mad for Bibrax. If you get separated, just head back as best you can. Wear your red cloaks as you get near the town so you can be recognized," Livy gave his final order.

The horsemen approached at the gallop, and Livy realised that there were at least 500 of them in a formless mass. Some were naked Gaesatae who had found mounts. The horsemen were mostly armed with spears. Livy felt a shudder of fear. He fought temptation to sound the retreat right away. A calmer side told him that the enemy would follow more slowly and cautiously if they were first stung.

At 250 yards, he took aim at the leading horse and released the first volley. Livy saw his target rear up and unseat the rider who tumbled backwards. The men followed his lead, and about two dozen horses went down. The leading ranks of the cavalry recoiled but quickly reformed just as another volley hit them this time with improved results. The enemy cavalry seemed disconcerted and reluctant to proceed closer under the rain of deadly shafts. Livy saw with satisfaction one of his arrows pierce an armour-clad rider. Armour was rare among the Belgae, and the man was probably a retainer to one of the chiefs. His pyramidal-tipped armour-piercing arrow had performed as designed.

More and more horsemen however gathered just out of range, and then Livy ordered a halt to save the remaining arrows. "They are going to charge us," Livy cried out. "When they come, give them two more volleys, then let's run! Get on your horses now."

The men mounted just as the enemy charged. Livy chose the leading rider and aimed for his torso. He loosed the arrow and reached for another shaft even before it hit. The horsemen were coming very fast. He fired quickly and saw the front rank of riders thinned by casualties. He then turned his horse around and fled. His men were already all running. They were seriously outnumbered, and staying to fight would be suicidal. The horses had a chance to recover so they made good speed. The scouts had already marked out the line of retreat, and Livy just followed the man in front and rode hard. It soon became too dark to see anything except for the man directly before and the man behind. There was shouting and torches were seen behind as the enemy cavalry tried to catch up with them in the darkness. Their torches danced like fireflies in the gloom, indicating their location. The Romans rode in the dark and in silence so that they could not be seen or heard. Livy's heart pounded, and he could feel the sweat drenching his face and body despite the cold night air.

There is nothing like running for your life to make the senses keener.

The horses made a regular rhythmic beat as they pounded along and seemed still unwinded, though they were starting to perspire with the exertion. Every man knew that if caught, there would be no mercy. The Romans had been briefed about the human sacrifices and didn't doubt that such a fate or worse awaited them. Most would prefer to die fighting. Livy on the other hand preferred to live and enjoy breakfast and a bath in Bibrax. "Always think positive," he remembered the remark of Xeno his teacher. He tried to clear his mind of fear and just concentrated on riding.

The Belgae horsemen were persistent and kept on their tail though they seemed to be spreading out and thinning their lines. A half hour hence, they started cutting east towards Bibrax, and looking back, Livy noticed fewer pursuers. They also seemed to have fallen further back.

Moments later, they came to a clearing. Livy ordered the men to ride to the far side, dismount, and seek cover. The men readied their bows. "Do not fire. Keep silent, and they may miss us and go off in another direction. If we shoot, we will give ourselves away. Pass my words down the line. Don't shoot unless I shoot first," Livy whispered.

They men hid their horses further into the trees and formed a skirmish line. At least the horses would get a few minutes to catch their breath. Everything suddenly became very silent.

Enemy horsemen appeared, probing in the shadows on the far side of the clearing. Livy could see their torches dancing amidst the trees. There were perhaps a dozen points of light. The enemy cavalry must have thinned their ranks to search a wider area.

He could just make out their conversation. They were calling to each other to see if anyone had seen anything. At least that's what Livy expected them to be saying.

Two of the horsemen ventured out into the clearing. They paused to look around and then slowly walked their horses towards the raiders' position. They moved at an agonizingly slow pace. Livy stopped breathing and prayed to all the gods that they would not come close enough to spot one of the raiders.

They separated and slowly crept their horses forward a step at a time.

Livy pulled his bowstring back in anticipation. His arm and shoulder muscles ached with the strain. If they came even ten yards closer, he would not have a choice. The rest of the Belgic cavalry seemed to be watching them intently from the other end of the clearing.

Then one of the horsemen stopped. He said something to the other. The other replied. The first man sighed and said something else. Then both men started back towards the other end of the clearing at a trot.

Livy slowly released the tension in the bow and put away his arrow. He leant back against a tree and took a deep breath. The raiders remained hidden and silent. After an interminable time which was probably no more than a sixth of an hour, the enemy horse moved away southwards.

Livy spoke to his men in a low voice, "Withdraw slowly and make not a sound. Everybody on foot till I give the word to mount."

The men got up and slowly disappeared into the forest, again leading their mounts. Everyone thanked the gods in his own way.

Their danger however had not yet ended.

Liqian, Han Empire, Winter, 36 BC

I was delighted. I felt like a child with a new toy. The new extension to my villa was complete at last, Mr. Ma, the builder, had taken six months to do the job. He had never seen anything comparable in all of the empire. His first impression when given the task was that it was a mad scheme, instigated by river demons. What would any sane imperial prefect want with a collection of large pools of water? Was he a necromancer predicting the coming of a long draught? He thought the prefect of Zhangye had lost his mind.

Furthermore, why did he have to build three pools? If storage of water was the intention, surely one would have sufficed. Then there was the matter of the large furnaces to boil the water and the elaborate copper pipes to bring the hot water into the pools. Was the prefect preparing to boil his enemies alive? What evil intentions lay under those mad schemes?

On the other hand, Ma wasn't going to complain. He had been paid enough silver coins to build another large villa. He had made enough money from that project to cover his business expenses for two years.

I took my new wife, Qingling, to try out the new bath complex which was built on a rise about fifty yards from the main house. It was connected by a covered pathway. Qingling was blindfolded. I wanted to surprise her. We were accompanied by two of her handmaidens.

I held her by the hand, and she had an amused smile on her face. When the blindfold was removed, she beamed in surprise. It was winter, but the bathhouse was appropriately heated. The water in the three pools had a deep blue colour due to the blue mosaic tiles which surfaced the bottom. The walls were decorated with paintings of rivers and craggy mountains shrouded in mist, dotted with picturesque villages.

Qingling had served at the imperial palace and was not unused to extreme luxury, but not even the emperor had such a wondrous bathhouse. "Let me explain," I said. "We start here with the hot bath." I pointed to one of the smaller pools. Steam was rising from it in wisps.

"It looks hot enough to cook someone," she said. Her eyes were wide open in wonder.

"Almost, but not quite. You must try it. The heat will open the pores and cleanse the dirt from the inner layers of your skin," I said as I began to disrobe.

Qingling blushed. "Perhaps we should dismiss my maidens?" she said.

"We should train them not to be embarrassed about nudity. Not today though. It is too sudden. You ladies may retire." They bowed and retreated hurriedly, blushing as they went.

I undressed my wife, slowly and deliberately. She turned away coyly and would not look me in the eye. I was surprised that she was still shy about her body. We had been married already more than a year, and I had taken her regularly.

When she was fully undressed, I took her by the hand and led her gingerly into the water. She jumped and danced a few steps at the unexpected heat. Her figure was still formidable despite the little bump in her lower belly. Her skin was porcelain, smooth, hairless, and unblemished. Her legs were well proportioned and slender though not as long as those of women from the west. Her breasts were not large but beautifully shaped. We sank chest deep into the water, luxuriating in the heat which contrasted with the chilly winter air. The combination was startlingly pleasant.

Qingling smiled. "So this is the big secret you have been keeping from me these last months. I think it is wonderfully luxurious. You should give the idea to our emperor. Even he doesn't bathe in such luxury! I don't think I can stay in this hot water for too long though. It can't possibly be good for me in my condition."

"Let me know once you feel uncomfortable and we will move to the next pool," I said.

Qingling got up after a short while, the water dripping off her pink labia. She was more relaxed now and made no attempt to hide her private areas as she emerged from the hot pool in a cloud of steam. I was reminded of the story of a Venus rising from the waves.

She waded into the adjacent pool and beckoned me to follow. Walking bravely, in she went to sit at one corner. "This water feels amazing after the last one. The degree of heat is truly comfortable," she said.

I smiled. "I have some ginger tea prepared. Let's sit in this pool awhile and take a drink." I got out of the hot pool and went to a small table which had a teapot and two porcelain bowls. I poured the tea and brought the bowls to my wife. She sipped daintily, her last finger raised as was the fashion in polite circles.

I got into the pool once more and sat right next to her, our shoulders touching. The sight of her naked body and her subtle fragrance had aroused my jade shaft. I reached over to caress her breast, which were plump with milk. She flinched.

"I am sorry, Master. I am overfull with milk, and my breasts are tender," she said.

I moved my hands between her legs, and she parted a little to allow access. I ran my fingers lightly over her smooth Mount of Venus. It was considered bad luck in Han culture to shave one's pubes, but Qingling knew my preference and had either shaved or plucked every hair away. I moved my fingers down between her lotus petals, and she threw her head back and gasped.

Her fingers crawled lightly over my jade shaft. She began to run them delicately and expertly, playing me like a musical instrument. I felt the sexual tension build rapidly. I forced myself to resist the urge to hurtle towards the precipice.

Qingling on the other hand flowed with the river and soon shuddered to a crashing climax. Her sensuous lips parted to gasp for air as she enjoyed the warm sensation flooding her being. She extricated her jade hair pin and let her lustrous ebony locks fall over her ivory shoulders. With a lascivious smile, she dove under the water between my legs. I nearly exploded as I slid over her slippery tongue into the warmth of her mouth.

Moments later, she surfaced for breath, gasping. Any longer and my dam would have burst asunder. With amazing agility she mounted me like a horse impaling herself on my jade staff. As I slid comfortably into her warm, slippery interior, I felt her pelvic muscles pulsate rhythmically as she rode me. Waves after wave of sublime ecstasy pulsed through my being. The climax felt as if the whole Yellow River had burst its banks and flooded the North China Plain.

For a moment I was catatonic. Unable to move or respond, I could hear my heartbeat ringing in my ears. Qingling was puzzled, then alarmed. "Perhaps the exertion had strained his old heart," she thought. "Have I exceeded myself and brought grief to my poor husband?" Perhaps he was not as fit as she assumed.

I, on the other hand, knew very much that I still lived. The pounding of my circulation in my ears was a sure sign of life. My body functions had just momentarily paused as if it had to rest a moment from such extreme pleasure. Qingling was calling out to me, but I heard nothing. Then I reached out and firmly gripped her hand reassuringly.

She sighed in relief and patted her breast. "I thought you had a seizure, Master," she said.

"I cannot explain what happened," I said. "It seemed that my whole body just shut down for a while." I smiled.

"You gave me a terrible fright," she said, looking a little angry.

"It's not my time. You gave such extreme pleasure. It stole my soul away for a moment." I smiled reassuringly at her.

We had a swim in the cold pool, which Qingling could not tolerate for long. I lingered, enjoying the contrasting sensation. Later, we lay on a couch in the warm room, sipping tea and indulging in a variety of steamed dumplings.

"Where did you learn such exquisite bedroom skills?" I asked abruptly.

Qingling choked on her tea and coughed violently. I waited for her to compose herself. She looked down demurely and then answered, "In the imperial palace, ladies of the court have to provide a large variety of services to the emperor and the imperial family. We were required to learn many skills. These included music, tea making, dancing, conversation, and of course bedroom skills." She looked embarrassed.

"Do not be disconcerted, Qingling, I knew you were not a virgin when you were presented to me as a gift from the emperor. After all, you are of imperial blood and I am a mere barbarian general. I consider myself honoured."

"Nevertheless, I am ashamed that I did not arrive intact," she said.

"I have no use for an unskilled virgin. I prefer a wife who can bring me to the heights of pleasure, which only a skilled exponent of the arts can confer." I beamed at her. "No doubt, you had the very best teachers in the arts of ying and yang."

She was in no doubt that she had found favour in my eyes and seemed content. An attractive blush warmed her cheeks.

"The days to come will be busy. Gan Yanshaou, governor of the Western Regions, will be paying us a visit together with his deputy, Chen Tang. They have military matters to discuss with me. It seems our friends, the Xiongnu, grow restless. They self-proclaimed *chanyu* of the Northern Xiongnu is arming for war, and we must soon face him," I said.

"War again?" She looked annoyed. "I thought you were done with the military life. Certainly it should be left to younger men."

"I will avoid involvement if I can. Believe me, I have no yearning to go campaigning in the desolate deserts and mountains of the western frontier. The Xiongnu are also a formidable nation which I do not look forward to facing again." I smiled reassuringly.

She looked as if she did not quite believe me. "Stay alive for me, Master. I cannot now imagine what paths our lives will take if you fail to return." She looked at me pleadingly.

"We get ahead of ourselves. Perhaps they just want me to provide strategic or tactical advice or to help them raise some military units. They may even be just paying a social visit to this veteran old general." I tried to melt her growing anxiety.

Her body language betrayed her unease. She had drawn away and her hands were crossed over her naked breasts. "You will no doubt be preparing a banquet."

"Of course, the governor is not of sound health recently. Prepare a rich and nourishing chicken soup with medicinal herbs and roots. He will appreciate that. Kill a suckling pig and have the cook roast it till the skin is crispy. I will have my usual roast goose with plum sauce. We should also make a beef stew in a large clay pot and steam a fresh river fish. I leave you to organise the dumplings and dessert," I instructed.

"What shall we do for entertainment?" she asked.

"I want the dinner to be substantial but not ostentatious. I do not want to give the impression of luxury or high living. This would violate the principles of Confucius. You will give a recital on the Gu Chen (Zither), and I will hire a small dancing troupe from the city. A few bottles of that rich rice wine we have in the cellar would smooth the conversation."

"Will we be required to provide female companions for them?" she asked plainly.

"Chen Tang is a young man and may have his needs. The governor is in his seventh decade and in poor health. Then again, one never knows. Are there any among your maidens who would be willing to provide the service? We will compensate them, of course," I enquired.

"I am sure there are some among them who will do it for extra coin. Perhaps we should hire some professionals from the city," she suggested.

"Yes, have them attend to the officials in the bath. If later either has the urge, they can serve them in the bedroom as well. Hire a half dozen so there will be some choice. Have them instructed on how to bathe the gentlemen properly."

CHAPTER 4

Take a roundabout route and lure the enemy with some gain: Start out after him but arrive before him. This is to master the crooked and the straight.

After riding for about half an hour, Livy had a premonition of danger. They had achieved a huge coup, but getting away was too easy. Surely the Gauls were not lacking in cunning. He began to think tactically. How would the enemy plan to intercept them? He knew they would not give up so easily and right now would be manoeuvring to cut them off from safety and exact their revenge. He searched the mind of the enemy.

There is no greater danger than that nearest home.

At dawn, the Belgic cavalry had laid a trap at the edge of the forest, a mere three miles from the walls of Bibrax. Deeper in the forest, a long, widely spaced line of skirmishers were well hidden and alert to give an alarm at the first sight of Livy's raiders. The rest of the Belgic cavalry were divided into three squadrons numbering 100 riders each. Each group gathered in a small clearing. When the alarm was given, the nearest group would engage and the other two would quickly converge on the spot, surround, and slaughter the raiders which had done so much damage and were no better than horse thieves. Revenge would be exacted in blood.

Murato was the leader of the war party. He was a veteran of many raids and battles, and his muscled body bore the scars to prove it. To that formidable warrior, life was battle and war was life. Typically, he fought nude as a mark of honour and courage. His sword fighting skills were second to none among the Gaesatae and he was an expert horseman. That day, he wore leather trousers as a concession to the discomfort of having to ride. He had quickly learnt that riding nude was deleterious to certain tender parts of his anatomy.

He wore his hair in two long blond plaits and sported a long downturned moustache but no beard. In his right hand was a heavy hunting spear with a wicked leaf-shaped steel blade. A long, straight Gallic sword was slung at his back in a leather scabbard. He wore a conical steel helmet decorated with wings and black horsehair plume. It sported large cheek pieces.

The ambush was Murato's conception. The Romans would get complacent as they neared their base and would not expect to be suddenly attacked so close to home. His warriors hid themselves well and were silent. Murato dismounted behind a tree as he waited for the raiders to appear. He was calm and ready.

The sun rose and still there were no raiders to be seen. The mist was dissipating. The Belgae had been crouching hidden for an hour and their legs were sore, but no one came through the forest. The other war leaders were looking at Murato questioningly. What's happening? Had the raiders somehow slipped past? Everyone was getting uneasy.

Suddenly there was shouting and sounds of battle in the rear. Two of the three cavalry squadrons were being attacked! Javelins, slingshots, and arrows were flying at the cavalry formations seemingly out of nowhere. The squadron commanders tried to form a line and charge their assailants, but the missiles were coming thick and fast. Men and animals screamed in terror. Arrows skewered flesh and stones crushed bones. The horsemen milled around, bewildered. Organisation crumbled. In frustration, the commanders blew the retreat and the horsemen fled. All three squadrons scampered northwards through the forest.

Murato's scouts had not been hit yet so they had time to form up. His men formed a skirmish line and then charged. After about fifty yards, he came across the Balearic slingers and ran his horses through them, killing a number with sword and spear. Murato thundered into the fray and skewered one of the slingers with his heavy spear right through the chest and out the back. He then drew his sword and beheaded another slinger with a mighty slash of his heavy sword. He chopped down on a third slinger as he turned to run and cleaved down on his shoulder, shattering the collarbone and cutting deep into the chest cavity, severing several major blood vessels which caused a fountain of blood to splash all over his large chestnut stallion. The resistance firmed up when they next ran into the line of Numidian light infantry. Javelins were hurled at close quarters, bringing down horses everywhere. The Numidians put up a stiffer fight with their javelins thrusting like spears into the faces of the horsemen. Murato saw several of his men get impaled and fall off their horses.

Two Numidians with dark faces and simple white tunics then ran towards him, javelins raised. He swerved his horse to charge towards the left one, who panicked and jumped to one side. At the same time, he parried the javelin of the Numidian on the right, then caught him on the back swing with a slash to the back. Suddenly he was on the other side of the enemy line, and he looked to see how many of his men had gotten through. He estimated there were about two dozen. They rode towards the sunlight, which marked the edge of the forest. As he cleared the last trees, what he saw made his heart sink and his blood grow cold.

Two hundred yards in front of them, a line of Roman cavalry was drawn up. Each man carried a bow with the arrow nocked and ready to fire. One second later, a volley of shafts impacted his men, and half of them were hit and fell screaming. Murato admired their accuracy. They were skilled bowmen. He hadn't a chance to reach them alive.

Livy and Murato stared at each other. Livy too acknowledged the bravery of that barbarian commander. Murato waved his men to withdraw and turned his horse. Livy gave the order to hold and lowered his bow. He drew his sword and gave a salute. Murato returned the salute, then turned and rode back into the forest with the remainder of his men. The Numidians and slingers were not organised to stop them from escaping.

Livy, felt strangely happy to see them escape. He was not sure why. Perhaps he should have hunted them down. He noted the noble bearing of that strange naked savage that had fought so well and so bravely. No doubt they would meet again in the field of battle in the coming days. Livy wondered if either would show each other the same civility the next time they met.

Exhaustion made him turn away towards Bibrax.

Cavalry Skirmishes

The raiders took the morning to rest and refit in Bibrax. Iccius was even more hospitable than the day before. The raiders were now returning heroes. What's more, the Remi were thoroughly impressed with the herd of captured horses, which were only now being transported in batches back to Caesar's camp. Livy wondered how they would manage so many animals.

He took the opportunity to commandeer the best hundred of the captured animals as remount for his men and then gave the next hundred to the Remi, who rejoiced at that unexpected bounty. That did much to ingratiate the raiders further with the local women, who were now falling over themselves to pamper their benefactors.

Anticipating the ambush prepared by the enraged Belgic pursuers, he had made a mad dash back to Bibrax, making a wide circle eastwards. They arrived before dawn and had just enough time to prepare an ambush for the ambushers. His men and horses were exhausted, and if they would have been forced to fight, they would not have come through unscathed.

Biorix and his Remi friends were lying exhausted by a campfire. A whole lamb was roasting, a gift from the town. The aroma of the roast was tantalising, but the men were too exhausted even to eat. Livy went up to them and lay down. He closed his eyes for a moment. When he opened them, he was staring into the face of Brigita. She was beaming brightly, and then she bent down and gave him a warm, wet kiss on the lips. Her breath was sweet, and her lips and tongue tasted of honey.

"I'm so happy to see you," she said. "Here, I have wine for you. The best I can find. All the way from the Roman province."

Livy levered himself up on one elbow and took the flask gratefully. He took a long draught, then a second. The wine was full and fruity, far superior to the vinegary wine of the legions. "That was what I needed. Thank you." He looked straight into her lovely grey eyes.

Brigita blushed. "I have something special prepared for you. Follow me. We can eat later"

She got up and walked off. Livy followed. She walked down the muddy main street of the town, then turned into a side street and then turned again. Their sandals made a squishing sound as they walked. There was a smell of wet animal manure in the air. Finally they came to a small wooden house with a thatched roof. "This is my house. Please come in."

The inside of the house showed a woman's touch. There was a stove which was alight. The floor was clean and boarded. There were curtains and cushions to sit on. The bed in one corner looked comfortable. There was a dining table and some well-made wooden chairs. On the table was a basket of fresh bread, and the table was set for two with metal plates and a flagon of wine. The room had the aroma of freshly cooked meat stew. Best of all, there was a large wooden tub in the middle of the room. Wisp of steam came from the surface of the water, and Livy could already feel its warmth.

"First I will clean you up, then we eat," Brigita said firmly. "You need good scrub. You have blood and dirt everywhere." She helped him out of his chain armour, belt, boots, and tunic and soon plonked him in the bath which was quite hot and just below scalding temperature.

Brigita gave him a sly smile and blushed. She then reached down to catch the hem of her tunic and pulled it off over her head. Livy drank in her lovely body. It was well proportioned with ample breasts, small pink nipples, narrow waist, and sturdy legs. She gingerly lowered herself into the large wooden tub behind Livy and proceeded to scrub his hair with a rough wet piece of wool, moving carefully so as to avoid opening the existing scalp wound.

"I didn't know Belgic maidens shaved below," Livy teased.

"They don't. I did it for you. I heard that Romans preferred shaven pubes."

"You are right. Tell me more about you," Livy luxuriated. He felt all the tension melt away as she tenderly massaged his scalp.

"I am the niece of the prefect. My mother was his sister, and my father used to be the chief of the town till he was killed in battle. I was given in marriage to a handsome young warrior. He was from a noble family who were retainers to the prefect. A year ago, he was also killed in battle. I was heartbroken because I loved him. Our people fight too much. Even before the Romans came, there was constant warfare between tribe and tribe," she ended on a sad note.

"You are young and beautiful. Why did you not re-marry?"

"There are not enough men in our town and even less now. Simply put, there was no one worthy, and I didn't want to just settle for any stupid country oaf. You can turn around now. I wash you in the front."

Livy had been enjoying the back scrub, especially so because he could feel her nipples occasionally rubbing against him. He turned around and faced her. She was pretty rather than beautiful. Her face had a symmetry that elevated her above her peasant stock. She looked more refined than one would expect for a village girl in a barbarian town. Youth, health, and simple living had given her a glow.

"How old are you?"

"I have lived twenty seasons. I married when I was sixteen, and my husband died a year ago." She looked suddenly pensive. "I am a little afraid to marry again as men have a bad habit of getting themselves killed these days." She gave a sardonic laugh.

While they talked, she scrubbed his chest, face, and arms, then moved down to his legs. As she cleaned higher up his thighs, Livy felt an involuntary reaction to her gentle massaging movements. Brigita did not fail to notice. She smiled and blushed.

"Please don't feel uncomfortable. It's a natural reaction." She laughed.

Livy drew her close to kiss her as he let her hands gently grasp his erect phallus. Her mouth smelt delicious and her lips were soft and sweet. The sensation of her gentle, warm hands on his member was exquisite beyond description.

Livy gave himself to the ecstasy of the moment, and they gave their bodies to each other with delicious passion.

After the bath and a very long and sensuous tumble on her straw bed, they enjoyed a hearty lunch of stew, fresh bread, cheese, and some apples. "Did you enjoy that?" Brigita mumbled with her mouth full. She was still totally naked, and Livy thought she remained so because she sensed that he liked looking at her body and wanted to continue giving him the visual pleasure.

"Yes, I did. Very much," Livy answered.

"It's been a long time for me, and women have their needs too. You are not without experience. Someone taught you to pleasure a woman."

"I had someone back home," he murmured shyly.

"A Roman girl? Was she a neighbour or a slave."

"No, she was Celtic. She was well tanned by the sun, not fair like you. She was a slave, but she was my best friend. She taught me about the ways of men and women, and we were close in other ways. It was not only about sex."

"Do you miss her?"

"Yes, I do, very much. I think about her especially in the lonely nights as I lie in my tent listening to the snores of my men." He laughed.

"What happened to her when you left?"

"I persuaded my family to free her. She remained in our house, and my mother promised to protect her. She says she waits for me, but I think after a while, my mother will find her a husband who will love her and care for her."

"And what about you? Do you look for a woman to call your own? I don't think so. You are a soldier and have sold yourself to the army for what? Sixteen years? And I believe you Roman soldiers are not allowed to marry."

"Not officially, but many of the older men and the centurions of course have a woman among the camp followers."

"I have no wish to be a camp follower."

Livy didn't remember asking her. Nevertheless, it was sweet of her to assume he would. She obviously liked him.

"It is a terrible life, and I think if your man is killed, someone else just takes over. Otherwise you can't survive. No, thanks, I think I prefer to stay in Bibrax, and when the war is finally over, I will marry someone with a farm, whom I can take to bed every night and keep safe."

"And have a whole bunch of kids and beat them every day?"

"Yes, and have a whole bunch of kids and beat them every day if they are naughty." She giggled. She took a piece of bread, dipped it in the rich stew, and popped it in his mouth.

They spent a few wonderful hours, and Livy was truly refreshed and felt human again. She was a skilled and passionate lover. Brigita was not about to run off with him, but as long as she was still single, he was welcome to come and enjoy her hospitality so long as he provided her some comfort in return. They could be friends.

In the early afternoon, Livy collected his companions and headed back to the main camp of Caesar's army. There were barely eighty men left. Four were wounded and left behind in Bibrax, and sixteen were missing. He knew some of them were killed in the Belgic camp, but he hoped at least a few had escaped and would rejoin in time.

Nevertheless, the night action had been an astounding victory. Nearly 2,000 horses were captured and several hundred of the enemy killed or wounded. "That's at least 2,000 less enemy cavalry to worry about in tomorrow's battle. The tiger had indeed lost a few teeth," Livy concluded.

The men moved with a new bounce. He had earned their respect in the last two days, and they no longer regarded him as an upstart youngster promoted prematurely from the ranks. He was a proven commander and he had led them to victory. Men liked nothing better than victory in battle. How suffering and horror are quickly forgotten, dissipated by the glow of glory! Each man had an extra horse, and some had gained valuables plundered from the beaten enemy.

As he rode along the track towards the main camp, he passed a convoy of slaves. Those were captives from the recent action. They were big men of pallid complexion. Most had been stripped naked and bound. There were chains around their necks and ankles, and they were escorted by mercenaries in the pay of slave dealers. Those jackals followed battles to make business and reap profits. They were scum, but they helped keep the army in pay as the money paid for the slaves went to Caesar.

He passed one lot which looked especially forlorn. There were several walking wounded among them. They sported crude bandages and were being supported by comrades. They moved slower than the rest, and their slave driver escorts were beating them mercilessly with whips. Livy rode up to one and yanked his whip away.

"What the . . . ? Who the fuck do you think you are snatching my whip?! I ought to give you a thrashing, you young guttersnipe!" He was a large black man in leather armour.

Suddenly he was faced with a half dozen arrows pointed at his chest. The man looked stunned and let his hands drop.

"You don't talk to Centurion Livy in that tone, you scum." Biorix gave him a cold hard stare and a shove with his boot.

"I'm sorry, sir. I didn't realise."

Livy cut him short, "I don't approve of your barbaric treatment of these prisoners. They may be spoils of war, but they are warriors and have fought bravely unlike scum like you. There are wounded among them. They should be loaded on to carts rather than whipped."

The man was cowed and looked down, ashamed.

"Biorix, go commandeer that cart over there and load the wounded on it. Also give the prisoners a drink from our canteens. We can fill up easily back in camp. Leave a few canteens with them to help them endure their misery. We are supposed to be liberating them from barbarism and bringing them Roman civilization. Let us not be wanting in showing simple humanity."

The wounded prisoners were released from their chains and loaded up on to the carts with the help of the raiders. Everyone was given a long drink.

A large naked prisoner with a bloody bandage over his head came up to Livy. "My gratitude, we are enemies, but I will not forget this kindness, Centurion," the man said.

"What is your name?" Livy asked.

"I am Drax. I command these men," the warrior replied.

"May your gods smile on you, Drax"

"And on you as well, Centurion." He extended his hand. Livy grasped it, then helped him ascend into the cart with his men.

The other prisoners were likewise moved. Many promised to add the raiders to their prayers, and some even tried to kiss their feet and their hands. Livy was moved as well. The attitude of the commander also made an impression on the raiders. War was inhuman, but it did not stop soldiers from individual acts of kindness.

Liqian, Winter, 36 BC

The Governor's Visit

Gan Yanshaou, governor of the Western Regions, arrived at my hilltop villa about a week after the baths were completed. He was accompanied by a bodyguard of a dozen crack cavalrymen dressed in the dusty blue Han colours, replete with bronze lamellar armour and ornate shiny helmets. They carried spears with colourful streamers and large blue silk banners with the Han ideogram emblazoned prominently.

The governor rode in a two-horse carriage and his deputy, Chen Tang, rode a white stallion. Chen Tang sported an elaborate steel armour suit coming down below his knees. His elaborate helmet was emblazoned with dragons, and he had a lustrous blue horsehair plume.

I was dressed humbly in my civil service robes and headgear with no sign of ostentation. I met the dignitaries at the foot of the steps which led to the entrance to my villa. "I bid you welcome to my humble abode, Great One," I chimed. I bowed deeply with palms held clasped in front.

The governor went into a fit of coughing. He composed himself, then answered, "Greetings, Prefect. We thank you for your hospitality. Your villa has good feng shui. You face the south, which is good. You don't want the north wind blowing in your face." He chuckled to himself, which triggered another bout of coughing. He bowed and greeted me in similar fashion.

"I am Deputy Commander Chen Tang," his young deputy introduced himself. He was handsome, clean-shaven, and well built. We were almost the same height. The governor had become hunched with age.

"We are honoured to have you as our guest." I saluted Chen Tang. I gestured for them to ascend the stairs. Chen Tang and I helped the governor ascend, each holding on to one arm. I showed them to my reception area.

As we sipped bowls of rice wine, the official discussions began.

"We have news from the other side of the Western Regions," Governor Gan began. His voice was slow and measured. "The Xiongnu made a raid on a Parthian city called Merv. The city was built using a large contingent of men from the Far West of the world. They are prisoners of war from Da Qin Guo."

That fact immediately caught my attention, and I sat up transfixed.

"I thought that would get your attention." The governor gave a wry smile. "These men have been conscripted forcefully, I expect, into the Xiongnu army of *Chanyu* Zhizhi, who is even now rearming them and training for offensive operations against us."

"How sure are you of this information?" I asked.

"Over the years, Chen Tang has developed a formidable network of spies in the Western Regions. Oh yes, we are confident of the veracity of our information," the governor said.

"These men are being used as the nucleus of a new army. I hear the soldiers of Da Qin Guo are formidable heavy infantry. These men pose a potential danger to the empire," Chen Tang said.

"Yes, they are, at this time, I believe the very best infantry in the world." I sat back and took a big gulp of my wine.

"How will our Han infantry stand against them?" the governor asked.

"A Roman legion will cut a Chinese unit of similar size to pieces," I said. "You may however seek victory through overwhelming numbers and choosing the right place and right moment to strike," I said.

"I feared this might be so." The governor looked worried "We must prepare ourselves. I believe the *chanyu* has designs on Han territory. My *commanderie* will be his next target."

"Your Excellency must be tired from the journey. Please let us commence dinner, and we can discuss business later." Handmaidens appeared and led the guest to the dining room, where the aroma of roast suckling pig tempted the palate and caused stomachs to groan with hunger.

After dinner, the two men enjoyed my bath facility. As we sat with bloated stomachs in the tepid pool, we resumed our discussion.

"I have ordered Chen Tang to recruit an army of 40,000. We will have ample infantry and crossbowmen. What we lack however is cavalry. Preferably we would like mounted archers. I believe you are somewhat an expert in this type of warfare," the governor said.

"I am no longer in the military," I protested. "I have retired and lead the peaceful life of a lowly prefect." I extended my clenched palms in respect.

"You diminish yourself too much," the governor said. "You are yet capable to lead our cavalry, and we will certainly need cavalry. A pure infantry army will not be able to bring a mounted Xiongnu army to battle," the governor reasoned.

"You are right. An infantry army without cavalry will be seriously disadvantaged," I said. The disaster at Carrhae came to my mind, making me wince involuntarily. "How many cavalry do you have?"

"A mere two dozen," Chen Tang replied.

"How many cavalry will you need for this expedition?" I asked.

"Preferable a thousand at least," Chen Tang replied.

"Will we be able to request them from the capital?" I asked.

"We already tried," the governor said. "None are forthcoming. We have been ordered to recruit our own. That is why we are here. We need you to recruit a cavalry unit and train them in the next three months for combat operations. We have the funding."

"That is a short time," I said.

"Can you do it?" The Governor looked at me earnestly, even desperately. I felt sorry for the old man.

"Yes, I can," I said with a reassuring smile.

"Will you lead them if we have to take them west?" he pursued.

"To fight against Romans?" I asked.

"If necessary, certainly against the Xiongnu," Chen Tang said.

"I will fight the Xiongnu any time. They are old enemies and I know them. I am not so sure about going against Romans," I said.

"We appreciate your sensitivity about this matter. If the occasion should arise, you may stand down." The governor was surprisingly understanding. "You are a man of great virtue and honour, and we will respect your feelings on this matter."

"I then see no reason not to accept your mission. Will you seek clearance from the capital and the governor of Gansu?" I requested.

"I will see to that," the governor assured me.

"What have I got myself into again?" I thought. I had my own private reason to fight one last war. I wanted to look up old friends.

CHAPTER 5

Belgica, Summer, 57 BC

The skilful warrior first ensures his own invulnerability.

The area around Caesar's camp had been denuded of trees for at least two miles around. Wood had been cut to build the camp and defences. The clearing also ensured that enemy forces could not sneak up on the Roman Army. The main Roman camp was in the summit of a ridge. The Roman Army was formed up on one face of the ridge facing north. The army looked small, so Livy surmised that it was just a guard and the rest of the legions were busy working on the defences. At the most two legions were formed up.

Perpendicular to the ridge on each flank, trenches were being dug and redoubts were being built as artillery platforms. Caesar was fortifying his flanks so that the Belgic host would have only one way to get to the Roman Army and that was up the ridge. Any attempt at flanking the Roman line would be met with a hail of artillery bolts from Ballistae and Scorpions. The whole encampment was a bustle of activity. The Romans bustled like beavers—digging fossae, erecting palisades, and constructing towers. The fossae or trenches were dug in concentric rings, and the bottom of each trench was further protected by sharpened stakes designed to brutally impale any unfortunate enough to fall in. Such special traps were called *Lilia* or Lilies. The openings to these traps were concealed with shrubbery.

The party of raiders finally arrived at the main camp. A party of Caesar's cavalry guard came to meet them. They were splendidly outfitted in polished silver cuirass and shiny helmets topped with black horsehair plumes.

"Greetings, Commander. Welcome back. Caesar would like to see you at once in his tent. Please follow me." The leader of the guards gave the military salute, bringing up his fist to his chest.

Livy returned the salute and motioned his men to follow.

"Just you, Commander, your men will be shown where they can set up their tents and pasture the horses."

Livy was escorted to a crimson tent decorated richly with silver trimmings. The two sentries outside saluted and pulled the tent flaps aside to let him in. Caesar was seated in his *curile* chair, bent over maps laid out on his campaign table. Several of his legates were present. Livy recognized Sabinus, Cotta, Quintus Pedius, and of course Marcus and Publius Crassus. The other officers he could not recognise.

Livy saluted smartly and waited to be addressed. He was somewhat reassured when Publius gave him a knowing grin. Livy was conscious that he looked dirty, dusty, and unkempt. He was confident however that after his recent performance that interview could in no way be negative.

Caesar was dressed in full uniform. He wore a gleaming silver—muscled cuirass with gold trimmings. His *subarmalis* and *pteruges* were of fine white leather. All the officers looked ready to go to battle at a moment's notice. Livy had noticed that even the soldiers at work had their chain mail on all the time. Caesar was making sure that the Roman Army would not be caught unprepared. Finally Caesar looked up at him.

"Well, young man, that was quite a performance last night. Your small band of *exploratores* knocked out a third of the enemy cavalry. That has somewhat evened the odds. As you know, we are desperately short of cavalry. I have a mere 2,500 horses, and only 500 are Roman cavalry. The rest are Belgic, Gaulish, and German. Now, we not only have deprived the enemy of nearly 2,000 horses but also have the horses to train another 2,000 of our own cavalry." Caesar gave him a satisfied smile. "You have our gratitude."

Livy stood at attention, not daring to respond. He was in the presence of the legendary commander himself—a man who descended from the Goddess Venus and whose family went back to the founding of Rome.

"At ease, Gaius Livius or rather Centurion Gaius Livius. Oh yes, I have decided to confirm your commission with two extra grades of seniority."

"Thank you, sir." Livy was stunned.

"I daresay there are not many nineteen-year-old centurions in this army, and I am taking a chance promoting you. You may have a little trouble with credibility down in the cohorts, but I have a feeling you have a special talent for unconventional warfare, and we will put you to good use in this war." Caesar paced around the centurion as he spoke.

"I'll try my best not to let you down, sir," Livy stammered.

"Good. I am attaching you back to the Seventh Legion under its new acting legate, your patron Publius Crassus here. You are hereby designated as centurion of the Sixth Century of the Eighth Cohort. The present centurion broke an ankle yesterday and will be indisposed. The century will however be commanded by your *optio* in your absence. I have a far more important job for you"

"At your command, Lord Caesar." Livy saluted smartly.

"I am impressed by your band of *equites sagitarii*, and I propose to expand your command to a full squadron of 300 horses. I will give you the authority to pick your men from any outfit in the army."

"I guess I will look for archers among the cavalry and riders among the Cretan archers." Livy remembered the answer from a previous interview.

Caesar smiled as he too remembered.

"I suggest you get on to it right away." Livy was dismissed. "Now, Labienus, let's talk about the cavalry deployment for tomorrow. I expect the enemy will probe us with cavalry before they launch their main attack, and we must be ready for a response." Caesar's attention had already moved on.

Livy saluted smartly and turned to leave the tent. Publius Crassus followed him. "A word, Gaius." He put a hand on Livy's shoulder.

Livy turned, looking stunned.

"I know that was somewhat sudden, but I do believe the promotion was more than overdue." Publius smiled and extended his hand.

"Thank you for your confidence, sir, and congratulations on your promotion to Legate of the Seventh," Livy said, taking his hand warmly.

"I've taken the liberty to have a centurion's tent prepared for you. There is a little surprise in there too. Come, I'll show you the way. I'm not a real legate yet. It's only an acting legate appointment. I believe Caesar wants me to take the Seventh on an independent action, though I know not where as yet." They walked away, Crassus's arm draped over Livy's shoulder.

Crassus led Livy to the encampment of the Seventh Legion. They came to a small white tent, stopped, and dismounted. Crassus led the way inside.

The tent's interior was cosily furnished with a camp bed, a *curile* chair, and a small desk. By the bed a full set of centurion's armour, helmet, greaves, cloak, and vine stick was set up. Everything was polished and in pristine condition. Livy beamed.

"I got the armourer to give you a brand new set." Crassus beamed.

"I am deeply touched, sir." Livy was lost for words.

"Well, get some rest, take your refreshments, and go rejoin your men. The raiders are an army asset but for the moment under command of the Seventh. I don't expect the enemy to attack today, but certainly we shall have to face them tomorrow. I'll see you later." They clasped hands again.

Livy was glad to see a pitcher of wine and a big bowl of fruit on the desk. "Compliments of Crassus," he thought to himself. He drank thirstily and then crunched into a luscious red apple. He then lay on the camp bed and almost dozed off.

"No time to rest," he thought to himself. He got up, splashed his face with some water from the pitcher, threw on his new centurion outfit, and hurried out of his tent. He left the heavy standard issue armour behind, preferring his own trusty lightweight steel chain mail.

A few minutes hence, he found the encampment of the raiders. Most of the men were lying dead to the world in their tents. He found Paulus and Biorix. They were busy tucking into a roast chicken, hunger overpowering exhaustion.

"Well, look at that! Mars himself come to visit us poor raiders!" Paulus smiled broadly and extended his hand. "Well, congratulations, sir. It's high time and well deserved if I don't say so myself."

"You look every bit the Roman officer now, sir." Biorix smiled with admiration.

"Thank you, but I don't feel particularly comfortable in this elaborate outfit and this ridiculous helmet." He was referring to the polished steel helmet with the large transverse crest made of red feathers, which would make him the target of every Belgic warrior in a fight.

"Not very practical, I admit," said Biorix. "But it would scare the hell out of little children," he crackled.

"I'd love to share your little joke, but work beckons. Caesar wants to expand our little troop to 300 for purposes best known to himself. So here's what we have to do . . ."

An hour later, Centurion Livy, Decurion Paulus, and Signifer Biorix were at the camp of the Cretan archers. It was a starry night, which added to the already bright illumination in the Cretan camp where dozens of campfires roared. There was an overpowering smell of cooking, and game could be seen roasting on spits. An unfamiliar smell of spice permeated the air.

Their leader was Kleon, a forty-something Greek with a big black beard. He sported an old-fashioned Corinthian helmet and a black iron-muscled cuirass. His own complexion was dark olive. He looked like a hoplite from an ancient Athenian army.

"I see we have a new centurion. Hello, Livius! What brings you to our humble camp?" Kleon greeted cheerily.

"I hope you were well entertained at Bibrax by our most hospitable Remi host," Livy said.

"Aye, my men and I were well looked after indeed. Fed and bathed and more for some. It was a real treat after such a bloody battle," Kleon said.

"I need your help, Kleon. Caesar wants to expand the squadron of my raiders. I need men who can shoot a bow and ride a horse."

"So you think it would make your task easier if you took men from me who already can handle a bow and you only need to teach them to ride, eh?" Kleon got the picture. "We're shorthanded as it is. I have barely 800 men. So how many men do you need?" Kleon asked.

"I need about 100."

"So many? And you think I should just hand them over just like that?" Kleon looked outraged.

"Actually I have an order from Caesar saying just that. On the other hand, we are friends, so I don't intend to use it. I'll trade you for the men."

Kleon's eyes gaped wide. "Now you are talking like a Greek. What do you have to trade with, my boy?"

"I've got here a really sturdy stallion just for you." Biorix led forward a beautiful grey stallion, one of the better horses liberated from the enemy. The horse looked lively and spirited.

Kleon looked impressed but tried, not too successfully, to look unmoved.

"I've also got two dozen amphora of the best *falernian* for your men. Will that sweeten the deal enough?" Livy offered.

"Not enough, but you have the right idea. What else?"

"You drive a hard bargain, my friend."

"Well, you want to take 100 of my men. I can't afford to lose them on the eve of battle, you understand?" Kleon narrowed his eyes.

"I won't take them till after the battle—if there is a battle," Livy said.

"You don't think the Belgae will fight?"

"We are in a prepared position, and all the advantage is on our side. Galba would be a fool to attack us here. I think they won't fight," Livy concluded.

"So now you are a bloody strategist too, eh? Thinking of making it to legate someday no doubt?" Kleon jibed.

"Back to the subject, why don't I throw in two more horses and 10,000 arrows from our store?" Livy offered.

"All right, you got a deal, but I get to pick the men. You can send someone to fetch them after the battle tomorrow or, if your prediction comes true, tomorrow evening," Kleon agreed.

"I thank you from the bottom of my heart, you old rascal. You should become a merchant after the war. You'd do well." Livy took his hand.

"Won't you stay for a goblet of wine and a bite?"

"No time, old friend. I need to find another 100 cavalrymen."

They clasped hands again. Livy looked at Kleon and then drew him near and gave him a hug and a pat on the back. "Take care tomorrow, old friend. May you live long and well," Livy said.

"Well, I hope you won't be a silly fool and get yourself killed. You watch your back, boy." He patted Livy warmly.

The next stop was the encampment of the cavalry. Caesar's cavalry commander was Labienus. Labienus was a good cavalry commander, but he was arrogant and intolerant. He also had the reputation of being devious and bad-tempered. Caesar and he were often at odds. Livy thought it better to see his old friend Decius instead.

Decius was now commander of a double squadron of 240 men, and they were doing drills in a flat pasture. The cavalry were practicing the diamond formation. That formation allowed rapid change of direction to any of four quadrants. Livy rode up to him. He had switched back to his plain cavalry helmet as he found the elaborate centurion's helmet totally unsuited to cavalry activities.

"Ave, Decius, your men are looking smart today."

"You can't drill them too much. We are expecting to meet the enemy cavalry tomorrow, and we need to be in top shape."

"A word, Decius. I need a favour." He showed him the authorisation from Caesar." I know this comes at a bad time and you need every rider. I don't need them till after the battle though."

"Labienus won't like this at all." Decius frowned.

"I expect not. Can you help me persuade him?" Livy looked at him hopefully.

"Your raiders are a great asset. I saw how effective they were at Bibrax, and I heard about your raid of the enemy camp. I think cavalry with bows definitely have an advantage over normal cavalry. Persuading Labienus will be a hell of a job."

"We must try."

"I'll help you talk to him, but I want a favour in return."

"Anything, Decius," Livy replied.

"I want to be part of your raiders. I don't even mind going back down to decurion of 100." Decius came closer on his horse. That would be a serious demotion from his present status as commander of two full squadrons.

"I shall be honoured to have you, old friend. I'll try and make it so." He wasn't all that confident he could swing it though. Labienus would never agree.

The interview with the cavalry commander was tense. Livy felt immediately that Labienus didn't even think he was fit to be a centurion, let alone commander of the *exploratores*.

The command tent was luxurious compared to Caesar's. There were gold plates and drinking goblets, an elaborately carved desk and bed, and several gold-trimmed chairs. The floor was covered by a beautiful crimson rug. The commander had obviously been drinking. He sat behind his desk, its polished top reflecting his clean-shaven face and carefully arranged white curls. Two smartly dressed cavalry officers stood to either side of him. He wore a finely made gold-trimmed tunic, and his purple cloak was held by a golden clasp at each shoulder decorated with the head of Medusa. Livy and

Decius looked distinctly scruffy in comparison. There was a smell of incense in the air, and the letter of Caesar lay open on the desk.

"I heard about your exploits last night. I suspect you were lucky that the enemy was so inept as to let you make off with all their horses. Nevertheless, my cavalry can now expand with the new horses, so I guess you deserve your little promotion." He sounded grudging. "Personally I like my centurions with more experience and years under their belt," Labienus grumbled.

Livy remained silent.

Decius chipped in, "Sir, cavalry with a missile capacity can be a great addition to your command, especially when the enemy has twice the number of horses. Numbers count in a melee, but if we can skirmish with arrows and run, we can reduce their numbers over time without losing too many men ourselves."

Labienus held up a hand. "Enough. I don't need a lecture on cavalry tactics. Horse archers are a barbaric concept from the east. They are the tactics of the primitive nomads of the steppes, like the Scythians and the Parthians. The Greek heavy infantry proved totally superior when they met such forces. Even Alexander didn't rely on horse archers. They are an outmoded concept. Whatever must Julius Caesar be thinking. I certainly cannot afford to lose 100 of my valuable cavalry just because someone comes up with a crazy idea."

Livy was livid. He tried hard to control his rage. "I would like to respectfully point out that modern Parthian armies have horse archers as their principal cavalry type with *cataphracts* in support."

"You presume to lecture me too? Pah! Those effeminate Parthians are no match for our legions. We can use the testudo formation against their arrows, and their infantry is no match for ours. Enough of this nonsense. I won't release my men, and I will speak to Caesar personally about this. You are both dismissed."

Livy and Decius were struck silent by the harsh remarks. They turned and left.

"Caesar must be out of his mind appointing a mere boy to head the *exploratores*. I'll bet they won't last two weeks against the Belgic cavalry," Labienus murmured to his aides.

"Well, that certainly went well," Decius remarked. "I don't think he likes you too much."

"I think that's a real understatement." The night was getting cold, and Livy pulled his cloak closer and rubbed his hands, breathing on them to keep warm. "Anyway I better let you go back to your men. I think you will have a heavy day tomorrow. We've done enough for one day." Livy suddenly felt the exhaustion sweep through him. He had not slept much for three days now.

They parted, and Livy made his way back to his tent. When he opened the tent flaps, he smiled at the pleasant surprise.

"Ave, Centurion." Brigita saluted playfully.

"Word does get around." Livy gave a tired smile. "How did you manage to find my tent?"

"I told them I was the Centurion Gaius Livius' woman. They allow centurion's whores to entertain their masters, it seems."

"I thought the role of camp follower was beneath your dignity," Livy remarked with amusement.

"It still is, but I have made an exception just for tonight. A brave warrior deserves comfort the night before a big battle." She leant back against his desk which Livy saw had a simple dinner laid out and two flagons of wine.

Livy walked towards her until he was leaning over her, looking down into her clear grey eyes. Her dark pupils were dilated, and she was clearly looking forward to what was going to transpire. They kissed passionately, completely giving themselves to the sweet taste and smell of each other's breath. Brigita pulled her loose tunic off her pristine white shoulders. She pressed her naked breasts against the cold chain mail.

"I've never made love to cold steel before. I must say it is a strange but somewhat titillating sensation." She unfastened the armour, then helped him out of his tunic. She took him by the hand and pulled him to the camp bed.

An hour later, they were lying naked together, eating succulent red grapes which Brigita had brought. They were both satiated and pensive. Brigita broke the silence.

"I like you, but the future you offer is fraught with danger and uncertainty. I don't want to become a widow a second time."

"You don't have to explain. I understand everything," Livy murmured.

"Who knows what tomorrow brings, so I have given you a memorable evening so that you will remember me either in this world or the next," she said.

"You are right to take pleasure whenever you can. I have seen too many lives cut short of late. If we win and if I live, will I see you tomorrow?"

"If you win and you live, I will be here." Brigita kissed him warmly.

CHAPTER 6

The fray can bring gain; it can bring danger.

The morning was bracing and cloudless and the sky a dazzling blue. Livy awoke to the shouting of orders, the tramping of feet, and the notes of trumpets and horns. Shortly, he was back with his century, dressed in full centurion regalia. His men were well turned out and stood in disciplined ranks. Large crimson shields decorated with lightning bolts stood in a neat row on the ground in front of each rank. The Seventh was placed second from the left in the Roman line. Six legions stood in line on a slope facing the enemy. Two legions, the Thirteenth and Fourteenth, were held in reserve in the camp. They were the newly recruited lads from Northern Italy. On both flanks, Livy could see the perpendicular row of trenches interrupted at intervals by artillery emplacements. Caesar and his staff officers positioned themselves in the centre.

The Belgic army was an amorphous mass. They looked like three to four times the size of the Roman Army. The mob was a tangle of colours, which contrasted with the uniformity of the Roman ranks. They tramped forward, beating their spears and sword against their shields, and made a huge din and a huge cloud of smoke. A marsh ran between the two armies, and the Belgic horde stopped as they reached it and started to form a line. They took their time, and the whole manoeuvre just to form a battle line seemed complicated as various chiefs negotiated their positions, each wanting a better and more honourable position in the line. Finally they were formed up.

There was suddenly a lull. Each side glared at each other across the marsh. Each hoped the other would attack and put themselves at a disadvantage, trudging through the wetlands. Neither was willing to make the first move. An hour went by. Livy noted that his men were getting nervous and thirsty. He ordered the water boys to bring water to his men. His fellow centurions followed. The day was getting warmer and still the two armies didn't move.

Suddenly a horn sounded on the Roman side. Several dull thuds were heard from both flanks from the direction of the artillery. The *onagers* and ballistae had starting firing. Large stones flew through the air at the Belgic mob, and flights of ballista bolts flew into the ranks of the enemy, impaling several men at a time. There were screams and shouts emanating from the enemy ranks. The formations under fire started to retreat out of range.

Suddenly enemy cavalry burst forth from both flanks and rode hard towards the artillery emplacements. The horsemen were a mixed bunch, some armoured and some naked from waist up. They carried spears and round shields. Their helmets were also varied. Some had elaborate ones with wings or animal decorations. There were at least a thousand horsemen on each wing.

Livy heard the sound of horns again, and immediately, Roman cavalry rode out from each flank directly towards the advancing enemy cavalry. The Roman squadrons looked about the same size, maybe 800 men in each wing. The opposing cavalry galloped full speed at each other. The Belgic horses cleared the marsh and were now accelerating eagerly to meet the Romans. The thunder of hoof beats was deafening. The two groups collided violently. The loud clash of weapons resounded. The Belgae seemed to have gotten the better of the initial exchange. Scores of horses and men on both sides were chopped down. The Roman advance had come to an abrupt stop. Moments later, the Roman horses seemed to be slowing pushed backwards. Then something inexplicable happened.

The Belgic cavalry suddenly disengaged and started galloping back to their lines. Labienus immediately rallied the Romans and signalled for pursuit. The Romans charged straight into the marsh after the Belgic cavalry.

Caesar who was watching groaned aloud, "Labienus, don't, it's a trap."

Publius Crassus beside him turned and said, "They look like they have the best of it, sir. What do you mean?"

"Watch and learn, young man," Caesar said flatly.

As soon as the Roman cavalry crossed the marsh, the Belgic cavalry immediately stopped, turned their horses, and charged back at them. At the same time, more cavalry emerged from within the ranks of the infantry, and the front ranks of the infantry also charged towards the now startled Roman cavalry. The front ranks of the Roman cavalry tried to reign in, but the horses behind crowded into them, not seeing what was happening.

Caesar growled as he watched. "Now the trap is sprung. Labienus is a fool."

Crassus was speechless as he watched how quickly a victory could be turned into defeat.

"Sound the recall for the cavalry," Caesar commanded. The trumpets immediately blared loudly.

Labienus had organised the front ranks to face the oncoming enemy and was signalling the rear ranks to withdraw. The Romans on the enemy side of the marsh were hit by cavalry and then charging infantry. The slaughter was painful to watch. Livy felt his heart sink into the ground. The combined Belgic force wrought total carnage.

At last, the Roman cavalry started to turn around and head back across the marsh. Stones from the heavy *onagers* were now falling amidst the Belgian attackers, punching holes in their ranks. Nevertheless, they pursued the Romans who were now fleeing in disarray, faces white in panic. Dead and dying littered the ground.

The Belgic infantry stopped at the edge of the marsh, but the cavalry pursued the Romans over the open ground in front of the legionary line. The legionary infantry opened their ranks to let the cavalry through. Their horses were blown and the unit was totally routed. The Belgic horses followed till about thirty yards when they received a volley of *pila* which skewered some men and a few horses. The rest reigned in their horses just as a second volley thinned their ranks further. They turned round abruptly and retreated out of range.

Caesar slapped his riding crop against his palm. "Dammit! We took a beating and now the enemy is encouraged. We can expect an all-out attack now. Tell all commanders to prepare to receive infantry. Order the artillery to open fire as soon as the enemy get in range. Tell Kleon to get his archers in front and form a skirmish line"

The Belgic army was greatly encouraged by the cavalry victory. There was wild cheering and hooting from the other side. Suddenly they began to bang their shields with their swords and spears, creating a rhythmic crashing beat. Slowly the whole mass of them began to move forward.

Livy watched with consternation. It was going to be a hard slogging battle—not hit and run like his raider sorties. Here he would have to stand and fight till they won or died. Suddenly the day seemed hot, and his sweat ran profusely down his face in rivulets.

"The men must not see me afraid," he told himself. He wiped his face with his cloak and tried to look strong and impassive. "Right, men, remember your training. Keep your shields up and don't let them get past. Keep your line intact, and they can't hurt you," he tried to encourage them.

He knew, however, that it didn't help much. Everyone knew that the Romans were outnumbered and that the struggle would be desperate. He looked at their young faces and pride swelled within his breast. They were all young Spanish lads no older than he was, but they were already tough, disciplined, and steadfast. Not a man uttered a word. They stood relaxed and confident with their shields and *pila* grounded. Livy decided that he could not let them down.

He turned to his *optio*, whose name was Galienus. He was a veteran from the Tenth Legion and was nearly thirty years old and due for promotion. "Well, Galienus, are we ready for this?"

"We won't ever be more ready, sir," he said with confidence. Livy almost believed him.

The *onagers* fired at maximum range, and huge stones were hurled towards the enemy army, falling just short of the front ranks. Suddenly the whole army came to a standstill. Livy expected them to resume their advance, but they stayed put just out of range of their artillery. They stayed there for the rest of the day.

Finally at dusk, Caesar ordered the whole Roman Army back to camp. Clearly Galba, the Belgic commander-in-chief, had decided not to attack that day. Perhaps the auspices were bad. Maybe there was some other reason. A small screening force was left on the hillside.

Caesar was clearly upset. He had planned for a great battle that day, which would crush all the Belgic tribes at once, bringing the whole region under his control. He had the advantage of position, and his artillery would have made mincemeat of any force trying to flank the legions. He even had two legions in reserve, which gave him huge flexibility. If they attacked across the marsh, he would let half of them cross and then attack that half while the other half was still struggling to cross. His legions would have broken the front half, who would then have to retreat back into the marsh where they would be caught and slaughtered. Now he felt cheated that the enemy had refused to give battle.

He retired to his tent to wash and freshen up. He then ordered his aides to round up all his commanders for a battle conference. They all came in a hurry. In his tent were all his legates, tribunes, the prefects of his auxiliary units, and the prefect of artillery. A light dinner was being prepared, but Caesar was in no mood to eat. There would be business before pleasure.

"First of all, it is obvious that our cavalry was bested today. What have you got to say, Labienus?"

Labienus looked sheepish. Some of his usual haughtiness had evaporated. It was obvious to all who had fucked up. "They ambushed us, My Lord Caesar. We were winning at first."

"They let you believe you were winning. You were outsmarted by a bunch of barbarians today, and they laugh at us in their camp tonight," Caesar said cuttingly. Labienus was speechless, his face red with humiliation.

"I want to see a better performance tomorrow by the cavalry. This time stick close to our lines and do not be tempted to pursue beyond the marsh. Next, why did they not attack today?"

"I think for the same reason we didn't march over and attack them," Crassus volunteered.

"Well, young man, tell me what do you think ran through their minds." Caesar looked at him intently, his eyes piercing.

"The first to cross the marsh would be at an obvious disadvantage. The other side would fall on the first part of the army coming across, and the rest would be slowed down. It's the same situation as a river crossing," Crassus explained.

"So I guess we have a stalemate, gentlemen," Caesar said in a resigned manner. "Neither side will be willing to make the first move."

There was a deadly silence in the tent. After thinking for several minutes, Caesar finally asked, "Anyone have any ideas?"

There was more silence. Finally Kleon spoke up, "Maybe we can tempt them over with a little bait."

"How do you mean?" Caesar shot back.

"Hear my plan, My Lord," Kleon began to elaborate. It was a cunning idea.

Livy retired to his tent. He was totally exhausted and parched. Biorix was waiting for him. "Greetings, Commander. I have good news. Kleon has picked out 100 new recruits for us. They are mostly from his new replacements, just came in a week ago. They are rather young but good lads all the same. Most are from Crete and Greece and other eastern provinces. A few already know how to ride, and all are pretty fancy with the bow."

"That's great, Biorix. I really needed some good news. Let me wash up a bit and get down a couple of bowls of water, then we can go over to the raiders' camp and meet our new men." Livy began to strip of his armour and then his tunic and washed from a basin of water left by Brigita. He then drank copiously from a flagon of drinking water. Feeling human again, he followed Biorix to the raiders' camp.

The new men were housed in tents pitched beside the old raiders. They were settling down for the evening meal when Livius and Biorix appeared. Paulus the decurion immediately fell in the men. They formed three lines, smartly dressed in green tunics and leather armour. Livy noticed that they were teenagers not more than eighteen years of age. He suddenly realised that he was not much older though he felt he had aged much since the beginning of the war.

"Men, welcome to the raiders. We are a special unit, and I assure you that if you are looking for excitement, you will find it here. Every man here is a chosen man with special skills. Every man here is an expert with the bow. Every man here should ride like a centaur. I know you are already marksmen with the bow and arrow, but now you will be taught to ride and to shoot from horseback even at the gallop. The training will be hard. You will be given little rest. You will train under your officers till you drop from exhaustion. When your training is over, each one of you will be worth ten ordinary soldiers."

There was a loud cheer from the both the new and the old men.

"I am your commander. My name is Centurion Gaius Livius. I will lead you to honour and glory and hopefully some loot and women as well."

At that, the men laughed loudly.

"Your reward will be fame and fortune. I welcome you this day to a great adventure."

The men cheered once more. "Paulus, see to their needs for the night and start training them hard on horse riding tomorrow. You may dismiss the men."

The men retired to their tents, and Livy sat down with his commanders for a drink in Paulus' tent. "Did you see our cavalry get bested today?" Livy asked at last.

"Of course, sir. Labienus made a bad mistake chasing those barbarians across the marsh. I'll bet things would have been different if we had been there or even Kleon's men. Some missile support would have made mincemeat of their cavalry," Paulus remarked.

"I feel the same way. There must be some way for us to play a part in the cavalry action," Livy said.

"Caesar wants us to train the men and expand the force. He has the long view," Paulus replied.

"Meanwhile our cavalry gets slowly whittled away." Livy frowned.

"I don't like it any more than you do, sir, but orders are orders," Paulus said. He emptied his flagon of army issue sour wine.

"Did Decius do all right?" Livy asked.

"Fortunately, he was kept in reserve today. He'll definitely be used tomorrow," Paulus added.

"If I get a chance, I am going to talk to Crassus about letting the raiders play a part. See if you can get the new men at least able to stay on a horse by the end of tomorrow," Livy decided.

"I'll see to that, sir," Paulus replied. "Well, let's drink up and go get some shut-eye. Here's to a better tomorrow."

"May the gods favour us," Livy returned the toast.

Livy was pleased to see a cart and horse beside his tent. As he opened the tent flaps, Brigita flew into his arms and gave him a long, wet kiss. On his writing desk was, once more, a home-cooked meal. There was the smell of a rich meat stew, fresh bread, and honey cakes.

"So you are still alive, and we have yet another night together," Brigita teased cheerily.

"There was no battle. Only a cavalry skirmish"

"I gather you were not involved."

"I had to stand all day in the battle line under the scorching sun and just watch," Livy explained.

"Stop whining. You are alive and we have another night together. What would you like to have first? Dinner or me?" She smiled coyly.

"Let's eat first. I haven't eaten all day, and my stomach feels like it will digest itself. After that, we can have each other all night."

She slipped of her tunic and proceeded to strip him. Livy realised that at least that night life was going to be good.

Cross salt marshes rapidly: Never linger.

The next morning the two armies deployed for battle once more on either side of the now critical marsh. For the first hour, the two armies stood and stared at each other. The Belgic army kept just out of range of the Roman artillery. Then there was a blare of trumpets, and a Roman formation started advancing towards the marsh. Livy was surprised. It looked as if Caesar had ordered a portion of the army to attack. That was a dangerous move, Livy thought, as it allowed the Belgae to deal with the Romans piecemeal. Livy frowned and creased his brow. "Could Caesar be really making such a big tactical mistake? Was he so anxious to bring the Belgae to battle that he was going to sacrifice a few thousand men?"

"Who are those men?" Galienus wondered aloud. "They don't look like legionaries. Most of them haven't even got armour on. Could they be the two reserve legions?"

"Not enough of them even to make one legion," Livy remarked. "I can also make out that some of the men are carrying bows and others the light javelins used by the Numidians. I think I know Caesar's plan."

"Auxiliaries disguised as legionaries. What will Caesar think of next?" Galienus shook his head in amazement.

"Watch and learn from the master," Livy said.

The small Roman force started to cross the marsh. Seeing that the force sent against them was puny, the Belgic army started advancing towards them. Livy noticed that the "Romans" were now slowing their advance. They obviously didn't want to get too far into the marsh.

Livy heard the loud thwacks of *onagers* being fired. Huge boulders were whizzing through the air. In seconds, they were crashing among the Belgae, raising large puffs of dust and smoke. He could see men splattered by the impact. The Belgae then began to charge at the Roman line with a loud roar that could be heard all the way to the Roman camp.

The Roman force came to an abrupt stop. Bows suddenly appeared and were raised to forty-five degrees to get maximum range. The first volley was fired at 300 yards. It hit about two dozen of the Belgae. The Belgae stepped over the dead and wounded and kept up their full-bodied charge. The second volley was well within range and fired with great accuracy. Scores of the barbarian warriors were hit, and the rest began to slow down and hide behind their shields. The enemy army was halfway across the marsh. They started to form up into a shield wall and continued to advance more slowly but very deliberately. The subsequent volleys of arrows were now having less effect.

On the hill, Caesar was smiling. Only a few hundred yards and the enemy would be across the marsh. He then intended to advance with the whole army and crush them. The two sides were now separated by about 100 yards. The Numidian light troops disguised as legionaries then ran forward and unleashed a volley of light lances at about fifty yards. A few of the enemy were impaled, but most of the lances embedded in the enemy shields, rendering them too heavy to carry. As the shields were discarded, the archers fired another deadly volley, this time at point-blank range into the unprotected frontline of the enemy. Men crumpled in droves screaming.

The Romans then turned and ran. With a roar, the whole enemy army surged forward after them. Caesar was delighted. Now he had to time the charge carefully. "Let them run half up the hill."

Suddenly a horn note sounded from the rear of the enemy formation. Everything seemed to stand still. The horn sounded again. The enemy stopped the charge and started to fall back. Caesar was aghast. Galba, the enemy leader, had not fallen for the bait. He was a canny old veteran.

Next, the roar of hoofs could be heard, and a huge cloud approached from the rear of the enemy columns. The enemy cavalry was being unleashed to ride down the poor auxiliaries, who were now running for their lives. He could see Kleon in his black-plumed Corinthian helmet at the rear of his archers, urging them forward. Cavalry suddenly burst from behind the Belgic infantry, galloping after the fleeing Romans.

Roman cavalry waiting at the flanks raced to intercept them before they reached the light infantry. Meanwhile, the batteries of ballistae opened fire, cutting down dozens of horsemen. Now it was a race. Would the Roman cavalry reach the scene in time to save the 2000 auxiliaries frantically fleeing for their lives?

Caesar realised that his latest plan had failed. Obviously Galba was not as impetuous as the average Belgic warlord. He had seen that it was a trap and had withdrawn his main army back behind the marsh to relative safety. Now his superior cavalry was going to cut down the bait that Caesar had offered.

Caesar signalled, and two legions moved down the slope towards the fleeing auxiliaries to shorten the distance they had to run. The men sensed the urgency and proceeded at double quick time. Agonisingly, the Belgic cavalry closed on the rear men, and suddenly they had caught up and started to settle scores, hacking at backs and necks. The rear ranks were brutally cut down by the angry horsemen.

Livy felt a wave of nausea sweep over him as he watched the fate of his Cretan and Numidian friends. If he had a horse and his raiders with him, he would have rushed down to assist, but stationed as he was in the main infantry line, there was nothing he could do. Providentially, Labienus and his cavalry now joined the fray and engaged the Belgic cavalry so that the light troops could now turn to escape again.

Livy could see his friend, Kleon, heroically putting one arrow after another in man and horse alike. Two other Cretan archers flanked him, holding off the enemy with spears. Suddenly one of his escorts was cut down, and two horsemen simultaneously attacked Kleon. He threw down his bow and unsheathed his sword. He avoided the first assailant as he slashed down and chopped his sword against the rear legs of the horse, which then tripped and fell tumbling its rider. The second horsemen had however got behind him, and a deliberate stroke caught Kleon in the back, and the brave auxiliary prefect dropped to his knees and then fell forward.

Labienus and his cavalry were now fully engaged with the enemy cavalry. There was a wild swirling melee of battling horsemen right in the middle of the battlefield. Livy could make out the naked Gaesatae horsemen. It would seem that many of them were now being used as replacement cavalry. He even imagined that he spotted the tall, blond-haired warrior in pigtails, who he had encountered the morning after the raid.

The battle hung in the balance for a few minutes. Slowly but inexorably, the tide turned in favour of the Belgae as their superior numbers and savagery slowly took their toll on the Roman, German, and Remi cavalry, who slowly began to fall back as their casualty numbers rose. More and more horses were now rider less, and many fallen men littered the field.

The surviving light infantry had almost reached the roman legionaries marching down the slope. Suddenly the sound of Roman trumpets pierced the air. Caesar had sounded the recall. The Roman cavalry disengaged as best they could and started to gallop back towards the legions. The enemy cavalry rode after them but after about 500 yards slowed to a halt, and then they raised their weapons and cheered. Once again they could claim victory after having chased the Roman cavalry off the field. This time they took their time riding back and forth, taunting the Romans and shouting insults.

Murato was among the riders. He felt a moment of exultation. The invaders could be beaten. They were not superhuman after all. He had personally killed half a dozen men that day, two of them Roman cavalry. His sword dripped with blood, and his naked body was wildly streaked with the blood of the enemies he had slain. He pranced his horse back and forth with pride. He had proven himself as a leader.

The Roman artillery fired a few volleys in reply, and their cheering soon turned to screams of agony as men and horses were skewered by ballista bolts. The horsemen were outraged. That was a cowardly act in their eyes. Had the Romans no honour? Nevertheless they turned and retreated in good order back across the marsh. There was silence in the Roman ranks.

Caesar turned to Quintus Pedius, one of his legates. "Hold two legions here in formation and march the rest back to camp. Send some men to pick up the dead and wounded"

"Yes, My Lord," the legate replied.

Caesar turned round in disgust and headed back to camp without another word. Inside he seethed with frustration. He was tempted to march the whole army down, cross the marsh, and engage the enemy. He took a deep breath, then forced himself to calm down. No, that would play right into their hands. A good general gave battle only when he was sure to win. He must have patience.

> The wise leader, in his deliberations, always blends consideration of gain and harm.

Livy decided to join the party retrieving the wounded as the Seventh Legion was one of those tasked to stand guard while the rest went back to camp. Some of his raiders volunteered to follow. The aftermath of a battle is never a pretty sight. The field was pockmarked with mutilated bodies, groaning, wounded men and dead and dying horses. Here and there were severed limbs and severed heads. Blood ran in rivulets.

They found Kleon in a clump of dead and wounded men and horses. Livy recognised the green tunics of the archers and a number of naked Gaesatae horsemen. Livy and Biorix found him lying flat on his back beside a dead horse. A pool of dark blood had collected under him.

They shook him to see if he still lived. Kleon gave a groan. "Is this Hades? Are you two fallen in battle too?"

"No," Livy replied. "We are very much alive, and you are too, for the moment. You haven't earned your place in Elysium yet, so don't die on us just now."

Kleon stretched out his hand, and Livy grabbed his forearm and pulled him into the sitting position. His back breast plate had been nearly transacted, and he had received a deep gash across the back which was bleeding profusely. Livy and Biorix removed the armour and staunched the bleeding with cloth and applied a bandage. They then flagged a passing cart and loaded Kleon inside, leaving a canteen of water with him.

"I am grateful, Centurion. If I live, I will repay your kindness," Kleon remarked after taking a deep draught from the canteen.

"Nothing to repay, Prefect. I will make good use of those young archers you sent me. Look after yourself. We'll come to see you when we have cleaned out this mess," Livy said.

Looting was very much a part of war, and those that volunteered to fetch the dead and wounded were also motivated by gain. The dead were systematically stripped of anything remotely valuable, including shoes, cloaks, weapons, armour, helmets, and of course any valuable personal effects. The friendly wounded were of course being evacuated to the field hospital. Enemy wounded were divided into two categories. Those with light wounds were shackled and then tended to, as they had value as slaves. Those that were too badly wounded or crippled were efficiently dispatched. Teams of executioners were wandering the field with sharp daggers.

Livy ordered his men to especially look for bows and arrows as his raiders would need them. They were also ordered to strip off any armour they could find to equip his new men. He then examined the dead Belgic warriors around where Kleon had fallen, but most had nothing valuable. Many were naked Gaesatae. He retrieved two gold neck torques and a gold ring. Those would be useful for trading for supplies. He then came across a well-armoured warrior lying in a pool of blood. His mouth was blood-stained and he was coughing. Livy noticed that he had stab wounds to his chest and abdomen. The wounds were mortal.

Livy knelt beside him and gave him a drink from his canteen. The dying warrior took it gratefully, took a gulp, and then coughed violently. "So to whom do I owe this kindness?" the warrior rasped.

"Gaius Livius, Centurion, Seventh Legion," Livy replied softly.

"You look like a boy. You Romans must be short of men to make a mere boy a centurion," he said. "Are my wounds mortal?"

"I'm afraid they are. You will be joining your gods in a while," Livy said sympathetically.

"Well, we all got to die sometime. Have you wine on you?"

"Yes, actually I do"

Livy took his flask of wine and brought it to the warrior's lips. He drank slowly, savouring each sip. "You Romans are not all bad. Let me do something for you before I go. In my saddlebag over by that dead horse, you will find a bag of gold coins. I guess you can also take whatever you find on me"

"You have good armour, a silver helmet, and a remarkable sword. You must be from nobility."

"I am Saraciacus, a prince of the Suessiones."

"Are you a son of Galba?"

"No. I am grand-nephew to the great Diviciacus, who was the most powerful King of Gaul and Britannia," Saraciacus gasped. He was weakening rapidly. He took one more sip of wine. "One last favour, please," he gasped. "Return my body to my people. Let me have a proper burial."

Livy held his hand. "I'll try my best. I promise you."

Saraciacus took a last drink of wine. He seemed to be more relaxed. He looked up at the sky and seemed to be mumbling some prayers. A few minutes later he died.

Livy searched his body. There was an impressive gold torque round his neck, a beautiful gold armband in the shape of coiled snakes, and a belt studded with gemstones. Livy retrieved the bag of gold coins from the dead horse, a fine grey stallion, and loaded all the loot into his own saddle bag. He also took the fine chain armour, sword, belt and helmet. He then lifted Saraciacus, slung him over his own horse, and started walking the horse back to his lines. A strange sadness hung over him like a cloak. A brave prince had met his end just like any common slave.

Livy went back to the raider's camp and found a simple wooden cart to deposit the body of Saraciacus. He also found a sheet to cover it from the flies. Shortly a message came for him to report to Publius Crassus.

He found Publius in his tent. It was a Spartan affair, crimson with no trimmings. Inside was a plain desk, a number of *curile* chairs, and a camp bed which was not much fancier than the one in his own tent. Clearly, this Crassus had not inherited the luxurious taste of his fabulously rich father. Publius had a worried look on his face.

He extended a hand. "I think you will have a chance tomorrow to prove the worth of your raiders," he said.

Livy smiled in puzzlement. "How so, sir?"

"Tomorrow you station with the raiders and leave your century under Galienus. You are to support the Roman cavalry. As you know, the last two days didn't go so well for the cavalry, but we have been reinforced by another thousand Remi and German horsemen, and tomorrow Caesar is determined that we drive the enemy cavalry off the field."

"Thank you, sir. This is just the opportunity the raiders need."

"How many of your new men can ride? I want to field as many raiders as possible."

"I think upwards of 150 men. I will see who else among our archers can ride a horse."

"Go get them ready and come back here. I will brief you about the tactics we are going to use tomorrow. I intend to give Caesar a pleasant surprise and show that grouch Labienus a thing or two." Crassus smiled slyly.

Livy spent the rest of the day working with the new raiders. As Kleon was out of action, another 100 archers had joined his team, and this time many of them could ride. Biorix took charge of those who were the worse riders, and Decius and Paulus worked with those who could ride. By evening, the men could at least shoot their bows stationary on horseback and then retreat at a trot. Livy kept a watchful eye on the training. He was not satisfied. Finally he called an assembly of all the new men and the veterans. He lined them up in two rows, veterans on his right and new men on the left.

Livy began his address. "Tomorrow you will face the enemy. You will kill a number of them by your archery. That will make them very upset. They will charge you with great ferocity hell-bent on vengeance, and you, my ladies, will try and trot elegantly away like a bunch of housewives. What do you think will happen?"

There was an embarrassing silence in the ranks. Livy trotted down the line of recruits, inspecting each one of them. Everyone looked down in embarrassment.

When he reached the end of the line, he turned back and trotted back. "They will catch you and rape you. That's what they will do! They will fuck you till you die."

He turned to his three sub-commanders. "I want these men to be able to gallop at full speed, do you understand? I want them to be able to run for their lives. I don't care how long it takes. I don't care if it takes all night. I want each man to be able to control a horse at full gallop by morning. Dismiss."

"You heard the man," Paulus repeated. "Back to the training field. You others, the veterans, go practice archery. I want everybody to be able to make back shots at the full gallop just like the Parthians."

Livy returned to the tent of Crassus, bringing Decurion Decius along. Crassus had an aide prepare a meal and serve with some watered wine. "I have been thinking long and hard how we can get an advantage over their cavalry. I've come up with some ideas which we might implement tomorrow."

The three of them huddled round the writing desk, where Crassus had made some diagrams. The discussion went on for several hours.

Finally the plans were fully agreed upon. It was obviously a revolutionary idea. Crassus would have to clear it with Julius Caesar, but all three felt it had a good chance of success and would tip the balance in favour of the Romans on the following day.

"I have one favour to ask," Livy added. "I retrieved the body of one of their princes today. He is nephew of Galba and grandnephew of Diviciacus, the Great King. I'd like to return his body to his people under a flag of truce."

Crassus looked up in astonishment. "That might not be a bad idea. It would give you a chance to have a look at their camp. I'll clear that with Caesar. You better go and prepare your men."

Livy saluted and left. Before he returned to the training grounds, he visited the *valetudinarium* (field hospital) to see Kleon. The hospital was located at a farmhouse near the river. There was not enough space in the farmhouse and adjoining barn, and many men were lying out in the open. There were hundreds of wounded. The sight of so many suffering men was heart-rending to behold. There was the smell of blood, sweat, faeces, and urine in the air. In one cowshed, the surgeons were amputating limbs on a blood-stained operating table. When one patient was done, the table was sloshed with water from the river to clear away the blood and excrement. In one area, the dead were lying in a forlorn row while nearby some civilians were digging a deep trench to bury them. It was easier than building funeral pyres. Livy fought down the urge to vomit as he passed through what seemed a scene from Hades.

Livy finally found Kleon inside the farmhouse, which was so crowded with wounded men that there was hardly space to walk between them. All around was the sound of wailing, moaning, sobbing, crying, and screaming. It was a macabre symphony. Livy knelt beside him and took his hand. "Hello, my friend."

Kleon opened his eyes. He was perspiring profusely and was hot from fever. "Ah, my young friend, how prophetic your words are! I await the boat over the Styx."

"Nonsense, old friend, only the good die young, and you certainly don't qualify."

"So have you come to insult a dying man."

"No, I come to bring you solace—in a flask. Best *falernian*. It ought to distract you from the pain." Livy placed the flask in his hand, then helped him to sit up.

"Ah, just what I was dreaming about. I get the most vivid dreams lying here with the fever. When you woke me, I was at a Dionysian-drinking orgy surrounded by the most beautiful hetaerae pleasuring me in every way."

"Drink, old friend. You will soon feel better."

Kleon took two deep gulps, spilling some of the wine down the front of his tunic. He sighed deeply. "I am in Elysium already. Thank you, my friend. So did Caesar get his battle?"

"No, my friend, your plan didn't work. They only sent over the cavalry. Galba is more intelligent than we give him credit for."

"So did Labienus beat their cavalry today?" Kleon asked.

Livy was embarrassed to reply. Finally he said, "No, we were beaten again like yesterday."

Kleon was quiet for a moment. "So it was all for nought. My boys died for nothing."

"They did not, Kleon. They took down many of the enemy with their arrows."

"I'll be with them soon." Kleon looked downcast.

"You are as strong as an ox, and you will certainly recover. Anyway, I have a plan to avenge your boys. We will give them a sting on the morrow."

Kleon did not look optimistic. "You do that, my boy, you do that." He lay back and closed his eyes.

Livy stoppered the flask and put it carefully by his head. He then gingerly worked his way out of the disgusting charnel house. He wondered how many of all the wounded men would eventually leave that place alive.

The rest of the afternoon and evening was spent supervising the training of the raiders. Livy concentrated on the new men. They practiced cavalry manoeuvres. The men learnt to canter and then to gallop. There were many spills, fortunately resulting in no serious injuries. They also practiced how to advance in formation, charge, and retreat. They drilled continuously under the demanding tutelage of Biorix, Decius, and Paulus till after sundown.

Just as it was getting dark, a messenger arrived from Crassus. Livy was given permission to return the body of the dead prince. He was also to agree to let the Belgae collect their dead. He was to be escorted by a party of four cavalrymen. Livy intended to take Biorix and three of his best raiders.

They left just after nightfall. The prince's body lay in a cart drawn by a workhorse. All the men carried torches so that the enemy would see them clearly and not think it was a sneak attack. A white flag of truce was carried aloft by Biorix, and Livy was in full centurion regalia so that he could pass as an official emissary.

They were halfway across the marsh when a troop of cavalry came trotting towards them. There were about a dozen Belgic cavalry. Half of them were naked Gaesatae, and Livy recognised the leader whom he had seen twice already. The Belgae surrounded them spears pointed at the small Roman party.

The leader with awesome pectorals and blond pigtails rode right up close to Livy and looked him up and down with scorn. "So what do you want, Roman pig."

"I am Centurion Gaius Livius, and I bring Caesar's greetings and something I wish to return to you," Livy spoke in Celtic.

The Gaesatae rode beside the cart and looked in. "You bring us a corpse?" He sounded outraged.

"Not just any corpse, it is a prince of your people—Saraciacus, nephew of Galba," Livy announced confidently in a polite voice.

"I am Murato, leader of the cavalry." Livy discerned a slight thaw in his manners. "We thank you for returning the prince to us. He was a brave and good man."

"May we escort the prince to your camp, sir? I have a message for your leader."

"I suppose we can return the courtesy. Your escort stays here. Just you and the wagon."

Livy rode behind Murato and was escorted into the Belgic camp. The warriors were clustered around campfires eating their evening meal. He noticed that there was ample wine but not abundance of food. Some groups seemed to be sharing a loaf of bread. He could see the hatred in their eyes as he passed them. Some even spat at him.

There were some tents erected, but many of the warriors slept in the open. Conditions were not as comfortable as those that the Romans enjoyed.

Then they passed the encampment of the Gaesatae. He was surprised to see that there were women warriors among them. The women were either naked or dressed only in blue war paint in swirling patterns. They looked more terrifying than sexually titillating, though Livy noticed that many of the women were young, slim, and shapely. Their standard of hygiene left much to be desired though, and the camp stank of unwashed bodies.

Finally they came to the edge of the Gaesatae encampment. Two female warriors barred their way. One was short and dark-haired; the other, a blonde, was taller. They were both naked except for blue paint. Livy noticed that the taller girl looked familiar. Her light blonde hair was cut short. She was slim, statuesque with pert breasts topped by small pink nipples. Her face was alluring with her azure eyes, long eyelashes, and luscious lips. She had a savage yet delicate beauty, which astounded Livy. She carried a bow which was nocked and the arrow pointed straight at him. The other girl carried a spear with a long metal point. She also pointed the weapon at him.

"Let us through, woman," Murato barked at the two sentries.

"No one is allowed into the king's encampment, especially Romans," the dark-haired girl, who looked the older of the two, challenged.

"I've seen this Roman before. I can't quite place him, but he looks familiar." The blonde girl squinted. "He looks too young to be a centurion. He must be one of those patrician kids. Did your daddy pay for you to be a centurion?" she mocked.

Livy was shocked that she made the last comment in Latin. "No, I earned it killing Belgic warriors," Livy retorted in Celtic. Her blue green eyes burnt with ferocity.

She stuck out her tongue and swept the pink tip over her upper lip in an obviously sexual manner.

Livy raised his eyebrow in bewilderment and blushed. She was truly a she-devil, but he could not help being fascinated.

"Let us through. We have with us the body of Prince Saraciacus. The Romans have returned him to us to honour. I bring this emissary before Galba," Murato demanded.

The two girls stepped aside. "The next time I see you, I won't hold back my arrow," the blonde girl said.

"The next time we meet, I won't expect you to," Livy replied.

"Shut up and move aside, Leuce. We haven't got all night," Murato said. His eyes narrowed in annoyance.

Leuce gave him a raised third finger, obviously an insulting gesture, stepped to one side reluctantly, and let the party passed into the Suessiones' camp. The Suessiones were the dominant tribe in Belgica, and they looked better equipped and organised. Many warriors had proper armour, shields, and weapons. Livy noticed many well-made spears, javelins, and long swords. They even had abundant helmets and some semblance of a uniform. Most of them wore trousers made of bluish cloth with square patterns and also wore a cape rolled into a band of a similar but darker blue colour. That they slung diagonally across the body.

Finally they arrived at a farmhouse. Outside was bivouacked what was obviously an elite unit of royal bodyguards. All the men were large and had uniform helmets and chain mail. They carried swords and spears of formidable quality. Their colours were the blue and yellow of the Suessiones. The wagon with the corpse was brought to a stop outside the house. Livy dismounted and was escorted inside. Loud, dissonant music emanated from the house.

The scene inside was pandemonium. The Belgic chieftains were having a feast. The amounts of food piled on the long wooden tables were a contrast to the meagre fare meted out to the rest of the army. The entertainment consisted of a few dozen nubile maidens. They were on the whole scantily clad, but some had been stripped topless or were even totally naked. The chiefs, many of whom were inebriated, were taking liberties with the women, chasing them around and trying to take off their clothes. There were half a dozen women dancing erotically in the middle of the hall, but no one seemed even to be noticing them.

Livy attracted a few curious glances, but most of the men were too busy partying to bother. Murato snorted with disgust and took him to the head table. Galba was sitting on a large fur-covered couch with three semi-naked women. "Next to him," Murato whispered in his ear, "are Bodougnatus, the king of the Nervii, and Commius, one of the leaders of the Atrebates." Galba was holding a large roasted leg of some animal in one hand and a woman's breast in the other. His beard was speckled with food debris. The floor around the table was filthy with food scraps. Livy came up to the three men, removed his helmet, and bowed to each.

Galba dropped the breast and the roasted meat, wiped his hands on his gown, and looked up at Livy.

"My Lords, I present Centurion Gaius Livius, envoy of our esteemed enemy, Gaius Julius Caesar, Proconsul of Rome," Murato announced.

Galba looked him up and down. "He is a mere boy. They must have sent him because he is expendable." Galba chuckled scornfully. Bodougnatus laughed loudly and Commius managed a smile. "So have you come to discuss surrender? I will give generous terms. You leave all your weapons and armour behind and we allow you to march back to the Roman Province with your lives. How's that? See we Belgae can be civilized too." Galba grinned menacingly, waving his hands for emphasis.

Commius and Bodougnatus laughed heartily. "Won't you join us for a bit of food, Centurion? You look half starved. Is your army a little short of rations perhaps seeing we have stripped the countryside bare?" Commius motioned hospitably to the food on the table.

"Perhaps he needs something else more urgently. Something one or more of these comely wenches could provide. Better enjoy while you can, Centurion. Tomorrow you may not walk on this earth." Bodougnatus guffawed and squeezed the glutei of the young maid beside him, causing her to jerk in surprise.

Livy fought to keep down his irritation at those insults. "Stick to your mission," he thought to himself. He composed himself, then, spoke as confidently and as calmly as he could manage.

"Caesar offers you peace if you submit to Rome. You are to lay down your arms and return to your towns and villages. Rome will henceforth provide you the protection of her legions. Rome offers you civilization, order, and wealth. Present leaders will retain their positions subject to Roman supervision of course," Livy said.

The silence was palpable. The mood in the room had completely changed. Livy felt a wave of fear sweep over him. He tried his best to appear calm and impassive.

Galba pushed the women aside, causing two of them to fall heavily on the floor. They dared not utter a sound. He stood up and towered over Livy. He was a big man with arms as thick as logs. His face had lost all humour and his visage became livid with rage.

"You can tell Caesar to go fuck himself! Tomorrow your puny army of dwarves will feel the wrath of the Belgae." He looked almost angry enough to attack Livy personally. He came close enough for Livy to inhale the putrefying smell of his breath. It was a disgusting combination of stale wine and rotting teeth.

"I will convey your sentiments to Caesar," Livy replied as calmly as possible. He could feel a bead of perspiration trickle down his forehead.

"Get him out of here!" Galba ordered Murato.

Livy turned, put on his helmet, and retreated as gracefully as he could. Murato and two royal bodyguards in chain mail escorted him out. As he was leaving, he heard the music come back on, and loud conversation resumed with the occasional scream from one of the serving wenches as she was assaulted.

Livy was escorted back the way he entered. There was no attempt to hide anything from him. The Belgae were confident of their superiority, no doubt after the cavalry battles of the last two days.

The men were sharpening their weapons and others were putting on war paint. Livy was convinced they would give battle the next day. That was valuable information for Caesar.

As he passed the checkpoint leading into the Gaesatae camp, he encountered the two women warriors once more. This time they did not challenge. Livy noticed that the tall blonde girl named Leuce was silently watching him. There was no teasing this time. He even imagined that she gave him the very hint of a smile. It was almost imperceptible. He was sure they would meet again.

Biorix and his escort were waiting for him in the Gaesatae camp. They were led to the edge of the encampment. Murato rode up to Livy. "You are brave to come. Our people don't always treat envoys with respect. You might have had only your head sent home to Caesar."

"I have you to thank for my life then. I suspect the respect you command among your people played a big part in my survival."

"We shall meet again." Murato saluted with his spear.

"I thank you for your hospitality, Commander Murato." Livy touched his riding crop to his helmet.

The small party of Romans rode back through the marsh, trying to pick their way through the drier ground.

Live spies are those who return with information.

Belgica, 57 BC

Sometime after returning from the Belgic encampment, Livy reported to Caesar. The tent was empty save for Crassus, Labienus, and Sabinus. The hour was late.

"I gather they refuse to surrender," Caesar remarked finally.

"They offered us surrender terms in return," Livy said.

"That's what I expected. The reason I offered to parley was to grasp opportunity to peer into their camp. What have you gathered about their situation?"

"Firstly, they are short of food. Most of the army is on short rations except for the chiefs and their retainers. Most of the army is not very well equipped, but there is a core of well-armed chosen men. Most likely they are the core followers of the chiefs. They appear to be preparing for battle on the morrow," Livy concluded.

"How know you this?" Caesar queried.

"They sharpen weapons and paint themselves. This together with the fact that their food runs meagre means they either attack or disperse. I'll wager my horse they mean to fight in the morning."

"I'll take you up on that, young Livius," Caesar countered. "If they attack tomorrow, we can finally crush them and end this war."

Caesar paused a moment to reconsider. Perhaps he had missed something.

"Somehow I don't think they will give in to our wishes so easily. I doubt they will charge across the marsh and assault us up on this ridge. They may have a surprise planned for us. We must be alert. Crassus, you better send out some scouts tonight," Caesar said.

"Yes, My Lord Caesar." Crassus saluted.

"Labienus, you better get your cavalry battle ready at first light. I want to be prepared for any surprises."

"I'll be ready, Caesar," Labienus said.

"You are dismissed, Livius."

Livy saluted and left. He made a stop at the training ground and looked up Biorix and Paulus. They were making a final briefing to the men after which the men were dismissed to rest and take their supper. Livy called a meeting of his officers. They sat around a campfire.

"Can they fight tomorrow?" Livy began.

Biorix replied, "They can stay on a horse. They can shoot from a horse when stationary, and they can run away. They won't survive a melee though."

"I expected so. Biorix and I will lead the new men tomorrow. We won't close with the enemy. Paulus, you lead the veterans."

"Some of the men lost in the raid came back, a half dozen of them. Four are fit for action," Paulus added.

"That's good news. So I guess you have about ninety or so, and I will have the 200 recruits. Let's try not to get any killed tomorrow. We fight with our head. I don't want any heroics. We just formed this outfit, and I want to keep my command intact for the moment, understand?"

"You needn't worry, sir, I'm not so fond of dying myself and you can depend on us to look after the lads," Biorix promised.

"Good then, I am depending on you two." He gave them both a hug and a pat on the back.

They drank a toast. "To victory on the morrow. May the gods protect us all," Livy prayed.

> Be ready for the unexpected.

He rode back to his tent and recognised Brigita's old mare tied outside. She had fallen asleep on his camp bed. Livy didn't want to wake her. She looked so beautiful and peaceful in her slumber. Livy smelt her hair, which had the aroma of fresh hay. She had left some bread and cheese on the table, and Livy suddenly felt ravenously hungry, so he helped himself to the food.

A few minutes later, Brigita woke up. "So you are back at last. I was beginning to worry that you had fallen in battle. I heard there was quite a skirmish this morning."

Livy looked at her with his mouth full of food. "I wasn't involved," he mumbled.

She joined him at the table and poured both of them a goblet of well-watered wine. "So when is your grand battle finally going to take place?"

"I fear it may be tomorrow." He took a long gulp.

"You've been saying that for the last two days. Not that I mind spending a few more last nights with you," she said with a grin.

Livy leant back in his chair and looked into her remarkable big grey eyes. The grey was the steel grey of an angry winter sea. "I have a present for you. I feel somewhat obligated after all the food you brought and of course for making my evenings memorable."

He took out the gold arm bracelet with the two entwined snakes.

"For me? It's beautiful. You must have lifted it off some Belgic noblemen. You thief," she taunted playfully.

"I didn't steal it. He gave it to me as he was dying. I eased his passing with some wine. He was a prince of the Suessiones."

"It's very beautiful and must be very valuable." She examined the bracelet with delight.

He slipped it up her left arm. "It looks good on your arm."

"Well, I accept your gift." She kissed him gratefully. "Now I have an idea. Let's go down to the river for a swim. You are filthy, and I won't couple with you till I clean you up." She pulled him out of the chair and dragged him out of the tent.

They rode down to the river on their horses. The river looked serene and cool reflecting the moonlight. They found a clump of trees to undress. The air was chilly and moist. They giggled like children and hand in hand slid into the water. The shock of the cold brought a pleasurable pain.

She pulled him close when they were chest deep in the freezing water. They embraced, and the warmth of her body contrasted with the cold. She kissed him hungrily, and he submitted to her desire. The musty smell of her breath awoke his lust.

A short time later, they were wrapped in blankets under a tree by the riverside having steamy sex. Brigita climaxed rather too loudly, and he had to kiss her hard so that passing sentries or worse enemy patrols would not detect their presence. After that, they cuddled under the stars, caressing each other lightly.

"Will you miss me after you leave?" Brigita asked after a long silence.

"Of course, I will," Livy replied. "These last days have been memorable."

"Yes, you became a centurion, got your command, and enjoyed the service of a woman every night without having to pay," she teased.

"Do I sense some bitterness in that last sentence?" Livy said gently.

Brigita buried her face in her hands and shook her head. "No bitterness. It's just that I will miss you terribly."

Livy held her close, putting her head against his chest. "My invitation for you to come along still stands," he said unequivocally.

"No. I'm safer in Bibrax. Your army will be fighting battle after battle, and I don't want to be involved in all that violence. I want to have a normal life and peace."

Livy didn't reply. There was nothing more to say. They would enjoy what is left of the night together. Who knows what the future would bring?

CHAPTER 7

Battle of the Axona (River Aisne), 57 BC

Dawn broke suddenly in a clamour of hoof beats, horns, and drums. The call to arms had been given. Livy tumbled out of bed and struggled into his armour. His head pounded from too much wine. Brigita's exposed naked body stirred, and she moaned. "What's that din?! Don't they realise people are trying to sleep?" She pulled the blankets over her dishevelled head to cover her ears.

Livy had no time for her. He got on his horse and rushed to the centre of the camp where the senior officers were gathering in a disorganised crowd. The legates, tribunes, prefects, and senior centurions were all gathered outside Caesar's tent. Livy rushed to join them, sneaking into the rear ranks.

"The enemy has been seen marching towards a ford upstream. They mean to cross the Axona and attack Sabinus's camp at the bridge. They want to cut our supply lines," Caesar spoke loudly and urgently.

"We need to leave right this moment. I shall personally command all the cavalry, including the new raiders. Livius, you are with me. Crassus, you bring all the light troops as quickly as possible. Cotta, you bring the two new legions, the Thirteenth and Fourteenth, immediately behind Crassus and the auxiliaries. Quintus Pedius, you are to remain here with the six remaining legions and guard the camp. They could be feinting to draw us away so they can come up and seize the camp."

Labienus was very obviously left with no role. He looked disappointed. Everyone rushed back to their respective units to get things moving. In a short while, the entire cavalry was galloping out of the camp by the back gate towards the bridge across the river. Caesar and his bodyguard formed the vanguard with Livy and the raiders directly behind. After that, came the Roman equites and then the Remi and German cavalry. After the cavalry, came the Numidian light infantry, the archers, and the Balearic slingers. At the back were the two legions. The infantry were marching at double time, weighed down by their armour, shields, and *pila*.

The sight that greeted them at the ford made one's blood freeze. The entire area was swarming with Belgae. They poured across the narrow crossing like sand flowing through the waist of an hourglass.

As they neared the ford, they saw that most of the enemy cavalry had already crossed. The enemy infantry was still on the other side. Huge columns of infantry could be seen converging at the river, crossing from far in the distance. It was obviously not a feint. The Belgae were trying to flank the Romans, seize the bridgehead, and make the Romans fight on their terms. Caesar had to stop them there and then.

Livy's raiders were ordered forward. He gave the signal for his men to form a skirmish line. The rest of the Roman cavalry formed a battle line right behind them. The veteran raiders already knew what to do. Livy hoped that the new men would be able to keep up. Livy commanded the left wing of the small force and Paulus the right. The Belgic cavalry were charging straight at them now, but they were coming as a mass with no particular order or formation. Clearly, they intended to sweep the Roman cavalry aside so that their infantry could cross unopposed.

Livy's men halted and raised their bows. He gave the signal to release as the enemy crossed 250 yards. Even at that extreme distance, the 300 shafts had a deadly effect. The front line of the enemy was decimated. After that, the archers fired at will as quickly as they could. The enemy ranks thinned visibly as deadly steel sunk into breasts of beast and men. Everywhere, horses screamed pitifully and crashed to the ground. Men tumbled violently.

Men and horses fell by the score, and the field was soon littered with wounded men and animals, taking the wind out of the enemy charge.

When the leading enemy cavalry were a mere fifty yards away, Livy ordered the retreat. The whole troop fled backwards at full steam and then broke left and right. That movement had been practiced interminably. At the same moment, the entire Roman cavalry charged straight at the disordered enemy. Julius Caesar himself rode at the centre, his red plume and cloak flying in the wind. The two sides met with a loud crash of steel on steel.

The Romans cut through the enemy formation like a knife through butter. The Belgae reeled back in disorder. The Romans and Remi were hell-bent on vengeance and slashed and cut the enemy mercilessly. Blood spilled in abundance as men and animals fought and died. Livy and his men had formed two horns on each flank of the enemy and were now pouring a steady rain of steel-tipped shafts into the sides of the enemy formation. They picked their targets, distinguishing friend from foe. Livy's men shot from stationary horses, thus improving their aim.

Finally, the Numidians joined the fray, throwing their short javelins at any remaining Belgic horse or stabbing the animals at close range. The battle had now degenerated to individual combat all over the field. The arrival of the Numidians tipped the balance. The Belgic horses had suffered enough. They broke off and ran in every direction. Some retreated back across the ford, causing disorganisation among the columns of infantry trying to cross the river. Some others decided to retreat upstream. The veterans under Paulus gave chase for a short while, sending a wave of arrows at their backs like a departing gift.

Caesar reformed the cavalry in preparation to engage the infantry, who were just spilling on to the near bank. They charged and the enemy counter-charged, yelling a blood-curdling war cry and wielding an assortment of spears, axes, swords, and knives. The archers, Numidians, and slingers sent a continuous rain of missiles at the advancing horde, thinning their ranks. The Roman cavalry struck them violently, scything down the infantry like wheat.

Livy brought his recruits forward and added their arrows to the fray. "Keep them at least 150 yards away from that horde, and if they charge in your direction, just withdraw 200 yards and then turn and let them have it with the arrows again," he yelled at Biorix, his voice hardly audible above the din of battle.

The ford was a choke point. It was a mere 100 yards wide and chest deep in the centre. The smaller Roman force could hold it albeit not easily as the Belgic army could not deploy. The Roman cavalry had driven the Belgae into the river now and were fighting furiously in the shallows. Thousands of dead and wounded lay at the water's edge. The fighting was savage and desperate. Livy concentrated on shooting his arrows as accurately as possible, thinning the flanks of the enemy. He was hitting one man with every shot, but his arrows were running out. Paulus and his veterans were doing the same.

When his men were finally out of arrows, he ordered Biorix to pull back with all the new men. He then galloped to rejoin Paulus and his veterans. "How are you for arrows?" Livy shouted.

"Almost out," Paulus shouted back.

"Fire your remaining shafts and then follow me," Livy ordered.

The men took aim and fired two last volleys, making each shot count. Livy then dressed them in a line and ordered the charge. The men drew their *spathas* and then advanced into the enemy flank.

Livy felt the wind in his hair and the exhilaration of riding a fine horse. That day they would show the Belgae what Roman cavalry could do. The raiders maintained a thin straight line that was parade ground in precision. Livy felt a wave of pride in those men. *Spathas* were drawn simultaneously with a loud coordinated swish. Livy pointed his sword forward, and the men began their charge into death or glory.

The pressure of numbers was forcing Caesar's cavalry back on to the bank, and more and more infantry were reinforcing the small bridgehead. Livy noticed that they were mainly Suessiones and Bellovaci. They were strengthened by well-armoured infantry from the chiefs' personal bodyguard.

Livy's cavalry took them by surprise. Only a few warriors turned before the charge ran home. Horses collided with bewildered infantry smashing them about and throwing some into the air to land broken. Livy singled out an armoured spearman who was just turning to bring up his spear. A split second later, Livy had slashed him across his throat, producing a spray of red.

Next he rode towards a clump of a half dozen warriors who were attacking one of the Roman equites, who was desperately trying to fend off their spear thrusts. One bare-chested warrior had dropped his weapon and was trying to drag the Roman off his horse. Livy surprised them from behind and dispatched two of their number with swift sword slashes to their unprotected backs. The Roman cavalryman fell off his horse, but before the Belgic warrior could dispatch him, Livy charged his assailants who fled. Livy let one of them have it from behind with an arrow. It pierced the back of his neck, the tip coming out the front. The half-naked warrior ran a few steps instinctively, then pitched forward. The whole episode happened so quickly that Livy didn't have time even to think till it was over. He had let his instincts take over, and they had served him well.

Livy dismounted to help the stunned soldier. "What's your name?"

"Lepidus, sir," the young Roman replied. He was slim, sinewy, and looked agile. "Thank you for saving my life," he said. Livy was too breathless to reply.

Livy helped him back on his horse and mounted up himself. Paulus and another raider had come alongside and were keeping the assaulting Belgic warriors at bay. The battle had disintegrated into every man for himself. "This situation favoured the barbarians," Livy thought to himself. The charge of the raiders had disordered the Belgae once more and allowed Caesar's cavalry to regain the initiative. More and more fighters were swarming over the ford. The numbers were overwhelming.

Just then several cohorts of the Roman infantry appeared. They were led by Sabinus, and Livy recognised the auxiliary cohorts from the fortification at the bridge. The Roman infantry advanced in closed ranks at the double and joined the fight. Several groups of cavalry were caught in front of the infantry shield wall.

One of those groups was Julius Caesar and a group of his staff officers. Their regalia attracted every Belgic warrior in the vicinity, hoping to win glory or booty. The small group of Romans were surrounded by about ten enemy infantry and about four or five horsemen clad in chain mail. Caesar himself was personally engaging two horsemen.

Livy, Paulus, Lepidus, and two other raiders were about 100 yards away. Livy immediately charged to Caesar's aid. His men followed, splashing through the shallows like river demons. He reached for his bow and found in his quiver one last arrow. As he nocked it, he saw one of the tribunes being dragged off his horse by infantry and another take a spear in the side. Caesar's party was down to five men. Livy loosed an arrow at one of the horsemen about to slash Caesar from behind. The arrow skewered his sword arm, and he dropped the weapon in shock. Caesar turned just in time to notice and then returned his attention to his other assailant. In a moment, the raiders were engaged, and the odds turned in the Romans' favour.

Livy engaged the armoured cavalryman whom he had injured. The warrior turned. A double-bladed heavy axe appeared in his left hand. Livy approached on his enemy's right side to gain maximum advantage. The axe man swung the axe ferociously at him, leaning to the right dangerously. Livy avoided the blow by leaning left, then struck him in the neck with the *spatha* as he sped by. The enemy horsemen remained on his horse, but Livy was sure he was dead as he left a trail of blood. After a few yards, he toppled from the horse. The war party surrounding Caesar melted away. Even the stalwart, armoured Belgic noblemen decided discretion to be the better part of valour. They broke off the attack and retreated.

Caesar glance caught Livy's eye. There was the most subtle hint of a smile and a slight nod. Caesar then spurred his horse for the Roman infantry line. The surviving tribunes of his general staff followed closely. Livy regrouped his men and headed for the right flank of the line. Most of the Roman cavalry were withdrawing.

The ford was a mass of floating bodies. The waters were coloured crimson. Viscera and faeces floated on the water. The Roman line was strengthening fast with the arrival of the Thirteenth and Fourteenth Legions. They formed a formidable line just about 200 yards from the bank. Sabinus's cohorts fell back in echelon in an orderly fashion.

The Belgae formed up on the bank for a charge at the Roman line. The light troops were running out of missiles now, so the two armies got ready to settle the issue hand to hand.

Caesar waited till about 10,000 of the enemy had crossed. He then unleashed his infantry, who marched forward at quick time. Within moments, they had closed to within thirty yards of the front line of the enemy. There they unleashed the first volley of *pila*. The Belgae took most of the javelins on their shields, which then became too cumbersome to hold up. As they tried to extricate the *pila*, the Romans advanced another ten yards and discharged a second volley, this time with the heavier *pila*. This time the damage was far greater, and many of the enemy warriors were impaled as they no longer had shields to protect them. Before the enemy could order their lines, the Romans drew swords simultaneously with a unified rasp. Shields were locked with a staccato of clunks. The Romans then advanced in precise ranks into the enemy just as if they had been on the parade ground.

The two legions broke through the Belgic line with ease. The Romans used their standard technique of hitting the enemy hard with their shields, then stabbing at any exposed flesh. The Belgae had no answer to that methodical, grinding type of fighting. They could hardly get at the Roman legionaries behind their large shields as they were systematically pushed back into their advancing comrades, leading to such severe crowding that they could hardly use their weapons. They could only take the punishment with hardly an opportunity to hit back. The slaughter was savage and frightful. After a short while, the Belgae broke and started streaming in disorder back across the river. They had clearly had enough. The legions pursued till knee-deep water when Caesar sounded the recall. Thousands of bodies floated on the river or lay on the banks. The cavalry pursued a little further but made no attempt to cross to the far bank. The enemy could turn and fight any time, and they had a big numerical advantage.

The Belgic army did not stop. They continued their retreat in the direction of their camp. They had obviously lost the heart to pursue the battle further that day. There was no cheering from the Roman side. They watched the retreat in silence. Caesar did not have the forces to pursue. The Romans countermarched smartly and formed ranks a hundred yards from the river bank.

One legion was left to guard the ford, and the rest of the Roman forces returned to camp. The Belgae did not make an appearance for the rest of the day.

CHAPTER 8

Brigita was happily riding back to Bibrax on her chestnut mare. The day was warm, and the sun was shining prettily through the trees, looking like shafts of gold. She was still fondly remembering the passionate lovemaking of the previous night, and she was further delighted by the obviously expensive arm bracelet that Centurion Livius had presented to her. Not daring to wear it openly, she had hidden it in her saddlebag. Birds were chirping and all seemed well with the world.

Coming around a bend in the road, she ran straight into a motley band of Nervii scouts. They were resting after the fight by the river. Most of them were light infantry, but there were half dozen horsemen, part of Bodougnatus's bodyguard. Brigita pulled up her horse in alarm. Both parties were startled into paralysis for a long moment.

"Look what the gods brought us, a Remi bitch and pretty one too," a large bearded Nervii warrior taunted.

"I wouldn't mind some Remi pussy at the moment," another fat and lecherous-looking Nervii added. "Come here, sweetheart. Come have a drink with us."

Brigita turned her horse and fled.

"Come back!" the first warrior shouted. Brigita urged her horse into a gallop in the opposite direction.

"Let's go get her," the fat one shouted. A half dozen of them quickly got on their horses and galloped after her. They had been humiliated at the river battle, and that was a chance to get back at a Roman ally and have some fun at the same time. The Nervii whooped with joy and gave chase.

Brigita knew she would not escape easily. Those men had rape on their minds, and it was a strong instinct. Unfortunately, she realised, the forest path was winding and she could be cut off easily. Still she refused to just submit. They would have to catch their pussy first! She looked behind and saw at least two men after her. She forced herself not to panic and think calmly. She was at least four miles from the Roman camp. Was there a short cut?

She could now see the Nervii horsemen creeping up on either side of her, cutting through smaller forest tracks. If she was going to cut away from the main track, she would have to make her move soon. She urged her mare on, squeezing as much speed out of her as possible. Coming to a sharp bend in the road, she tore into the forest rather than take the right bend. The move caught her pursuers by surprise, and suddenly they were all behind her once more. Tree trunks whizzed past in a blur as she sped along.

Brigita looked back and smiled in triumph. She had outrun them and would soon be back in the Roman camp and safe. Surely they would not pursue much longer for fear of meeting a Roman patrol. She bounced along as if in a dream.

The next moment, she was flying through the air. Her poor chestnut had stumbled and she was pelted forward. For an instant in time, she noticed the shafts of golden sunlight and a cool breeze. Then there was a sharp pain in her head, and everything went black.

Livy had returned to his tent after the morning battle. His raiders had been stood down in recognition of their significant contribution to the victory by the river Aisne. The men were told to rest and refit. A work party from the recruits were left behind to retrieve arrows from the dead and wounded enemy. Brigita was absent. She had left a note that she had decided to go back to Bibrax and invited Livy to come visit her if he could that evening.

That rang alarms in Livy's head as he realised that there were loose bands of Belgae roaming the countryside. She would have been far safer not travelling that day. He immediately decided to go to Bibrax and make sure she was safe. On the way, he rounded up Biorix and five of the veteran raiders. They replenished their quivers, and Livy took along a spare quiver of arrows and a long cavalry lance for protection.

They then set off quickly down the road towards Bibrax. After about two miles, they came across Brigita's chestnut mare. The horse was limping but otherwise not badly injured. She was still hot and sweaty, which meant she had just been ridden hard. Livy surmised that Brigita must be close. He moved his men off the road and proceeded on either side of the road in the forest. After a short distance, they could faintly perceive voices carried down the road. They heard rough voices cheering and jeering.

Livy motioned the men to advance with care. As they got nearer, he could make out some words in Celtic. "The bitch was good. Everyone should go for another round." That was followed by laughing and cheering. Livy was livid. The bastards had had their way with her. They would pay.

The raiders readied their bows. The spread out and advanced on the Nervii camp from three different directions, firing arrows as rapidly as they could. Livy's first arrow took one of the Nervii in the eye socket. The man screamed and stumbled about aimlessly, trying in vain to pull out the shaft. His next arrow took a rather fat warrior in the upper thigh. The man stumbled and fell.

There was pandemonium in the camp as the Nervii caught by surprise ran around in confusion. Some brave ones reached for weapons and rushed towards the raiders. They didn't get far and were felled before they closed. Others, less courageous, beat a hasty retreat into the forest. Livy let his men mop up the band of Nervii. He was looking for Brigita. He found her under a tree some way from the main group. Two Nervii warriors were with her. One had his pants off and was flaunting an erect penis. The other reached for his spear. Livy took out the spearman with an arrow through the neck, then, turned upon the half-naked man with his *spatha* drawn.

The man was huge. He had long black hair and a black beard. He pulled on his pants and took up a long sword and took a few practice swings. He looked calm and deadly.

"Come on, boy. She your woman? We've all had her. Twice. She ain't bad," he sneered.

Livy didn't bother to reply. He kept his distance, then dismounted. He knew if he came at him on horseback, the giant would just chop his horse down like a twig. That was no time to be brave.

He brought up his bow, took aim, and shot the first arrow into his right thigh. The man screamed and charged, sword raise above his head. In one fluid motion, Livy reloaded and fired his second arrow. That one pierced his left thigh. The giant slowed down but kept stumbling forward towards him. He sunk the third arrow into his right shoulder. The arrow went right through the point, coming out behind the man. The man sunk on to his knees. He had stopped screaming.

Livy walked up to him and pointed the *spatha* at his neck. The man dropped his sword. "Make it quick," he said in a resigned tone.

Livy hit him as hard as he could with the hilt of his sword, square on the face. The man dropped backwards, blood pouring from his nose. Before he could react, Livy had sliced off the ties of his trousers and pulled them halfway down his thighs, exposing his genitalia. The penis was still semi-erect. Livy grabbed it.

The man realised suddenly what was coming. "No, please, not that." Livy was so very tempted to slice off the huge erect penis at its root. He stopped himself. That man was going to live as none of his wounds were really mortal. What he was about to do was less than civilised. It was below his dignity. Was not that whole war about bringing Roman civilisation to the barbarians? He decided not to sink to their base level.

He released the penis, got up, and gave the barbarian a hard kick in the testicles. The man groaned loudly. It was half from pain and half from joy and relief.

His men came running to see what had happened. Biorix came up to him. "You are a kind soul. My people would have cut off both his balls together with his cock and made sure he lived to enjoy it," Biorix spat. Livy gave him a sheepish look.

He then got down and looted him. The man had two silver wrist guards, a golden torque round the neck, and a belt decorated with gold discs. The belt was of an ingenious and unique Celtic design. Livy stripped him bare of valuables. "What's your name, barbarian?" Livy asked him.

"Garactus," he groaned.

"My name is Centurion Gaius Livius. Remember this name. You don't deserve to live after what you did to that poor girl, but if I meet you again, I may not be so merciful." He kicked him quite viciously in the side.

Livy went over to Brigita. Her face was buried in her hands. They were blood-stained. She was naked. He covered her with his cloak and peeled her hands away from her face. She was badly bruised and there was swelling around both eyes, and she had a bloody nose and a split lip. They had beaten her. Livy tried to wipe some of the blood away with water from his canteen. She was sobbing hysterically and pushing him away. In the end, he just held her tightly and put her head against his chest. There was nothing he could say to make the pain go away.

None of the raiders were injured. That was lucky because Livy felt bad about having risked their lives for a personal matter. It was however far from safe to linger. They recovered four of the enemy horses, so anything valuable recovered from the dead and wounded Nervii were loaded on the animals. That included weapons, armour, and any trinkets found on the enemy. The wounded warriors were left only with water canteens. They were in no condition to join battle any time soon.

The raiders mounted up and headed down the road towards Bibrax at a brisk pace. Brigita was helped on to one of the Nervii horses, and her chestnut mare was tethered behind Livius. She hadn't uttered a word since her rescue.

The sentries at Bibrax were alert. They were spotted as soon as they emerged from the forest. The gates were opened without the Romans having to hail, and Iccius himself came out to meet them. He saw at once the sorry sight of Brigita, semi-naked and bruised. He immediately guessed what had happened.

"Who did it?" Iccius asked. His face was grim.

"Nervii war band," Biorix replied. "We got most of them. Some are wounded and still alive, about four miles down the road."

"I'll send a party to get the survivors. They must be made to suffer before they die," Iccius decided.

Livy realised that his Remi allies would not exercise any restrain. The wounded Nervii would be subjected to the most barbaric torture imaginable. It would have been kinder to have dispatched them on the spot.

"Bring my wife and my sister. They must take care of Brigita," Iccius ordered.

Some women came, and Brigita was bundled off. "I thank you for saving my niece, but it would have been kinder if she had not survived."

Livy was shocked. "I understand not your meaning? She is not badly injured"

"You don't understand our ways, young Livius. It's different for you Romans. A Roman girl who gets assaulted is no less honourable if she survives the experience. Among the Belgae, such a woman is permanently and irreversibly tainted. Not fit for any decent man. She is better dead."

"Your ways are harsh. Perhaps she is better coming away with us. She will not suffer so much contempt with the Roman Army."

"She will be just another army whore. Not much to look forward to in any case," Iccius retorted.

Livy thought for a while. "I could look after her. Centurions have the privilege of having a woman though not a wife."

"Best give her some time to recover from her ordeal, then you can make your offer. She is in no fit condition to think seriously about her situation as yet. My women will look after her in the meantime. She is safe in my house." Iccius made to leave.

"One last thing, Prefect, I will instruct my men that all valuables taken from her assailants will be hers. I think this much restitution is owed her," Livy requested.

"I shall see to it," Iccius concluded.

Livy saw to Brigita's chestnut mare. The horse had a sprained ankle but was otherwise not seriously hurt. He left her another of the horses taken from the Nervii. He then collected all the torques, rings, and armbands taken from the Nervii and placed it in the care of Iccius's sister, Terentia. Terentia was a widow in her thirties. She too had lost a husband in the interminable tribal wars. She never remarried though she was buxom and still attractive. She had a calm and sweet manner. Terentia promised to take good care of her niece. Livy gave her ten dinars to help with expenses, but she refused to accept. Iccius would provide, she assured him.

"At this moment, she is being bathed, and the *medicus* will soon see to her injuries." Terentia put her hand on his. "It is best you come back another day. Believe me, I know these things," she reassured him.

Livy rounded up his men. They were gathered in the large wooden town hall by the main square. The villagers provided a quick lunch of bread and fruits. Some of the men had a chance to spend a few minutes with their new women friends in the town. They then rode off towards Caesar's camp. Livy expected that after that day's victory, something was going to happen. Either the Belgae were going to chance an all-out attack or they would retreat. His raiders would be badly needed in both eventualities.

On the way back, they stopped at the Nervii encampment. Remi auxiliaries were scouring the forest around the campsite. Some were on foot and others on horseback. The Remi had adopted the dark-red livery of the Romans, and almost all the men had chain mail. They were beginning to look like Roman troops, but Livy knew that if they caught any of the Nervii, somewhat less than civilised standards would apply.

Livy approached an older man who seemed to be the leader. He wore a conical helmet with a large red plume. He gave a stiff-armed Roman salute as Livy approached. "Ave, Centurion, Fortuna favours us not today in our search for the Nervii scum. We found only dead ones. Some of their comrades must have come after you left and taken the wounded," the commander spat on the ground. "Damned Nervii, scum of the earth they are. The only good Nervii is a dead Nervii, I always say."

"Thank you, Commander. I am sure the Nervii are still about. You may yet catch them. I wish you luck in your hunt," Livy said. Those men admired him. He was the hero of Bibrax. It would not do to disillusion them by revealing his true feelings. He was somewhat relieved the wounded men had escaped.

He rejoined his men and rode briskly back to camp. Only two legions were deployed in front of the camp, but inside the camp, the army was on alert. All the legionaries were in full gear and ready to move at a moment's notice. Livy checked in on his century in the Seventh Legion. They were all young men in their late teens. He was cheered when he entered their camp area. Galienus his *optio* was all smiles and came to him with hands extended. "Please let me be first to congratulate you. We heard your raiders tipped the scales of battle today. Damned good show, sir!" He shook Livy's hands in both of his. Several of his young boys also plucked up the courage to come up and touch their hero. The adoration was lost on Livy because he was still in shock over Brigita.

Finally he collected himself. "You men fret for action. Believe me, the time will come soon enough. That mass of barbarians out there is far from beaten. They still control all the countryside around here, and this war won't end till we can bring them to a pitched battle."

The legionary called Crispus put a goblet of wine in his hand. "Nevertheless, sir, we beat them today, and the men would like to drink a toast to you."

Livy was reluctantly won over. "To victory then!" He raised his goblet.

"To victory!" the men chimed as one.

Sometime later, Livy was resting in the tent of Publius Crassus, Acting Legate of the Seventh. He was sitting stunned and silent for a long time. Finally Crassus ventured, "One thing I have learnt over the years is not to be fixated over any one woman. It invariably leads to grief. Actually in my experience, anything to do with women usually leads to grief." He smiled sympathetically, handing Livy a goblet of wine.

He was met by silence. Livy was obviously in pain, too much pain even to reply.

"Surely you're not in love with her!" Crassus exclaimed. "She is only a village girl from a barbaric backwater Belgic village. Certainly not someone to settle down with. Let me teach you about women."

Livy looked up. His eyes were red. "So tell me."

"There are two kinds of women in this world, well, in the Roman world anyway," Crassus intoned philosophically.

"Continue."

"Those you marry and those you merely enjoy. The first kind must be from a good family. You only marry for one of two reasons—for money or for the blood line. A good marriage for either reason earns you a place in society and helps your political career. Of course, you hope the bitch will produce a few offspring to continue the family line." Crassus chomped an apple as he mumbled.

"And the second kind?" Livy probed.

"The second kind brings you pleasure. The second kind makes the world go round. She warms your bed at night. She brings you to ecstasy. She brings quality to your life," Crassus went on with a smile and a distant look.

"You must have many an experience with this wonderful second kind, and I would guess with quite a few."

"With these you enjoy, but you never marry. They are pleasures of the flesh. They come and go. They are always replaceable."

"Until you fall in love," Livy sighed.

"Then you are truly undone," Crassus added definitively. "All reason goes out the window and only misery remains."

"There you are right, sir," Livy said miserably.

"There is good news though," Crassus said sympathetically.

"I can't wait to hear," Livy replied, unconvinced.

"Firstly, the hurt subsides with time. It invariably does, oh yes, every time." Crassus paused. "The second is that another one invariably comes along. Oh yes, they always do." He smiled.

"No one can replace Brigita." Livy remembered Aurora as he said that.

"So you say now," Crassus said thoughtfully. "So you say now," he repeated.

Just then the guard at the door looked in. "Lord Crassus, you have visitors."

Crassus smiled. "By all means show them in."

Two blonde girls with long pigtails entered, dressed in short tunics. They were very young, Livy observed. Late teens, he speculated.

"Meet my German friends, Gunda and Avila." Gunda was taller and very slim with long, well-trimmed legs. The other girl was shorter but also very well-proportioned. Her most prominent feature was a pair of perky mammaries visible under her thin tunic. They both had large, beautiful sky blue eyes and freckles. Crassus grabbed both of them and held one in each arm.

"These beauties don't speak a word of any civilised tongue, but they have nevertheless been providing me my creature comforts of late. In gratitude for your exemplary action this morning, I invite you to spend the night with us." He grinned broadly.

The girls smiled enthusiastically. They were obviously pleased at the new company.

"Now, Gaius, pick your partner. Do you prefer Gunda or Avila? We can always switch around later." He motioned the girls to fill up the wine goblets and get the party rolling. "The best way to forget a woman is in the arms of another," Crassus toasted and took a deep draught.

Livy was stunned. The girls looked willing and enthusiastic, and they were both desirable. "I think Gunda," he stammered. He was certainly in no mood to party, but it would have been impolite to refuse the legate.

She stepped over to him, put her arms around his neck, and kissed him warmly on the lips. She felt soft and wet and smelt clean. Soon Livy was lost in the Dionysian dream of wine and women.

Meanwhile in the Belgic camp, a counsel of war was being held. The warlords sat glumly around the hall of the big farmhouse they had appropriated. It stank of stale wine and rotting food from the previous night's feasting. Finally Galba got up. The others fell silent and waited for him to speak.

"This devil Caesar is no fool. We have an army more than five times his numbers. In ordinary circumstances, we will trample the Romans in the dust. The Romans are cowards. They hide on that hill behind their artillery and their defences. They want us to attack them. Many of us will die trying," Galba spoke loudly.

"Even if we win, more than half of us will die. There will be crying and wailing in every town and village in Belgica," Galba continued.

There were loud murmurings among the chiefs. "We came here to fight, and I say we fight," Bodougnatus challenged. "I'll lead the right wing with all the Nervii and take the trenches and the artillery. You, Galba, do the same on the left. All the rest of you run straight up the centre, smash through the legions, and drive into their camp. We have the numbers, the courage, and the right on our side. Tomorrow we teach them such a lesson that no Roman Army will dare set foot in these parts again."

There was cheering and loud beating of knives on the table and stamping of feet. The chiefs were obviously fretting over the inactivity of the last few days.

"Hear, hear," one cried.

"Kill them all," another shouted.

"Wait, wait!" Galba held his hands out to try and calm their enthusiasm. "That's just what Caesar wants us to do, you fools," Galba fought to restore reason. "Don't you remember what happened to the Helvetii and the Germans under Ariovistus? Where are they now, huh?"

There were murmurings, but the chiefs quietened down as they remembered the recent slaughter of those two huge armies by smaller Roman forces.

"Numbers mean nothing with those Romans. If we fight them the way they planned, we will be either dead or slaves, just like the Germans and the Helvetii. We must make them fight on our terms. Fight them in a place and time of our choosing."

Commius got up. "Galba is right. We Belgae are great warriors and fighters. We depend on our individual skills, courage, and honour to win battles. These Romans fight like no other army we have seen. They stay in formation. The soldiers act not as individual warriors but as part of a whole. They fight as a team. And then there are those infernal machines, stone throwers, bolt throwers, fire throwers. With those things, it's no longer honourable warfare. It's just murder." He paused.

There was silence. "I agree with Galba. Bodougnatus, if you and your Nervii want to slug it out with the Romans tomorrow, you go ahead. My men are sitting this one out." Commius crossed his arms emphatically.

There was a roar of protest. "I always knew you were a yellow belly, Commius. You've got no balls. You're scared of those puny Italian dwarves," Bodougnatus jeered.

Commius refused to be provoked and turned away.

The rest of the chiefs immediately broke into arguments with one another. There were a dozen different opinions, and the result was pandemonium. The whole room rang with angry altercations, each chief trying to shout down his colleague. The Nervii, Atrebates, and Viromandui were all for giving battle. The Bellovaci and Suessiones were much less keen. Finally Galba motioned for silence.

"There is one other vital matter to consider." Galba rapped his spoon on the table to appeal for order. Finally the chiefs gave him an audience. "We've run out of food."

It was around midnight. Livy was lying naked in Crassus's tent. The two nude girls were lying beside him. Gunda had her head on his right shoulder and Avila on his left. He could smell their wine-soaked breaths. Crassus had passed out some hours ago, and both girls had then turned on him with a vengeance till they both became too intoxicated to continue. Livy had had a serious education about the sexual habits of German women.

Suddenly the tent flap came open, and a helmeted head poked inside, took in the scene, and politely withdrew. "Lord Crassus, Centurion Livius, Lord Caesar wants you both in his tent right now," the praetorian officer commanded loudly. "Right now!" he exclaimed once again loudly.

Livy who had a horrible headache replied, "Yes, of course, right away. We're coming." He pushed the two girls aside and shook Crassus awake. "Let's go, sir. Caesar wants us. Must be something important."

They dressed frenetically and made their way quickly to Caesar's headquarters tent. The senior officers of the Roman Army were hurrying from every direction. There was already a crowd in front of the tent, and Caesar had got up on a platform to speak to his commanders. He was already dressed in armour but bareheaded. The adjutant called for order, and Caesar started his briefing. "Gentlemen, I am sorry to disturb your evening, but the enemy is moving. They are breaking camp and seem to be retreating. This may be an opportunity for us to attack them. If we move fast, we can catch them before they disperse and destroy their army."

There was quiet. Most of the officers were only half awake. Finally Labienus spoke, "I think it's a trap. They want us to go down there after them, and then they'll suddenly turn round and overwhelm us. They outnumber us six to one, and at night, they will have the advantage."

"You are right to be cautious, Labienus, but if you are wrong, we miss a great opportunity. Are there other views?"

No one dared contradict the testy Labienus as that was sure to secure his wrath. Livy knew that that move was unlikely to be a ruse. The Belgae were out of food. Not being able to bring the Romans to an even fight, they had simply given up and gone home. It was an excellent opportunity to strike. To point that out would make an enemy of Labienus, he was sure. Labienus already disliked him because of his recent successes and also because he considered him a provincial upstart.

"I know why they are retreating," Livy's voice came clearly from behind. Everyone turned to look at the source of the unfamiliar voice. Labienus glared at him. Caesar looked directly at him and motioned him to come forward.

"Tell us what you know," Caesar ordered.

Livy could feel the glare of all the legates, especially Labienus.

"I think they can no longer sustain this large number of men in the field. They have scoured the land bare and they are out of food. I think they starve," Livy said loudly for all to hear.

"In that case, we should attack at once," Caesar proposed.

"I would advise caution, My Lord Caesar. Are we going to risk the whole army just on the word of one junior centurion? Someone who till recently was just a mere legionary?" Labienus scoffed.

"Centurion Gaius Livius has my confidence. His performance of late has been exemplary. On the other hand, it is dark and foggy tonight and a perfect night for an ambush. Hannibal would love such a night, though I doubt Galba is the same calibre as our legendary Punic hero." Caesar was undecided. "So what do the rest of you think? Cotta?"

"I'd send out scouts and wait till morning," Cotta mumbled.

"Sabinus?"

"I think we should probe them, sir." Sabinus looked far from sure of himself.

"Crassus?"

"I'd attack, sir. Catch them on the run."

"Ha, the enthusiasm of the young." Caesar smiled. "Quintus Pedius?"

"Hold back till morning."

"So the majority prefer caution. My instinct is to attack, but I suppose we can't risk an ambush in the fog. Fine, we will send out the cavalry to see what's happening and nip at their tails if they are retreating. No major engagements and retreat if they appear in force. Labienus, you are in charge." Caesar wanted him to have a chance to make up for his shoddy performance of late. "Livy, your raiders are the spearhead. I place you under the command of the cavalry wing under Labienus for the time being."

Livy could see Labienus smile in triumph. He was the last commander he wanted to work under.

"The rest of you get ready to break camp at dawn and march after the enemy army." Caesar stalked back to his tent.

The rest of the commanders broke up silently and returned to their units. Reluctantly, Livy reported to Labienus. He was still engaged in giving orders to his cavalry commanders. Livy waited politely for him to finish. Labienus deliberately took his time. Finally, he turned to Livy.

"So I have the honour to command the great hero, Gaius Livius. Now what shall we do with you?" Labienus opened with sarcasm. "Well, I have just the job for you. Take all your men and check out the enemy camp and pick up their trail from there. I'll follow behind. If you see any large body of the Belgae, send word to me, and I'll come to your aid. Get moving," Labienus ordered.

Livy knew he was going to be put in the position of maximum danger. If it was a trap as Labienus believed, they would be the first to get hit. It was also likely that by the time Labienus arrived with the main body of the cavalry, it would be all over for Livy and his raiders. Nevertheless, Livy felt up to the challenge, and if he was right and the Belgic army was dissolving, Livy and his raiders would have rich pickings.

Livy got hold of Biorix and Paulus and told them to ready the men. He went back to his tent to change into his old raider outfit. He took off his centurion regalia and put on the light chain mail his father had given him—a simple cavalry helmet with no decorations and his belt and *spatha*. He looked no fancier than a ranker in the cavalry. He looked around his tent and found it strangely empty. The smell of Brigita lingered. Maybe it was only in his imagination. A strange sadness descended on him. He forced himself to move on and join his men.

CHAPTER 9

They rode out an hour later. It was yet dark, but the waxing moon gave some light to the endeavour. A chill pierced the armour and tunics of the horsemen. Livy divided his 300 men into three troops of a hundred. Biorix and Paulus had continued the training of the recruits, and most of them could ride passably by then. Livy's troop was the vanguard, and he appointed one of the veterans, a Roman named Valerius, as his second in command. Valerius was only a trooper but was a veteran cavalryman from the north of Italy. He was blond and had a light complexion and, Livy suspected, could have Gaulish blood. They rode quickly but stealthily. Livy moved the troop from cover to cover, avoiding ridge lines where their silhouette would be spotted from afar. The soft clinking of equipment and muffled hoof beats were the only sounds in the night.

He made his way up a small hill which overlooked the Belgic encampment. The men slowed to climb the hill. Livy sent Valerius and another veteran ahead. They were soon challenged. A small troop of Remi scouts led by a Roman decurion had staked out the hill. They were the ones who had sent the message to Caesar about the retreat. The decurion's name was Licinius. He had wrapped a heavy brown scarf over his dull chain mail. His helmet was dark with age, and his red plume had darkened to nearly black. His stubble was at least a week old.

"Centurion Livius, greetings," Licinius greeted warmly. Livy had never even met him. "Please follow me."

Biorix and Livy followed Licinius up to the top of the hill. It had a panoramic view of a large part of the Belgic camp, most of which looked abandoned.

"Where's the Roman Army?" Licinius asked. "We should be pursuing and attacking their rear. We will slaughter many of the sons of pigs if we attack in force forthwith."

Livy was red faced. "Caesar fears an ambush. Are there signs?" Livy asked.

"I see no trap. One can never be sure," Licinius answered.

"Only one way to find out, and that's to spring it," Livy said in a determined voice. "Are you with me?"

"Of course, to the River Styx if it comes to that," Licinius grinned.

Livy probed with sixty men. Thirty of those were the Remi scouts led by Licinius and the other thirty were the pick of his veterans led by Valerius. They fanned out into a widely spaced line and swept through the camp slowly in pairs. Biorix and Paulus formed the rest of the men behind the hill, ready to charge down to their aid at the slightest sign of trouble. The camp was quiet. All the tents were gone, but some campfires still burnt, and there was litter everywhere—half-burnt wood, animal bones, broken pottery, empty wine casks, excrement, and every kind of remnant from human passage. Everything seemed unreal and too quiet. There was no sound except the hoof beats of the horses. The smell of urine and excrement polluted the air.

Livy could feel the hairs at the back of his neck stand and his skin crawl. Labienus could have been right after all. They were walking into a trap. Any moment now, Belgic warriors would rise from the ground and overwhelm them. All his men looked about nervously except Licinius who seemed to be in cheerful oblivion.

A lone horseman materialised like a ghost from the dark. Livy recognised the rider immediately. "If it could ever be said that one can be immaculately turned out in the nude," Livy thought, "then Murato deserved that description." His hair and moustache were finely groomed, and his body looked pristinely clean and scrubbed. He even had a glow. He looked like a Germanic god.

"Greetings, Centurion Livius. Stop right there and come no further. If you intend to attack our retreating comrades, you will have to go through me!" Murato challenged.

Livius motioned to his signaller, who blew a note on his horn. Immediately the raiders appeared on the top of the hill and started galloping towards them.

Murato's horse reared. He looked annoyed. "I see you came prepared. Too bad. I respect you for your courage, Commander, but now we have no choice but to battle." He charged towards Livius, his huge sword raised. At that moment, there was a loud war cry and hundreds of screaming naked Gaesatae rushed out of hiding towards the thin Roman line. Most were on foot, though about a dozen were on horseback. All were stark naked, including a score of woman warriors who wore only blue war paint.

Livy reacted quickly. In a flash, his bow and arrow were aimed at Murato. Something made him hesitate. He lowered and shot Murato's horse in the chest. The horse collapsed, bringing Murato into the dust. Murato lay stunned. Livy loosed another arrow, bringing down another naked horseman. This time he hit the rider.

The enemy infantry were nearly on them now, and the raiders retreated quickly. Some of the Remi scouts failed to move in time, and Livy saw the naked warriors throw themselves at the riders, clawing them off their horses. They then dispatched the unfortunate Remi most violently, hacking off their heads brutally, spraying blood in warm red fountains which smeared their bodies in grotesque patterns.

Livy retreated 200 yards and calmly took down two more Gaesatae riders. He selectively aimed for the cavalry because he knew his men could easily outrun the infantry. He saw to one side a naked blonde girl with a spear sprinting in a blur towards one of the Remi scouts. He swung his bow and was about to drop her with an arrow when he suddenly realised who it was.

Leuce was in the war band, tasked to stop any Roman pursuit so as to allow the Belgic army to disperse. The chiefs had taken the decision to each disperse to their own territory and reassemble to defend wherever the Romans attacked next. Leuce felt it was a bad decision as that gave the initiative to the Romans. It would be hard to assemble an army of a few hundred thousand again. The main reason for that dispersal was hunger. The troops needed to go home to resupply. The more warlike tribes like the Nervii, Atrebates, and Viromandui were furious.

"Anyway, I am only a warrior. My job is to fight, and that's all. What do I care about grand strategy?" Leuce thought to herself. She had seen the Romans come. There were not many and only cavalry. Some were Remi and others clearly Roman. She had seen Murato talk to their leader. She recognised the young centurion who had come to her camp. His outfit was different—no decorations. She liked this simple look better than when he was all decked out in gilt and plumes. She couldn't hear what they were saying.

Suddenly, more horsemen were coming at a gallop. Then Murato had given the signal to attack. Leuce commanded a squad of twenty women warriors, and they rushed out to engage the enemy. They had an assortment of weapons including bows, spears, axes, and curved short thin swords. Leuce preferred to trust her seven-foot long spear which had a long polished steel blade sharpened like a razor. One of the Remi went down to an arrow fired by one of her sister warriors. She singled out the Remi for killing. They were all traitors after all.

One Remi horsemen was engaged by one of the Gaesatae men. The Remi parried the spear thrust and slashed at the Gaesatae with his heavy *spatha*. The warrior went down, blood spurting from a shoulder wound. Leuce rushed at the Remi, spear thrusting forward. Suddenly an arrow slammed into the ground at her feet. She was startled but focused on the Remi. From the corner of her eye, she saw that the archer was one of the Romans, approaching fast on a massive black charger. She thrust at the Remi, who parried with his sword. Seeing the fate of her comrade, she whipped her spear in a circle and hit the Remi over the back of his neck with tremendous momentum, which knocked him off the horse. In a flash, Leuce had leapt into the saddle. The stunned Remi was staggering on to his feet when Leuce rammed the spear point right through his neck. She put a leg to his chest and withdrew the spear, which was smeared red and dripping with blood. The mortally wounded man rocked a few times, then collapsed like chopped timber.

Livy watched in consternation as the Remi was slain. He drew his *spatha* and charged at the mounted girl. She saw him coming and swung her spear in a wide arc at Livy's head. He ducked and just avoided the blow. Then he went on the attack with his *spatha* against her spear.

They crossed weapons furiously. His sword made deep cuts in the spear shaft, but the wood was hard and stood up to his blows. The air resounded with the thud of steel against hard seasoned wood. The girl was a seasoned fighter and counterattacked with skill and determination. She thrust again and again, striking like a cobra. She was more than a match for Livy's sword fighting skills, which were never his strong point. He parried desperately while at the same time trying to maintain his seat on Nero.

Leuce lunged suddenly with lightning speed, and the spear glanced off his armour on his right side with a loud clang. It did not penetrate, but Livy felt the acute pain from the blow. In a flash, she had the spear tip pointed at his throat. Livy went cold and expected to die.

Leuce hesitated, then, smiled. Her sparkling eyes laughed at him. "Any other Roman pig and you would be dead. You spared my life some nights ago, so I let you live today. Besides it would be a waste. I have some other plan for you." She laughed impudently and was gone in a flash.

Livy was stunned. He couldn't afford the luxury of being in that state for long. The battle was raging around him. The Remi scouts and their Roman leaders were heavily engaged in hand-to-hand combat and were not faring well. The Gaesatae were picking them off one at a time by attacking in groups.

The raiders had gone into skirmish mode, keeping their distance and using their bows. They were having a deadly effect on the Gaesatae. Livy decided that this was one battle he did not want to see to its conclusion. They were heavily outnumbered, and his mission had already been accomplished.

He found the signaller and blew the retreat. The men disengaged as best as they could and rode for the hill. Livy was one of the last to follow. Valerius was with him along with two other Remi scouts. They had just managed to disentangle from some Gaesatae infantry. Suddenly an arrow was protruding from the back of one of the Remi. He screamed and fell off his horse. Livy turned around and saw a party of female Gaesatae firing at them.

He returned fire and saw a naked figure crumple. Then Biorix and the remaining horsemen thundered towards them. They were outnumbered three to one, and Livy decided that discretion was in order. He galloped off after his men. Licinius followed. After some distance, Licinius began to fall back, and the Gaesatae were gaining on them. Livy noticed that his horse had an arrow protruding from its rump. He shouted at the Remi in Celtic, "Go get help. I will stay and protect your commander"

Licinius looked desperate but was overjoyed to see Livy turn around. "You are the hero!" he shouted excitedly. "Bad choice though. I fear we both cross the Styx arm in arm."

Livy let off two arrows in quick succession downing two horsemen and then charged with his *spatha* raised. Licinius charged with him. The first naked warrior had a spear aimed at him. He avoided the thrust and slashed the warrior's torso under the arm. The man rode past, bleeding profusely from the wound. With no armour, the Gaesatae suffered grievous injuries when struck. His next opponent was Murato, who brought his sword down from overhead with great force. Livy parried but felt his whole arm vibrate and become numb after the blow.

"You should have taken my advice, young friend. I have no choice but to kill you now." He had an icy glint in his eyes. His men had formed a circle round the two Romans. Licinius had killed one man on the first pass, so there were now five against two.

Murato held back, and the other two pairs charged at the two Romans. Livy and Licinius positioned their horses side by side. Livy knew they had no chance. Both the Romans braced themselves to go down fighting.

At the last moment, both men charged and slammed their horses into the horse of one Gaesatae each. Both horses went down with the impact, bringing down their riders. The Roman horses were bigger and stronger than the Gaesatae ponies. The odds now were almost even. The turn of events startled the Gaesatae. Livy charged his second opponent, yelling at the top of his voice. The man turned his horse and ran. Licinius engaged his second opponent and seemed to be holding his own. Livy then turned on Murato, who smiled.

"Looks like the winds blow in your favour once more," Murato said in a resigned manner. He sheathed his sword. "We shall meet again."

Livy saluted him, and Murato rode back to his men. The other Gaesatae disengaged and followed. At that moment, Livy heard a familiar shout. Biorix pulled up next to him together with about ten raiders. "Shall we go after him?"

"No, it's dark, and we need to report back to Labienus that there isn't any great trap waiting for the Roman Army. You could have come round a little faster, you know. We were nearly raped and roasted."

Biorix blushed in embarrassment. "Came as fast as we could, sir. Sorry, sir."

"Let's go home," Livy grunted.

It was already dawn. There was a feeble glow over the horizon, colouring the distant hills purple. There was still a chill in the air, and mist lay thick on the ground. The entire Roman cavalry force was mounted and ready to move. Horses neighed restlessly, and equipment jangled in the still morning air. They deployed outside the gates of the Roman camp, and the camp was already in the process of being torn down. Legionaries buzzed around like busy bees. Caesar and Labienus and some other legates were conferring in what looked like an orders group in a large white tent erected in front of the dismantling camp.

Livy rode up with Licinius and dismounted. He went up to Caesar and gave the stiff-armed Roman salute. "Ave, Caesar," he greeted.

"Ave, Gaius Livius, what have you to report?" Caesar replied. He looked fresh and alert and was in full armour and red cloak. He wore his Corona Civica on his head.

"The Belgic army has dispersed and is in full retreat, sir. They are not deployed for an ambush as far as we can tell," Livy reported.

"How can you be so sure? "Labienus challenged. "Looking at your appearance, you look as if you have been attacked."

Livy flushed. "It was a small blocking force of Gaesatae. I believe they are the rearguard. I do not think they would have offered significant resistance to a determined Roman pursuit," Livy defended.

"How many men?" Caesar asked.

"Perhaps three or four hundred," Livy replied.

"You deliberately disobeyed my orders not to engage, Centurion Livius. I told you to avoid an engagement. I think this youngster should be disciplined," Labienus demanded.

"Begging your pardon, sir," Licinius interjected. "It was dark, and the Gaesatae surprised us, sir. The centurion did not deliberately seek battle"

"Then you were clumsy to allow yourself to be ambushed. That's just plain incompetence," Labienus continued.

"If you did not think he was up to the job, you should not have sent him," Caesar retorted. "It's a dangerous mission. Reconnaissance in the dark is hazardous and ambush is not easy to avoid. I think the centurion has fulfilled his mission. You are wrong, Labienus, and this is no grand ruse by the enemy. They have run out of food and decided to go home. We, on the other hand, have let most of them escape."

Labienus was seething. Caesar paused to think. He walked around in a circle. "Quintus Pedius and Lucius Cotta will take the cavalry and pursue north. Destroy any bands of enemy warriors that you catch. Labienus will follow with two legions and mop up. The rest of the army will march west into the territory of the Suessiones. We're going after their leader, Galba," Caesar decided.

Caesar turned to Livy. "Come with me, young man." They walked to Caesar's horse together. "The men will take most of the day to break camp, and we will probably march tomorrow. Our target will be Noviodunum. Your raiders will be attached to me for this stage of the operations. I want you to dine with me this night. I have organised a special party in my tent. Let's say the seventh hour after noonday. Just come in your tunic." Caesar mounted his horse, and Livy gave him a leg up. Livy saluted, and Caesar touched his riding crop to his brow.

Livy went to look for Crassus. He found him at his tent which was being taken down. The two German girls were helping to pack the furniture and other paraphernalia into a cart. They both smiled and waved sweetly to Livy when he arrived. "Looks like that pair have taken quite a liking to you." Crassus smirked mischievously.

"They are wonderful, sir. You have chosen well. I want to thank you for last night," Livy said gratefully and reddened with embarrassment at the same time.

"Think nothing of it, Gaius. You can call me Publius. We are friends."

"Thank you, sir, I mean, Publius." Livy beamed. "It's a great honour for me to be called friend."

"Come, help me load up, and then I'll send the girls over to help you pack your tent," Crassus offered. "After that, let's go get some breakfast."

Livy cheerfully warmed to the task. The two girls were marvellous workmates. They giggled and flirted with him during the whole exercise, making the work seem light and the time pass fast. The girls knew a smattering of Latin, so there was rudimentary communication, but mostly they relied on their bodies to do the talking.

When the packing was done, the four of them lay under a tree for a picnic breakfast of bread, fruit, and some cold roast chicken. Gunda came to kneel beside him and started feeding him with grapes. Avila did the same with Publius. "I heard you saved the life of a young decurion named

Lepidus," Crassus finally remarked with a grape in his mouth and after some breathless kissing with Avila.

"Yes, as a matter of fact I did," Livy replied with his mouth full.

"He's the son of a senator. Important family. They will be grateful. You'll get the Corona Civica for that," Crassus said matter of factly. "A stunning award to possess. It gives you the right to attend the Senate and wear it, the damned thing. The senators have to applaud when they see you. Quite an honour really. Wouldn't mind having one myself."

"You can have mine if you want. You've been good to me," Livy said earnestly.

"No good. You've got to earn it. It's not transferable." Publius laughed. "Anyway you deserve it. You have been a real hero in the last days. Didn't know you had it in you."

"I'm sure you would have performed even better in my place, Publius."

"Not sure that I would, Gaius. Not sure that I would," he mumbled almost to himself.

Later, the girls followed him to help take down his tent and pack his things. A couple of legionaries from his century came to help, and Biorix had managed to find him a cart for his furniture and baggage. The two young legionaries were entranced by the two Germans. Soon they were following the girls around like puppies and taking orders from them. Livy left them to their task. He had a more important task to perform.

Around midday, he arrived at Bibrax. The place looked cleaner and tidier than the last time. The wall had been repaired. The bodies had been buried and the damaged houses fixed. The townsmen had been busy.

The town guards recognised him and opened the gates for him immediately. As he rode in, men, women, and children smiled and waved to him. He was made to feel welcome as if he were returning home. His heart warmed to the Remi. He headed for the home of Brigita. He stopped outside the door and dismounted, tying his horse to a pillar. He knocked on the door, and after a few moments a woman peeked out. It was Terentia. "Greetings, Honoured Lady, is Brigita in residence?" Livy asked politely.

"Yes, she is in and frantic to see you. We hear the Roman Army is on the move and the camp is being torn down. Come in, come in." she pulled him inside.

Brigita was sipping some soup at the table. Her face was swollen and bruised. There was so much swelling around the right eye she could hardly open it. She looked up at him longingly. "I am so pleased you have come." She held out her hand to him. He took it firmly and sat down.

They were silent for a while. The situation was awkward, and Livy didn't know what to say. Finally she said, "I missed you. Thank you for saving me from those terrible Nervii." She gave his hand a squeeze.

"You look . . . well," Livy finally said.

"You're lying. I look terrible. Would you still want to make love to a woman who looks like this?" She gestured at her own face. Livy realised that her nose was broken and out of shape and probably several of her facial bones as well.

"As a matter of fact I would," Livy reassured her, trying to sound as sincere as possible.

"Ahem." Terentia coughed. "Maybe I better be going. I will come back later, dear. Take care of yourself."

"Good-bye, Terentia, and thank you for looking after me." Brigita waved.

Terentia left, shutting the door slowly. "Now I have you all to myself." Brigita smiled. "I hear you are leaving. They are dismantling the camp."

"Yes, our Belgae friends have given up and gone home. I think Bibrax will be safe now. Caesar is pursuing, so we are leaving. Would you like to come along?"

Brigita sighed. "Part of me wants badly to come with you. I have no longer much future in this town as no one will touch a woman who has been multiply raped by the enemy."

"Then come with me," Livy implored. "I promise to take good care of you."

"I know you mean well, but you will be too busy with your war. Besides, an army whore's life is not for me. Furthermore, there is always the chance that you will get killed!" she added emphatically.

"What will you do then?" Livy asked gently.

"Iccius will arrange for me to stay with relatives in the Roman province, Galla Narbonensis, in the south. I am his niece after all, and he feels responsible. My father was his brother. No one will know about my misfortune there, and perhaps they can arrange a marriage for me."

Livy was sad. "I guess it is good-bye then." He smiled.

"Not yet. Stay with me awhile. Spend some time with me." She looked at him imploring. "I may not see you again," she pleaded.

"All right," Livy said. "I will stay"

Livy helped her undress and cleaned her many wounds. He made a bath and gently helped her into it, then scrubbed her gently, taking care to avoid the painful areas. They talked for some hours till the sun sank low in the sky.

In the late afternoon, Livy rode back to Caesar's camp. He galloped along the forest track because he had overstayed in Bibrax. The parting was hard. He did not know when he would have the chance to see Brigita again. He would miss her. Their relationship had been very physical and very sexual. There had been no time to explore other aspects of their relationship. It was short and intense. Livy felt that if they had more time they could have really bonded. Perhaps she could even be the life partner that he sought after. Then again he was not really ready for a life partner yet, was he? Life still held much to explore. There would be other women. Nevertheless Brigita was memorable. He would not forget her just as he would always remember Aurora. The weather was getting cold, and a brisk wind blew as he hurried home, his red cloak flying behind him. The shadows of the trees were already long. He hoped there would be no marauding bands of Belgic cavalry scouring the countryside.

The main Roman camp had been almost entirely disassembled except for the wooden parapet. In the middle of the camp around Caesar's headquarters a few tents still stood. Livy headed for them. The headquarters area had been cordoned off with wooden mantlets for security. Livy dismounted at the entrance and was met by a tribune in shining silver-muscled cuirass and a rich red-plumed helmet, one of Caesar's staff officers.

"Come for the *cena*?" the tribune enquired.

"Yes, Centurion Gaius Livius of the Seventh Legion," Livy reported.

"Oh, yes. You are on the guest list for tonight. Please follow me. You will need to freshen up before dinner." He led Livy to one of the tents. Inside Livy found several wooden bathtubs filled with water which had steam emanating from the surface. Beside each tub stood a young slave girl in a short white tunic.

"You may choose your attendant," the tribune said in a rather formal manner. There were six of them. Livy chose a slim brunette with almond-shaped eyes and an ivory complexion. She looked different, like from another world. He had never seen anyone so mysterious and strange before. "Good choice, Centurion. You'll enjoy her. She is from a tribe called Han. They're from way out in the east, the Land of Silk." The tribune smirked and left. The other girls who looked like Gauls of Germans melted away, leaving him with the slave from Han.

"Do you speak Latin or Celtic? What's your name?" Livy tried.

"I am called Jasmine. I speak a little Latin." She kept her head bowed and spoke in a very soft voice. "May I help you out of your clothes, Master?"

Livy nodded, and Jasmine started by helping him out of his *caligae* and then his armour, *subarmalis,* and tunic. She wore a tunic which only reached to her upper thigh, revealing a pair of trim, ivory-coloured legs. The material was smooth, shiny, and thin enough to make out her shapely body and see the outline of her small but shapely breasts and erect nipples. Her touch was gentle and cool. Attentively, she helped him into the bath which was hot but tolerable. Livy let his body sink into the tub and luxuriated in the sensation. Jasmine gave him a drink from a small beautiful ceramic cup. The liquid was hot and slightly bitter but had a marvellous aroma.

"What is this?" Livy asked.

"Our people call it cha. It is a drink made from special dried leaves from the east. Drink it, Master. You will feel refreshed." She began to scrub his back.

"Tell me about this faraway land which you come from."

"We call it Zhong Guo or Middle Kingdom. It is also called the land of the Han because it is ruled by emperors of the Han Dynasty. It has many cities and millions of people. The empire, some say, is the biggest in the world. It lies at the other end of the earth from here and takes several years to get there."

"So tell me, Jasmine, how did you manage to end up here in Belgica?"

"It's a long story, Master. I need time to tell you, and you don't have time. You have to go to dinner with my master Lord Caesar, and he doesn't like to wait," Jasmine said emphatically. She used a rough cloth to scrub his chest and arms.

"Nevertheless, I want to hear your story. Can I seek you out after the dinner?"

"Be so kind as to raise your legs and rest them on the rim of the tub," Jasmine commanded. Livy complied.

"Aren't you going to take off your clothes and join me inside the tub?" Livy asked hopefully.

Jasmine blushed. "I am sorry, Master, but I am not that kind of slave. If you wanted sex, you should have chosen one of the others." She sounded apologetic.

"I am really sorry to assume," Livy quickly apologized as respectfully as he could. "My limited experience with women who give baths . . ."

"We are not all the same," Jasmine interrupted. "Please stand up." Livy complied quickly. Jasmine began to wash his upper thighs, buttocks, and then his testicles and his penis. She was thorough but not sexual. Nevertheless, Livy could not help but have a normal male reaction. Jasmine ignored the effect she was having on him.

"If you start something, you should finish it," Livy remarked. Jasmine wriggled her nose and smiled sexily.

"No time, Master. I must get you dried and dressed. Caesar is expecting you." She gave his organ one last squeeze. Livy almost exploded. She helped him out of the tub, towelled him dry, and helped him put on a fine light blue tunic of the same shiny material as her own tunic. His was finely embroidered with a strange animal which looked like a snake with claws and wings and the head of a lion.

"What material is this? It's amazing. So soft, light, smooth, and shiny," Livy asked.

"It's called silk, Master. My country is also known as the Land of Silk. Its origin is a well-kept secret. I will explain another time. Please let me dress you." She was doing her best to hurry. "Look for me here after the party if you are not too tired."

At that moment, the tribune returned. "Ah, Centurion Livius. You look ... er, well, nice and clean. Time to come to dinner. Caesar awaits," The tribune marched ahead and motioned Livy to follow.

Livy looked back and saw Jasmine give him a warm smile, then bow her head quickly.

The tribune came to Caesar's tent and was immediately admitted by the two German guards. Caesar relied on German bodyguards as he trusted them more than the Romans around him. He lived in constant fear of assassination by his political rivals in Rome. The guards were dressed as Roman cavalrymen but were taller and had neatly trimmed beards and long hair tied into a bun.

The tent was large, perhaps equivalent to six command tents. It was specially put up for the party. The floor was luxuriously carpeted, and it was brightly lit by a dozen braziers and scores of candles. Soft music from flute and lyre filled the air, and the subtle smell of perfume and incense tickled the nostrils.

The tribune announced him as he entered. Inside were Caesar, Publius Crassus, and another Roman whom he did not recognise. There were also a dozen ladies in near transparent silk chitons. All had heavy make-up and elaborate hairdos. There were five expensively draped divans arranged in a horseshoe shape with Caesar's divan at the bottom of the U. Serving slaves of both sexes stood discreetly behind. In the centre was a long rectangular table laid out with food, wine, and fruits. The meal looked sumptuous though not luxurious. It was well known that Caesar prided himself on not being ostentatious. Livy noted that the main course was a roast wild boar. There were also roast ducks and geese, blood sausages, and an abundance of bread, cheese, and fruits. Livy's stomach growled merely at the sight as he had not eaten since morning.

"Come and sit next to me, Gaius." Caesar pointed to the divan to his left. The unknown Roman was at his right. Livy was placed between Caesar and Crassus.

"Let me introduce everyone. Publius Crassus, you know." He motioned to the handsome well-built Roman to his right. "This is the famous Marcus

Antonious whose exploits are already legendary, unfortunately for the wrong sort of things. He is just visiting for a few weeks, but in that time I hope to set him straight," Caesar said. "I give you Gaius Livius, our young hero of the day. I've invited young Gaius to get to know him better as he has done astounding things of late."

"It's an honour to meet you, sir." Livy bowed to Marc Antony. Livy had heard about him. He was mainly famous for scandals and reckless living but was a relative of Caesar.

"This is my faithful companion, Servilia Caepionis." Caesar gestured to the older woman sitting beside him on his divan. She was well kept for her age and elegantly dressed in a low-cut *stola*. Her face had hardly a wrinkle and her hair was elaborately turned out in fashionable ringlets. Livy was certain she had been beautiful when younger. Livy surmised that she was Caesar's mistress. "Servilia here traces her ancestry back to the legendary Gaius Servilius Ahala. Do you know the story, Livius?"

"The murderer of Spurius Maelius, the man who would be king during the time of Cincinnatus. Yes, I know the story, My Lord Caesar," Livy replied. "I am honoured to meet the descendant of such a great man, My Lady." Livy bowed to Servilia.

Servilia smiled and looked at him, impressed. She was obviously flattered. She leant forward a fraction.

"You surprise us again, Livius. You are far more educated than I would have expected from your provincial background. I understand your father served with Pompey?" Caesar leant over closer to him and handed him a goblet of wine. Livy sipped it. It was *falernian*; it had a fruity flavour with a fine bouquet and a touch of spice but was well watered.

"Yes, he was, both in the wars against Sertorius in Spain and the Mithridatic wars in Pontus"

"What was his appointment in the army?" Caesar enquired.

"In Spain, he was a senior centurion in one of the legions, but he did not make *primus pilus*. In Pontus, he was prefect of artillery."

"That's an important appointment." Caesar looked somewhat impressed. "Was your father skilled at engineering?"

"One of the best, Caesar."

"Did he teach you anything?"

"I am familiar with the construction and use of *onagers*, ballistae, spiders, and other heavy weapons," Livy said in a matter-of-fact way.

"You are indeed a young man of many talents. I hear you speak Gaulish and Belgic too."

"My mother was Celt-Iberian, so I know some Gaulish and Belgic, but I am not fluent. I can get by in a simple conversation," Livy said.

The slaves had begun to pass around the food, and the other guests had fallen into conversation and were eating and drinking. One male slave came with a big platter to Livy and Caesar. Caesar picked what looked like the leg of a roasted goose; Livy took the other leg. They continued to talk as they ate. The meat was fragrant and not overdone, the skin browned to a delightful crisp.

"I know that you saved the life of Lepidus, and I have the honour of bestowing on you the Corona Civica. We have planned a little ceremony for you tomorrow. Your own legion, the Seventh, will parade as will part of my legion, the Tenth."

"I am deeply grateful, My Lord." Livy could hardly conceal his pleasure.

"As you know, the award allows you to sit in the Senate. It gives you honorary senatorial status even without the requisite wealth requirements," Caesar said.

"I am deeply honoured. I do not think that as a soldier I would ever qualify on financial criteria." Livy beamed.

"Well, young man, I always believe that promotion and rewards should go to the capable, not just the rich or well connected. Too often, the Roman Army has had the wrong kind of commanders and suffered ignoble defeats. I intend to make some overdue changes if I get the chance. My enemies among the conservatives, the so-called Optimates, would try to thwart me the best they can. It's to their interest, these armchair generals, to keep the status quo."

"I believe the system you propose would definitely improve the army, sir," Livy commented.

"Spoken like a new man. You are a fan of Marius, no doubt."

"Of course. His campaign against the Germans was amazing reading," Livy replied enthusiastically. "Also I am a firm believer in meritocracy, that a person's position in society should match his deeds rather than his birth."

"That's too modern and radical a view to hold in this time and this world," Caesar replied. "Although I have the same sentiments, in our Roman world it's still all about name and blood. They note who of your ancestors were consuls, praetors, *curile aediles*, and so forth. With the right blood, you smooth your way up the *cursus honorum*, towards high political office," Caesar said. "New men like Marius and even Pompey Magnus were and even now always slightly looked down upon as sons of peasants and provincials. Even their legendary deeds cannot quite erase their background."

"Your enemies in the Optimates should not mind you then, My Lord," Livy said.

"They fear me. I am one of them. My blood is as old and famous as the best of them. I do not have the disadvantage that Marius and Pompey had, and thus they cannot limit me. This they understand and cannot tolerate. That is why they will do everything they can to stop me."

"With your stream of victories, you will have the support of the people and your rivals in the Senate will not find it easy to oppose you," Livy analysed.

"You have insight! That's why I can't afford to lose this war," Caesar said. "On that note, I have another matter to discuss with you." Livy waited as Caesar seemed to gather his thoughts. "You did save my life back by the river, so I am immensely in your debt."

Livy blushed in embarrassment. "I was only doing my duty, sir. I expect nothing for this act. It was my honour to serve."

"I hate to be ungrateful, young Livius, but I do not think you will benefit from a second Corona Civica. I cannot publicly acknowledge my debt for political reasons, but I offer you something far more valuable."

Livy waited and wondered what that could be.

"I offer you a favour from Caesar. That is to say, one day you will want something very badly and you will need me for it. It could be an appointment, political help, money, influence, getting out of trouble, anything. When that day comes, just ask and it will be granted by me."

Livy was bewildered. A favour from Caesar, anything he could wish for? His mind boggled at the possibilities. He was speechless.

Caesar took a heavy gold ring from his finger and slipped in on to the fourth finger of Livy's right hand. "Look at the ring," Caesar commanded. "It has the image of Venus on it. She is my patron goddess. Some say the Julii are descended directly from her. This ring has been in my family for generations."

"I am deeply honoured, Caesar." Livy was awed.

"Wear it on the fourth finger for it is the finger of Venus. When you need your favour, just show me this ring to remind me. Meanwhile you will find it will open many doors. Just say you are from Caesar and show them the ring."

"Do not ask too hastily for your favour and do not waste it. Wait till you really, really need something and it is not possible to get it any other way," Caesar cautioned.

"I will not waste it, sir, and I will use it wisely," Livy assured him.

"I am sure you will. I'm very sure," Caesar concluded, his face suddenly taking on a distant look. "I am remiss as a host. You should be allowed to enjoy yourself. My dear Servilia runs a unique business. She provides female companions for Romans of wealth and rank. Today she has brought six of her best for us to enjoy. The expense is on me. Believe me, they are usually affordable by only the wealthiest of my legates and tribunes. Have you heard of the Greek term *hetaerae*? I believe Servilia has trained them in the Greek tradition. They provide mental as well as physical pleasure. You will find the young ladies remarkably conversant on any subject." He motioned to Servilia to join them. "Well, some of them anyway."

Servilia sashayed over, brandishing a fan. Livy bowed to her. "My Lady," he greeted. She offered him a goblet. He drank and recognised that it was *conditum*, wine flavoured with honey and spices. It was delicious.

"I'll go over and entertain my good friend Antony over there. You look after our young hero, Servilia." Caesar got up and moved over to Antony's couch. Servilia sat herself on one end of Livy's couch. She smiled but only with her lips. Her eyes did not smile.

"Well, as you are the guest of honour tonight, you have the right of first choice. Let me introduce my girls. The two sitting on the couch with Crassus are Drusilla and Portia. They are both Italian girls, the first from Brundisium and the other from Arpinum." The girls looked in their early twenties, both brunette and curvy with full figures. They had reasonably pretty faces which were heavily made up. Livy decided that they were not his type.

Servilia sensed his sentiment and continued, "Those two with the notorious Marc Antony are Fulvia and Artemisia. Fulvia is the blonde girl. She is from Cis Alpine Gaul and has obvious Gaulish blood. Artemisia has an interesting background. She is Spartan, and when I first met her, she was training to be a *gladiatrix*. I bought her over because I felt she would be wasted in the arena given her great beauty. I think she realises that her life span would be longer as a whore," Servilia said. "She speaks good Latin and Greek, by the way. Do you speak Greek?"

"Yes, I do, madam," Livy replied politely. Fulvia was vivacious and somewhat slutty. Her tunic was almost totally transparent, and even then she had let it fall off one shoulder, revealing one full breast topped by a pretty pink nipple. Antony was fondling her unashamedly. Artemesia was on the other hand appeared cool. Her tunic was very short, revealing beautiful, long, tanned, and muscled legs. Her breasts were fully covered, and Livy observed that she probably did not have large ones. Her aloofness and nonchalance captivated Livy.

"Lastly, the two sitting alone at the end, those are new girls. They are very young, sixteen and seventeen, I believe. A good age for a young man like yourself. Both were gifts to me from Caesar. The blonde girl is German and a captive from the war against Ariovistus. She is still in training. Like all Germans, she is quite enthusiastic in bed but a little deficient in education and culture. Her name is Gisila. The last girl is Celtiberian like you. She was captured by Caesar when he was suppressing the Spanish tribes. Her name is Stena, and I believe she is daughter of nobility and thus quite learned. She has a noble demeanour which slavery and prostitution hasn't been able to suppress."

Livy summed up the two last girls. Stena was truly interesting. She held herself with poise and breeding. Her long brown hair was shiny and well groomed, though not elaborately done up. He would be able to speak to her in Celtiberian, which was his mother tongue. The German was very pale and very blonde with thin lips and much attitude. Livy anticipated that sex with her would be of the rough animal variety.

"Well, Centurion? What would be your pleasure."

Livy smiled and answered. "I would like the Spartan and the Celtiberian girl, Stena and Artemisia."

"You have a good memory for names." She motioned for Stena to join them. "Please give me a little time to get you Artemisia. I'll have to pry her away from Marcus. Get to know Stena for the time being." Servilia gave up her seat for Stena and glided towards Marc Antony.

"Please take your time," Livy said. She smiled.

Stena came up to Livy and kneeled beside his couch. Livy looked closer at her face and noticed large brown eyes with long lashes, flawless complexion, and her lightly tanned colour, kissed by the Mediterranean sun. Her hair was slightly curly about her face, and she smelt of fresh olives which reminded him of home. "Come sit beside me on the couch," Livy spoke to her in Celtiberian. She brightened in surprise and got up to sit beside him.

"My name is Stena," she started. "What would be your pleasure, Master? Please be patient with me because you are my first client. My mistress has had me under instruction till today, and I have not been allowed to perform any sexual services till tonight, although I have attended at her parties to serve food and drink," she said apologetically.

"My name is Gaius Livius, and my mother is Celtiberian. I grew up among your people." He didn't reveal that she even had the same name.

Stena looked pleased. "It's good to meet someone from home. Which town are you from, if I may ask."

"I'm from Tarraco. Where are you from?" Livy asked.

"Clunia. I was the daughter of one of the leaders of the town," Stena replied.

"How did you come to be one of Servilia's girls?" Livy asked.

"My family was on the wrong side when some tribes rebelled against the Romans when Caesar was governor of Spain. He crushed the rebellion, and all those involved became slaves. I was only a little girl then. My father and brother were killed in battle. My mother took her own life shortly after that, and I was orphaned. Caesar found me and took me as one of his household slaves."

Livy was shocked. "I am sorry. You have had it rather rough, haven't you?"

"Not as bad as some others. I was treated well in Caesar's household," Stena said. "I was companion to his daughter, Julia. Then Servilia became Caesar's mistress, and he was obliged to help her when she started her business, so I was given away as a gift to her," Stena said sadly. "So that's how I ended up a whore."

Livy felt sorry for her. "Well, we can just talk, you know. You don't really have to serve me that way, not tonight anyway."

"No, please, Master. You should not pity me. It's just postponing the inevitable. There must be a first time, and if you don't take me, someone else will. I was rather glad you picked me because I liked you when I first saw you, and I was hoping you would be my first customer. I know you won't treat me unkindly, and I would really like you to be my first," she pleaded. There was anxiety in her eyes. "At least let me have a fond memory of my first experience as a whore." She sat closer, coming into contact with his shoulders lightly. She then picked up a couple of grapes and started popping them into his mouth.

Livy smiled but did not reply. He concentrated on enjoying the succulent fruit.

"Did you pick another girl to join us?" She held a goblet of *falernian* while he sipped.

"Yes, Artemisia the Spartan. I expect she will attend us shortly."

"You chose well, Master. She is one of Servilia's best. She is quiet and doesn't speak much, but her customers invariably ask for her again. She's an ex-*gladiatrix*, did you know?" Stena asked while caressing Livy's forearm.

"Yes, Servilia told me."

"She is one of the girls actually happy to be here. I think she must have had some horrifying experiences in her former profession," Stena added.

The free flow of wine was starting to have its effect on everyone despite the fact that Caesar had watered the wine well.

Crassus was sandwiched by the two Italian girls, who were taking turns to kiss him very passionately. Antony, almost completely drunk, had almost completely stripped Fulvia naked. Fulvia was obviously also very drunk and only putting up a token resistance and giggling continuously. The German girl had joined that party but seemed only interested in a roast chicken which she was devouring ravenously. Artemesia was plying Antony with another goblet of wine.

Caesar was lying on his face having a back massage by Servilia and being fed oranges by one of the slave serving girls. Suddenly Antony got up, pushing Fulvia away.

"I propose a toast to Gaius Julius Caesar, my great friend and conqueror of Gaul and Belgica. May your exploits live forever in the annals of Rome."

"Hear, hear," everyone repeated around the room.

"And may his wine be always as good as tonight but less well watered," Antony challenged, staggering and finally falling back on his divan.

"I water the wine well for good reason, my dear Antony," Caesar replied. "First of all, I find my dinner guests much more interesting when they are not totally inebriated, and secondly, as you are also my officers and we are at war, I prefer you thinking clearly without a massive headache in the morning." He raised his glass and took a very tiny sip.

"Oh yes, I want to have a chance to fight tomorrow. Kill some Belgae and win some glory," Antony demanded. He looked totally sloshed.

Caesar looked at him with disdain. "You will have your chance if you can function in the morning, which I doubt you can. I give you command of the cavalry. I remember that you like to go prancing around on the Campus Martius in Rome."

Antony took another goblet from Artemisia, raised it in salute to Caesar, then to all the rest of the guests and then collapsed on to his divan. Servilia got up and went over to Antony's couch. She whispered something to Artemisia, who put down yet another goblet of wine which she was about to serve Antony and walked towards Livy's couch.

Livy took notice as she walked towards him. She was tall, had a very erect posture, and her gait was confident and rhythmic. There was no obsequious shuffling like many female slaves. Her hair was light brown, long, and straight. It was tied up in a long ponytail held at the top by a silver clasp. She also had a thin silver armband on her left arm and no other decorations. She was tanned but lighter than Stena and wore a very short tunic which barely covered her private areas. Her svelte legs were deliberately displayed for all to see.

She stopped right in front of Livy and extended her hand. "Good evening, Centurion Livius, I am Artemisia of Sparta. I am told you requested my company tonight."

Livy took her hand and kissed the back of it. He liked her very direct and confident manner. "Please join us." He motioned to the empty space on the couch. Artemesia took her place at the end of the couch chastely keeping her legs together although Livy had already glimpsed that she had no loin cloth on. Her short tunic was of a silvery, greyish black silk which moulded to her body contours, and she had silver slippers on her feet.

Livy felt mysteriously drawn to her. She had attitude and looked him directly in the eye, challenging him. The eyes were a beautiful emerald green with long lashes. Livy felt speechless for a while, then began, "So how did you come to be one of Servilia's girls?"

"So you want a story, Centurion," she stated rather than asked. Livy noticed that she didn't call him master or sir. He decided to ignore the slight. She was in her own way demanding that he treat her as an equal and not a slave.

"I hear you have an interesting one," Livy replied. "Please share it with us."

"Since you ask so politely, I will favour you thus." She gave him the slightest smile which already sent Livy's heart racing. "Men are so easy," Artemisia thought to herself. "He is not quite a man even, only a boy, but he is polite and has a kind face, yet he is a hero," Artemisia analysed to herself.

"I am Spartan and my father was Spartiate and had been through the Agoge, a full citizen trained in the Spartan military tradition"

"I have read about your history and society. In school, we read about the Peloponnesian wars and the two Persian wars. Your people are legendary." Livy demonstrated his education.

"I see you are not just an illiterate sword wielder like most men of the legions I have met." She gave a more spontaneous smile.

"As I was saying, my father was a *homoioi*, an equal. As members of the warrior cast, we lived by strict rules. We were not allowed commerce and had to live by agriculture. We had a few bad years, and my father ran into debt. When he died, he left us in penury. I have no brothers, only a sister. We three women tried to keep the farm going and slowly pay off the debts. Then my mother became ill and soon died."

"The fates were far from kind to your family," Livy said.

"We could no longer pay off our debts, and the Roman moneylenders brought soldiers who took us, confiscated our farm, and sold the two of us into slavery. I was only fifteen years old and my sister was only nine. I never saw her again." Her expression changed to one of deep sadness.

"Then what happened?" Stena had started to feel a little left out and started caressing his upper thighs, working ever so closer to his groin. Livy reacted involuntarily, but he wanted to hear the rest of the story. He took hold of her soft hands and held it firmly but gently.

"Since I had received the training of a Spartan, was skilled in combat, and looked very fit, the slave dealer decided he might make more money selling me to a gladiatorial school, a *ludus*, rather than as a household or sex slave. I thought it was a blessing at the time. How silly could one have been?"

"You would have a real advantage with all that Spartan physical and weapons training. I bet you were a top *gladiatrix*," Livy said.

"I took to the training like a bear to honey, and since a *gladiatrix* was not allowed to be pregnant, no one tried to rape me. That was the good part. Where I became undone were the live matches. Most of them were fought to the death. They made me fight almost naked with only a helmet and two curved thin swords. We were called *dimachaeria*. Men came to see female bouts not just for the combat but to leer at our naked bodies."

"I am sure it was not the nudity that bothered you. I hear Spartan girls trained naked."

"No, you are right. You know a lot about our culture. It was not the nudity. I always won and I never fought to kill, only to wound the other girl so that she could not continue. At least that way she would have a chance to procure a *missio* if the crowd liked her and felt that she had put up a good fight."

"I see. You seem to have met with some success."

"Up to a point," Artemesia said. "Then one day I was in a death match with a Macedonian girl. As you know the Macedonians are our historical enemies. She was young, blonde, and pretty. She fought well, but I managed to wound her several times till she could no longer lift her sword. I closed in for the kill, then looked to the master of the games for the verdict. The whole crowd cheered for her life, and I was pretty confident that she would get life."

Livy and Stena were transfixed by the tale. They could not comprehend that that slim beauty before them could be a fearsome *gladiatrix*. The music had become softer and more soothing. Stena made another foray under Livy's tunic, and he was too entranced by Artemisia's story to stop her.

"I looked to the editor, the chief of the games, and he gave the sign for death. I was shocked. I looked at the girl. Her eyes were silently pleading, and she was shaking her head slowly and tears were beginning to well up in her eyes," Artemisia continued.

Livy and Stena were leaning forward anxiously. "Did you do it?" Stena asked.

"I removed her helmet, then stroked her hair. Then I held her close, our naked breasts touching each other, and whispered into her ear in Greek. Then I kissed her and at the same time thrust my sword into her heart. My own heart broke at the same time."

Livy discerned a small tear at the corner of Artemisia's right eye. She made no move to wipe it. "I think the *lanista* must have told the editor that she would be useless alive because of her wounds. Just another mouth to feed. I had wounded her too severely, and she would not be able to fight again. So it was my fault."

"What did you say to her?" Livy sat up in amazement.

"I told her I was sending her to Elysium. It will be a better place with no pain or suffering. I will make the transition as quick and painless as possible. She gasped in surprise as I ran her through. Then she seemed to smile, her hands came up to caress my cheeks, then her eyes clouded over and she died. Her blood spurted all over my breast, and she voided water all over my thighs."

"That's so, so very sad," Stena commiserated as she caressed Livy's shaft with a feather-light touch, which resulted in an exuberant blossoming.

"I lost my will to fight after that. I refused to come out of my cell, wouldn't eat, cried most of the day. At first, the *lanista* tried to talk me out of it. Then he threatened. Losing patience, he had me beaten. I still refused to fight," Artemisia continued.

"Finally he said if I didn't fight he would have all the gladiators and guards gang rape me. He gave me a day to think about it."

"So I gather you gave in?" Livy asked.

"Yes, the next morning I turned up for practice. They scheduled me for the games two weeks hence. It was another death match. My opponent was a Scythian girl from the grasslands to the east. She was tough and well trained. I had lost my edge. We fought for a long time till we were both exhausted. I managed to cut her on the right arm, but she was ambidextrous and fought just as well with the left. She kept attacking, and I couldn't bring myself to finish her, so it went on and on. Finally we were both so tired we could hardly get up to continue. We just swung uselessly at each other. The crowd was bored and started hooting and jeering and throwing things at us."

"What did the editor do?" Livy asked.

"He stopped the fight and declared a draw."

"Your *lanista* must have been furious," Livy added.

"He was. I was beaten again, not too seriously though, and locked in my cell without dinner. They scheduled me for another match the next day. I think the *lanista* had given up on me and decided at least he could fight me till I was killed and get as much money as possible for my death. I later heard the Scythian girl was given a severe beating. She survived though and went on to become a champion *Gladiatrix*."

"So what happened the next day?"

"I went on the sands again, this time against a Gaul. She was young and pretty but not overly skilled. She wielded a long Gaulish double-edged sword which gave her the reach, but I knew that if I closed with her she would be seriously disadvantaged. She relied on brute strength which she had an abundance. I relied on skill and agility. I quickly cut her in several places on her arms and legs, slowing her down. The match was clearly uneven. A few moments later, she charged wildly giving me an opportunity. I kicked her hard in the right knee, and she went down with a thump. I quickly jumped on her as she lay on her back and sat on her abdomen with one sword point to her throat. She lay still, not daring to move. I could see wild fear in her clear blue eyes."

"How was the mood of the crowd?" Stena asked.

"They were baying for blood after the draw the previous day. They wanted the poor girl killed. I looked at her, and she was clearly not prepared to die. She started to beg for mercy piteously. This was of course bad form. A *gladiatrix* should accept her fate calmly and silently. I couldn't understand a word she said, but the thought suddenly came to me that she would make a lovely wife and mother. She was very pretty. I looked to the editor."

"I guess he would not want to upset the crowd," Livy commented.

"He signalled for death. I raised my sword, and the girl closed her eyes and sobbed softly. I couldn't do it. I just dropped my weapons and walked out. I walked calmly towards the gate of life. The crowd was furious and started to throw fruits and other things at me. I ignored the insults and missiles and walked on."

Livy listened, impressed by her courage.

"At the gate, two huge guards took me, one by each arm. They threw me into a tiny cell. Shortly after the *lanista* came, and I was given the worst beating I ever endured. As a Spartan girl, believe me, I had endured many."

"What happened then?" Stena asked.

"I was left half dead in my cell. That evening, some girls came to clean my wounds and bathe me. I was given some wine and some bread. I wondered at the change in treatment. I was dressed in a clean tunic and taken from the cell to the *lanista*'s office. There was a well-dressed Roman lady there. It was Servilia. 'I was going to have you executed, thrown to the lions. This important lady from Rome however has been watching your performance the last two days and has decided to offer you an alternative to death,' the *lanista* said."

"I was of course relieved that I wasn't going to be fed to the lions. I bowed graciously to the lady. 'I will be pleased to serve mistress,' I said."

"She laughed sardonically. 'You may not be so pleased once you know my alternative, young lady,' she said. 'I run a very high-class whore house for rich Romans. I am offering you the job of a high-class prostitute, my dear. You will be hetaerae. It's a Greek concept, so I am sure you understand. Don't worry. You will not have to service dozens of dirty, grimy customers every day like a common whore. The type of establishment I run will not require you to service more than one customer on any evening and more likely only once or twice a week. What's more, your customers will be the elite of Rome and will mostly not smell too bad,' she said in jest," Artemisia recounted.

"I guess you had no choice but to accept," Livy said.

"It took me only a moment of thought, then I thanked her and accepted. I've been a whore ever since."

Livy smiled. "That's quite a story. How long have you served milady?"

"Almost a year now," she said.

"And what do you think of your new line of work?"

"Much better than the arena, as you can imagine, and nobody gets killed," she said.

"I'll bet your austere Spartan soul revolts at the dishonour of selling your body."

"Strangely, I feel less repulsed by this work than my background suggests. It's not always unpleasant. I have some nice regular clients, and sometimes I have the luck to meet a handsome young man like yourself." She gave him a sad smile.

Livy blushed as no one had ever thought of him as handsome. He didn't have a well-muscled body and his features were scholarly rather than Apollonian. "Is there any hope of regaining your freedom?"

"Yes, of course. Servilia lets us keep a tenth of our fees, so we should be able to buy our freedom after some years. The sad thing is that freedom might not have much meaning by then. It would be difficult to find a husband because of our past, and we won't know any other trade. Most freed whore slaves seek re-employment at three-tenths of the taking. Some manage to save enough to start a small tavern of their own but still continue to sell their bodies."

"So I guess once a whore always a whore," he said.

"That about sums it up, my dear Centurion. I hear once a soldier always a soldier as well." She laughed.

"Well, my father did manage a transition to olive farmer," Livy remonstrated.

The party was slowly winding down as the guests became more inebriated. Suddenly Servilia rang a small bell to get everyone's attention. "It is time, my ladies and gentlemen."

Suddenly all the torches were extinguished, leaving three or four candles burning. The spacious tent was thrown into relative darkness although one could still make out figures in the darkness. Livy who was looking in the direction of Caesar saw Servilia undo the jewelled clasp of her chiton which fell gracefully to the floor, revealing her almost flawless figure.

Simultaneously, every other girl took off their tunics or chitons. For a few minutes, the men were treated to a wonderful view of beautiful naked bodies all around the tent. Livy noticed that Stena still had a little baby fat around her waist and thighs although she had beautiful glutei and full breasts which were not overly large. Artemisia on the other hand was near flawless. She was slender compared to more curvaceous classical standards in Greece and Rome. Her breasts were precisely proportioned to her athletic figure. Livy was pleasantly surprised. Both girls were well shaven with absolutely no body hair. Livy could not make out any details of the other girls.

Caesar spoke out of the dark, "Servilia and I are leaving. You, my friends, can continue the party here or adjourn to the adjoining tents if you prefer privacy."

"I'm fine right here, Gaius Julius." Antony's voice rose from the darkness. That was followed by female moaning. Livy was not sure if it came from Fulvia or the German girl. The candles were now being blown out one at a time.

"I'm fine as well, My Lord." This last came from Crassus. After that, there was darkness as the last candle was blown, and only the sensuous moaning of the girls broke the silence in the tent.

"So, ladies, what will it be?" Livy asked. "Shall we join the festivities or shall we seek some privacy."

"I don't care either way," Artemisia said flippantly.

"It's my first time, Master, and I'd prefer some privacy. That's if you and Artemisia don't mind," Stena pleaded.

"I'll lead the way," Artemesia volunteered. Livy wrapped Artemisia in his cloak and took the sheet from his divan to wrap Stena. They threaded carefully through the tent, taking care not to step on anyone. As they were about to exit the tent, they heard one of the Italian girls cry out in ecstasy. Score one for Publius Crassus!

Outside there was a steady drizzle and the air was chilly. Artemesia led them to one of the adjacent tents. All three were drenched by the time they got into the tent. The tent was small but comfortable. It was about the size of Livy's centurion's tent. A small brazier was lit which gave some warmth, and an oil lamp gave light. There was a large mattress in the centre as well as a small low table with a large bowl of fruits and a flagon of wine. There were grapes, apricots, figs, apples, and peaches in the bowl. The tent was unguarded.

"This looks like a nice place to spend the night," Livy remarked. His head was spinning with wine, but the alcohol was wearing off after the drenching in the cold rain. Stena helped him off with his wet tunic, and Artemisia used a towel to dry his hair. The girls then dried themselves out by the fire as Livy admired their magnificent anatomy. The girls' faces seemed to glow in the firelight, and he realised that they were both really alluring girls.

The two girls were aware they were being watched and admired and felt a little embarrassed. They finished drying themselves off, and then the three of them sat watching each other and waiting. All three were totally naked, and Livy could feel life coming back to his *priapus*. The girls were watching it as it grew slowly.

Almost as if by signal, they both joined him on the big mattress in the centre of the tent. Stena cuddled up on the left and Artemisia closed up to him on the right. "We are going to give you a night to remember," Artemisia said emphatically.

"We like you and we want you to remember us," Stena added. "Just lie back and enjoy." She started to kiss him passionately, using her tongue and lips enthusiastically. The feel of her body on his was soft, warm, and yielding. He was swept away by her unbridled passion. She really wanted to make that a night to remember.

Artemisia then turned him around. "It's my turn," she murmured as she kissed him gently and softly on his wet lips. She kissed him several times very lightly. Her lips had just the right texture, and the smell of her breath was intoxicating and arousing. At the same time, her hands explored his body, caressing and titillating him most exquisitely. Livy was driven mad with desire and was about to ravish her there and then when suddenly she pulled away.

"Stena has the first round. This is important. You are her first customer, and she needs a wonderful experience to initiate her into the world of hetaerae. Please be gentle with her," Artemesia said. She then took up a peach and starting eating. "Don't worry, my handsome Centurion. We have the whole night."

The experience with Stena was warm, friendly, and comfortable. Livy took her slowly and gently and tried his best to make the experience enjoyable for her. She had been a virgin when she was first captured and then had been brutally raped several times before being sold to Caesar. Caesar had protected her and used her only as a household slave without any sexual duties. This was her first voluntary sexual experience, and Livy wanted her to learn that it can be a wonderful experience for a woman as well as a man. He kissed her frequently and used his hands to pleasure her. Soon she was moaning with pleasure, and the moans slowly increased in frequency. Her breathing became quicker, and she closed her eyes to concentrate. She climaxed with loud groans, her body quivering. She parted her legs, and Livy slipped effortlessly inside her compliant crevice. He enjoyed the symphony of sensations as he rhythmically explored her tumescent interior. He felt his climax approaching like a brewing volcano. She gasped in synchrony with each thrust, accelerating towards an explosive finale. Livy wondered who would first breach the finish line. Stena crossed the finish line just a moment ahead. She seemed paralysed for a moment, lying totally still. Then she opened her eyes, batted her eyelashes, and smiled.

"That was unbelievable. Thank you, Master."

"It was my pleasure to serve." Livy bowed in mock courtesy, smiling broadly.

"I am suddenly so tired. I need to rest now. Go play with Artemesia." She gave one more radiant smile and turned around to sleep, pulling the sheets over herself.

Livy was a little nonplussed. This was a reversal of usual events. It was usually the man who turned around and went to sleep after sex, leaving the woman stranded. He laughed to himself and then turned to Artemisia, who had gone through several peaches and a bunch of grapes.

"What? I was hungry. I was too busy entertaining that creep Marcus Antonious to eat anything," she murmured defensively.

Livy smiled at her. "Go ahead and eat. I don't mind. You can eat the whole bowl if you fancy." Livy decided she looked even more beautiful when she was angry. Her face was exquisite. She could have been Helen of Troy or Aspasia of Athens, who was mistress of Pericles. Perhaps she looked like her namesake, Artemisia of Caria, who commanded ships at the Battle of Salamis in alliance with King Xerxes.

"You need a little rest anyway. I don't think you'll be able to perform for a while." She looked derisively at his flaccid member.

Livy covered it self-consciously with the sheets.

"Don't be shy, my dear. I've seen lots of flaccid ones before." She laughed. It was a charming laugh. She then came and sat close to him. She lay on his shoulder as he put his arms around her, cupping one naked breast. She did not seem to mind and put her head beside his so he could smell her hair.

"We're leaving tomorrow. Going after King Galba and the Suessiones," Livy finally remarked after a long silence.

"I know. Servilia told us. We are to follow in your baggage train. It's all very convenient. Servilia gets to renew her relationship with Caesar whilst we make money for her, servicing his senior officers," Artemisia said.

"On the bright side, I get to see you," Livy said.

She looked taken aback. "You would really like to see me again? We haven't even had sex yet."

"Seriously, I like you already." Livy smiled shyly.

"Whores can't afford to have friends, only regular customers. Servilia tells us repeatedly, 'No boyfriends allowed,'" she said emphatically.

"I'll be your regular customer then," Livy said.

"You can't afford me," Artemisia said dismissively.

"Don't be too sure," Livy retorted. "I have a plan and a few favours to pull." Livy smiled knowingly.

Artemisia looked sceptical. "Well, we'll see what magic you weave."

"It'll be a surprise," Livy said.

The sex that followed surpassed all expectations. It was hungry, wild, and unrelenting. Their passions ebbed and flowed like the tide. Artemisia was by now expert in the sexual arts, and she had many things to teach Livy about how to give pleasure to a woman. She herself held back nothing. She gave herself wholly and completely. Livy never even imagined such exquisite pleasures as Artemisia bestowed on him.

They finally fell asleep exhausted in the early hours of the morning. Livy's last memory was of Stena cuddling up, embracing, and kissing him on the lips. "Good night, Master," he remembered her saying before she fell asleep on his left chest.

> The art of war can be mastered more easily than the art of seduction.

CHAPTER 10

Livy awoke instinctively a few hours later. It was near dawn and still dark. The girls were fast asleep, one on each side, and Stena was snoring softly. He got up quickly, washed his face and hands in a water basin, and put on his tunic. He quickly exited the tent and went to the bath tent where he left his uniform and armour.

To his surprise, Jasmine was there to greet him. "Good morning, Master," she said in her soft, delicate voice. "I trust you slept well. I have organised a quick bath for you and have had your clothes cleaned and dried," she said. The bath was tempting.

"I am deeply grateful, but I fear I might not have time. It is near dawn, and I must get my men ready to move out," Livy said.

"Don't worry. There is time. It will take but a moment." She stripped his clothes off before he could object and plunged him into the tub. It was steaming hot but just tolerable. He deduced that she must have woken early to heat the water. Sweet girl!

Jasmine looked down shyly and then said very softly, "It will be faster if I join you in the tub to scrub you."

Before Livy could either agree or not, she had stripped naked and lowered herself carefully into the tub facing Livy. She started to scrub his hands and then came closer to wash his face and his chest. Livy could smell the scent of flowers in her hair. As she washed lower down, her forearm accidentally, or maybe deliberately, as you never know with women, brushed against his erect member. Livy had the normal morning male reaction.

Jasmine gasped. "You are not spent yet after all that activity last night?" Her eyes were wide with astonishment.

"Apparently not," Livy smiled cheekily. He was aware he still reeked of secretions from the two girls.

Jasmine quickly returned to her usual inscrutable calm demeanour, but she started to stroke or scrub the erect *priapus* which of course got only bigger. She suddenly realised that she could soon provoke a point of no return. She suddenly released the object of her fascination and ordered him to turn around. She quickly scrubbed his back and his hair and then popped out of the tub. She looked clearly embarrassed though Livy didn't sympathise with her as she had clearly put herself in that predicament.

"So how did you come to be so far from home?" he asked.

"My father was an explorer and a trader. He wanted to see what was in the Far West. We fitted up a trading ship and sailed westwards. We passed through the Spice Islands and the Indian subcontinent. Finally we landed in Arabia. We traded out silk cargo for gold, gems, and silver, and then my father decided to return overland. We joined a caravan heading east. Unfortunately, we were ambushed by bandits near your province of Syria. I was kidnapped and sold into slavery. My father and his men escaped, but I never saw him again."

"That is such a tragic tale," Livy said.

"I was bought and sold several times. Fortunately, my owners realised my value, and no one violated me. Finally I was presented to the Roman governor of Syria. He purchased me at once and brought me to Rome as a domestic slave," Jasmine continued.

"How came you to be in Caesar's possession?"

"One evening after Caesar was elected consul, he was invited to dinner at my master's house. My master owed Caesar many political favours, and at the dinner, he asked Caesar if he could do something in return. I was serving Caesar all evening, and he was somewhat fascinated by me. I could already speak some Latin by then. Caesar made my master an offer to buy me. My master told Caesar he could have me as a present on one condition," Jasmine related.

"What was the condition?" Livy was curious.

"He told Caesar that he could have me provided he promised not to violate me and to eventually find me a suitable husband and give me my freedom," she said. "Caesar agreed and here I am. He has kept his promise so far." She smiled sweetly.

Livy rinsed himself off one last time, dunking his head under the water, then got up and dressed himself quickly. He was just buckling on his chain mail when a tribune came in. Jasmine was still naked and helping him pin on his cloak. She gasped and quickly covered herself in a towel.

The tribune gave her a look of disdain, then addressed Livy, "The commander wants you in the command tent at once. Briefing."

Livy saluted, and the tribune left, probably to collect some other senior officer. He turned to Jasmine, took her right hand, and kissed it. "Thank you for the refreshing bath and scrub. I really want to get together with you and talk about the Han Empire. I think there are many fascinating things which I can learn from you."

"It would be an honour, Master," she said. "You can find me usually in the proximity of Caesar's tent as I am his household slave. I will be happy to talk to you any time." She gave a shy smile. "Good luck today and may you be safe."

Livy pulled her close and kissed her on the cheek. Before she could react, he was out of the tent.

Caesar's tent was empty save for Crassus, Sabinus, Marc Antony, a few slaves, and his secretary. Crassus looked bright and eager, but Antony was bleary-eyed and looked a little ill. All three were already in full uniform with armour. Caesar looked confident and in high spirits. Livy marched in and saluted.

"I am moving six legions towards Noviodunum." He pointed to the map on the table which had counters representing Roman and enemy units on it. "This is the capital of the Suessiones, and if we take it, their coalition is likely to go to pieces." Caesar rapped his cane on the map for emphasis.

"Isn't the Suessione army also heading in that direction?" Crassus asked.

"I am sure they are. Barbarian armies move slowly, though, and without much discipline. If we force-march, we can be there before them and take the city before they arrive. With the city in our hands, the army will have nowhere to go and may just surrender. That would take 50,000 men off the playing field."

"What are your orders then?" Antony asked.

"Antony, you are in command of what remaining cavalry we have. This includes Livy's 300 raiders and half of my 200 German bodyguard. Divide your forces if necessary but find the Suessione army and harass them and delay them. Destroy all small bands but avoid a major action with their main force. Livy's men would be ideal for this task. Hit and run. Use your arrows to prick them, then disengage if they counterattack in force."

Antony smiled. "Thank you for the opportunity, sir. I will not let you down."

"Try to delay them from getting to Noviodunum till I get there and take the town," Caesar emphasised.

"The six legions stationed here will force march straight to Noviodunum. Crassus and the Seventh will be the vanguard. I will assign the remainder of my bodyguard to you as scouts. They will make sure we don't run into an ambush. I will follow with my Tenth legion. Sixth and Eighth will follow next, then the baggage train, and then Ninth and Twelfth will bring up the rear."

"What about the artillery, sir?" Crassus asked.

"We'll split them into two, light and heavy." Caesar decided. "Light artillery to follow after the Seventh. Set them up to fire on the town as soon as you arrive. Heavy artillery will come after the Eighth just ahead of the baggage train."

The secretary was busy writing everything down.

"Get all that down in writing, and let me make my mark on each order and send it to the legates and prefects," Caesar ordered. "All units are to be ready to attack at once on arrival."

"Excuse me, Caesar. Can I ask about Licinius and his small band of *exploratores*?" Livy asked.

"Hmm, I guess their task is a duplicate of yours. You want them attached to your unit?" Caesar asked.

"My thoughts, exactly," Livy replied.

"Very well, you get them for this stage of the operations. Licinius to be under Livy and Livy to be under Marc Antony," Caesar summarised for the secretary. "Orders to go out forthwith."

"Will that be all, sir?" Sabinus asked.

"No. We have an important ceremony to perform before we quit this camp," Caesar said, glancing at Livius.

The Seventh and Tenth Legions were on parade in the centre of the camp. The other legions were busy doing the last bits of demolition and packing. Caesar stood on a wooden tribunal with the eagles of the Seventh and Tenth behind him. His own personal standard and the standard of the Army of Gaul were also on display. Behind him were several *curile* chairs on which the senior officers sat. All the legates were present except Labienus, Quintus Pedius, and Cotta.

The band played a fanfare, and the legions stood to attention. The honour guard gave a salute with their heavy *pila*. They were the men of the Seventh Legion Eighth cohort, Sixth Century, Livy's personal command. Caesar stood up and strode to the dais.

"Stand at ease," the camp prefect commanded. The two legions stood at the easy position with legs apart and spears forward at an angle with shield grounded.

"The Corona Civica is the highest award given by the Senate and people of Rome," Caesar declared loudly. His voice was high-pitched and carried well. His rhetorical skills were already well honed. He was wearing his own Corona Civica, which helped to disguise his balding pate.

"It is awarded for a soldier who saves a comrade in the face of the enemy at great risk to his own life. Today we come to bestow this honour on an exceptional soldier of the Seventh Legion. A few days ago, Centurion Gaius Livius saved the life of Decurion Marcus Lepidus in a desperate cavalry action on the plains in front of our camp. Centurion Livius attacked a band of six Belgic warriors single-handedly, killing three of them and driving off the rest without thought for his own safety." Caesar paused to catch his breath.

"By his actions he saved the life of Decurion Marcus Lepidus, who is from a distinguished senatorial family. He has also brought great honour to the Seventh Legion. This is the first Corona Civica to be awarded to the Seventh."

The men of the Seventh cheered. After a few moments, their acting legate Publius Crassus motioned for silence.

"By receiving this award, the Senate and people of Rome bestow upon the recipient the right to sit in the Senate as an honorary senator, not subject to the normal financial qualifications."

Another cheer broke out. This time the Tenth chipped in as well. The Tenth Legion (Legio X) was the elite force of the Army of Gaul. They were Caesar's veterans from his Spanish campaign, and they were all tough, disciplined, and superbly trained.

Caesar nodded to the camp prefect.

"Legions, attention." the prefect commanded.

The trumpets and horns blew another fanfare.

"Centurion Livius and Decurion Lepidus to the front," the prefect shouted.

The two officers were dressed in full parade regalia with red plumes, feathers, red cloaks, and shiny armour. Livy's centurion crest was transverse while Lepidus wore the sagittal red crest and two white feathers on his gleaming silver helmet, which denoted his decurion status. Lepidus had on silver scale armour which looked expensive. Livy had on the steel chain mail given by his father. He also wore a red sash for the occasion, which was usually worn only by senior officers. Caesar had insisted on that small touch.

The two officers marched to the platform, stood at attention, and gave the stiff-armed Roman salute to Caesar.

Livy's mind was a plethora of fleeting thoughts. He ought to have been feeling unbelievably proud and honoured. Instead he just concentrated on performing his drill perfectly. It would be bad form to cock up. He noticed the mist on the ground and a cool breeze. He laughed inwardly at his own silliness.

A tribune came and handed Lepidus a beautiful wooden box. He took it and opened it, displaying the golden oak leaves of the Corona Civica. Caesar stepped down from the platform and took it from Lepidus.

Lepidus took Livy's hand and said, "My deepest thanks for saving my life, Centurion."

"Think nothing of it," Livy replied.

"Congratulations and well done, Centurion Livius," Caesar said.

Livy removed his helmet, and Caesar ceremoniously laid the crown on Livy's head. He then shook Livy's hand.

Livy and Lepidus then returned to their positions.

The trumpets blew another fanfare.

"Officers, return to your unit," the prefect commanded.

Livy and Lepidus saluted, took a step back, did an about-turn, and marched back to rejoin their units. Livy noticed the raiders lined up at one end of his legion. Their presence somehow mattered more than the presence of the rest of the two legions. Those were the men he shared life and death with.

Livy rejoined the men of his century, who were decked out as the honour guard.

"Legates, rejoin your men," the prefect commanded.

"At my command, the legions will take your position in the marching order. Command will revert back to your centurions."

"Parade dismissed," the prefect gave the final order. The men took a right turn and started marching off in their respective units.

Livy took off his Corona Civica and turned to Galienus. "Take command, Galienus. I have to join the cavalry to make up the vanguard."

"Certainly sir, and congratulations," Galienus said. There were murmurings of congratulations from many more of the legionaries. They all smiled proudly at him.

"Thank you, men. I will see you when we reach Noviodunum," Livy promised. He ran off to rejoin the raiders.

Biorix was holding his battle helmet. "Here, put this one on and let me stow the loot for you. Reckon these would fetch quite a price if sold, eh?" Livy gave him a half-serious frown.

"Shut up and mount up. We've got work to do." Livy got on his horse and the other followed.

CHAPTER 11

Appear in the place he must hasten. Hasten to the place he least expects you.

Livy gathered his forces and took to the road. He rode side by side with Marc Antony, who looked a little less green and seemed to have settled into his role. Behind them rode Licinius, Paulus, and Biorix. The men were alert and well rested and moved with well-ordered precision.

The weather was cool after the rain, and the morning was still chilly as the sun had not yet made its appearance felt. The ground was still damp from the rain, and a light mist gave the impression that the horses were riding on clouds.

As they rode out the gate, Antony asked Livy, "Where shall we start looking for the Suessiones, Livius?"

"I would start on the north bank of the river, sir. Our bridge here and the ford further down are the only crossing points around here, and we control both. If I were Galba, I would march west and try and find another crossing closer to Noviodunum. If we move fast, we will probably catch them before long"

"Good thinking, Livius. Signal the men to hurry along now," Antony said.

"A word of caution, sir, the Belgae are masters of ambush, and we best send out some scouts in front so that we don't stumble into a trap," Livy suggested politely.

"Ha, ha, you learn fast. I heard you got ambushed yesterday at their camp," Antony laughed. "Go ahead. Deploy a vanguard."

Livy ordered Licinius to take half a dozen men and deploy forward in pairs, scouting a wide arc.

As they rode along, they could see the legions which had been pursuing the enemy north coming back. They were accompanied by long lines of prisoners. Many of them were women, elderly men, and children. Livy didn't see many warriors. There were also many wagons of loot. Here and there he spotted squadrons of Remi and Roman cavalry.

"Looks like Labienus and his pursuit forces have returned," Antony commented. "I hope they slaughtered a good number of the enemy. They got quite a bunch of prisoners there."

Livy did not entirely agree. The pursuit was too late, and he was sure that most of the Belgic Army had escaped to fight another day. He kept his own counsel.

"That was some party Caesar organised last night," Antony resumed. "I kept my two going the whole night. They are both super whores. Very slutty and willing to do anything. Very game," he reminisced fondly. "How were your two? A bit skinny for my liking, but that Spartan bitch looked interesting. How was she?"

"She performed satisfactorily, sir," Livy replied as civilly as he could manage.

"Only satisfactory, eh! I was thinking of trying her out next, but now I have to give it a second thought. I like them screaming for more, you see."

Livy found the conversation somewhat distasteful and kept quiet, hoping Antony would change the subject. He was relieved that his assessment of Artemisia had somewhat quelled Antony's ardour.

"Actually, I plan to do the whole lot before this campaign is over. Maybe I'll even have a go at Servilia." Antony laughed.

Livy was astonished. "Caesar would hang him out to dry," he thought to himself. This Marc Antony seemed to him a rather impulsive man, driven by reckless passions. Livy wondered about his fighting abilities. He would find out soon enough.

CHAPTER 12

The forest was covered by a thick mist which was beginning to dissipate as the sun rose. Murato and his Gaesatae were well camouflaged, hiding on both sides of the forest track. They had given the Roman cavalry the slip in the night, but his scouts had just moments before spotted a patrol scouting towards them, trying to re-establish contact.

The Gaesatae formed the rearguard to the Nervii and Atrebates contingent, which were moving north towards the Sabis River which was the border to Nervii lands. As usual they, being expandable, were given the unenviable work of slowing down the Roman pursuit. The previous day had been one long running fight.

Murato and his naked warriors had made the Romans pay every time they met, but numbers were on the side of the invaders, and a third of his warriors were dead or wounded. That included some of the woman warriors. The Romans and Remi had shown no compunction in killing women. There were many good friends to mourn, and he was determined to make the Romans pay.

Leuce and her women comrades were ready. Their arrows were nocked and their bare bodies were painted to blend in with the colours of the forest. Murato couldn't help admiring her marvellous figure. "She has such perfect thighs," he thought to himself. He would take her that night if both were alive and unwounded. The anticipation brought a pleasant feeling to his groin. There were hoof beats in the distance. The Romans were proceeding carefully at a walk. The trees cast ominous shadows and the birds suddenly stopped their chirping. Only the wind rustling in the trees and the clipety-clop of the enemy horses could be heard.

The smell of nervous sweat permeated the air as the Gaesatae waited to spring the trap. A few of the Roman cavalry could be seen silhouetted against the light at the end of the path. More joined them. It was a substantial patrol. Murato could discern the decurion with his black horsehair plume and scale armour. A decurion meant at least a *turmae* of thirty men. Murato had less than a hundred warriors left.

A shrill war cry was the signal for the attack. Murato threw his spear at the leading cavalryman, hitting his horse square in the chest. The animal screamed and reared, throwing the rider. Leuce loosed an arrow, which took another of the horsemen in the chest, penetrating the chain mail. The soldier managed to remain on his horse and withdraw. After that, all hell broke loose as screaming naked men and women launched themselves at the astonished horsemen who tried their best to fend off the blows with their large oval shields and struck back with either spears or heavy *spathas*.

Murato took up another spear and launched himself at the decurion. The decurion was a veteran and blocked the thrust with his shield. The spear penetrated, making the shield useless. Both men drew swords and prepared to engage. Murato however aimed his first blow at the horse's nose. The pain-stricken animal went wild. The decurion was caught off balance and fell.

"Decurion Decius! Watch out," one of the cavalrymen yelled and rode quickly to his leader's aid. Murato positioned himself to the right of the horsemen which was the unshielded side. The young cavalryman swung with his *spatha* at Murato's head. Murato ducked, avoiding the blow, and landed a heavy blow at the man's flank. The slash penetrated the chain mail and the man went down. He then turned to finish of the decurion.

The man was just getting up and seemed to be stunned. Murato was about to swing at his neck to behead him, but then changed his mind. The blow fell on the back of his helmet and was heavy enough to knock the man unconscious. Murato now had a prisoner.

The Gaesatae had almost finished wiping out the first *turmae* of thirty when a second *turmae* appeared and joined in the fight. They were Remi auxiliaries who did not have the same mettle though they were bitter enemies of the rest of the Belgae for having allied with the Romans. The Gaesatae launched themselves at the Remi with a vengeance quickly killing a dozen of them. Leuce jumped on a horse behind one of the horsemen and slit his throat. The spray of blood from the man's carotids drenched her, making her look like a demon from hell. The shrill war cries of the women warriors drove the Remi to panic. Murato pulled one of the Remi off his horse and then stabbed him with his dagger through his eyeball, the blade driving into his skull.

The furious attack had totally panicked the Remi horses. They retreated in disorder. The Gaesatae gave chase with Murato in the lead but had little chance of catching the horsemen. Finally one of the Remi turned round and threw a javelin at Murato, who managed to throw himself to one side to avoid it. The man behind him was less lucky, and Murato turned around to see him skewered through the abdomen.

The naked Gaesatae who was a handsome young man sank slowly to his knees, his hands grasping the *pilum* but not sure what to do with it. Both Murato and Leuce ran to his side. Both realised at once that the wound was mortal.

The young man took a long time to die. Leuce gave him some strong wine to ease the pain and made him as comfortable as possible. "Don't leave me," the young man whispered. "Stay with me. I have no one."

That last statement stung Leuce to the heart. He wasn't the only one to have no one and no place to go. The Gaesatae were all lost, homeless souls. They were tribe-less warriors just waiting their turn to die. She felt hot tears in her eyes.

Murato had to rally his remaining forces. They stripped armour, weapons, and anything valuable from the Romans and Remi. Any surviving horses were also appropriated. Enemy wounded were dispatched. That was not always done quickly or mercifully. Horrible screams shattered the quiet of the forest.

Leuce stayed with the young man, offering what comfort she could as his life slowly ebbed away. He held on tightly to her hand and refused to let her go. He could not be moved without causing excruciating pain. The *pilum* also could not be pulled out. Leuce kept plying him with as much wine as he could drink, and slowly he relaxed a little and the pain seemed slightly better.

After a while, she was lost in her own thoughts and not even thinking of the poor boy. She remembered the happy days of her childhood with her parents and her brothers and sisters. She thought about their beautiful little farm near a small village. The farm had a stream running beside it, which was full of big fat fish which her father used to catch and bring home for dinner. They had been far from rich, but they were never short of food. Her mother was a good cook and made the most delicious white bread and cakes.

Her father was one of the literate people in the village, and he took pains to teach his children to read. She remembered that she was best at studies, and her father was always amazed how well she could read and write. There were Roman traders coming and going through the area. One of them was a friend of her father and agreed to teach her some Latin whenever he was around. There were also Greek traders, and she picked up a smattering of Greek as she had a good ear for languages.

Then came the Germans raiders from across the Rhine. They burnt, pillaged, raped, and killed. Most of her village was massacred. Her father and the other men formed a militia and fought them off for several hours before they were overpowered. Both her brothers were killed in the battle. The Germans were incensed by the resistance and treated the survivors with great brutality. Her sister was raped in every orifice. They gang raped her for days before she finally died. Her mother was subjected to every degradation in front of her father before they slit both their throats. Leuce was only a child, too young to arouse any sexual interest, and the whole episode was now like a lurid nightmare.

For some reason, they kept her alive, perhaps intending to keep her as a slave or sell her. One night, she found a loose plank in the hut where she was kept and managed to escape. The neighbouring villagers had employed a band of Gaesatae mercenaries to help them rid themselves of the German scourge. A combined Belgic and Gaesatae war party attacked the Germans a few days later and managed to drive them away. The Gaesatae found her hiding in an empty hut and adopted her. They taught her the ways of the warrior and the Gaesatae code of life.

Leuce finally snapped out of her reverie. The young warrior was quiet and looked entirely peaceful. He had passed while she was daydreaming. Leuce took the *pilum* and pulled it out of the dead warrior. Some men came and took him and buried him in a mass grave by the side of the road. Leuce found a bunch of wild daisies and left a bouquet over the grave.

Marc Antony was exhilarated. This was his first war time command, and he was thrilled to be given the opportunity to do something important. He was determined to win honour this day. The whole countryside showed the devastation consequent to the passage of the Suessiones. Farms were abandoned, despoiled, or burnt. Crops were destroyed. Many civilians lay dead and unburied.

Livy felt a deep sense of sorrow for all that unnecessary death and destruction. Antony's reaction on the other hand was pure rage, and Livy could see that he couldn't wait to get hold of the Suessiones to exact his revenge. Licinius on the other hand was dead pan, and if he did react emotionally, he didn't show it.

Sometime later Livy saw a pair of scouts riding back in a hurry. Livy looked hard behind them but could not see anyone in pursuit. "Better call a halt, sir, and find out what's going on," he advised Antony, trying his best not to sound presumptuous. Antony put up his hand and the column halted. The Remi scouts rode straight up to Antony to report.

"There is enemy cavalry in a small village ahead. They are looting the villagers, looking for food," the Remi scout said.

Antony brightened. "How many"

"Quite a large force—150, maybe 200 men," the Remi replied.

"We can take them, can't we?" Antony said in Livy's direction. "We are more than 400 men"

Livy composed himself to reply. "Yes. We can take them, sir. We would succeed in killing many of them and of course suffer a number of casualties ourselves, more if this scout's numbers are wrong. The bigger question, sir, is how that would slow down the Suessiones. This is their rearguard, and if we vanquish them, it'll only hurry them along back to Noviodunum. Caesar's whole plan is to get there before their main army." He prayed to Hermes that that didn't sound too impudent. He was beginning to like Antony, who was impulsive and brave but mostly sincere.

"Irrefutable logic, my dear Livius. You've been reading the Greeks no doubt." Antony seemed impressed, and Livy breathed a sigh of relief. "Have you any ideas how a small force of cavalry can slow the huge Suessiones army? We are less than 500 against 50,000," Antony asked.

"The only choke point is the river crossing. They need a big ford for that size army. The only one is about ten miles downriver. If we can cross the river around there, we can be waiting for them, and that's where we can stop them, at least for a while."

"Hmm" Anthony thought a moment. "Sounds like a good idea." He turned to the scout. "Where's the closest ford."

"About half a mile downstream, sir, where the village is," the scout replied.

"Looks like we might have a brush with that lot at the village after all. I suggest we just keep them busy while the main force crosses," Livy said.

"Let's hear your plan, Centurion." Antony reverted to his commander's voice.

"I'll take 100 of my best men to keep the enemy cavalry busy and cover your crossing. The scout will take you across the ford and on to the big ford further downstream where the enemy army has to cross. I will disengage after a while and hurry to join you."

"I'd like to ride with your party, Livy, if you don't mind. Decurion Paulus can take the rest of the force across the ford. I would like to observe your men in action. I have never seen horse archers in combat before."

"Sir, you are the commander, and I suggest that the main force needs your leadership, sir," Livy politely suggested.

Antony was slightly annoyed. "Nevertheless, I will participate in the covering action. Bring me two light *pilum*," he ordered Paulus.

Livy felt further protest was useless. Antony wanted action and wanted it now.

"Decurion Paulus, you bring the main force across the river and wait under cover near the main ford. I hope we can reach the spot before the enemy starts crossing. If we are delayed, you are to try your best to delay the Suessiones from crossing the river."

Livy ordered Biorix and the 100 veterans to form up, and the rest under Paulus headed for the river. Antony and his 100 men approached the village cautiously.

As they closed on the village, they could hear shouting and screaming. The Suessiones warriors were having fun with the village women. Some of the buildings were on fire, producing a thick black smoke.

Livy stopped the men for a short briefing. "May I brief my men?" Livy asked Antony for permission.

"Carry on, Centurion," Antony replied.

"Our task is to cover the crossing of the others. So let's keep between the village and the ford. Everyone is to stay mounted. Let's form a skirmish line two deep. We sweep towards the village and position ourselves 500 yards south of the village. They will spot our people trying to cross if they are at all alert. They will come charging out to engage. We will then shoot anyone emerging from the village and hold them back as long as possible. Do not melee with the enemy, understand?"

The men nodded.

"If they get too close, we retreat another 200 yards, then turn and shoot again. We keep doing this till we reach the ford. Half will cross and half stay to cover. When the first half gets to the other side, they cover the retreat of the remaining half. Is everyone clear?"

There were several "yes, sirs' murmured softly.

"Good plan," Antony murmured, giving Livy a light slap on the shoulder. "Let's go, men," Antony ordered.

The men formed a skirmish line and waited. Livy stationed himself with Antony. He turned to see Paulus and his men beginning to cross. The German heavy cavalry crossed first with the Remi scouts.

Suddenly there was shouting from the village. A few moments later, he could see cavalry forming up. They had no doubt been spotted. The cavalry looked well armed and armoured. They were probably Galba's retainers.

They formed a line and started trotting towards the Romans. Livy's men fired the first volley at 250 yards. The effect was devastating. Horses and men went down in scores. His men had become very accurate with the daily practices. As the enemy came closer, the men started to pick off the riders rather than the horses. Soon there were rider less horses running about everywhere and many men on the ground.

Antony gaped in astonishment. He was used to heavy cavalry tactics where horsemen charged at each other to fight at close quarters. He could hardly believe what Livy's raiders could achieve with their skirmishing tactics.

The enemy reeled at the onslaught and withdrew. Their armour had done little to protect them as the arrows penetrated when fired at less than

200 yards range. The survivors stopped about 100 yards from the skirmish line and started to withdraw. A few defiantly threw their javelins, but the shafts fell well short.

Suddenly Anthony shouted, "Come on. Let's go round up their horses." He then galloped forward, expecting the raiders to follow. Livy and Biorix looked at each other in shocked astonishment. The enemy were far from finished. They had only withdrawn to regroup.

"Take half a dozen men and protect the tribune," Livy called out at Biorix, who immediately gestured to the men around to follow him after Antony. "The rest form up on me. Maintain skirmish line and shoot at anything that moves," Livy ordered.

Two hundred yards in front, Antony cut down one of the walking wounded enemy, then started to chase down the half a dozen rider less horses. Biorix and his men quickly took the horses from him as soon as he gathered them.

The presence of Antony on the field with his silver cuirass and plumed helmet acted like a red flag to a bull. A dozen heavily armed Suessiones cavalry immediately charged out towards him, spears levelled. Biorix and his men immediately began taking them down with accurate fire. Livy galloped forward, firing, and hit one of the horses, bringing down both horse and rider. Soon there were only three of the enemy left, but they were determined to take down Antony.

Biorix shot down one, but the other two were almost on Antony. Antony took a light *pilum* and launched it at the leading man, piercing him through the chest. He did not have time to throw a second. The Suessiones warrior was a large, tough-looking man with a long yellow moustache. He galloped straight at Antony, the spear aimed straight at his chest. Anthony had no shield and was holding only a light *pilum*.

Livy was about to shoot him down, then he hesitated. He had a feeling that Anthony could handle that one. At the last moment, Anthony twisted to one side, avoiding the spear. As the Suessiones swept past, he turned around and plunged his *pilum* into his back. It was expertly done.

"The man can fight," Livy decided, and a new respect formed.

The Suessiones were cowed and hesitated to press their attack further. Anthony deliberately provoked them by getting off his horse to retrieve the two javelins. He had proven himself in front of the men, killing two heavily armed men in solitary combat. The Suessiones did not take up the challenge, having had enough of the deadly arrows of the raiders. They melted away. The screaming from the village stopped.

Antony pulled out the first *pilum*. There was no movement from the impaled man who was obviously dead. He took the gold torque from his neck as a souvenir. The second man was still alive. He was still struggling with the *pilum* stuck in his back. Antony stepped on him and pulled out the javelin. There was a scream of agony and a gush of blood.

Antony turned him around to take his torque. The man was richly adorned and obviously a nobleman. Antony was about to dispatch him with his *gladius* when Livy interrupted, "He might make a valuable prisoner, sir. Looks like nobility or at least a retainer. Could be close to Galba."

Antony lowered his sword. "Good thinking. Can we keep him alive."

"Worth a try, sir. Back wounds are survivable if nothing vital is penetrated," Livy added.

Biorix and one of the other men came and carried the wounded man, slinging him over one of the spare horses. "Better get out of here, sir. Those Suessiones pigs are just waiting to pounce on us again," Biorix grunted.

"Yes, we better get a move on," Livy said, looking in the direction of the village. "Paulus and the others must be across by now and we should hurry to catch up."

Antony mounted, and the raiders formed up and headed for the river crossing.

CHAPTER 13

Decurion Decius woke up with a blinding headache. He found himself naked in a wooden cage about four feet square. It was not even big enough for him to stand up. They hadn't even left him a loin cloth. He was in the middle of the Gaesatae camp, and everyone else was stark naked as well. That strangely did not make him feel much better though.

His bladder was full, and he had no choice but to urinate through the bars. He looked around and noted that he seemed to be the only prisoner. His throat was parched and he was famished as well.

The Gaesatae had not even bothered to post a guard on him. He examined the cage and found that it was solid, and there was a large iron lock on the door which he could not even get at from the inside. Escape would be difficult.

There was nothing to do except lose himself in mental reverie. Decius remembered his childhood in southern Italy. His father had been a marine decurion attached to the Roman fleet. His mother ran a tavern by the docks. He was looked after by the tavern girls who sold not only wine but their bodies as well. Even his own mother sometimes plied the oldest profession during his father's long absences. He didn't have a future except for a military career and he was prone to sea sickness, so the navy was out of the question. One of her mother's lovers was the prefect and commander of the local auxiliary cohort. She provided him exceptional service, and in turn, Decius got a position in the local troop of Roman equites. Most of the cavalry men were sons of wealthy men of the town, and he suffered their scorn during the entire training.

Fortunately the whole troop was sent to Spain, where he campaigned under Caesar. He was a brave and resourceful cavalryman and soon distinguished himself. Caesar promoted him from the ranks to decurion, and he had been grateful and loyal ever since.

A sharp rapping on the bars awoke him from his daydream. "Wake up, Roman!" a female voice called to him in Latin. His eyes focused on her. She was pale blonde, and her short hair was cropped short to just below her ears.

Other than a golden armband and a leather belt attached with two curved blades, she was totally nude. Despite her blue war paint, Decius could see that she had a figure like a Greek goddess and an exquisite face like Aphrodite. He looked up into her clear blue eyes, and she met his gaze defiantly.

"I brought you some bread and water, Roman. We haven't got much food ourselves, but I loathe to see a condemned man starve, not even a Roman pig." She slipped the food and a mug of water through the bars, and Decius took it gratefully.

"Where am I?" Decius asked after taking a long drink and a few bites of the bread.

"You are with a Gaesatae band commanded by Commander Murato. We have joined the combined army under the Nervi," she answered.

"And what's to be my fate, lady?"

Leuce smiled. No one had called her a lady before. "I don't really know, Roman. I think it hasn't been decided. First, you are to be taken before King Bodougnatus of the Nervii. He will decide your fate."

"I guess it won't be pretty."

"A quick execution would be the best you can hope for. They may torture you for information. Worse of all is to be sacrificed to our gods by the Druids," she said flatly.

Decius squirmed inside with horror, but he tried to appear calm and unafraid. The Gaesatae girl would not be impressed if he fell apart. She could still be the key to his salvation.

"What's your name, lady? I want to remember your kindness and put a name to my benefactress."

"They call me Leuce. I have no tribe or family. We are homeless soldiers fighting for pay."

"You don't even wear clothes, I see."

"Our nudity is our honour. We don't value material things. We live only to fight. There is purity in that," she tried to explain.

"I find your customs strange."

"No stranger than we find yours," Leuce countered.

Decius remained silent for a while. "When do I meet your king?"

"They will come for you tonight, after sundown," Leuce replied.

"Will you be with those that come for me?" Decius asked hopefully.

"No, I have other duties." She didn't look forward to providing sexual services to her male comrades, but there was no point in shocking the poor prisoner. "If you still live, I will bring you more food after they return you here. Meanwhile take this canteen. You will need the water more than you need food." She threw him a leather canteen. "I need to go now."

She left before Decius could protest and made her way back to her tent. Suddenly, strong hands grabbed her by the arm and pulled her aside. She looked up into the face of Murato.

"Sweet on that Roman, are you? You know better than to fraternise with the enemy." He gave her a hard shake. "What's the matter? Your own people not good enough for you?"

"Let me go, Murato." She shook herself free. "I speak to whomever I like, you brute." She tried to slap him, but he caught her at the wrist.

"You bitch, I gave orders that no one was to talk to him." He slapped her hard so that her head spun and she bled from a cut lip. He held back from hitting her with all his strength because she could have been knocked unconscious. He was a strong man.

"You bastard, I hate you," she yelled.

"I'm going to fuck you till you scream anyway." He laughed.

"I'm never going to couple with you ever again," she shouted.

"Like I'm going to give you a choice, you slut," Murato retorted.

She wiped the blood from her lips and spat. "I'll remember this," she concluded and ran off.

"I hope you do, bitch," Murato yelled after her. He had half a mind to run after her and rape her there and then, but he had other work to do. He had to attend a meeting which the chiefs were calling, so he departed reluctantly for the camp of the Nervii.

Late Summer, 36 BC, Fortress City of Zhizhi

> Success in war lies in scrutinising enemy intentions and going with them.

Chanyu Zhizhi stood atop one of the defensive towers atop the new walled city which he was building. It would be the capital of his new Xiongnu Empire. There was a fierce pride in his breast as he looked down at the formidable walls creeping ever so higher daily. No more would he be known as a barbarian nomad chieftain, living in animal skin tents. He was on his way to be a true "Son of Heaven', a King of Kings.

The top of the tower had been furnished as a Central Command Headquarters. There was a large table with the surrounding terrain modelled in sand and clay. Rivers and hills were accurately depicted as was the shore of Lake Balkash. His Generals Modu and Dagu and his new auxiliary commander Murato stood around the table.

"What news of the Han?" The *Chanyu* inquired.

"We tortured that dog of a spy till he died. He didn't tell us much. The Chinese are definitely mobilizing. I expect them here latest by next spring. They could be here even earlier," Dagu said.

"What sort of army will we meet?"

"Our spies in Gansu say that the entire army is infantry, spearmen and crossbowmen. Unless they are hiding them somewhere, they have hardly any cavalry except for a small contingent of the Governor's bodyguard," Modu reported.

"How big an army are we facing?"

"Around 40,000, our spies estimate," Modu said.

"What of our special weapons?" The *Chanyu* asked.

"Our engineers have built forty bolt throwing *ballistas* and ten stone throwing *onagers*. We also have about a hundred light bolt throwers called scorpions. Your enemies will be in for a nasty surprise," Murato said with a smirk. He had shaved his shaggy beard and sported only his downturned Gaulish moustache.

"I knew the Romans would be a tremendous asset,"The *Chanyu* thought to himself. "Will the Kangju aid us?"

"Yes, your majesty, they will send a contingent of horse archers and some heavy cavalry," Dagu confirmed.

"I am confident we have the means to take on any Chinese Army," Modu said emphatically. "They have numbers but they are only light infantry armed with *Ji* and *Qiang* and crossbowmen."

The *Chanyu* looked thoughtful. "Our archers can outrange their crossbows and our rate of fire is three to five times. Our artillery will tear holes in their infantry formations, then our heavy cavalry will crush them and the Kangju will chase down the survivors," His eyes glowed as he spoke.

Yes, we will send them running back to Gansu with their tails between their legs," Dagu said.

"Let's drink to our victory," Murato said.

The four men lifted their silver bowls and drank deeply of the fermented horse's milk. Murato privately thought that it tasted like piss and missed the beer and wine of Gaul. There were other things he missed here in this God forsaken wilderness. His thoughts flew to a certain golden haired Gaesatae woman. She was what he missed the most.

"Please come to the terrace," Murato invited the *Chanyu*. "My men have organized a small demonstration for you."

The four men followed him to the balcony which overlooked an open area in front of the walls. The thousand Romans were paraded in original armour and uniforms with banners and standards. The tunics were not the same colour as their previous uniforms. They were a brownish red hue. Plumes and feathers however were still the blood-red of the Roman Army. All the standard weapons of the Roman Army had been restored from caches found near Merv. Legionaries had their bronze helmets, *scutum*, *gladii* and *pila*. Even the centurions had their distinctive helmets with the red transverse crest. The subunits even had wolf-skin clad signifiers carrying the yellow banners of the Xiongnu and *cornicens* carrying the G shaped horns called *cornu*.

The horns sounded and the two cohorts formed an open order triple line. The drill was synchronous and precise. "I give you your Roman Infantry," Murato presented proudly. Murato signalled the *cornicens*. There was another blast from the horn. The men snapped into close order and locked shields. The rear rows swept their *pilums* back ready to throw.

"The two Senior Centurions shouted. "Release," A few hundred *pilum* flew forwards impaling a row of straw targets set up for the occasion. At another command the men drew their *gladii* with an impressive combined rasp that echoed off the city walls. They then formed a large square, then a circle. Finally they deployed into a wedge formation.

The *cornicens* blew again and the men snapped into *testudo* (tortoise formation) with shields all round and forming a roof over the heads of their comrades. This formation protected the soldiers from incoming showers of missiles.

The *Chanyu* smiled. He nodded in approval. "Excellent General Murato, I think your men will give the Han army a nasty surprise."

Murato was flattered to be addressed as General. He had always longed to be a Great Warlord. "I have another demonstration for you, Great One," He motioned the Generals to another side of the tower.

In the plain below were half a dozen *onagers* and a dozen *ballistas* set up to fire. The targets for the onagers were a dozen carts lined up in two rows. At a signal from Murato the commander of the *onagers* gave the order to fire. Half dozen huge rocks hurled through the air in an arc coming down among the wagons in an explosion of dust and rock. When the dust lifted the many of the wagons were completely pulverized.

The Generals were awed and talked approvingly among themselves in Xiongnu.

"I have one final demonstration, Great One," Murato said. "Please observe." He raised his hand.

The dozen *ballistas* fired their bolts into ranks of straw men. Each bolt brought down entire files of men, sometimes passing through three or four at one time and pinning the targets together. The straw formation was decimated.

"I commend you on a very impressive show," The *Chanyu* said. "Will it be possible to train Xiongnu warriors to become Roman style infantry?"

Murato thought carefully. The Xiongnu are horse warriors, used to a very different style of fighting. The task would not be easy. "The Xiongnu are excellent cavalry. I have seen none better. To train them as infantry would be a waste of their skills which each one has honed since childhood," He said

"We face 40,000 Chinese infantry. Your little band would be overwhelmed no matter how good you are in drill and tactics," The *Chanyu* said.

"We need to combine all our assets to achieve victory," Dagu said. We have good infantry, excellent cavalry, archers and now artillery. We have to use them in clever combinations."

"My soldiers have one more weapon which should not be disregarded," Murato added.

"And what else can your remarkable soldiers do?" The *Chanyu* asked.

"They can dig, Great one. They are experts with the shovel," Murato grinned.

The *Chanyu* tweaked his moustache. He understood. "Well I leave you fine military minds to work out the tactics which we must use against the Chinese. I want a full tactical plan within a week. Meanwhile I have other pressing matters to attend to."

The *Chanyu* stalked off followed by two bodyguards. He never walked alone. Too many people wanted him dead. The floor below housed his living quarters. He stayed here rather than at the unfinished palace when he was supervising military preparations.

He came to an imposing wooden door. The guards opened the heavy door, closing it after the *Chanyu* and waited outside. The room was dimly lit and there was the smell of musky perfume in the air. He could see the outline of the Parthian princess spread out on his bed, hands and feet tied to each bedpost. She mumbled angrily and incoherently as he came towards her. Her mouth had been gagged with cotton to prevent her from bringing the house down with her screaming.

The *Chanyu* slithered on to the bed till his face was just hand span away from her face. Her smell was intoxicating. He kissed her hair which had the odour of oil and sweat which excited him. She wriggled in disgust but in vain. He stuck his tongue into her ear which made her struggle even more. The leather straps around ankles and wrist just became tighter and more painful.

"If you promise not to scream I will remove the gag and allow you to talk," Zhizhi raised his eyebrow and smiled from the corner of his mouth. "Nod, if you agree"

The princess stopped moving awhile. She nodded. The *Chanyu* removed her gag. "You son of a street whore, unbind me this instant," She hissed.

"Why should I, I think you are most useful in this position, naked with all your beautiful parts exposed," He sniggered.

"I'll starve myself to death," She threatened.

"You have neither the tolerance nor the patience for such a course of action," He laughed. "I saw you eat like a pig when food was offered."

He was right. She could not tolerate the pain and agony of slow starvation. She had to change her strategy. "I'll make you a deal, monster," She said.

"What could you possibly offer?" He countered dismissively. "I can fuck you any time I want and that's your only use to me."

"I will not struggle when you take me and I will even try and make it pleasurable for you," The Princess desperately offered.

The thought filled her with disgust but she saw to her satisfaction that the *Chanyu* was at least caught off guard and was spinning the idea in his mind."

"You mean you won't try to gouge out my eyed the moment I release you?"

"I give my word. Release one hand and I will show you. If I misbehave you can tie me up again."

He carefully released her left hand. "Take off your breeches," She commanded. He obeyed revealing an erect penis. She caressed it gently with her hands and he groaned with pleasure. She then bent down intending to put the throbbing, pulsating rod between her luscious lips.

The *Chanyu* grabbed her by the wrist to stop her. She looked up defiantly at him. "What's the matter, afraid that I will bite off a piece?" She sneered.

The *Chanyu* raised his hand to backhand her across the face but checked himself at the last moment in an uncharacteristic show of self restraint. He gave her a sinister smile. "We'll stay away from your teeth for the moment," He said.

She glared at him with her dark brown eyes then spat saliva on her free palm and began to stroke his rod smoothly and rhythmically. Her touch was light and sensuous and the *Chanyu* became intolerable aroused. He groaned involuntarily as the tension built till he was almost exploding.

She increased the pace of her strokes till he looked as if he were about to explode. He pushed her back on to the bed and holding his staff thrust it between her legs. She screamed. He failed to penetrate her as her opening was contracted and she was dry as dust. The *Chanyu* spat on to his own rod to lubricate it then rammed at her gates repeatedly as if assaulting a fortress till at last he penetrated her fully. He pounded her brutally.

The Princess moaned and gasped. He was not sure whether from pain of pleasure. He didn't care. He was too near the precipice. She did not struggle, protest or resist but seemed to bend to his will. Her submission gave him deep satisfaction.

Finally he erupted in a stupendous climax the likes which he had not experienced before. His heart was pounding and he was breathless. He felt drained. She seemed catatonic, her mouth open, her eyes glazed.

Moving like a cat he sprung off the bed and untied all her bonds. She was still half paralyzed, regaining her senses. When she sat up he was already dressed.

"You have earned your release. Don't do anything stupid or I will have you bound again," He opened the door and commanded the guard. "Bring her some food and some wine. Don't let her leave this room and be careful you don't let her escape when you go into her. Remember, she bites. She is not to be allowed any clothes, understand," The *Chanyu* barked.

The Guard bowed in response. "By your command, Great One," he said.

In a flash, the *Chanyu* was gone.

The Princess retched in disgust. She could taste bitter bile in her mouth. She swore to herself. "Someday I will kill that spawn of the devil."

Belgica, Summer, 57 BC

> When defending against a large force with a tiny one, choose your terrain well. It makes all the difference.

The squadron of cavalry under Antony had reached the large ford which the Suessiones were soon to cross. The army had not reached the ford but was fast approaching as indicated by a large cloud of dust. Most of the enemy were infantry, and they had not used their cavalry to secure the crossing but instead to serve as a rearguard. That was a mistake which Antony could exploit.

"Can we hold them, Livius?" Antony asked.

"We're too small a force to hold them for long. We need reinforcements. With two or three cohorts, some Nubians, slingers, and archers, we could hold them off for hours," Livy observed.

"Caesar's army can't be too far off. Paulus, gallop with all speed to Caesar and ask him to send what reinforcements he can. Light troops and four legionary cohorts if he can spare them," Antony commanded. He seemed much more focused after his recent combat experience.

"I'll go at once, Commander." Paulus saluted and sped away in a cloud of dust.

"We need to strengthen our defences here. Any ideas?" he asked Livy.

"Let's plant stakes in the muddy water on this side of the river. Biorix, get the men moving. I want every man to cut some branches and sharpen them on both sides. Plant them at forty-five degrees facing the enemy bank"

"Good idea, Livius," Antony assented. He had come to rely heavily on Centurion Livius' good tactical sense. "Anything else?"

"Get the Germans to lay caltrops all along the bank in the shallows." Livy showed Antony a caltrop. It was a nasty piece of metal with four spikes designed so that no matter how it fell, one spike would always point upward to impale the enemy's feet or his horse's hoofs. "I've brought a few sacs of these nasty things. We also have lots of spare arrows loaded on the remounts."

"I guess we can hold for a while." Antony smiled.

"We'll make it tough for them to cross, sir." Livy smiled back.

"How do we deploy the men?" Antony asked.

"The raiders will form a skirmish line hidden in those trees and shrubs. The horses will be held 100 yards back. The Germans will remain mounted and take position in that clump of trees. If the enemy break through our line, the Germans will charge and take out any of the enemy that cross. We'll distribute all the spare arrows to the men."

"Sounds like a plan," Antony concurred. "You heard the man. Get to it," he yelled at the sub-commanders.

During the next hour, everyone chipped in to prepare and plant as many stakes as possible. The stakes were planted so that they were invisible and the points were below the waterline. Antony himself lent a hand to the task. Livy warmed to him. At least he was no armchair general.

The first enemy to appear were a band of light skirmishers. They were bare-chested and wore trousers with square patterns of blue and grey. Each man carried a small round shield and several light javelins. They approached the river bank at a run and were in loose formation.

Livy and his raiders were well hidden among the trees and shrubs along the bank. The enemy force was about 1000 strong, and once they entered the water, they were slowed by it. Livy waited till they were knee deep, then gave the order to fire. The arrows did their deadly work. The enemy light infantry had no defence. Their shields were too small to offer general protection.

Livy aimed for their leader and saw his arrow pierce him through the neck. He clutched at the shaft, and Livy sank another arrow into his chest. The man collapsed, staining the water red. Hundreds of the half-naked Suessiones were hit, and the raiders kept up a steady fire that decimated the light infantry. Slowed by the water, they could not get close to the archers, and though many tried to throw their javelins, the missiles fell short and had no effect. They did not even reach the row of submerged stakes.

Soon the river was red with blood and covered with floating bodies. The Suessiones gave up and retreated to the far bank, carrying their wounded with them. Livy ordered a cease fire. "Save your arrows, men. More will come. Our mission is to buy time," Livy reminded everyone.

"I am truly amazed what a few missile troops can do," Antony said. "Certainly puts into question the dominance of heavy infantry on the battlefield."

"Arrows are great against light troops and cavalry but less effective against heavy infantry with large shields and armour. I think we shall be sorely tested by all types today," Livy replied.

Meanwhile on a hill north of the river, Galba and his retainers were observing the action at the river.

"The Roman pigs have deployed on the south bank, My King," an old retainer spoke.

"I can see for myself, you idiot. We should have rushed a few battalions of heavy infantry over to hold the other side last night. Now we will have to dislodge the pest at a cost of men and time. Vindiacos, you are my war advisor. This is totally your fault. I should have your neck for this." Galba was furious.

Vindiacos was truly alarmed. "Your Majesty, the men were tired and short of food. We needed to rest."

"Rest! Rest! This is what happens when you rest. The Romans never rest. This whole campaign has been one disaster after another. We gathered the greatest army in our history, and what happens? We run out of food and have to disperse, and the Roman Army still walks through our land at will. It's all the fault of you so-called wise advisors. I ought to throw the whole lot of you to the dogs!" Galba ranted.

Vindiacos was speechless. He looked down in humility.

"So what do we do now?"

"I suggest we send several battalions of heavy infantry in close formation and make a frontal attack across the ford. Our archers can return fire from this bank," Vindiacos suggested softly.

"You are a fool once again, Vindiacos. Their bows outrange ours and our archers will fall like flies, then our infantry will just be used for target practice. Even if we do secure the other bank, we will take heavy losses. Besides, our men will then run into their heavy infantry again and be repulsed just like the day before on the Axona."

"You no doubt have a better plan, sire."

"Bring up all the cavalry. I don't see any cavalry on that side. It's time for my nobles to do some work. The horses will move over more quickly, and then we will close with their archers more quickly suffering fewer casualties. Once over, they can make mincemeat of any infantry on the other side."

Vindiacos had his reservations. The arrows would take down many horses, leaving the riders stunned and wallowing in the river. He dared not contradict his king though, and if that was his plan, he wouldn't be able to blame anyone if it didn't work. "I will send word to your nobles, My King."

"How many royal cavalry do we have?"

"Close to a thousand, My Lord"

"Doesn't seem to be a strong force over there. They are my best troops, and they will soon destroy them. We must act quickly before the rest of the Roman Army arrives."

"It would take maybe an hour to prepare the men."

"See to it," Galba ordered.

Vindiacos scurried off.

On the southern bank, Livy and Antony waited in apprehension. The first assault was a disaster for the enemy. Surely they would come up with the right solution. A large phalanx of heavy infantry could plod across almost unscathed, leaving the raiders no choice but to withdraw. The Germans could charge them, but they were a small number and would die nobly, but nevertheless die.

"What would your men do if they send in the heavy infantry?" Antony asked.

"We would try to take down as many as possible while they are crossing. We would aim for legs, arms, heads, and any exposed part of the body not covered by shields. We could also shoot high to drop arrows behind their shield wall, though they would put up their shields above their heads against this tactic."

"I wonder if they know about the testudo formation," Antony remarked.

"I hope not. That would be pretty impervious to arrows," Livy answered.

"Well, we'll find out pretty soon. I wonder when your decurion is going to come back with some reinforcements. We need some heavy infantry badly," Antony said.

"Look, the second wave is approaching." Livy pointed across the river. He smiled. "They've sent the wrong kind of troops."

"Heavy cavalry and well armoured," Antony observed. "Can your men handle those?"

"Just watch us. Their armour can be penetrated, and the horses are easy targets. They will soon pay a heavy price for sending the wrong kind of troops against us."

Livy turned to Biorix. "Tell the men to start firing at 300 yards. Aim for the horses first. When they get near enough to be accurate, take out the riders. Ignore the ones that fall off their horse."

"Aye, sir," Biorix said and went off to pass the message to the men.

"Sir, I would greatly appreciate if you would join the Germans and charge on my signal. Yours would be the decisive blow that would finish them."

"Of course, Centurion. I will be happy to execute the final blow." Antony was smiling broadly.

The enemy horses walked their steeds deliberately forward. They looked magnificent in their armours, shining helmets, and blue plumes. They formed a column of about forty horses wide. That was about the width of the ford. They had animal head banners with streamers of many colours. He saw the front rank lower their spears and start to trot. After a while, they broke into a canter.

Livy was not worried. There was no way they could charge across the ford with any speed. The water was neck deep in the centre, and the river was at least 200 yards wide at that point.

The raiders started firing even before the horses reached the river bank. The result was carnage as hundreds of horses went down or went berserk and threw their riders. The following ranks were disordered as they tried to pick their way through the dead and wounded horses and men.

The raiders fired a volley every five seconds, decimating the cavalry on the bank. About two score of the surviving horsemen managed to get into the water and started to wade across.

Livy shouted to his men, "Keep your fire on the enemy on the far bank." He then tapped a few of the nearest men. "Come with me. Let's try and take out those in the water." Livy nocked an arrow and fired as he spoke, hitting one of the horsemen in the forehead. He toppled backwards. The small band of raiders kept a steady and accurate fire on the men in the river, thinning their ranks. About sixty or seventy horsemen were now in the river, making their way quickly to the Roman bank.

On the far bank there was confusion, and some of the nobles were already retreating, not willing to risk the storm of arrows any further.

To Galba watching from the vantage of the hill, the effect was shocking beyond belief. His best troops had just been cut down mercilessly by a bunch of cheap archers. He was speechless. How could this disaster happen?

Vindiacus beside him was also silent. To say anything at that point would bring down the king's wrath for sure.

The king covered his face for a while, then turned to Vindiacus. "I am sorry, old friend. We have lost our best troops, our brave noble cavalry. We must cross the river. Caesar may already be attacking Noviodunum as we speak."

"Shall I send in the heavy infantry?" Vindiacus asked for confirmation.

"Do so at once."

Vindiacus motioned to a messenger who rode off immediately.

Only about two score of the horsemen managed to make it to the shore. Some of the horses screamed as they ran into the sharpened stakes. Others got past the stakes and stepped on the caltrops. Horses were going down everywhere. Livy signalled for the Germans to charge. At the same time, he shot his last arrow square into the mid-chest of the nearest enemy horseman. He then drew his heavy *spatha* and launched himself at the next rider. The man was splendidly kitted in a steel suit of mail and a shiny bronze helmet with black plume. He had a round shield with a boar's head painted on it.

The man took his spear and threw it, hitting one of Livy's men in the leg. Livy was on him in a flash. The man turned his horse to face his new assailant, but Livy not pausing brought his *spatha* down on the horse's nose. The horse reared in shock and pain. The rider tried desperately to keep his balance, and Livy immediately grabbed his belt and yanked hard, pulling the man off his horse. He fell on his back, winded. Livy immediately sat on him and raised the *spatha* to dispatch the man.

The man put up both his hands in supplication and yelled, "Spare me. I am a nobleman. I surrender." The words said in Celtic registered in Livy's brain one split second before he plunged his blade through the man's neck.

"Turn around," Livy ordered. The frightened nobleman complied. Livy stripped off the belt from one of the dead bodies and tied his hands behind him. Meanwhile, the German heavy cavalry had slaughtered the surviving Suessiones cavalry, who were already exhausted after the swim across the river.

There were dead and wounded lying all over both banks of the river and many floating in the water. Biorix came up to Livy. "Permission to help ourselves, sir," He gestured to all the bodies lying around.

"Carry on, Biorix. Ask the men to help themselves but be quick about it. I want everyone back in position as soon as the enemy appear." Livy knew that a little loot would certainly help the morale of the men. The Germans joined in as well. He turned to his prisoner.

Quickly he stripped him of torque, rings, wrist bands, armbands, sword, dagger, and jewelled encrusted belt.

The man spat in disgust, "You are nothing but thieves."

"Sorry for that. Spoils of war. You'd do the same thing were the positions reversed," Livy spoke in Celtic. "What's your name?"

"Lugurix," said the nobleman. "I am cousin to Galba and member of the council of elders. It's something like your Senate."

Livy laughed. "You compare your little village gathering to the Senate of Rome? That's a little presumptuous."

The man scowled. "Your arrogance knows no bounds, you impudent young pup."

"This impudent young pup just spared your life. Your memory is short," Livy retorted. "Nevertheless, I will be sure to treat you in a manner befitting your rank. That means I don't strip you naked."

The man scowled. "What do you intend to do with me?"

"I haven't decided yet. Maybe we can keep you for prisoner exchange. On the other hand, perhaps you can be useful as an emissary to persuade your Suessiones brothers to give up."

"You can eat shit and die," Lugurix mumbled.

"Well, if you have that attitude, I might sell you to some slave merchant as a bath slave to some homosexual rich Roman. Then perhaps Caesar will spare you the indignity and just take your head." Livy smiled mischievously.

"Aarghh," the man screamed. "You mock me, you monster."

His agony was interrupted by a few screams as the enemy wounded were dispatched and some pitiable neighing as wounded horses were put down.

Biorix returned. "What's the butcher's bill?" Livy asked.

"Three dead and eight wounded on our side. One of the dead and two of the wounded are Germans," Biorix reported.

"How bad are the wounded?"

"Most of them will live to fight another day. One of the Germans is wounded bad though. Might not make it. Chest wound," Biorix elaborated.

"What about the other side?" Livy asked.

"Several hundred dead or wounded, half of them light infantry and half the horse. We accounted for quite a few of their leading men," Biorix answered.

"How about captives?"

"We got about two dozen prisoners, not counting this lord here. The rest of their wounded who could not walk we finished off."

"Lots of loot?" Livy asked nonchalantly.

"Rich pickings, sir, very rich pickings." Biorix was smiling from ear to ear.

Just then someone shouted, "Riders incoming." Livy looked south and saw a trail of dust. Someone was coming in a great hurry.

"Looks like half a dozen riders, sir," Biorix commented.

"Paulus returning with help no doubt," Livy said. Antony came running. He too had been helping himself, looting the few Suessiones he had personally killed.

The party comprised Paulus, a tribune, and several tough-looking men in armours and helmets, which were definitely not regulation.

"Decurion Paulus reporting," he addressed Antony. "Let me introduce Tribune Caepio. I bring greetings from Caesar."

"Who are these men?" Antony demanded.

"They are gladiators in Caesar's service. He uses them as bodyguards, but he says they are the very best gladiators he owns."

"Does Caesar expect us to hold out against the whole Suessiones army with four gladiators?" Antony asked, incredulous.

"There are more coming," Paulus assured. "Caesar's last hundred German cavalry and then two cohorts of the Tenth behind them marching at double time"

"No light auxiliaries?" Antony asked.

"I'm afraid not. He is already at Noviodunum and is preparing to assault the town even now. The light troops are needed to repel the defenders from the walls," Paulus added.

"I guess our job now is to buy enough time for Caesar to take the town."

"That's about the picture, sir," Paulus said. "I think I see the Germans coming over there."

"About fucking time," Livy swore. "Here come the Suessiones as well. Take your position, men.

Antony quickly briefed his small force. "All the German cavalry will fight dismounted. This goes for Tribune Caepio and the four gladiators. We have to be the heavy infantry till the cohorts of the Tenth arrive. The raiders under Livy will try to do as much damage as possible with arrows. Try to thin their ranks. Once they hit our bank, we will charge and try and drive them back into the water. The bank is about two feet high, so we have a slight height advantage. Keep it. Stay on the bank and don't run into the water. There are caltrops in there."

"What should the raiders do once the enemy close with us?" Biorix asked.

"The hundred veterans who are all trained in hand-to-hand combat will stay to help the Germans fight. The rest who were till recently Cretan archers will move to the flanks and keep hitting those in the water with your arrows," Livy replied.

"Is everyone clear?" Antony concluded. There were murmurs of assent from everyone. "Then to your positions, men, and may Jupiter bring victory," Antony said with as much conviction as possible.

"Any chance the reinforcements will get here in time?" Livy asked Paulus.

"They will, sir," Paulus assured.

Livy had his doubts. He had hoped that they could just withdraw if things got too sticky, but Antony now wanted to hold as long as possible. "It's 300 of us against all of them, Paulus. Have you heard of the Spartans at Thermopylae?" Livy asked.

"No, sir, never heard of them. What happened?"

"They got wiped out. Every single one was killed," Livy replied tersely.

"I'm sure it was a good death, sir," Paulus replied.

"There is no such thing as a good death," Livy replied.

Vindiacos had organised his infantry in columns. Each column was just wide enough to negotiate the ford. The whole army deployed in the pasture just before the ford, just out of arrow range. Galba and his senior retainers rode to the front, and he stopped in front of his army.

"We Belgae are called the furious ones. Among the Celts, we are the bravest of the brave. And among the Belgae, we Suessiones are the greatest nation. Our former King Diviciacus was ruler of all Belgic lands. He was king of kings and you are his people," Galba addressed his men.

"The Romans are invaders. They've come to enslave our people, burn our villages, and rape our wives and daughters. We are here to protect our loved ones, our country, and our way of life," He continued

"Oh yes, I concede the Romans are also good fighters and well organised, but they are not gods. Look at their size and stature. Man to man, any Belgic warrior can beat any Roman soldier. They win because of cunning and discipline. These traits we also have in abundance.

Across that river lies our capital Noviodunum. Many of you have wives and children there. The Romans are even at this moment preparing to storm our town and destroy or take everything we hold dear. Only you can prevent this catastrophe and rescue them. Only you!" Galba shouted.

There was a combined angry yell from the whole army. Weapons were raised in the air and beaten upon shields, causing a huge racket. Vindiacos motioned for silence.

"Over on the other side of the river is a small force of Romans. We must crush them to get across. The survivors of the last two attempts have told us there are only light troops and a few cavalry. There are no heavy infantry there. We have 50,000 heavy infantry right here. They cannot stop us.

There across the river lies home. Do you want to see your loved ones again? Sweep those Romans away, and we shall be home by sundown," Galba said.

The whole army cheered enthusiastically. All they wanted was to go home and protect their loved ones. They started to beat on their shields in unison. It was a complicated rhythmic beat. The first columns started to march towards the river in close formation, their long hexagonal shields swinging by their sides.

The sight from Livy's perspective made his blood run cold. Even the usually unflappable Antony looked worried. A never-ending river of heavy infantry seemed to flow down towards the far bank of the ford. Livy strained his eyes to see what sort of troops he was facing. If they threw the elite heavily armoured champions at them, the arrows would make little impact and they would get across relatively unscathed. The subsequent melee would be truly one-sided.

Again the Suessiones had got it wrong. The bare-chested spearmen and swordsmen were in the fore. That was typical of the hierarchy-bound Belgae. The cheap troops made of poor peasants had to do the dying first while the richer, better equipped troops fought later. That tradition was going to cost them. Livy managed a wry smile.

"I see your boys get another chance to do some more damage before they dislodge us," Antony remarked. He was learning fast.

Livy briefed his archers quickly. "I don't want any blind volleys. Shoot like on the range. Every shot to count. Aim for any exposed flesh. Hit their legs, arms, heads, necks, anything you can see. Don't waste arrows on their shields. If they lock shields, angle your fire so that your arrows fall from above. Make every shot count."

The first column came within range on the far bank. The archers started their deadly work. The arrows came at random, so there was no order to lock shields to the front. Several scores of the bare-chested spearmen went down. Their formation was disrupted, and they went into the water in relative disorder. Livy's men picked them off mercilessly. They hit any part of the body that was exposed. Even wounded men were taken out of the equation.

The river became red with blood again. The wounded men started to withdraw, getting into the way of the following ranks. All formation was lost. The raiders soon found they could take down the scattered spearmen at will. The casualties multiplied as the whole formation lost cohesion and could not close ranks or make a proper shield wall.

Livy noticed that the spearmen carried clubs as their secondary weapon rather than swords. Those clubs would be dangerous at close quarters as the men who wielded them were taller and stronger than the average Roman legionary. He doubled his efforts to shoot down as many as possible, grateful that he had made provision for triple the usual supply of arrows. The enemy were in mid-stream now, and the water was almost up to their necks, making it difficult to hit as they held their shields up over their heads.

Livy shifted his aim lower, shooting into the water just in front of the advancing men. The arrows hit the water and drove into their unprotected chests and abdomens, and he was relieved to see his targets collapse. The other archers soon discovered the same strategy, and the advancing ranks were soon full of gaps which could not be plugged. As they clambered up to shallower water, their legs became visible, and the archers shifted their aim lower and started hitting shins and calves.

The enemy lines were thinned further as some walked into the hidden underwater spikes or trod on caltrops. There were many loud screams, and men toppled into the water in agony as their feet were injured.

The remaining warriors charged the last few yards, desperate to close with the Romans. Antony and the Germans counter-charged and repelled them back into the water. The Belgae were vulnerable as they tried to climb the steep slope of the bank. They were also tired out after fighting their way over the river. The full-bodied charge of the heavily armed Germans was the last straw. Those who were not killed outright turned and fled. Antony was furiously slaughtering the enemy, and the momentum carried him into the shallows. Looking across the river, he realised that the time for celebration had not arrived. The next formation was already beginning to cross. This time they had locked shields and were moving slowly in formation, trying to keep a continuous line.

"Back to the bank, men," Anthony shouted. "Keep behind the archers. Retrieve as many of these bloody shields as possible." Anthony took hold of one of the long hexagonal shields of the enemy and retreated up the embankment.

The next formation had learnt from their predecessors. They kept in tight formation and moved slowly and steadily. They were bare-chested swordsmen and had the same kind of hexagonal shields. They carried long double-edged broad swords.

This time the raiders had trouble hitting the swordsmen. They were careful not to expose any parts of their bodies. Livy managed to hit two of them in the legs, which caused them to fall away, but new men quickly took their place, and the formation moved inexorably forward. Very few of the warriors were falling. There was some effect from the Cretan archers on the left flank, who were shooting against the uncovered right flank of the dense formation. Even there, the warriors were soon protected by a wall of shields as those on that flank switched their shields to the unprotected side. The archers switched to dropping arrows from above, but even then the effect failed to disrupt the formation though there were some screams from the middle of the formation as men were wounded.

Antony turned to Livy with a worried frown. "Looks like this is where we go down fighting gloriously, eh, Livius?" Livy had no answer. The situation couldn't be worse. It looked as if there would be one desperate melee on the bank and then the enemy would just annihilate them. There were at least 3000 men in that formation alone, and more and better armed were coming.

Livy looked to the prisoner who had been bound and gagged. He had half a mind to execute him before the final battle. The man seemed to read his mind and was furiously mumbling something incoherently. He seemed frantic.

"Don't worry, Lugurix. I leave your fate to your gods. If we lose, your kinsmen will rescue you," Livy finally said.

Over on the hill above the enemy bank, Vindiacus looked pleased. "The commander of the sword contingent is making good headway. They are halfway across the river and in good order. We should sweep the Romans away with this wave."

"They'd better. The performances of the previous units were dismal, and I aim to have the heads of their commanders if they are not dead already," Galba spoke with determination.

Vindiacus was aghast. He hoped that the king's words were mere bluster, but what if he meant what he said?

"I see the glint of metal coming from the far side to the right," Galba said, squinting to make out what was coming from that direction.

They both looked hard in that direction, and every member of the nobles in their party was looking hard to see what was coming. The glint of metal became more frequent and increased in numbers, looking like a string of stars coming round a small hill and some trees.

Finally one of the braver officers said, "Looks like men in armour carrying spears"

Vindiacus felt all his hopes suddenly dashed. They would not see home that night, and that battle was fast becoming a horrible battle of attrition. How would they get across the river now?

Galba looked furious. "Fuck. Someone is going to pay for this." He looked menacingly at Vindiacos.

"Don't despair yet. Those legionaries are still at least two to three miles away. If we can capture the other bank, we will be able to form up and meet them at least on fair terms. Let me go down myself and lead the army across."

"You better get going then," Galba said dispassionately. He had lost faith in the man. The bald middle-aged man looked bent and pathetically weak.

"And don't come back," Galba thought to himself.

Vindiacos galloped off down to the river followed by his retinue of six personal retainers. They were all young fit men and heavily armed and armoured. Their helmets shone with polish and their black plumes flew in the air impressively.

CHAPTER 14

At the river's edge, the Germans had formed into two lines, 100 men in length. Another 100 raiders had gotten into line behind them. Most of them carried the hexagonal shields liberated from the first wave of the enemy. Antony stood in the centre, Livy was on the right and Paulus at the far left. Licinius and Caepio led the second line and Biorix the third. The four gladiators stood two on either side of Antony. They would be his bodyguard.

The Remi scouts had already brought to the attention of the defenders the news that help was coming. At most, they would have to hold for less than half an hour, though Livy realised that this would be the longest half hour in their lives. He hated hand-to-hand fighting. It was just too unpredictable and costly. His German allies looked supremely confident and menacing and brought him a little confidence. Nevertheless, the terror he felt underneath was palpable, and he tried his best not to show it.

The Belgic swordsmen had passed the deepest part of the ford and were now in the shallows. The archers were taking down the odd victim, but the massed shields were, to a large extent, impervious to arrows. They came on inexorably and slowly, then rushed forward in a body, screaming a fearsome war cry. At thirty yards, the Germans unleashed a volley of *pila*. The spears killed a few but largely stuck into enemy shields, making them unmanageable. The frustrated swordsmen tried to pull out the deformed *pila* but found it almost impossible, and most just discarded their shields. At this point, the raiders poured in two or three volleys of arrows at the unprotected swordsmen.

This caused fearsome casualties, disrupting the enemy line. Some men screamed and fell aside as they were impaled by the hidden stakes which were in waist-deep water. The water near the bank began to redden once more. The rest plodded on, only to step howling on the caltrops. Many stopped to pull the wretched devices from their feet. The entire enemy line was badly disrupted and now fell prey to a storm of arrows zipping about all through their ranks. Before they could recover, the whole Roman line—Germans, gladiators, and raiders alike—charged just as the enemy were struggling on to the bank. The Germans had their second spear levelled, which gave them considerable reach.

The front ranks of the swordsmen were mowed down by the German spear charge. Most of them didn't even have shields raised for protection. The impetus of the charge carried them through the second rank into the third. By then, the Germans had their heavy *spathas* drawn and were expertly cutting a swathe through the Belgic formation. The swordsmen dropped their shields and tried to fight back with their heavy long swords, but in the crowded bank, they did not have the space to swing their weapons. The Germans, however—trained in the typical Roman fashion—relied on running hard into their opponents with their shields and then stabbing them. They were in their element.

Antony was in the forefront of the fray. His flanks protected by the four gladiators, he was now invincible, and the five of them cut a broad swathe through the disorganised enemy ranks. The gladiators found the Belgic infantry easy meat and massacred them mercilessly. They moved economically and expertly, thrusting and stabbing everyone in their path. Heavily armoured, they were unstoppable.

Livy skewered his first opponent through the abdomen with his *pilum*, then drew his *spatha* and rammed another huge warrior with his shield. The man hardly budged. He raised his sword to strike, but Livy stabbed him in the left side before he could bring down his sword. The man stepped backward in surprise, and Livy hit him hard on the face with the pommel of his sword, bringing the man down. His mind had gone blank, and he just fought instinctively to stay alive as he rushed into the enemy ranks, thrusting and stabbing whenever he saw any bare flesh. His face and body was splattered with blood and gut contents, and he felt a devilish spirit take over as he waded into the shallows.

Antony was in his element. He was a well-trained swordsmen and this close-order hand-to hand-combat was totally to his liking. He struck smoothly and swiftly with deliberate strokes and economy of movement. Each time he thrust, he drew blood. He had already personally accounted for half a dozen of the enemy, and the Germans around him were slaughtering the rest. He could feel the enemy reeling and moving backwards.

"No pursuit," Antony called out. "No pursuit. We stick to our bank." The disciplined Germans stopped going any further and the Belgae retreated, not having much stomach to continue any further after the severe drubbing from the Germans, who were fearsome warriors and their traditional enemies. The Germans were, on the average, even bigger and taller than the Belgae.

At this moment, a group of well-dressed horsemen arrived. They came up on Livy's flank and started to rally the half-naked Belgic swordsmen. Livy could hear their leader shouting in Celtic. "Turn around and fight, you fools. There are so few of them. Press forward, and we can still win the day."

Hardly any of the Belgic soldiers heeded the rallying call, and everyone continued to drift backwards. All the shouting attracted the attention of the archers on the bank, who started to fire arrows at the small group of horsemen. Two horses were hit and threw their riders, and two more riders went down to arrows. Vindiacos's horse soon had two shafts protruding from its side, and it started to topple. Livy ran towards him, but one of the remaining horsemen turned to intercept him.

The rider swung his sword at Livy, who ducked. The sword glanced off his helmet, producing a sharp pain. Fortunately, the helmet, though dented, did not get penetrated. The man turned his horse for another blow but suddenly sprouted two arrow shafts in his back. He managed to hang on to his horse but turned his horse around and made off towards the far bank.

Livy turned his attention to Vindiacos, who had slid off his dying horse and drawn his sword. He turned to face Livy as he approached. "Give it up, old man. It's a lost cause. Your army will never get to Noviodunum on time, and your war is lost."

The man circled warily, his sword still pointed towards Livy. Two tall, muscular Germans now approached, swords drawn. They were huge men and quite intimidating.

Livy tried talking in Celtic again. "Don't die needlessly. There has been enough death today. Your people need you to make peace with Caesar and to keep it. There will be a new beginning. It's not our intention to enslave your nation."

Vindiacos seemed to be wavering. "What would happen to me?" he asked, still on guard.

"You will live. Maybe you will be reunited with your family again. I can't guarantee it, but with life there is always a chance. While you are my prisoner, I promise you civilised treatment. After I hand you to Caesar, I am no longer in control of your fate. I hear he is clement to those that surrender and make a deal with him. He wants to pacify Gaul, not destroy it."

The man thought for a few moments, then dropped his sword to the side. "All right. I am in your hands."

"You can keep your sword, sir, if you promise not to use it against us."

"You have my word," Vindiacos said.

"It's good enough for me," Livy said.

On the banks of the river, the two cohorts of the Tenth had already formed up in perfect lines. They looked smart and impeccably turned out, just like when they were on parade earlier.

Antony waded over to Livy. "We've done it. We've stopped them and they can't cross to interfere with Caesar." Antony was elated.

Livy was suddenly exhausted. "Good work, sir. Your first combat command was an outstanding success."

"I appreciate your help and advice, Livius," Antony acknowledged, slapping him on the back.

"I'm only glad to be alive, sir, and that most of my men seemed to have survived," Livy replied, still breathless.

"Tonight we will celebrate with Servilia's girls, right? At my expense," Antony promised.

Livy nodded and continued to try and catch his breath. He felt the dent on his helmet. That was far too close!

A tough-looking centurion dressed in sparkling silver scale armour inundated with decorations splashed through the water towards them. He saluted. "Centurion Caius Marcellus, commander of the Ninth and Tenth cohorts of Legio X reporting, sirs." Antony and Livy returned the salute.

"My men are in position on the bank. We will have no trouble dealing with that lot." He motioned to the army on the opposite bank. They had seen the legionaries deploying, and after the many defeats, they had decided to call it a day. The whole army was retreating.

"There are another four cohorts of auxiliary infantry coming, sir. We force-marched all the way to get here as quickly as possible. Caesar orders you to retire and meet up with him in Noviodunum. Sir. We can take it from here, sir" Marcellus addressed Antony breathlessly.

"Thank you for relieving us, Centurion. We'll get organised and be on our way," Antony replied.

Livy went back to his men and looked up Biorix and Paulus. "Butcher's bill? Paulus?"

"Five dead and twenty-five wounded on our side. Two of the dead are our veterans, Tertius and Severus." Paulus looked saddened. They had shared many adventures.

"How bad the wounded?"

"Most of them are light except for two. One will probably lose a leg. The other may be mortal," Paulus replied.

"How did the Germans fare?" Livy asked.

"Much worse," Biorix answered. "They lost a dozen dead and about forty wounded."

"I'm not surprised. They bore the brunt of the hand-to-hand combat. You always take more casualties in a melee," Livy said. "They are excellent fighters, though. Their whole unit should get battle honours."

"There is some good news, sir." Biorix smiled slyly.

"And what's that?"

"We got a lot of loot. Lots of torques, armbands, rings, fancy swords, belts, helmets, enemy *signum* made of gold and silver, and high-quality armour," Biorix said in triumph. "We're all quite rich."

"So it seems." Livy smiled.

"One-quarter goes to you, you being our commander. We'll share out the rest, eh?" Biorix asked.

"Some should be given to Antony. I know he has a lot of debts," Livy said.

"We offered him already. Wouldn't take it. Says Caesar will reward him."

"I guess he would at that. Nevertheless, I will make him a present from my share," Livy concluded.

Livy went over to his two important prisoners, Vindiacos and Lugurix. They were guarded by two fierce-looking Germans, who looked ready to slaughter the two at the slightest provocation. He spoke to Vindiacos first. Lugurix was still tied up, though his mouth gag had been removed.

"Come over here, sir," Livy addressed him politely. The man complied.

"I need you to take off your helmet, sword belt, armour, and your entire valuables, sir," Livy ordered.

The man complied with a resigned look. After he had stripped, Livy further searched him and relieved him of a pair of gold wrist bands and several large rings decorated with precious stones.

"Please remove your shoes now. After that you may remove the shoes of your colleague," Livy ordered once more.

Vindiacos complied. Livy motioned for all the personal effects of the two men to be taken away by one of the raiders. "Ask Biorix to store those for me," he ordered the young raider.

Livy then went to one of the bodies and removed the man's simple leather sword belt and scabbard. He took Vindiacos's fine sword, stuck it into the simple scabbard, which fortunately fit, and gave the sword, belt, and scabbard to the surprised man.

"I keep my promises, and I hope you will as well. You may keep your sword, but if you try to escape or hurt any of my men, I will hunt you down like a dog," Livy said, looking him straight in the eye.

"I have given my word as a Belgic nobleman," Vindiacos affirmed.

"As for the other one, he remains tied up," Livy ordered the two German guards. "Watch them closely."

He then turned to the young raider. "Get them some water. I don't want it said we are cruel to our prisoners."

Treat prisoners of war kindly and care for them.
Use victory over the enemy to enhance your own strength.

On the hill, Galba was totally demoralised. Vindiacos had failed, and his army had been beaten again. The man was either captured or dead. He hoped the latter was true. The stupid man had cost him dear. There was no question of crossing the ford now. Not with heavy infantry guarding the bank. His whole army had to backtrack to the east again and cross at a point much further up river. It would cost them a day, and he was afraid his capital would have fallen by the time he reached it.

In his mind, he could picture the burning, killing, looting, rape, and destruction that the Romans would visit on his people. The gods must have abandoned the Suessiones. What had they done to deserve this? Maybe now was the time to turn to the priest.

He watched as one by one his army contingents marched eastwards. They were hungry, tired, and demoralised. Not the kind of army he would have liked to lead against those terrible Eagle men.

He turned to his aide-de-camp. "Get me Bratronos the priest. Tell him I want to see him at once!" he ordered. The man obeyed quickly.

Sometime later, Bratronos appeared. He was dressed in the hood and long grey robes of a Druid. He carried a long, gnarled oak staff and had a limp. "You know what happened today, Priest?" Galba asked.

"Our army has once more suffered misfortune, Your Majesty," the priest replied.

"You told me this whole venture was sure to succeed. You told me we would lead the Belgae to victory, and I would become king of kings. You lied, and I have half a mind to sacrifice you to the gods for your treachery." Galba fumed.

"The signs were clear, You Majesty." The priest defended desperately. "You are to lead your people to salvation from the Romans. Perhaps you misinterpreted the words of the gods?"

"What else could it mean but that I should unite the tribes and drive out the Romans?" he challenged.

"Perhaps there is another alternative." Bratranos hedged.

"What other alternative? You, son of a whore!" Galba was getting annoyed.

"The Remi have fared well, coming to an accommodation with them, Your Majesty," the priest probed.

"Well, why the fuck would they want to come to an accommodation with us now? They got us by the balls. They are poised to take our capital and enslave all our women and children and, our army is already out of supplies and they can just watch us starve or hunt us down individually when we dissolve. If I were Caesar, I would not need to make an accommodation at this time." He was so furious that he gave the priest a kick.

The man collapsed and got a few more kicks in the belly. Galba turned to his aide. "Get this scum out of here till I decide what to do with him. He is to be under guard. Let's hurry and get the army home."

Noviodunum 57 BC

> Ultimate excellence lies not in winning every battle but in defeating the enemy without even fighting.

Antony and Livy reported to Julius Caesar in his headquarters, which was sited on a hill overlooking Noviodunum. The town was being assaulted. Caesar had hoped to catch them by surprise and had launched an immediate attack on the hill fort.

Livy could see that that the fortifications were not paltry. The walls were made of a combination of wood and masonry and were twelve feet high, and there was a moat filled with water on three sides. At the front, there was no moat, but the attackers had to negotiate a steep slope leading to the walls and the gate.

Caesar had brought up mantlets and all the light artillery, which were sweeping the top of the walls, clear of defenders, with a hail of ballista and scorpion bolts. The major part of the Tenth was poised to assault the front whereas the seventh had been divided into two, and one-half each were assaulting the left and right walls of the town. Caesar left the back untouched. He had the idea that if the town panicked, they might just withdraw through the back, leaving the town to him. The survivors would not survive long in the open country as they would be hunted down easily.

"Antony, Livius, you are just in time. I gather the main enemy army is nowhere near?" Caesar greeted them.

"Last we saw of them they were still across the river. They can't arrive till tomorrow, Lord Caesar," Antony reported.

"I gather you made a terrific stand at the river, Antony. You inflicted thousands of casualties on Galba and his men." Caesar beamed.

"It's my honour to serve, Caesar." Antony looked elated. This was what he came for. Real combat experience.

"I am sure this will go far towards your political aspirations back home, which, of course, I will support in other ways as well," Caesar offered unreservedly.

"We owe this victory to the excellent men you assigned to me. I want to commend Centurion Livius and his raiders in particular. They completely changed my view about the usefulness of horse archers, sir. They are unusually versatile troops," Antony said.

"I already know their value, dear Antony. How did my Germans perform?"

"They were outstanding, sir. The best cavalry I have seen and the best infantry too. We were badly outnumbered, but together we prevailed."

"I will make sure that all under your command are rewarded, most of all Gaius Livius here. Come and see me after the battle in my tent," Caesar ordered.

"My Lord, let my men and me go down and help clear the walls," Livy pleaded.

"You have done enough for today. I don't want any more casualties in your command. The Cretan archers and Balearic slingers will suffice. Besides, I have a large number of light artillery that will decimate any defenders daring to show themselves over the walls."

"As you wish, sir," Livy was disappointed.

"Rest here awhile. I will get my orderlies to bring some refreshments for you." Caesar went back to his battle.

The orderlies laid out a small table under a tree. The food was simple: bread, cheese, and fruit and a flagon of watered wine. To the thirsty and starving officers, it tasted like ambrosia from Olympus. Antony, Livy, Paulus, and Biorix ate and drank their fill. They hadn't eaten the whole day.

The artillery had stopped their bombardment, and the infantry assaulted on all sides at a run, bringing ladders to climb the walls. The defenders immediately appeared on the top of the walls and started hurling rocks, bricks, javelins, and anything they could get their hands on at the assaulting legionaries. The Cretan archers who followed behind the infantry started picking the defenders off with arrows.

The Tenth Legion struggled up the hill and laid their ladders on the walls. Soldiers started to climb up the ladders, but the defenders used poles with a forked end to push the ladders off the walls. One by one, the ladders were pushed away, and the legionaries fell in a heap below the walls. Soon only two ladders were in place. On one of this ladder, one centurion had actually made it to the top and had slain the defender who was trying to push the ladder off.

"That man will get a *Corona Muralis*. First over the walls!" Antony said excitedly. Livy and the other officers were also watching in quiet fascination.

The defenders quickly rushed to that section of the wall where the centurion and two legionaries had captured a toehold. The three men fought desperately as defender after defender rushed at them with spears and axes. The three men dispatched one defender after another, but they kept coming and there wasn't any space for the following legionaries to get on the ledge behind the top of the wall. Just as he had disarmed two more defenders, the brave centurion was hit by an arrow through his front armour. The two defenders were unarmed, but they rushed at him and toppled him over the wall. The two remaining legionaries were soon overwhelmed, and then the ladder was pushed off the wall and it came crashing down.

Unbelievably, the Tenth had failed to take the wall. There were no more ladders, and the men were just helplessly taking missiles, crouched under the wall. The Seventh was doing no better, and Livy was looking hard for his men. The moat was proving too much of a challenge, and heavy missile fire was making it impossible to get the ladders across the moat. Too many men were being wounded or killed.

Caesar decided to sound the recall, and the two legions withdrew in good order, walking backwards, shields facing the enemy, and archers continuing to take a toll of the defenders.

There was a loud cheer from the walls. This was answered with a volley of ballista bolts, which swept away many of the prematurely elated defenders. After that there was quiet.

Caesar walked over to them, took a goblet of wine, and drained it. He looked frustrated. He bit his lip and then looked at Antony. He then undid the straps of his heavily plumed helmet and took it off. His bald pate was soaked in perspiration.

"I miscalculated, Antony," he said. "These cursed *oppidums* cannot be taken by a cursory assault. They need to be reduced by slow, methodical means. It will require engineering. I won't make the same mistake again," he said in a distracted manner.

"Report to my tent at the eighth hour. Go get some rest and see to your men in the meantime," Caesar ordered and then stalked off.

The Romans formed a ring round the Oppidium and made three camps housing two legions each. The Seventh legion was lodged with the Twelfth, and Livy decided to park the raiders with the Seventh as usual. He found a comfortable spot for the raiders to encamp within the palisade and left them to Biorix and Paulus. He then went off to look for Galienus and his century, the Sixth Century of the Eighth Cohort.

He found his men comfortably camped and starting their dinner. Acting centurion, Galienus, spotted him and immediately came up with

Optio Decimus. "Greetings, Commander," Galienus greeted with a broad smile. "We heard about your heroic stand by the river. Took on the whole Suessione Army and stopped them dead in their tracks. The men are all very excited about your exploits. They feel that your victories are also somewhat theirs."

Livy was too exhausted to return the enthusiasm. "How did our boys do at the assault today?"

"We got off light, sir. It was damned close thing. They got us pinned in the moat, and getting those clumsy ladders across was hell. Fortunately, none of your century was killed, and we got four men wounded but all will recover. Fortuna was on our side today," Galienus reported.

Livy was relieved. "The raiders weren't as lucky Galienus. I am truly relieved the century got off lightly."

"We never even got near the walls. They were hurling everything they could lay their hand on at us. We did account for a few with our *pila*, though," Galienus added.

"Right, let the men eat and get an early night. I am sure Caesar will renew the assault tomorrow."

"Will you join us for the evening meal?" Galienus asked.

"Certainly, I'll just go to my tent awhile and freshen up."

Livy found his tent all set up with the furniture arranged neatly, ready for use. Even his camp bed had been made. His legionaries had obviously been concerned about the comfort of their now-famous commander. There was a basin of water to wash, and Livy tried to wash off as much of the blood and dust from his body as he could. He had just stripped naked when a voice came from the door flaps.

"Centurion Gaius Livius, may I come in?" It was a woman's voice, and before he could respond, Servilia came in and gave him the once-over with a smile. She took in the sight of his well-toned naked body with some satisfaction. Livy was too tired to try and cover up and just looked at her with nonchalance. He was sweaty, and streaks of blood smeared his body.

"I see for myself what my girls have been raving about," she said teasingly.

"Welcome to my humble tent, lady. To what do I owe this honour, and how can I help you?" Livy grinned. He continued to wash himself. "Can I offer you some water?" He gestured to the pitcher. "I doubt I have any wine about the place." He looked around.

"Well, I happen to have a wineskin right here. The best *falernian*," she replied. "We can have a portion together to celebrate your victory today. Caesar told me all about it."

"By all means. Goblets are over there. Do pour us a glass," Livy said.

Servilia poured two goblets, un-watered, and sat herself on his camp bed.

"I came to thank you for saving Caesar's life. Not many people know about it and you have been surprisingly discreet, but as you know, Caesar and I are rather close," she began.

"I understand he has a great fondness for you, and you have a relationship spanning many years." Livy smiled politely, staring unabashed at her impressive cleavage. Her *stola* was cut so low that her two globes seemed about to liberate themselves at any moment.

Servilia was impressed that he had answered in a neutral, polite, and non-judgemental way. Once more she smiled charmingly. "You are astute for one so young. For political reasons, Caesar cannot openly reward you or promote you as you so richly deserve, but he is not ungrateful. I have come to offer you an interim small reward, which we hope would show our gratitude till we can show our appreciation more fully."

Livy was curious. "I am your servant, My Lady."

"I notice you were rather fond of two of my girls. They in turn have told me you were a perfect gentleman and both were positive about you after the first encounter. I will send you both girls tonight at Caesar's expense, of course."

"I am deeply honoured, My Lady."

"There's more. You may keep one of them as your personal companion till the end of the campaign or till my establishment withdraws from the army. Furthermore if you are not satisfied with the two girls, you may replace them with any of the others from my collection." She said all this with a straight face like a teacher explaining to a young student.

Livy drained his wine as he considered his good fortune.

Servilia poured more wine into Livy's goblet.

"I am speechless," Livy said. "On my pay, I wouldn't have been able to afford even one night with your lovely girls. It is a most generous gift."

"Caesar realises you have your normal male needs, and he does not want you to have to resort to the common *lupanaria* among the camp followers," Servilia continued. "Now that you are of senatorial rank, though not of senatorial means, he feels that you should have your basic needs met like any other Roman of some substance."

"Please convey to him my deepest gratitude." Livy bowed graciously. "Of course, this would be useful to you as well."

"Certainly, I now have one regular assured customer." She laughed.

They toasted and drank deeply from the un-watered wine. "Excellent vintage, My Lady," Livy complimented. "*Falernian*, and at least five years old," Livy commented.

"You know wine?" Servilia asked.

"My father used to make some though his main crop was olives." Livy obliged.

"You never cease to amaze me, young man. I have half a mind to have you for myself." Servilia teased him with a naughty grin.

"It would be an honour that I wouldn't dare accept, My Lady," Livy said.

"How courteously expressed! You have the silvery tongue of a serpent, Centurion. I think you may be dangerous," Servilia said with a pout.

"Not at all. I think you are a most remarkable lady, and I would really like us to be friends."

"So would I, young man. You'll need a political ally as you move up the ranks and join the senate."

"I'm only a common soldier, My Lady."

"I don't think you will remain one for long. You have talent. I have known many men." Livy caught the double meaning. "And I can always spot the good ones."

"I would hope to prove you right."

"I have no doubts you will," Servilia said with conviction. "I will take my leave now." She held out her hand.

Livy took it gently and kissed it. To his surprise, she leaned forward and gave him a light kiss on his cheek. Her floral scent was tantalising.

"I look forward to talking more with you soon."

"And I likewise, My Lady."

"The girls will be delivered to your tent by the ninth hour." She reverted to the voice of a madam once more.

She turned around and headed for the exit. Livy parted the flaps as she passed. Outside, a male slave was waiting with her horse. She was given a hand to mount her beautiful white mare. As she rode off, she turned to take one last look at Livy.

Livy smiled to himself and looked forward to the evening. First, there were a few duties to perform. He suddenly realised that he had been stark naked all this while.

Livy joined his century for a simple dinner. One of the soldiers had managed to trade for a couple of chickens from the camp followers, and the century were treated to a rich chicken stew to eat with their hard tack or *bucellatum*. Several pieces of the rock-hard bread had been mixed in the stew to thicken it. Some locally gathered herbs had gotten into the stew to give it a delicious fragrance. It was a simple meal supplemented with some fruit, bacon, and cheese.

Livy contributed several wineskins, which he managed to trade from the quartermaster for a few looted trinkets. The men were grateful for this. After the meal, he had gone over to check on the raiders, who had also made themselves comfortable. Most of them were dead tired and had already gone to sleep. Biorix and Paulus were still awake, however, and had posted pickets all round the camp. He found his two commanders sitting by a fire with two Belgic girls. He recognised the girls, who were from Bibrax.

"Greetings, Centurion, what brings you to our humble abode?" Paulus greeted.

"I thought you might like some good red wine to go with that fine bird there." Livy motioned at the large bird roasting over the fire, giving off the most delicious aroma. He threw them a large wineskin.

"That, sir, is a roast goose that hunter Biorix here shot just this evening," Paulus replied.

"Smells incredible," Livy said. "What did you put on it?"

"Rosemary and thyme, sir," Biorix replied. "Picked it off the forest, I did."

"Biorix here is not only a great hunter but an expert chef," Paulus said proudly at the same time giving a firm squeeze to the breast of one of the girls.

She squealed and slapped at his hand with a loud smack.

"This is Eala, by the way, and that one is Sabia," Biorix introduced. "This is our commander, the famous Centurion Gaius Livius." He took a deep gulp from the wineskin and passed it to Eala, who also drank deeply.

Livy started to notice the two women. Eala was with Biorix, and she had dark long hair and a fair smooth complexion. She was a little plump for his taste, but she had a pair of formidable breasts, the top of which were visible over her low-cut tunic. Sabia was slim, petite, and blonde. Paulus had already stripped her topless and was busy nibbling her nipples.

Livy sat himself down and took a swig from the wineskin when it came his way. Paulus was obviously past caring about formalities and had his head buried between Sabia's breasts. Livy addressed Biorix. "The men did really well today. I am sure Caesar will award the raiders unit honours."

"Aye, I'm sure he will, but the men are happy already. We got a whole bunch of loot, and the lads all feel pretty rich. Besides, they are flush with victory."

"Have you had the stuff valued?" Livy asked.

"We had the merchants from the camp followers over, and he valued the stuff for us. Guess how much?" Biorix winked.

Livy held up his hands. "You tell me."

"More than 200,000 dinars worth of gold and silver," Biorix exclaimed in triumph. "As commander, you get a quarter, which still leaves lots for the rest of us."

Livy was stunned speechless.

"You're quite a rich man now, Centurion Gaius Livius. You've got nearly 50,000 dinars." Biorix slapped his open palms. "We are the richest unit in the army. It came mostly from those noble cavalrymen we slaughtered."

"I guess the men will be wanting to survive this war now."

"You can bet your arse on that, sir," Biorix said.

"Call me Gaius," Livy said. "We're partners now, Paulus, you, and me. We can go by first names. Well, in private anyway." Livy smiled broadly.

"Just try not to get us killed from now on," Biorix joked. "We will convert the lot into cash with the merchants and have them bank the money for us back in the Roman province. We can all go collect our share after the campaign, if we still live. The merchant will give each of us a signed receipt with the amount stated on it. Don't worry, sir, I'll organise everything."

Eala had put a hand under Biorix's tunic and the man suddenly fell silent. He was enjoying her ministrations.

"You guys have your evening cut out. Maybe best I get going." Livy suddenly felt a little embarrassed.

"Aw, don't be shy, Gaius, we got all night to poke these gals. They'll both be sore by the time we finish with them." Biorix chuckled. "Tell you what, let me cut you a piece of this excellent goose here before you go. It's about done now."

Biorix took up a sharp knife and quartered the bird. He wrapped one quarter in a cloth, burning his fingers in the process. He tied up the bundle and gave it to Livy.

"My compliments, Gaius, and thanks for the booze." Biorix offered the meat nicely packed and tied into a package.

Livy was touched and gave him a long hug. "I am glad I have friends like you, Biorix,"

"Me likewise, Gaius, me likewise,"

Livy turned to go. "Bye, Paulus,"

There was no reply. He noticed that Sabia was completely naked now, and Paulus was on top of her. He raised a hand to wave. Realising he was no longer needed, Livy decided to make his way home.

Back in his tent, he laid out some fruit and bread on the table. He unwrapped the delicious roast goose and arranged it on a plate. He also got out a few goblets for wine. He had two wineskins left to entertain his guests.

He then settled down on his camp bed to await his guests. While waiting, he dozed off.

He was awakened by a male voice. "Begging your pardon, sir?" the legionary spoke politely. "You have visitors, Centurion."

Livy awoke with a start. "Let them in."

The brazier had burnt down somewhat, but there was still enough light to make out the two feminine figures coming in through the tent flaps. There were both clad in cloaks and hoods. The legionary stuck his head in. Livy recognised the man.

"That will be all, Priscus. You may return to your station."

The man saluted and left after giving the two girls a quick once-over. "These officers get all the best bitches," he thought silently to himself as he compared Stena and Artemisia to the skanky ladies among the camp followers.

"We heard about your big battle at the river," Artemisia began as she started taking off her cloak, revealing a low-cut, silk, Greek chiton underneath. The long skirt had been slit to her upper thighs, revealing her smooth, perfect legs. "It reminded me immediately of my ancestors at Thermopylae, three hundred against the Persian host of Xerxes. The bravery of you and your men will live down in history." She looked at him triumphantly.

"Not quite the same, my dear. Firstly, there were only 50,000 of the barbarians and not two million as at the Fiery Gates of Thermopylae. Then my men were not heavy hoplites like Leonidas and his men, though some say they fought in the nude. Thirdly, we had the help of some very large and competent Germans." Livy smiled amiably.

"Leonidas had the Thespians and other Greek contingents, but it will be the Spartans who will be remembered, just like your raiders. 'Livy's raiders' they are called now."

Stena had now undressed, revealing a short black tunic which barely covered her groin. The dress was semi-transparent, and her breast was visible through the cloth.

"That's a very sexy dress, Stena," Livy said admiringly.

"I wore it just for you, Centurion." She laughed a tinkling laugh.

"Can we eat? We're famished," Artemisia said.

"That roast looks delicious. What is it?" Stena asked.

"Help yourselves, ladies. That's roast goose with Thyme and Rosemary, compliments of my Remi chef," Livy declared.

The girls were delighted and tucked in immediately. Stena was thoughtful enough to detach the drumstick and serve it to Livy. She looked at him somewhat adoringly, and Livy was somewhat alarmed that the poor girl might be infatuated with him.

Artemisia was devouring the goose with relish. "Your Remi chef is excellent. I would like to meet him and learn his recipe," Artemisia mumbled between mouthfuls.

Dinner was spent retelling the battle by the river. Artemisia seemed fascinated by the military details while Stena was awed by the description of blood and gore. They ate all the food and finished most of the wine. The girls lost most of their inhibitions and started to dance erotically with each other. It was strange because there was no music. Livy decided that they probably danced to an imaginary melody.

The effect of the wine started to get to him. Slowly he drifted to sleep. The last thing he remembered was seeing the two girls kissing each other. He dreamt of his home in Tarraco. He was a twelve-year-old boy again splashing in the sea with Aurora. He chased her along the surf, and her bare feet made lonely imprints on the beach. A gull screeched overhead, and the clouds looked like fleece against the azure sky.

He was awakened by a loud male voice. It was Galienus, the acting centurion. "Wake up, sir. I am sorry to interrupt, but Caesar wants you." He shook Livy awake. "I am truly sorry, sir. I didn't realise you had company."

Stena was lying naked beside him with one arm draped across his chest. She was snoring softly. Her breath was heavy with alcohol. The tent was dark as the brazier merely glowed with the dying embers. He nearly stepped on Artemisia as he got up. She had passed out just beside the camp bed. He noticed a streak of saliva smearing one corner of her luscious lips.

"What happened?" he asked finally.

"The enemy army has arrived. Looks like they marched through the night." He helped Livy into his *subarmalis*, armour, belt, sword, and helmet. "I've brought your horse so you can ride quickly to headquarters."

"Thanks so much, Galienus. Take care of the men while I am gone and tell these two to stay here. I don't want them wandering around alone in the dark."

"Of course, sir. These two are hot! Where did they come from?" Galienus could not help but to ask.

"They are out of your reach, Galienus, out of my reach as well. They are meant for the legates, tribunes, and senatorial types," Livy remarked.

"How come they're in your tent then, sir?" Galienus remarked.

"It's a long story, Galienus. I'll see you later." Livy jumped on his horse and rode off.

Caesar's headquarters was bustling. There was already a whole crowd of officers present. The adjutant motioned for silence, and Caesar addressed his officers.

"The enemy army is only five miles away. Numbers-wise we are evenly matched, but the quality of our troops is far superior. A small force of raiders and German cavalry turned back their whole army yesterday."

Livy glowed with pride as Caesar looked in his direction.

"If we engage them, we will surely destroy them. There is no doubt about that. We will take significant casualties, however. They will fight hard to come to the rescue of their city." Caesar paused for breath.

"I have a better plan which will achieve victory at minimal cost to us. We will not engage them in force. We will harass them with light troops continuously, but when they attack, we will withdraw. We will allow them to fight their way into Noviodunum. They will think they have succeeded when the whole army gets into the city."

The officers could already see what was coming, and many nodded and murmured their approval.

"Once the army is in the city, we will close the trap and complete the blockade on all sides. No one will be able to get out. There is insufficient food for the whole army and the inhabitants, and they cannot withstand a siege. We will bombard them with artillery, and they will soon capitulate. What I intend to achieve is a bloodless victory, at least for our side."

There was unanimous agreement for this brilliant plan.

The adjutant handed orders to the various commanders involved in the night operation. The enemy would be subjected to a series of hit-and-run attacks, which would melt away once the enemy organises a counter-attack. The idea was to give the impression that the Romans were trying their best to stop the army from reaching Noviodunum. In the confusion of the darkness, Caesar hoped the ruse would not be discovered till too late. Once the army was ensconced in the hill fort, it was doomed. The town was already surrounded on three sides with ditches, sharpened stakes, and palisades. It would not be too difficult to seal off the remaining side. The Suessiones would then be trapped like chickens in a coop.

Livy was given his order in a sealed scroll. His raiders were to be the third wave of attackers. No doubt other auxiliary units were to make their demonstrations first. A path had been cleared for the Suessione Army to reach Noviodunum, but Caesar had planned all manner of distractions for them.

CHAPTER 15

The skilful strategist defeats the enemy without doing battle, captures the city without laying siege.

Galba was riding behind the first contingent. These were his best troops. Right in the front were heavily armoured spearmen, 3,000 strong. This was followed by armoured axemen, 2,000 strong. Then came Galba, riding with his household cavalry, which numbered about 500 horses.

The whole army was exhausted after marching at a fast pace all day. They had been desperate to get to Noviodunum, which, the last messenger said, was under siege by the Romans. Galba prayed to Thanatos, the god of Thunder, that he would reach his people in time.

Although occasional enemy scouts were seen there had, till now, no major activity from the enemy. The tramping of the army made a loud din that shattered the night. The men carried torches to light the way as the moon was hidden by clouds.

About a mile away, the Roman prefect of artillery gave the order to light the fireballs. These were rocks wrapped in cloth soaked in flammable oil. Once the missiles were alight, he gave the order to fire. There were loud thwacks as the heavy *onagers* were fired, and the flaming missiles arched upwards and down on the enemy army. About a score of the flaming incendiaries fell all round and some into the enemy army. There were loud screams as men caught fire or were crushed. Formations dissolved as men dove for cover.

One missile landed squarely into the formation of household cavalry, flattening a group of horsemen and setting a few others on fire. The artillerymen reloaded and fired a second volley, causing even more havoc.

Before the Suessiones could recover, they were hit by a storm of arrows fired by the Cretan archers, who were hiding in the surrounding brush. Dozens of warriors were hit before they could put up their shields. The enemy officers quickly organised protection from the arrows, locking shields and forming shield walls.

The warriors then charged the archers, who immediately ceased firing and ran for their lives. The lightly armed archers easily outran the tired warriors. Just to be sure that they escaped, a second echelon of archers now opened fire on the pursuing warriors, hitting many. Most of the rest withdrew back into the ranks.

The few impetuous warriors who continued to pursue, fell prey to more arrows or roaming Roman cavalry.

Galba immediately issued orders for the army to stay in formation and not to pursue any attacks by light troops. The army continued their march towards the town.

There was a brief respite. Galba and his men breathed a sigh of relief. They had beaten off the Romans, and there didn't seem to be any sign of big formations between here and the town. His scouts reported that the Romans may have neglected to defend this route heavily. He may yet save his capital, Galba thought. He felt encouraged. He had led this phase of the operations himself rather than rely on his stupid advisors. Perhaps he had regained the favour of the gods.

A few moments later, his confidence was shattered once more. Heavy metal bolts started flying in from everywhere. The Romans had brought up their ballistae and scorpions. Whole files of men were skewered by the heavy weapons. Once again, the army was thrown into confusion as men screamed and died all round. There seemed to be no defence as the projectiles flew with such force that they pierced shields easily and impaled several men simultaneously.

The warriors went to ground, keeping low to avoid the missiles, and sought shelter behind trees and rocks. Once again, the organisation dissolved and the army stopped moving forward. Galba shouted and screamed for the men to get up and keep moving forward. Few obeyed.

Then the missiles suddenly stopped. Galba knew he could not relax. What was next?

Suddenly, there were ululations all around, and javelins started falling all round the army. At the same time, rocks and pellets seemed to be coming out of the dark. Galba saw several of the heavy axemen skewered by javelins and the dark shapes of Numidian light infantry flitting about in the darkness.

Suddenly there was a loud thud, and he turned to see the face of the cavalryman next to him turned into bloody pulp. He had been hit by a slingshot and collapsed a moment later. A stone hit his horse, and the animal reared in pain. Galba just managed to hold on.

The warriors got back into formation and advanced on their tormentors in close formation, shields locked to defend against stones and javelins. The Numidians were using Roman javelins which deformed on impact. They were also impossible to pull out once stuck in a shield, and many shields were lost, leaving their owners totally vulnerable.

The Numidians and their companion Balearic slingers withdrew quickly in the face of the counter-attack. The Belgic warriors threw their spears at them and some fired arrows, but it was difficult to hit anything in the dark as the light troops were in skirmishing formation and well dispersed.

Soon they gave up, got back into marching formation, and continued trekking forward. Galba hoped that this was the last attack and that there would be little opposition getting into the town itself. As the town came into sight, the terrain expanded into an open space. Galba ordered the army to deploy, in case they faced final opposition just before the town. The plain seemed empty though, and he was elated. The town seemed to be still in Belgic hands. "We have made it," he thought.

Just then a line of cavalry appeared before him. It didn't seem like a large force. In the dark, he could not make out their identity.

He ordered his remaining cavalry to deploy in front. He addressed his army.

"There lies our capital Noviodunum. The Romans have failed to capture it. There lie our women, our children, and all we hold dear. It is a mere league away. You have suffered much and come this far. We are almost home. Let's make one last effort and sweep this tiny Roman force away, and we will sleep in our homes tonight."

The army cheered. They could see the end of their suffering.

"My noble cavalry will lead the way. We will charge and all of you will follow." Galba raised his jewel-encrusted sword and pointed forward.

At that moment, fireballs descended from the heavens as the *onagers* started their barrage once more. The whole army gave a war cry with all their strength and charged for the safety of the town.

Livy watched calmly as the whole Suessione host careened wildly towards his thin line of men. He had briefed them thoroughly, and they knew exactly what to do. At 300 yards they fired the first volley, hitting mainly horses who went down dislodging their riders. After that, it was fire at will, mainly aimed at the riders.

At 200 yards, the Belgic horsemen met with a catastrophic surprise as they hit a well-camouflaged ditch, and most of the horses fell into it. The sides were too deep for the horses to climb out. A few horsemen managed to jump the ditch at the last moment as they were somewhat behind. Livy's men preferentially shot them down. Livy could see the fancy black plume of Galba's helmet. He had just reigned in short of the ditch.

Livy targeted him and shot his horse from under him. The horse took the arrow in the chest and collapsed. Galba fell heavily on his back and was struggling to get up. Livy notched another arrow and shot it into his leg. That would reduce his mobility a bit, he decided.

The cavalry was all but obliterated, and the rest of the army clambered into the ditch and out the other side and continued running for the city. Livy motioned for his men to withdraw to let the panicked host run by. The Cretan archers and the Numidian light infantry had now gathered at the sides to pick off any stragglers and encourage the army to move straight towards the town. The people of the town were gathered on the battlements, shouting encouragement. The gates were opened wide, and the army started to stream towards it. The Romans did nothing to discourage them. Within a short time, the whole army had retreated into the town. The Romans ceased firing, and two legions immediately closed the trap, deploying just beyond the ditch in solid lines. More soldiers began to build a barricade behind the legions. The Suessiones were now trapped.

Livy's men helped the light troops sort through the enemy wounded. More experienced now, they concentrated on the cavalry and the elite infantry, where there were richer pickings. Several thousand enemy warriors were captured. Most of them lightly wounded. The badly wounded were dispatched, and the dead were piled up together within sight of the town.

Livy rode off to report to Caesar. It was still a few hours till dawn, and Caesar had taken off his armour and was dealing with paperwork in his tent. Servilia was with him. Livy was one of the first to report in.

"Centurion Livius, I am glad to see that you survived once more. The plan worked well and the hungry, demoralised enemy army is now trapped in that town with insufficient food. Did you sustain any casualties?"

"None, My Lord," Livy answered. He was exhausted.

"I hear you had a personal encounter with King Galba."

"I killed his horse and put an arrow in his thigh," Livy said.

"Why didn't you kill him?" Caesar asked.

"I thought he might come in useful once his tribe surrenders."

"Good thinking, young man. You might be of use to me in the senate yet." Caesar gave a sly smile.

"I guess you didn't have time to enjoy the delightful present I sent you."

"We were interrupted, sir."

Caesar turned to Servilia. "I think it only fair that we make up this evening, don't you think?"

"Certainly, My Lord." She smiled at Livy. "Have another night at my expense," she said generously.

"Tomorrow I will need you to help me negotiate with the enemy. We will need the cooperation of those noble prisoners. Did you have any problems with language the last time you met the king?" Caesar asked.

"I think we understood each other, My Lord," Livy assured him.

"Well, run along then and go get some rest. The Suessiones aren't going anywhere. By morning, they will be completely surrounded with palisades, stakes, several layers of ditches, and firing platforms for my artillery. They will soon realise their position is untenable." Caesar was confident. "Report to my tent at the eighth hour," he commanded.

Livy saluted and left. Servilia waved goodbye and smiled at him.

Back at the tent, the girls had woken up and were openly happy to see him. They both jumped on him very quickly, removing his armour, weapons, and tunic. They then sat him down and proceeded to clean him with water from a basin. Artemisia got behind him and scrubbed his back while Stena washed his front. She took pains to clean the dirt from his face, ears, around his eyes, and his neck. At one moment her face was really close to his, and he was looking into her eyes. She closed her eyes and kissed him very passionately. Livy closed his eyes and enjoyed her soft lips and fragrant breath.

Artemisia gave his flanks a sharp poke, which made him jump. "Now let's not get romantic, you two," she said, sounding a little jealous. Livy turned around, grabbed her head, and gave her a long wet kiss. Artemisia struggled slightly with surprise, then just relaxed and enjoyed it. Livy realised he had to be a little careful with the girls and take pains to be somewhat impartial. Yet, he would have to choose between them soon. It was a difficult choice. Both girls had a lot going for them. Both would make excellent companions, but he would enjoy them in different ways. He was happy for the reprieve. He didn't have to decide till the following morning.

The girls finished with his toilet. They both stood staring at him. A pillar of flesh had arisen between his legs. Stena looked on with silent fascination, one hand over her mouth. Artemisia, on the other hand, licked her lips with her pink tongue and then said, "I think it's my turn to go first."

The next morning, Livy left the two girls sleeping on his couch. He covered their naked bodies with a blanket. Their bodies were intertwined as if they were coupling. He washed his hands and face in a basin, then hurriedly dressed in the full centurion's regalia. Today, his duties would be diplomacy rather than combat.

The *actuarius* who was assigned to his century was waiting outside his tent. "Good morning, Centurion. Would you have the time to go through some of these accounts and reports, sir?" Livy realised that he had been neglecting the paperwork.

"I have more important duties at present," he said. "See if Galienus can look through some of this stuff, and I will certainly take a look at them later," Livy said.

"But, sir," the clerk persisted.

"I said, later." Livy looked him in the eye and tried to appear as intimidating as possible.

"Yes, sir." the clerk finally gave in.

Livy felt a little guilty for neglecting the affairs of the century, but it was true that he had more important matters to attend to of late. He realised that he had conveniently also included cavorting with whores as priority activities. He didn't feel guilty for long. The girls were special.

It was still chilly and mist lay on ground. The sun, however, was up early today, and the day would soon warm up. There was a strange tranquillity around as he passed through the Roman camp. The soldiers were having breakfast or kitting up, but they moved with a strange silence.

Caesar's tent was as usual already bustling with activity. Livy arrived just before the eighth hour as appointed. The guards recognised him and saluted as he went into the tent. Crassus and Mark Antony were present as were the two Suessiones noblemen whom he had captured only yesterday.

"Good morning, Centurion Livius, you are just the person we need. Your language skills are crucial at this stage of the game." Caesar looked preoccupied.

"I am at your service, sir." Livy saluted smartly. He also nodded to Crassus and Antony, who were also dressed in full regalia.

"You three are going to be the chief negotiators. Antony will be my spokesman. I think he has earned his role after yesterday," Caesar explained. "Now, about these two gentlemen," He pointed to the two enemy nobles. "How can we make some use of them."

"I gather they have been well treated?" Crassus asked.

"I gave them a good breakfast this morning," Caesar said.

"More than we can expect if the roles were reversed," Antony added.

"We should take them along. I think both of them see the futility of resistance and may help to talk some sense into King Galba," Crassus offered.

"All right, make sure they are heavily guarded and give orders to their escorts to kill them if they try to escape," Caesar ordered.

"Livius, all you have to do is translate. Let Antony do the talking. He knows what to say," Caesar said, looking at Livy.

Sometime later, Livy waited with the negotiating party behind the Roman lines, which faced the front gate of the town. Horns and trumpets sounded, and a half-dozen huge siege towers started to move forward. The trenches had been bridged to allow the monstrous contraptions to be pushed across. Caesar also had a dozen heavy *onagers* ranged in front of the town walls. Large braziers were lighted next to each artillery piece, leaving the defenders no doubt that incendiary was going to be used. Two dozen ballistae were also brought up.

Caesar had recovered all his eight legions, and he now paraded all eight of them in a never-ending cordon, two on each side of the town. When the defenders looked out, he wanted to strike fear into them that what faced them would be total annihilation if they resisted. The legions decked in full regalia with all their banners fluttering and drums beating were an awesome sight. To the Suessiones, they looked like an army from another world.

Galba was carried on to the walls to view the Roman host. His leg wound was festering, and he was in considerable pain. He looked out on the plains around Noviodunum and shuddered. He had never before seen such monstrous machines as the siege towers, and he was awed by the number of ballistae and *onagers*. His men had already had a demonstration of their deadliness the previous night.

The town behind him was crowded with soldiers and civilians. There were thousands of wounded moaning and screaming in pain. Their cries added to the cries of the bereaved women whose husbands, brothers, and fathers had perished. The people did not have enough food to last long. It was a scene from Hades. He knew that the Romans could set the town alight with their infernal incendiary machines. A fire breaking out in the town would be catastrophic because it was so crowded and there was nowhere to run.

Galba missed his advisor Vindiacos. He never felt so alone. "Bring me the cursed priest Bratronos," he ordered his aide.

There was a moment of embarrassed silence. One of his aides then finally spoke. "The priest is nowhere to be found, Your Majesty."

Galba was furious. "Didn't I order him to be kept under guard?" he screamed.

"Yes, My Lord, but he overpowered the guard and escaped."

"I am surrounded by imbeciles," Galba growled. "No wonder the Romans have so easily got the better of us." He felt suddenly beaten and depressed. His leg really hurt.

"Look there, Your Majesty. They are sending an emissary. Perhaps they want to talk." Everyone was excited. Perhaps there was a way out without blood.

The emissary was Biorix. He had a fast horse and carried a white flag. He rode bravely up to the walls. "I have a message for King Galba," he said loudly in the Belgian tongue.

"I am King Galba," the king replied from the walls.

"Caesar offers you terms if you surrender. If you wish to parley, we will meet between our lines in one hour," Biorix added.

Galba thought for a moment. There really was no choice. "Tell Caesar I accept."

"Bring no more than ten men in your party. Our side will not exceed this number. Personal weapons only, no bows, shields, spears, or javelins. Do you accept these conditions?" Biorix asked.

"Yes. I accept," Galba confirmed.

"Thank you, Your Majesty. We will meet in an hour then." Biorix waved and galloped back to the Roman lines.

Antony prepared his party. The three officers would be Crassus, Livy, and himself. The two Suessione nobles would come along as bargaining chips. Biorix would be included in case there were language difficulties, and then four German bodyguard cavalry, in case there was trouble. Everyone would only be armed with their personal swords.

Exactly one hour later, the gates of Noviodunum opened. A cart pulled by a single horse escorted by eight well-armoured cavalry came out and rode towards the meeting area. Galba was sitting in the cart.

There was a deafening silence as both sides watched the proceedings anxiously.

Antony motioned his party forward. They walked their horses slowly and deliberately.

The Suessione party stopped, and only Galba came forward in his cart with his driver.

Antony motioned his party to halt and came forward only with Livy.

"Greetings, Your Majesty. I bring you best wishes from Caesar," Antony said cheerily. "I am Marcus Antonius, tribune and senator of Rome." Livy translated.

Galba looked pained and annoyed. "And I am King Galba, son of Diviviacus, ruler of the Suessiones, and overlord of all the Belgic tribes. Get to the point, Roman."

Livy continued translating softly.

"I know you." Galba looked at Livy with recognition. "You're the boy who came to our camp. Why is it every time I see you bad things happen."

"It's a pleasure to see you again too, Your Majesty," Livy replied.

"Do you wish to surrender, You Majesty?" Antony asked amiably.

"What are the terms?" Galba asked.

"Caesar asks for unconditional surrender," Antony said firmly.

"Those are harsh terms," Galba replied.

"It's worse if you don't," Anthony reasoned. "I can assure you that Caesar has a magnanimous character. There will be no further loss of life. None of your people will be killed."

"Enslavement?" Galba asked.

"That would be up to Caesar," Antony said.

"We would be entirely at his mercy." Galba was outraged.

"It's that or be totally annihilated." Antony gestured at the siege towers and artillery. "If you don't agree, we will begin our assault immediately. Once the first siege tower or battering ram touches your walls, no surrender would be accepted.

Galba's countenance went dark. He was struggling within himself. He was so outraged that he felt like throwing himself at the Romans and going down fighting. Then he remembered that all his people would die. At least the Romans had promised not to kill anyone.

"All right, we surrender. Promise me on your honour that no one will be killed."

Antony smiled. "I promise you on my honour. Tell your men to throw down their arms."

Galba signalled, and his escort threw down their swords and dismounted.

"Please wait here, Your Majesty. I will bring Caesar, and he will tell you what he requires of you." Antony lifted his sword high and waved it.

There was a loud cheer from the Roman Army. There would be no more killing today. Livy was delighted. More delighted than any of his previous battle victories. It was wonderful to win bloodlessly.

He got down from his horse and went to Galba. "May I have your sword, Your Majesty?" he requested politely. Galba unsheathed his sword and gave it to him. It was a heavy sword made of the best steel. The handle was rich with carvings and encrusted with precious stones. This would be a valuable trophy for Caesar.

"You made the right choice, Your Majesty," Livy assured him. "I think Caesar will treat you and your people better than you expect. Much better than if you were defeated by your rival Belgic or Gaulish tribes or, worse still, the Germans."

Galba looked defeated and morose. "I hope you are right, young man. I hope you are right," he said.

Sometime later, a tribune rode down to them. "Caesar invites you to join him in his tent," The tribune said. "The king's escort is to remain here. You three officers are required to escort His Majesty."

The cart bearing Galba was escorted into the Roman lines stopping at Caesar's tent, which had been spruced up to receive the visitor. Galba was helped into the tent by Crassus and Livy and sat on a couch facing Caesar, who was sitting on a well-crafted *curile* chair. He was dressed in his white uniform with silver armour and helmet.

"I bid His Majesty welcome," Caesar began. Livy translated, and Galba bowed. He looked totally resigned to his fate.

"You have shown great wisdom in putting yourself and the fate of your people in my hands," Caesar said. "You have also demonstrated trust in my mercy."

"This leads me to the belief that Rome and your people have some future together," Caesar continued.

Galba started to take interest, and his demeanour suddenly changed. "What do you mean, Caesar?"

"I will give you much better terms than you deserve," Caesar said. "Firstly, your army will give up all their arms. No exceptions. Secondly, Noviodunum will open its gates to us. I promise there will be no raping and pillaging. Your nation will become a protectorate of Rome and our ally. You will accept Rome to be your overlord and a Roman prefect will be appointed to administer your region. You and your nobles may form a council to advise him. You will be allowed to keep your title as king but will be subordinated to my prefect. Some of your warriors will be inducted into my army as auxiliaries. We will select the best of them. They will serve for the duration of this war."

Galba suddenly had hope. He was to remain king, and there was no mention of slavery. "Your magnanimity is unbelievable, My Lord Caesar," Galba said.

"Don't be too happy. There is more," Caesar said. "We will exact compensation in gold for raising arms against us. There will be a one-time payment and then a yearly tribute. My staff will work out the amount payable. You are further to provide me 500 hostages. I want the children of all your nobles, including your sons."

Galba seemed pained by this last. "I suppose it's a small price to pay for peace," Galba said.

"Don't worry. I will treat the hostages well. They will not be enslaved. I also need a number of your nobles as hostages."

"Agreed," Galba said in a resigned tone.

"There is one last thing. My men have fought long and hard and endured much hardship. No doubt your men have as well. We are the victorious, however, and there must be a price. Your people are to help keep us supplied for the duration of this Belgian campaign. Furthermore, your town will be responsible for our needs while we are encamped here. This includes the services of your women," Caesar said with a straight face.

"What do you mean? You said there will be no rape or pillaging."

"Oh, of course there will be no rape. Your women will give themselves to my men willingly. I leave it to you to persuade them," Caesar said.

Galba was outraged, but he quickly saw that any other alternative would be worse.

"As a concession, we won't stay for more than two nights as I intend to move on to your friends, the Bellovaci next." He smiled reassuringly.

"I think your women won't mind putting themselves out for just two nights. I further guarantee that your people will not be enslaved, besides the ones we have already captured in battle. There will be no executions and no further bloodshed," Caesar said.

Galba's emotions ran back and forth from relief to outrage. Finally he calmed himself. "Shit, this leg still hurt like Hades," he thought to himself.

"Will that be all, Caesar?" He fought to keep his anger to himself.

"For now," Caesar replied. "Deliver His Majesty back to his town, Antony," Caesar ordered.

"If you decide to comply willingly with all my demands, just open your gates," Caesar concluded.

Antony and the tribune escorted Galba back to his carriage for the trip back to the town.

Caesar turned to Crassus and Livy. He smiled. "That went rather well. The Suessiones have surrendered without us having to lose any more men."

Crassus and Livy were looking a little uncomfortable. Caesar noticed and asked "Are you two concerned about the last demand?"

"I agree with every demand, except the last, My Lord. It seems somewhat less than civilised." Crassus put it as politely as possible.

Caesar paused to gather his thoughts. "Livius, you agree?"

"Yes, My Lord."

"I appreciate honesty in both of you," Caesar said. "I have no choice but to do this. The men require some reward after all they have been through. I cannot give them gold because I need it myself to continue the campaign. If I do not look after the men's morale, they will soon be asking what they are fighting for."

The two men still looked somewhat disturbed.

"I am well aware that this makes us appear somewhat less civilised than we claim. Think of it this way. It is better the women come somewhat willingly, convinced that their sacrifice would save the lives of their men and children, than to let the men put the town to the sword. The women will get fucked one way or the other, but this way it's done without bloodshed on either side."

"I guess it's the lesser of two evils," Crassus said, convinced.

Livy kept his own counsel. He objected on moral and philosophical grounds, which could not be brushed away on the basis of pure expediency.

"I have news on another subject, Livius." Caesar changed the topic. "A good friend of yours, Decurion Decius from the Roman Equites, was ambushed by your Gaesatae friends and captured. Even now, the Gaesatae are holding him prisoner, and they have joined the Nervii Army."

Livy was immediately alarmed. Nothing good could come of being a prisoner of the Gaesatae or the Nervii. Horrible stories had circulated of torture and human sacrifices. "May I have permission to mount a rescue?"

"I understand your consternation, Livius, but your chances of success are nil if you just run off with your raiders north into enemy territory. This requires some thought and planning. We may need the help of our new Suessione allies, and you will need to go looking like Suessione cavalry and not Roman *exploratores*."

Livy checked himself and said, "I am at your disposal, My Lord."

"We will, of course, include you once I work out the details and get an expedition together. I won't be sending the raiders as a unit. If we do mount a rescue at all, it will be by a small special operations team," Caesar said.

Livy had some misgivings but again decided not to rock the boat for the time being. He would wait to see what Caesar had in mind.

"Today, we will be busy disarming the Suessiones and exacting our tribute. Tonight, the men will have their celebration. There will be a parade tomorrow morning at the ninth hour to award some unit citations. After that, I want to have a meeting with all the legates and prefects to plan our move against the Bellovaci."

"Will you be requiring my assistance in anything further today?" Livy asked.

"No. That will be all, Centurion. You may return to your unit."

Livy saluted and left.

Servilia slipped in from the back entrance of the tent. She came behind him, put her arms around his neck, and planted a kiss on his cheek. Caesar grabbed both her arms to pull her close.

"Did I do well, my dear?" Caesar asked her.

"You did brilliantly, like always," Servilia affirmed.

"It was close. We were almost out of money and supplies. Now the Suessiones will help finance the continuation of the campaign and not a moment too soon."

"If only they knew our situation," Servilia said. "What would you have done if they resisted."

"I would have pounded them with fireballs till their whole city was aflame then taken the city with an all-out assault. Many on both sides would have died. I think this outcome is the best for both sides. The Suessiones will not lose any more people and would slowly build up their economy once more with a little help from us."

"What about all their poor women?" Servilia teased.

"If I were them I would make the best of it. I have managed to seize a large quantity of wine from the surrounding vineyards, which should lessen their ordeal. I expect a lot of half-breed babies would result from tonight, which may in the long run aid the assimilation of this tribe to Rome," Caesar said with a smile.

"You always have the knack of looking at the bright side of things." Servilia laughed.

CHAPTER 16

Livy and his men watched from a hill as the legion tasked to administer the requisition of arms, food, and treasure went about their job. The legionaries were making a house-to-house search under strict supervision by their centurions, who had orders not to aggravate the residents of the town and to go about their task as politely as possible.

Livy watched as a long train of carts laden with treasure and food flowed from the town towards the Roman camp. An equally long train of empty carts went in the opposite direction. Officers from both armies supervised the work. Caesar had promised that a sufficient portion of food and a third of the treasure would be returned to the Suessiones. Galba had been allowed to send some of his retainers to oversee the distribution of the food and treasure.

"I heard about poor Decius," Biorix began. "Bad luck, getting captured by the Nervii. They are known to do terrible things to their prisoners."

"I had half a mind to take all the raiders after him, but Caesar has other ideas. On thinking it over, he was probably right. We wouldn't have stood a pig's chance of making it."

Biorix was somewhat amused by the expressions and laughed. "We would have been roast pig ourselves. I hear the Nervii sacrifice their prisoners to their god by roasting them in a wicker cage."

"I hear they let their dogs have you. Can't imagine being ripped about by dogs!" Paulus shuddered.

"For Decius's sake, I hope Caesar comes up with something quickly," Livy said.

"What do you want the men to do the rest of the day?" Biorix asked.

"I want the new boys to do more riding practice and some sword practice. I need them to be able to defend themselves in a melee. How are the wounded doing."

"Not so bad," Paulus replied. "Some of them may be rejoining us in a couple of days. I think we can put them on light duties. Any word about Kleon?"

"Last I heard, he too is recovering. The old goat must be an immortal." They all laughed.

"I just got an idea about the sword-fighting practice. I think I can produce a truly expert trainer."

The two other men raised their eyebrows. They knew that Livy himself was far from expert.

"Gather all the men after lunch by the river. Find a nice shady spot," Livy instructed them, then walked off.

Back in his tent, the two girls had prepared a light lunch and were busy playing dice with each other. "Hello, Centurion," Artemisia called out. "I hear the war is over." She looked delighted.

"The war with the Suessiones is over, but we still got all the rest of the barbarians to deal with," Livy said, smiling.

"Here, have some bread and fruit," Stena offered.

Livy took a luscious-looking red apple and took a big bite.

"We got instructions from Servilia," Artemisia stated. "You get one more night with us since we were so rudely interrupted last night. We are to stay with you till tomorrow morning."

Stena looked totally happy and was beaming.

"Somehow I have the notion you already knew that," Artemesia added.

Livy did not reply to that and decided to change the subject. "How would you girls like to go on a picnic by the river? We'll bring all the food in a basket and a wineskin to share."

"I'd love that!" Stena said excitedly.

"Seems to be more than what meets the eye here, Centurion. What's really happening?" Artemisia said.

"That one is clever," Livy thought to himself. "The truth is, I am curious to see how good a fighter you are, being Spartan and an ex-gladiatrix. My men are having sword practice by the river, and I thought we might have some fun joining them."

Artemisia raised one eyebrow and wrinkled her nose. "Hmmm. Might be fun. I am a little tired of sex all the time. Might be good to have some outdoor fun for a change," she said.

"Can the two of you ride?" Livy asked.

"Of course," Artemisia said.

"I can ride too," said Stena.

"I have an extra horse. You two can ride double or one of you can ride with me," Livy offered.

"I'll ride with you," Stena volunteered quickly.

Artemisia got on to the chestnut mare which Livy had brought along, and Stena rode with Livy on his black stallion with the white marking on its forehead. Stena was riding in front with Livy holding on to the reins from behind. Their bodies pressed closely together, and Livy could not help feeling a wave of excitement.

It would be really hard to choose which girl to keep when the time came. Artemisia rode on, oblivious to them. She was enjoying the sensation of riding and feeling free once again. To a Spartan, the state of slavery was intolerable and a total affront to their very being. Spartans were always the masters, never slaves.

They reached a very scenic spot by the river where some large trees provided shade to a grassy patch. The raiders were broken into three groups and officers were attending to sword drill in each of them.

Livy and the girls alighted under a tree from where they could watch all three groups, and they proceeded to lay out the picnic.

"Do these activities bring back memories?" he addressed Artemisia.

"Yes, the good memories of my time in the Spartan *agoge*. Especially the training with the wooden swords," she had a wistful look on her face.

"Come, let's go have some fun with my young novices." He took her by the hand and led her to one of the groups.

The officer stopped the demonstration bout and called the group to attention. "Attentiom, Commanding Officer present," he shouted.

"At ease, men," Livy replied. "I have a surprise for you today. This young lady is Artemisia, a Spartan who has attended the famous *agoge*, where they train the best swordsmen in the world. I would like her to demonstrate her skills in the hope that you and even I will learn some fine points. I need a volunteer. Who is the best swordsmen here?" he asked the decurion.

"Telemachus, sir," He pointed to one of Livy's veterans.

"Ah, another Greek. Where are you from, soldier?" Livy asked.

"I am from Argos, sir."

"Amazing, an Argyve, historical enemies of the Spartans. This should be an interesting match." Livy smiled enthusiastically.

He turned to Artemesia. "Would you honour all of us with a small demonstration against this rogue from Argos, madam?" Livy asked politely.

Artemisia pulled her lips into a half-smile. "I accept the challenge, Centurion."

The decurion announced, "Weapons will be wooden *spathas*. No hitting at the head. Match ends when one contender makes what is deemed to be a fatal blow, the other surrenders, or is put in an impossible position."

The two fighters took their positions. Both were wearing only tunics and no armour. They both had round cavalry shields. Artemesia felt at home as the shield resembled a Greek *hoplon,* only smaller, and the wooden sword felt familiar as well. She was dressed in a short white tunic.

"*Pugnate*," the decurion yelled for them to begin.

They circled each other for a while, each looking for an opening. Suddenly Telemachus rushed in with a series of quick blows, which Artemesia parried expertly or took on her shield. She was testing him out and seemed very collected and steady. Telemachus withdrew slightly. He was thinking how to penetrate her defences. He rushed forward bodily and slammed his shield against hers. This was standard infantry tactics. He hoped to knock her down as she was lighter than he was.

Artemisia reacted with almost blinding speed. She stepped aside and kicked him in the shin, tripping him and sending him sprawling. A loud cheer came from the spectators. "Ooh, that must hurt," one soldier commented.

"Silence in the ranks," the decurion admonished.

Artemisia didn't go in for the kill. She stood back and let him get up. Her chivalry impressed the boys. Telemachus got up slowly and painfully. There was big bruise just under one knee. He looked angry and embarrassed.

Artemisia beckoned him to come and finish it. He was hesitating. To encourage him, she threw her shield aside and just stood there swirling her wooden blade around. Telemachus had no choice but to attack or lose face.

He launched himself forward with a yell, sword raised to strike from above. The move was too obvious. Artemisia moved fast against his left, ducked the blow as his sword swung against her, and struck hard to the back of his knee. Telemachus toppled heavily backwards, losing both shield and sword.

In a split second, Artemisia was sitting on him, sword pointed at the throat. Telemachus was too stunned to react.

"That's a kill," the decurion announced, and there was enthusiastic clapping from the audience. Livy looked to the side and saw that his two friends Biorix and Paulus had joined them together with Stena, who was smiling and waving at him.

"That was a magnificent demonstration of Spartan fighting skill," he announced. "Who would like to try next?" Livy asked.

"Would you like to continue?" Livy asked her. She nodded.

None of the men volunteered this time. No one wanted to be humiliated by a woman. Finally Paulus put up his hand. "If you don't mind I'd like to learn from this young lady," Paulus humbly offered.

"I think I would like to give her a shot," Paulus volunteered with a grin. He started to shed his armour, greaves, belt, and helmet. "I think I would like to try her without shields," Paulus said.

"Do you agree?" Livy asked her.

"Why not?" she said with a defiant look at Paulus. Artemisia threw her shield aside.

"On guard," the decurion shouted. "*Pugnate!*"

Paulus took on a fighting crouch facing his opponent. Artemisia looked very relaxed, standing erect and twirling her wooden sword. She waited for Paulus to attack.

Paulus did not rush in. He moved slowly and deliberately, testing her defences. Livy could see that their technique differed greatly. Paulus slashed like a cavalryman. Artemisia parried easily and counter-attacked by thrusting and stabbing. Her movements were economical. She never wasted a move and conserved her energy.

They probed each other for a long time. Paulus began to tire as he tried harder and harder to overpower her by quick series of slashing attacks. Artemisia was very quick, either parrying the blows or just ducking aside. She kept her movements minimal, only moving aside at the last moment.

Paulus was beginning to look breathless while Artemisia was unfazed. This irritated him and he feinted to his left then changed at the last moment and tried to slash at the left side of her abdomen. Artemisia sidestepped back and then to his right, bending her body backwards with unbelievable agility. At the same time, she swung her sword backhand and hit Paulus hard over his sword arm.

Paulus yelled loudly and dropped his sword. "Maim your opponent, and he is yours eventually." She remembered the painful lesson of the *ludus*.

She withdrew to allow Paulus to pick up his sword. There was scattered clapping from the spectators.

Paulus was a little red with embarrassment. He was larger, stronger, and taller and a veteran of many battles. This was a mere teenager, worse, a girl. He had to admit she was good. He was tired and panting. He decided to make one last try to take her down.

He launched himself at her bodily and dived at her legs. He swung his sword at her legs, hoping to hit one of them and bring her down. It was a desperate move.

Artemisia was surprised, but her instincts were well honed. She jumped high, bending her knees, and Paulus just missed striking her bare feet. He flew under her and hit the ground with a thump, sliding forward a few feet. Artemisia landed, turned around, and jumped on to his back, her sword pointing to the small of Paulus's back.

"Point and match to the Spartan," the decurion called. There was loud applause. Artemisia got up and gave Paulus a hand and pulled him to his feet. He was winded but no worse for wear.

"You fought well, young lady. If all Spartans fought like you then I am glad we never went to war against your people," Paulus said sportingly.

"You fought well, likewise. You are a worthy opponent, and I am honoured to have the opportunity to spar with you," Artemisia said politely. She gave him a polite bow.

Paulus shook her hand and pulled her close to give her a friendly hug and a kiss on the cheek. Artemisia blushed a little and looked down.

"She is quite amazing," Paulus said to Livy. "We should recruit her," he said jokingly.

"You are closer to the mark than you realise," Livy said giving Paulus a wink. "Anybody else want a match with our champion here?" Livy asked loudly.

Men were shaking their heads everywhere. No one wanted to be humiliated by a girl.

"Come on, you big, brave men. All scared of a little girl?" Stena cajoled.

Still there were no volunteers. Livy was getting a little embarrassed.

"What about you, Centurion? Dare to take me on?" Artemisia finally asked, loud enough for all to hear.

"You can take her, sir," Biorix encouraged with a sly grin.

"I don't see how you can refuse," Paulus added with a laugh, rubbing the bruise on his back.

Livy hesitated then finally said, "All right, last match, then back to your training."

Artemisia grabbed the hem of her tunic and pulled it with one swift motion over her head. "You, I fight naked, like in my *agoge*."

The men gaped at her impeccable body. There was suddenly perfect silence, and everyone admired or lusted for her.

"Take off your clothes, Centurion," she challenged.

Livy was a bit hesitant but complied. He was a bit embarrassed to show his manhood. He had seen bigger, especially on Marc Antony.

Artemisia didn't react at all. "I fight with two swords and no shield. That is my preferred configuration. You can choose whatever you like."

Livy knew his limitations. Sword-fighting wasn't his forte, and he knew she would be quicker and more agile than him. His best chance lay in defence. "I choose *spatha* and legionary shield. He picked up the oval, standard Roman infantry shield with the truncated top and bottom. He would find plenty of cover behind it.

"On guard," shouted the decurion. "*Pugnate!*"

They circled each other. Livy crouched behind the shield with only his forehead and eyes looking over the top. At the bottom, the shield covered everything except his feet. Artemisia looked at him with her head to one side, trying to figure how to get at him. Unlike the first man, he did not try to charge her and hit her with the shield. He advanced slowly, step by step, trying to get under her guard. He also did not slash about with his sword, keeping it held close to his shield.

Artemisia was a little nonplussed by his tactics. She needed him to attack so she could find an opening in his defences. Livy just kept plodding towards her, all the time guard up. She tried probing his defences with her two swords, trying to get him from his right non-shielded side, but he always saw her coming and was able to parry her blows.

The audience was getting fidgety. It looked like a boring stalemate. Artemisia would attack and try to find a way around the shield, but Livy blocked easily. She was getting impatient and attacking more, and this suited him fine.

Suddenly she feinted to the right and Livy shifted his shield to block her blow, but instead, she somersaulted left and slashed at his unguarded right shin. It was a brilliant manoeuvre. Livy just managed to lower his sword to block the blow. It was hard enough to numb his arm. Artemisia rolled away and recovered into the standing position.

Before Livy could get his guard up, she attacked again, this time on the run and screaming a war cry. This was the break Livy was waiting for.

Artemisia was barrelling in on his right side, and there was no way to bring his shield around in time. Furthermore, she had two swords to his one, and she would definitely penetrate his defence. In a split second, Livy realised that he had no good defence. Fortunately, it was only a practice match.

Livy lunged forward at her. Since he had never ever attacked, she was caught off guard. Their bodies crashed together, and they both went down. Livy was on top of her when the dust cleared. Artemisia had lost her left-hand sword. Livy had the tip of his sword against her left chest and she had her sword against his belly. In real life, they would have killed each other.

There was a moment of silence as the audience remained stunned, then Biorix began to applaud and the rest followed.

The decurion announced, "The match is a draw."

Livy began to notice the wonderful sensation of their two naked bodies lying skin to skin. He smiled at her, and she smiled back with genuine respect.

"You two going to get up, or are you going to copulate right here on the sand?" Paulus's rude comment interrupted the moment. Livy got up and gave her a hand up, pulling her on her feet. They both parted to their respective corners to retrieve their clothes.

Paulus and Biorix came up to him. "So this is the mysterious sword instructor?" Paulus asked. "She's pretty good. The men can learn a lot from her and everyone will enjoy the lessons too."

"Can we get her to teach naked?" Biorix asked with a smirk.

Livy gathered up the two girls and resumed their picnic under a shady tree. The soldiers went back to their training with renewed enthusiasm. They had now seen some really expert sword-fighting. The men were paired off to test their skill against each other. Biorix and Paulus were invited to join Livy and the girls.

Artemisia did not bother to dress but went straight into the water to wash.

The rest sat by the bank enjoying fruit and wine. Stena was happy to serve the men and seemed please by the attention of the three. She was a simple, sweet girl and uncomplicated. Livy felt she was more suited to be the wife of a merchant or a rich farmer. She would pamper her husband and take good care of the children. Her time would be spent sewing and weaving and making sumptuous meals in the kitchen. Her charming manner was endearing her to both Paulus and Biorix. Her noble heritage showed clearly in her good manners, and she had none of the roughness of the typical camp follower.

Artemisia was washing her hair and her body as if she were the only person around. She was oblivious to all but her own thoughts, and she seemed one with nature. She was not in anyway a lady of the city. She would find city life boring and pointless and would reject it just as she rejected make-up. She would be an ideal companion on campaign. She was used to the rough life and would not complain at any hardship she had to endure. Basically, she was Spartan.

"So, do you think you can persuade yon Amazon to become the trainer to our boys?" Paulus asked.

"The decision may not lie with her," Livy said.

"How did you get to know her anyway?" Biorix asked.

"Friend of friend of Caesar," Livy replied.

"Well, she is well connected then," Paulus said.

"More than you think," Livy preferred not to gossip.

Artemisia returned to the bank. Her hair was wet, but she looked cleaned and scrubbed. She dried herself and put on her wet tunic, which she had just washed in the river. The material clung to her body, showing every feature. The men smiled in admiration.

"Had a good swim?" Biorix asked.

"Just what I needed," she answered as she tried to dry her dark brown hair.

"The centurion is wondering if you would like to join us as trainer of sword skills," Paulus offered.

"My fate is determined by others," she replied.

"And if your master or mistress were to approve? Would you be pleased to serve with us?" Livy asked.

Artemisia smiled. "I wouldn't object," she said. She sat down and started to eat ravenously. "Fighting makes me hungry," she said to Stena.

CHAPTER 17

Livy, Biorix, and Paulus watched from their favourite position on the hill overlooking Noviodunum. All day, carts bearing treasure and food had been coming out from the city. Towards the evening, the carts bore a different cargo. The women of Noviodunum were being transported to the Roman camp. The women were on the whole silent. Most had accepted their fate. They would make a sacrifice for the survival of their people.

There were loud cheers from the camps as each contingent arrived at a Roman camp. The men were looking forward to their reward for victory over the Suessiones. After all, why do men enlist in the legions if not for loot and women? This was payment in kind for all the hardship endured and for risking their lives.

The sun was a fiery red as it sank over the horizon, casting long shadows. In the Roman camps, music and singing could be heard. This was to be a night of merrymaking. There were no sounds of merrymaking from Noviodunum, however. Only silence.

"Well, let's go back to camp and see what kind of Suessiones wenches they sent us," Biorix decided.

"I agree with that," Paulus said. "You coming with us, sir? I believe you got better things waiting for you in your tent."

"I do, but I will join the men for a while," Livy said aware of his need to bond with the men.

The three men rode down to the raider encampment. The men were preparing for the orgy, cooking up a feast with what was available. Livy noticed that the men had been hunting and he recognised roast hare, ducks, chicken, quail, and other birds. There was no shortage of meat tonight.

The raiders were sent about 50 women. They alighted from their carts and huddled together in fearful groups. The lads seemed also too shy to approach them. Finally Biorix took the initiative. He went up to a group of them where there was an older woman in her thirties. He started to strike up a conversation in Belgic, and the women seemed to relax. More of the lads followed his example. Some of them offered wineskins or beer to the ladies.

Livy noted with satisfaction that the Suessione women were being courted politely. There was no evidence of aggression. After a while, the women were invited to the campfires for dinner, and they started to mingle with the men in groups, being enticed with food and drink.

The women knew full well what they were here for, but the courteous behaviour of the men would do much to take the sting out of what must be a humiliating experience. He already noted that some of the women were far from willing and could not be placated by the appearance of civility which the men strove so hard to keep up.

Biorix came up to him, offering him a wineskin. "Our men seem to be behaving. If any lot deserves a reward it's our lads."

"I wonder how the lads feel consorting with women of the erstwhile enemy," Livy pondered.

"I don't think you need worry too much, sir. To the men, women are women, and they haven't had any for a while. I told them to treat the ladies nice and show their manners. I think most of our boys know how to get into their loincloths without resorting to force. I've made loads of wine available to dull the senses of the women." He laughed.

"Nevertheless, keep a close watch on things. If any of the women fiercely objects, I don't want her to be forced, understand?" Livy emphasised. "I am sure there will be enough willing ones."

"Aye, sir. Leave it to Paulus and me to keep order. Would you like some dinner, sir? I have wild ducks prepared, with herbs and spices, roasted to perfection."

Livy's stomach rumbled at that suggestion. "Sounds good. I'll stay for dinner, and this will also give me an opportunity to keep an eye on the boys." Biorix led him to a large campfire which had cushions ranged around it as well as some low tables laden with bread and fruit. A row of ducks were spitted and roasting on the fire, giving an aroma to die for. Paulus was already there with the two regular Remi girls, Sabia and Eala. A number of decurions were present and about half a dozen of the prettier Suessione girls. The men were trying their best to get the girls to drink. The women were, on the other hand, attacking the food ravenously. The food situation in Noviodunum must not have been too good, which explained the quick capitulation.

Sabia got up and served Livy a generous portion of the roast duck. He ate it with bread and washed it down with watered wine. Biorix had exceeded himself. The skin of the duck was fragrant and crispy. The meat, soft and not overcooked, melted in the mouth. The fragrance of rosemary was intoxicating.

The girls tucked in lustily, and, by the look on their faces, they were in gustatory rapture. Livy examined them closely and noted that they were mostly young, below thirty. They were reasonably pretty with hair ranging from dark brown to blonde. They mostly had blue or green eyes, and a few were freckly. They had generally fair complexion and full bosoms. They were taller than Mediterranean girls like Spanish, Italian, or Greek and had more robust figures. Most of the girls were now looking more relaxed and less apprehensive. The men were, on the whole, courteous.

A young blonde girl came to sit beside Livy. "Hello, Centurion. My name is Lila," she introduced herself. "What is your name?" She spoke in rudimentary Latin.

Livy was surprised at her knowledge of the language. "You can call me Livy."

"Strange sounding name, Livy," she repeated.

"How did you come to learn Latin?" Livy asked.

"My father was a merchant, and he used to go south to the Roman lands to trade."

"What did he trade?"

"He brought down horses, beer, and wool and brought back wine, cloth, glassware, and olive oil. He bought a Greek slave one year, who started a school in Noviodunum. The children of the richer families were then given the opportunity to learn Latin, Greek, reading, and writing."

"You father is a wise man. Is he in the town?"

"He was on one of his trips to the south when the war broke out. He hasn't come back, and we hope he is all right."

"I really hope so too, Lila." The girl looked about sixteen and had blonde hair in two pigtails and big blue eyes. She was the prettiest of the girls in the group.

"Centurion, I know we are here to be given to your men for sex, but I really, really would resent to be gang-raped." She suddenly started to shed tears. "Please protect me, Centurion."

Livy was startled by her sudden outburst. He pulled her close and gave her a hug. "I sympathise with the unfairness of the situation, but then this is an imperfect world, dear," He held her close against his chest for a while.

"The best course of action is to find a young man that you like, preferably an officer and just give yourself willingly to him. With some luck, and if he is kind, he will keep you for himself for the next two nights. Who knows, you might even find love."

She pulled back and looked at him pleadingly with doggy eyes. "Won't you please be my protector? I would give myself willingly to you and serve you well. You can take me as many times as you want, and I will try my utmost to please you."

Livy laughed. She seemed so earnest. "I am honoured that you choose me, Lila, but I have pressing duties this night." Livy held her hand. "Otherwise, I would love to take up your offer." She was really charming in her childlike innocence, and Livy was beginning to think how best to help her.

Around him, the alcohol had done its work and inhibitions on the part of the men and the girls were already loosened. Many of the men and women had paired off, and there was much kissing, fondling, and some disrobing. The women were mainly too inebriated to resist, and some were plainly enjoying the orgy.

Livy turned his attention back to the girl Lila. "I cannot make an exception of you, my dear."

"You have other women to bed tonight?" she asked astutely.

"Are you yet a virgin?" he asked.

"I am saving myself for my husband, which my father has yet to find."

"I think virginity is overrated, and personally, I prefer a girl with some experience and so will your future husband if he has any sense. All the girls I know can't get enough of sex after they have experienced it!" Livy laughed.

The girl blushed. She obviously knew little of such matters.

"Consider tonight a pleasant education in the art of how to please your future husband. I will find you a gentle and considerate teacher, someone who is as handsome as Apollo. A man no woman can resist and possessing a *priapus* superior even to mine," Livy said.

The girl was shocked speechless. Livy called Biorix over before she could reply and whispered in his ear.

A few moments later, a tall, handsome youth arrived, who really had the look of a Greek god. His body was perfectly muscled, and he had the perfect proportions of a classical statue. He was tanned with dark curly hair and blue eyes. He was dressed only in a short tunic which barely covered his groin and a shadow of what lay beneath could just be discerned. Livy introduced them.

"Sit down, Cleander. I have a present for you. This sweet young thing is Lila. She is a well-educated daughter of a merchant and will make a good wife to some lucky rich man one day. She is, however, unschooled in the ways of men, and in this area you are ordered to educate her for the next two days. Be gentle with her, though not too gentle." Livy laughed. "But, try to keep her to yourself if possible. Is that clear?"

"It will be my pleasure, Centurion. I will teach her well," Cleander said with a broad grin. Livy could see the girl blushing, but she didn't seem at all displeased. After all, if one was to be taken involuntarily, then a Greek god may turn a nightmare into a fantasy.

"Take off your clothes, girl." Livy ordered. "Let's see what you have got."

The girl was too stunned to do anything but comply. She doffed her tunic and had no underwear beneath. "Not so unprepared after all," Livy thought to himself. Her figure still had the vestiges of puppy fat around the abdomen and thighs but was otherwise comely enough. Her assets were her ample breast and her curvaceous hips.

"Now, you should take off your clothes," she challenged Cleander. "I want to see what I get."

Cleander was amused but unfazed. He took off his tunic in a flash, revealing a near-perfect body, well-muscled but not overly buff. His manhood was formidable. Lila gasped in appreciation.

"Take care of her, Cleander. She is your responsibility for the next two nights," Livy ordered. He took hold of Lila's hands and pulled her close to kiss her on the cheek, then handed her to Cleander.

He then sat back down with his men to enjoy his roast duck.

Caesar was sitting with Servilia on his divan. He had organised a small dinner party and had invited Galba and some of the Suessione nobles. The food was sumptuous but not overly ostentatious. Servilia had brought along four of her girls to entertain the Belgic nobles, and two of them, the Italian girls, were busy entertaining Galba himself. One was feeding him grapes as he reclined while the other was giving him a back massage.

"I hope the nobles will be distracted enough by this party to temporarily forget about the service their women are providing to our men tonight," Caesar said softly to his mistress.

"I have scoured your army's *lupanaria* and could come up with only half a dozen girls of sufficient standard. I only took the Mediterranean ones as a change for your guests from the pale blondes they are used to. I hope they will serve well," Servilia grumbled.

Caesar surveyed the women. They were all dark haired with skin colour ranging from lightly tanned to dark olive. "The Belgic nobles seem to be having a good time."

The girls were scantily clad, and some of them had stripped down to the waist to show a variety of breast shapes, and a few were already nude.

"I hope this softens the pain of defeat," Servilia said.

"I hope it softens it enough for them to be our allies or at least remain strictly neutral."

"I think it will take a while before they get hold of enough arms to rise again."

"I won't be surprised if they have arms hidden somewhere. That's not what worries me most though," Caesar said.

"The price you exacted is small. You could easily have annihilated them."

"The greatest victories are bloodless. Yet, I fear the Gorgon's head, which is revenge."

"Can you trust Galba?" Servilia asked.

"You know the answer to that, my dear. I have a trump card, however." Caesar smiled.

"I should have expected that of you." Servilia caressed his cheek playfully. "What is it?"

"I hold his two sons hostage," Caesar replied smugly.

Caesar rose with a goblet of wine. "I propose a toast." The room fell silent, and the nobles were given filled goblets by their female escorts.

"I toast to a new era of peace between Rome and the Suessiones. May we join together to create a Belgica where men can live in peace and pursue prosperity and happiness," Caesar declared, raising his goblet and drinking deeply.

The nobles raised their goblets and drank. "I toast to noble Caesar," Galba replied.

"Let there be peace between our nation and yours. Let there be peace based on a spirit of mutual respect and fairness," Galba said.

Caesar caught the hidden meaning. "To peace," Caesar replied, and everyone drank.

Caesar walked down from his place of honour to Galba's divan on his right. The girls made a place for him to sit. "How is your leg, Your Majesty?"

"It gets better daily, though walking still presents a problem." Galba replied in Celtic and Caesar's translator rendered in Latin. He suddenly missed the services of one Centurion Livius. He never knew how accurate these slaves translated.

"I want to assure you that I will personally see to the fair treatment of your people. Trade will resume immediately. I will start road building projects and schools, and we will undertake to defend you from your traditional enemies."

"These are fine promises while your men rape my women," Galba said bitterly.

"Well, you and your nobles get to rape the best of ours tonight in return," Caesar retorted. "In two days, we move against the Bellovaci, and then the Ambiani comes next. I intend to pacify the whole of Belgica, Galba. You will soon realise that your people are lucky to be out of it and will shed no more blood."

"This, at the price of our independence," Galba said.

"I do not intend to enslave your people. I seek to bring you civilisation, peace, and prosperity under Roma," Caesar said with firm determination.

"We have heard of your civilisation which comes with taxes and corrupt governors," Galba said.

"I will appoint the prefects myself, and any corruption will be punished, I assure you," Caesar said.

"We wait to see if you can keep your promise, Caesar."

The girl refilled his cup, and they both drank. "Enjoy this night, Galba."

"I intend to, Lord Caesar."

Much further to the north in the Land of the Nervii, Centurion Decius had just received the worst beating of his life. His naked body had been whipped, bludgeoned, and kicked. Several ribs were broken. He had bruises everywhere, and he could not even stand or sit. He was dragged to his filthy, soiled cage and thrown inside. He did not know how long he lay between consciousness and unconsciousness. Every part of his body ached badly.

Many hours later, he opened his eyes and looked up into the dark blue-green eyes of the Gaesatae girl, Leuce. She had a bucket of water and a wet cloth and was gingerly cleaning his wounds. "Hang on, Centurion. Don't despair." she gently washed the blood from a cut on his forehead.

"I think death would be merciful at this point," Decius murmured and then gasped in pain.

"I am sorry. I will be gentler," Leuce said in Latin.

"I couldn't help it. I told them what they wanted to know. No one can bear torture like that," he said in disgust.

"I really hope I haven't done too much damage to my side," Decius said.

"What did they want to know?" Leuce asked.

"Caesar's order of march. It's always the same anyway. Everyone knows it," Decius said resignedly.

"Don't lose heart, Centurion. Your ordeal may end soon," she said.

"Are they going to execute me? Probably sacrifice me to your gods, eh? Can't say I mind too much at this point. Death would be a release. Why don't you sneak in a knife and just do me a favour, sweet lady."

"I can't say more and don't ask me anything. Your friends are coming for you."

"I can't believe it. I am deep within enemy lines."

"Do you know a centurion called Livius?"

"Yes, I know him well. If anyone can get through, he can." A small spark of hope kindled in Decius's breast.

"Yes, I know him too," Leuce said. Her amazing eyes seemed to glimmer more brightly for an instant.

Livy spent his last night with his two hetaerae. He had left the orgy at its zenith. Nearly everyone was drunk. There were copulating couples everywhere. The alcohol had suppressed every shred of resistance among the women, and he did not see a single woman being forced. Most were just too drunk to care. Others were willing participants anyway.

As he was walking back to his tent he was intercepted by a tribune. "Centurion Livius, I have a message for you from Caesar. Your raiders are to assemble at the sixth hour at dawn. There will be a parade at the seventh hour, and your unit will receive battle honours."

"I stand informed, sir, and my men will be there," Livy replied.

"There is more. After the parade, there will be briefing for you and your three best men from your raiders. A special mission is planned, and you are only to select men who look Celtic in appearance."

"I understand, sir," Livy replied.

"I'll see you in the morning then, Centurion." The tribune got on to his stallion, which had a beautiful leather saddle and red saddle cloth with gold trimmings. Livy noticed he was still smartly turned out in full uniform and had probably no time to enjoy the evening's festivities. Livy felt a little shabby in comparison, only clad in his red tunic. Perhaps he ought to pay more attention to his turnout if he aspired to senior rank.

Livy went back to look for Biorix. He found him almost nude, dancing with three Suessione girls, who were obviously drunk. Music was coming from some of the Cretan boys playing drums and wind instruments. One of the women was strumming a lyre. The music was winding and sinuous, Doric sounding.

Livy waited for him to finish then pulled him aside. "I hate to spoil your fun, but a few of us have to move out on a mission tomorrow."

Biorix rolled his eyes. "Again? I thought we are stood down and can have some rest and recreation. Haven't we done enough the last days?"

"Yes, you are a hero already, and you will have your chance to rest. Nevertheless, you and I move out tomorrow. We're going after Decius. Remember our friend Decius?"

Biorix nodded, though not with much conviction.

"I also need four of our veterans. They should be Remi and look as Celtics as possible. You know the type, big guys with blond hair and long moustaches."

Biorix nodded in half-understanding. "Get back to your party and have a wonderful time." Livy pushed him from behind and gave him a slap on the bum.

Livy hurried back to his tent. He too had a private party to look forward to, and this time he didn't want to forfeit his reward. There would be no more opportunities, and he also had an important decision to make.

CHAPTER 18

Bodougnatus had an important guest. There was a party of Eburones in his camp, led by their King Ambiorix. The Nervii had encamped next to a small village, and Bodougnatus and his retinue had occupied the largest house. The poor villager had been turned out, and he moved his family into a barn. The Nervii had appropriated all his food and animals, and his pigs and chickens were even now being roasted. His wife and daughters had already been raped by multiple warriors but had kindly been returned to him alive, though somewhat worse for wear.

The king was feasting, and his guests were at his table. Serving wenches were pouring large amounts of wine into cattle horns and distributing to all the guests. The Nervii were back in their lands, and food and drink were once again in abundance.

"Well, Ambiorix, are you joining us in our war, or are you going to skulk around like frightened children in your towns?" Bodougnatus challenged.

Ambiorix fought down the urge to strangle him with his bare hands. "Bodougnatus is nothing but a stupid fat pig," he thought to himself. The Eburones were no less brave or courageous fighters than the overrated Nervii. He breathed deeply and swallowed his rage.

"As you know, great King, our nation is ruled by two kings. My colleague, Cativolcus, does not believe in your enterprise as I do and prefers to sit and watch on the sidelines. I, on the other hand, share your opinion about the Roman scourge and have come to offer you the services of my personal bodyguard," he replied, speaking in slow, measured tones.

"We are damnably short of cavalry, so your tiny contribution is accepted. I had hoped for more." Bodougnatus noticed that Ambiorix was a man in his forties with a well-toned, muscular body, which he was proud to show as he went around topless save for a thick golden torque around his neck.

Ambiorix noted the slight. "This man is an utter fool," He thought. He had second thoughts about joining this bunch of idiots. No wonder the Romans were winning.

"Gentlemen, we have with us tonight another honoured guest. Bratronos, high priest of King Galba of the Suessiones. Tell us what has befallen our brethren, the noble Suessiones."

"The Romans stole a march on us and reached our capital Noviodunum before us. They besieged it. When Galba and the army arrived, he surrendered rather than fight the invaders. He betrayed all of us."

There were angry murmurings all round the room. Everyone was shocked because the Suessiones were the biggest Belgic tribe with the largest army, and they were also the richest.

"Tell us what else that coward did," Bodougnatus commanded.

"He gave over all our women to be defiled by the accursed Romans. Every woman that was not too old to be used for carnal pleasure."

There were loud groans from everyone.

"All our women given up for rape!" Bratranos emphasised. "That is what will happen to all your women should you think to surrender to the Romans."

"We, the Nervii, will never permit such an outrage. We will fight the Romans till they are destroyed. We will bring them war to the very gates of Rome itself," Bodougnatus screamed.

"Our brothers, the Atrebates and the Viromandui, are here standing with us. Side by side we will stand up to Caesar and crush his army. Then it will be we who rape their women and enslave their men. Even the Aduatuci now march to our aid. With the three tribes present, we number more than 100,000 men and more with the Aduatuci. Caesar has barely 50,000. This time we will crush him."

The nobles cheered and beat the tables with their swords. "Death to the Romans! Death to the Romans!" they chanted in unison.

"What about the Bellovaci and the Ambiani?" Ambiorix asked.

"They cower behind their walls," Bratranos sneered. "Caesar will go after them next."

"Shouldn't we march to their aid?" Ambiorix asked, concerned.

"No, they have to take their chances," Bodougnatus said. "We can't rush everywhere, rescuing every town. We have only one chance to defeat Caesar, and that is here in Nervii territory where we can prepare and be well supplied."

"Hear, hear," the nobles affirmed.

"Here we stand the best chance, and I have already a battlefield in mind," Bodougnatus said. "Furthermore, we must now regard the Suessiones as enemies. Those that are not for us are against us. Any Suessione warriors must be regarded as hostile and attacked. No quarter is to be given."

"What about those wanting to join us?" Bratranos asked in dismay.

"Those we will disarm and bring here to be questioned. We must be sure they are not Roman spies." Bodougnatus decided.

"What role do you see for my Eburones?" Ambiorix asked.

"Ride south and scout. See what Caesar is up to. Get word to us immediately if he starts to move in our direction. Furthermore, destroy any Roman or Suessione scouting parties."

"Will you be sending your men with us?" Ambiorix asked.

"I can't spare any men right now, but there is a band of Gaesatae that will be a useful addition to your horsemen. They have been given all the difficult missions lately and their number has dwindled to less than 500. You can take a hundred of them with you if you can find them enough horses. Their leader is Murato. He is a big strong lad like you." Bodougnatus smiled slyly. "You two should work very well together. Ha! Ha!"

"Very well, King, I shall take my men out tomorrow." Ambiorix couldn't get out of this madhouse quick enough. He was peeved that all Bodougnatus could spare him were a bunch of naked savages. There will be reckoning one day with the Nervii, but presently, the Romans were the greater threat.

"Enough talk of war. Now we drink and see how many women we can fuck before morning. I'll bet you this old man can still outdo most of you young uns," Bodougnatus concluded and then dove on top of two young girls with blonde pigtails.

Late Winter, Ganzhou, 36 BC

Ganzhou was a prosperous walled city located strategically in the middle of the Hexi corridor which led out of China towards the Western Regions and the Silk Road to the west. The journey passed through a rugged landscape of red hills and mountains devoid of any vegetation. Speckled over this beautiful bleak terrain were small brick-and-mud villages amidst pockets of cultivated fields.

I travelled with six picked bodyguards armed with bows and long curved scimitars. They were all veteran Han soldiers from my previous command. Each of us had a spare horse as we were moving fast and travelling sixteen to eighteen hours each day.

Finally the imposing dun-coloured walls of Ganzhou lay ahead. From the outside, the city looked like a bleak outpost. Towers with upturned roofs looked out over the desolate landscape. We passed through the gates unobtrusively, as I had dispensed with official robes and headgear. The security was slack after such a long period of peace.

The streets were bustling with people from many tribal groups. The Han were a minority here. There was the varied smell of cooking in the air, layered over the stench of animal and human waste. Thousands of burning fires brought warmth and a haze to the city. Perhaps it was the accumulated heat of thousands of bodies in close proximity as well. There was certainly a sense of cosiness here, a haven amidst the freezing wasteland outside the walls.

The building I sought lay in the centre of the bustling commercial district amidst a row of taverns, tea-houses, and restaurants. A gaggle of voices greeted the ear from the loud conversation of a thousand patrons, eating, drinking, and making merry. What else was there to do in a dreary winter evening?

The Golden Lotus Inn was a three-storied affair made of grey stone with a long wooden balcony on the second floor and a green tiled roof with elaborate eaves shaped like dragons. There were rich blue banners with golden lotus motifs hanging from the balconies. It was the classiest tea-house on the street and perhaps in the whole city.

My party was greeted by two demure maidens in white silk gowns embroidered with birds and flowers. "Good evening, Prefect Li. The two mistresses are expecting you. I bid you welcome to our humble tea-house," the taller one spoke in a musical voice. She gave me a warm smile and a deep bow.

I was led into a large hallway decorated with indoor plants and flowers. There were fountains and pools with decorative carp gliding in pristine clear water. There was faint music in the air from the zither and the lute. The whole effect was subdued, tasteful, and tranquil. The guests drank their tea and enjoyed their entertainment in private rooms. It was all very discreet.

I accompanied the two maidens to the top floor while my men were taken to the dining room for tea and a meal. I was shown into a spacious suite with a polished wooden floor and walls decorated by murals depicting lovely Han maidens entertaining guests at a tea party amidst the red and gold of autumn.

The two ladies who owned the tea-house had both dressed up for me. The taller one had lustrous brown hair and exceeded my height. Her heavily brocaded silk gown was a bright azure. Her confident gait was unmistakable, and she looked at me out of the most amazing emerald green eyes.

"General Li, we bid you welcome to our humble establishment," she said in perfect Han Chinese.

The second lady gave a polite curtsy. She was slim and dainty and wore an equally richly brocaded jade-green gown. Her hair was jet-black and her skin pale ivory. Her lips were lotus buds. "It has been too long, Master. Your onerous duties keep you very busy, no doubt."

"The both of you are ever in my thoughts." I bowed to them both and extended my folded palms in traditional greeting.

The taller woman kissed me affectionately on both cheeks. "You lie as usual, but we are both nevertheless very happy to see you," she said with an amused smile.

"The ravages of time have hardly touched either of you," I said. "You both look as lovely as the spring."

"You flatter us, Master," the smaller lady replied. "We have become adept at covering up the ravages of time with some discreet cosmetics."

"Come and recline at the table," the taller lady invited. Her name was now Ai Tingmei. There was a low table elaborately laid for dinner. Around the table were soft cushions with back rests. They looked like legless divans.

I reclined at the table, and the two women positioned on either side. "We made you your favourite dishes. There is roast goose with plum sauce, steamed bread, chicken cooked with ginger and sesame in clay pot, and steamed river fish with mushrooms and scallions," Tingmei said.

I was ravenous after the long journey and was reaching with my chopsticks to attack the food.

"Master, we should first make a toast," Molihua interjected. She raised her porcelain bowl. "To old friends and good times," she proposed.

"Old times and good friends," I replied, taking a deep draft. The wine was superb.

"Please, let's begin," Tingmei said.

The three of us dined quietly for a while. The food was excellent. They had a really good cook here. The ladies topped up my bowl generously whenever it was empty and picked the choicest morsels for me. The hospitality was faultless.

"So to what do we owe the honour of this visit? It cannot be solely because you miss the company of two old ladies. Neither do I think it is to enjoy the pleasures of our establishment," Tingmei said, then popped a small dumpling into her delectable mouth.

I was caught by surprise at these direct remarks and choked on a piece of goose. "I do miss the two of you, but you are right. I have an ulterior motive. War is brewing in the west with the Xiongnu."

"I thought you were done with playing war," Moli said as she swept rice from her bowl into her mouth with her chopsticks.

"Yes, I believed so as well, but this is a special request from the governor of the Western Regions. Besides, there is a special reason for my involvement," I said.

"You have played this game too long, Master Li Bi," Tingmei said. "A truly wise warrior knows when to quit." she smiled. Crow's feet appeared at the corner of her emerald eyes.

"Only one possible reason could arouse me from my present contented state," I continued.

"I cannot imagine what that could be," Moli said.

"There are Romans involved," I said.

This time it was the turn of the ladies to choke in surprise. Both went into fits of coughing as tea or spirits challenged their windpipes.

Tingmei recovered first. "I thought we agreed never to talk about Da Qin Guo ever again," she protested. "We have a new life here and no chance of returning to our old lives."

"I'm afraid our past has come back to haunt us," I replied.

"Are they part of the lost legion? The missing 10,000 of Crassus's men?" Moli was quick to infer.

"I suspect they are the very same. We have old friends among them," I said.

Tingmei looked thoughtful for a while. "I guess we have no choice but to help then. These men must have suffered greatly in the last dozen years under Parthian captivity. If there is a chance to win their freedom, we must do all we can," she said.

"Tingmei was so much the product of her training. So much bound to duty as always," I thought to myself. I savoured the snow-white steamed rice which tasted so plain by itself but exploded with flavour when sauce from the dishes soaked into it.

"We have a surprise for you, Master. Let's finish the meal, and we will take you someplace relaxing." Moli smiled mysteriously.

An hour later, I was led to a rooftop atrium. In the centre was a small pool lined with shiny dark blue tiles. Steam wafted off the surface. The room was open to the elements, and the air was chilly. A handmaiden helped me out of my clothes, and I stepped gingerly into the pool, slowly letting my body acclimatise to the heat. The contrast of frigid winter air and singeing water was intensely invigorating. There were rose petals floating in the water. I settled in and put a hot towel on my forehead, closing my eyes to savour the pleasant sensations.

I heard female voices laughing. Moli and Tingmei appeared, clad in fur coats. In a flash, both discarded their furs and slipped into the water, one on either side of me. I had a glimpse of their familiar naked bodies. Both women had preserved their figures well. I noticed slim legs, taut bellies, tight glutei, and breasts which still defied gravity.

The three of us luxuriated in the pool for a few moments. I was beginning to become aroused by the presence of the two naked women. I had always found both rather desirable. Tingmei resumed the conversation. "Are you going to mount a rescue expedition?"

"The matter is rather complicated. Our friends are now part of the Western Xiongnu Army under the command of our old enemy *Chanyu* Zhizhi. They were liberated when the Xiongnu took Merv in the Parthian province of Margiana and pillaged it. Chen Tang is mounting a Han expedition to crush the Northern Xiongnu with nearly 40,000 infantry. He asked me to recruit a unit of cavalry and command it," I explained.

"I hope you are not expecting us to join you in this expedition? We might end up fighting our own friends," Tingmei protested.

"No, I don't expect you to come along unless you choose to. I now have about 600 raw recruits whom I need to train, and I can't think of two better trainers than the two of you," I said.

"Do you know that Moli here now has a school of Wu Shu or Chinese martial arts? We have more than a hundred students learning all types of fighting skills, including unarmed combat. I think we can train your recruits for the right price," Tingmei said.

"What are your rates? I need three months' training for 600 men."

"I'll give you a special bulk discount. 100 silver pieces per man," Moli said.

"I can agree to that. I need them proficient in bow, sword, and spear," I said.

"Perhaps crossbow might be better. They will never be able to outshoot the Xiongnu," Moli said.

"Perhaps," I conceded.

"I have another condition," Moli looked at me squarely. "I want to be second in command."

"You can't be serious!" Tingmei exclaimed.

"I am totally serious," Moli said. "If I train them, I get to command them."

"You have a death wish," Tingmei said.

"There was a girl called Mulan, who disguised herself as a man to join the Han Army to fight the Xiongnu and finally became a general. She was always my hero."

"The Han Army doesn't allow women to be soldiers, let alone officers." I tried to dissuade her.

"I will dress as a man. I have done that before, twenty years ago, remember?"

I didn't argue further. I needed her to train my recruits. Time for a change of subject. "I don't intend to fight our Roman friends if I can avoid it. I hope to persuade them to defect to our side."

"If you can achieve that, it would be good," Tingmei said. "They deserve a better fate than to be wiped out in battle after surviving enslavement all these years."

"I wonder who of our friends are left alive," Moli pondered aloud.

"We will find out soon," I said. "There are a few dear friends I really hope still live."

Tingmei motioned to a serving girl. Several porcelain bowls were brought.

"Let's toast to our new endeavour then. May the gods favour us and bring us success," Moli said.

"To success," Tingmei said.

"To old friends." I raised my bowl and drank deeply of the excellent wine.

"It's late. We should make preparations to retire," Moli said. "Master, as you are our honoured guest, we do not expect you to sleep alone."

"Is this a proposition?" I asked.

Moli gave me a negative look. She never fancied me in that way. "I believe Tingmei may be yet willing to share your bed, but we are, after all, an establishment of pleasure and we have someone to suit every taste. Let me show you a selection of our best," Moli proffered.

She gestured to one of the handmaidens, and moments later about a dozen young ladies were brought in. They stood in a line beside the pool. At a gesture from Moli, they allowed their gowns to slip to the floor. The girls stood shivering naked. Two-thirds of them were Han Chinese with lustrous black hair, almond eyes, and ivory complexion. The others were clearly barbarians from Central Asia. One or two may even have been Xiongnu. I noticed the neatly trimmed triangles of black pubic hair.

I sipped my wine as I took in the amazing sight. The girls were nubile and all pretty, but none came remotely close to the near perfection of my own wife, Qingling. I politely declined. The girls looked a little disappointed as they filed out. I wondered why? I was a middle-aged man and no longer a romantic figure. Actually, I wonder if I ever was a romantic figure. I can't complain though. I did have my share of amazing women over the years.

"I think I will pass on your generous offer," I said with a wry smile. "I prefer to spend the night with Tingmei, if she is so inclined." I looked at her hopefully.

She seemed to be thoughtful for a moment. She looked down shyly and replied, "I am ever at your disposal, Master, and will be honoured to spend the night in your bed. I am, however, in declining years. I may not be as satisfying for you as I was in my youth."

"You will always be satisfying for me," I countered.

"Nevertheless. I have a special present for you." She gestured to the handmaiden.

I waited expectantly. Moments later, a tall, blonde, white girl entered and stood beside the pool. She was a stunning creature, a goddess from the north. She let her ermine coat slip off and stood before us in nude splendour. Her light blonde hair was short—falling just below her chin—her eyes were deep blue, her complexion was the colour of milk, and her body was perfectly proportioned with smooth slender legs, ample breast topped with pink cherry-sized nipples, and curves which made my blood boil. Her face could launch a thousand ships. I was speechless. She did not even shiver in the cold like the rest of the whores.

"I see she finds favour in your eyes." Tingmei gave a satisfied smile. "Who would you rather spend the time night with, honourable Prefect of Zhangye? This stunning creature from the frozen waste of the north or little old me?"

It was a loaded question. My mind raced to find a diplomatic answer. "You were my woman for many years, dear, and I travelled a long distance to relive good times spent with you. I would not give up a night with you even if Aphrodite herself propositioned me." I put on my most sincere face.

Tingmei looked pleased. She smiled. I missed that smile. It brought back many pleasant memories. "Very well, I shall spend some hours with you but not the whole night. When I retire, Vesna here will entertain you." Her tone discouraged further protest.

I was assigned the best guest room in the house. It was spacious and boasted a large four-poster bed. The walls were decorated with immaculate calligraphy and paintings of scenes depicting rivers and mountains. The mattress was, however, a bit too firm.

Sex with Tingmei was familiar and friendly rather than wildly passionate. Nevertheless, she responded with surprising enthusiasm. I began by taking her up the mountain by playing the lute strings, then sipping the vast spring with my lips and tongue. I did this till I released the tide of yin. As waves of pleasure flowed through her every fibre, she gasped and dug her nails into my arms, drawing blood.

I turned her around before she recovered her breath and probed her jade gate from behind with my turgid turtle's head thrusting deep into her slithery celestial palace. The lovely aroma of her juices assaulted my nostrils, releasing a thousand memories. Ten thousand sexual encounters exploded into consciousness. I pounded her like a war-drum, holding back my own tide by sheer will. She ascended to the heavens and burst like a rain cloud. She wept.

Moments later I exploded like a volcano, flooding her with hot lava. We collapsed, spent.

We lay speechless for a few moments, as if dead. Life slowly crept back into our bodies. Tingmei was first to recover. "Was it always so intense? It's been so long, and I can hardly remember."

"It was always good between us, but tonight, we transcended to another level," I said.

"I have not had it for some time. We run a house of pleasure, but I seldom participate personally," she said. "I heard you got married once again."

"Yes, the emperor gave me one of his court ladies as a retirement present," I said.

"I heard she is young and quite lovely. Does she please you?" she asked.

"I would be remiss to deny it. She brings great comfort to my old loins," I said, tongue-in-cheek. I felt so comfortable and relaxed with Tingmei. It was like old times.

"I have a question that I always wanted to ask," I said. "That first time we sparred in front of my men, did you let me win?"

She gave the brightest smile, like a ray of sunshine at dawn. "Yes, I did. I didn't want to make you lose face in front of your men. I could have beaten you easily. You had no kung fu." She laughed.

"I have a second question. I offered you marriage many times, but you always refused. Why? Did you ever love me?" I asked.

"You talk like a girl, Master." She laughed again, her crow's feet showing. "Not at first but I slowly grew to love you over time. I certainly love you now," she said reassuringly.

"Then why did you refuse to marry me? I think we would have made a good married couple," I said.

"I have good reason. Firstly, you had fascination for a certain blonde barbarian bitch. Besides, you were never faithful to me. You fucked every pretty girl that came along," she said.

I was put in my place. She was right.

"Despite that, I would have forgiven you and married you, but I have an even higher reason. I am Spartan, and I value freedom above all else. As your wife, I would belong to you once more like a slave. Our society is still too patriarchal. Remaining unmarried and being financially independent, I can do as I wish and answer to no man."

"Your logic seems irrefutable," I answered ruefully, stroking my beard like Confucius.

She laughed again. "You look like a Han philosopher."

I gave her a half-serious pontificating look.

She took hold of one of my hands with both hers, curling her fingers around mine. "We will always be best friends, and you will always be welcome in my bed," she said with a naughty smile.

"You are only interested in my jade staff," I said playfully.

"Count yourself lucky that I like yours. I don't spread my favours around like you do," she said. "I am tired now, and I need my beauty sleep," She swung her magnificent legs off the bed to get up and wrapped her silk gown around herself. "Lie down and rest awhile. The second shift will soon be here," she said.

She was out of the door in a flash, leaving behind a whiff of subtle perfume in her wake.

I dozed for a few minutes, then heard a discreet knock at the door. My eyes blinked open. The door opened, and Vesna stood in the doorway. She was a Nordic apparition clad in ermine. She let the coat fall at the doorway. I noticed she had immaculately shaven pubes as she walked elegantly towards my bed, head held high and breasts bouncing delectably. I held my breath in awe.

She stopped at my bedside and awaited my command, her body proudly on display.

"Can you speak Han Chinese?" I asked.

"*Ee tian'* (a little), she said.

"Don't stand there in the freezing cold. Come to bed," I ordered. She slipped in beneath my blanket and cuddled up to me. Her cold hands reached for my jade staff. It had dozed off.

"Don't worry, honourable Master," she said. "Let's sleep awhile, and when you are strong again, I will show you how we entertain each other in the icy winters of the North." She gave me a fetching smile.

Tingmei was right. Vesna was totally my type. I kissed her luscious lips, breathing in the smell of her musky breath. Her lips were soft and yielding, her mouth moist, and her tongue smooth as silk. We kissed long and deeply. It was like draught of the finest wine. I kissed till I drifted asleep.

The next morning, I had breakfast with Tingmei and Moli. There was steaming hot tea, steamed dumplings filled with meat, and delicate steamed bread. My mind flickered to the activities of the night before. Vesna had allowed me to sleep. Each time I awoke, however, she would "play the flute" expertly with my yang weapon till I was near bursting; then she would take me up her golden gully deeply as far as her vermillion chamber. I had never had so much sex in one night for decades.

"You have a smug and a satisfied grin," Tingmei commented. "Things went well last night."

"Your hospitality is matchless as usual, and your girls are clearly the best in all of Gansu and perhaps in all the Imperium." I raised my glass to the two of them.

"Now that we have agreed to train your men, I guess we will be seeing much more of you," Moli said.

"Indeed," I replied.

"Who is training your men in horse skills?" Tingmei asked.

"Biao Li, of course, I tracked him down in Jinchang, where he runs a blacksmith shop and a popular wine tavern." I said.

The ladies smiled warmly. "I guess you have the very best team then. It will be like old times," Moli said.

"Like old times indeed," I said.

Belgica, 57 BC

Livy returned to his tent in a troubled state. He looked forward to enjoying his two hetaerae, but he had the difficult decision of deciding which one to keep. On entering the tent, only Artemisia was present. She was setting up the table with wine, bread, and fruit as usual. Livy had brought roast chicken from the party to share with them. Stena was apparently out to get more wine as they anticipated a long night of revelling.

"Good evening, Centurion," Artemisia said rather formally. She was in a short white tunic with gold trimming, and her lustrous brown hair was let loose, cascading over her shoulders. Livy was once again struck by how much she resembled a Greek goddess. She looked like Artemis the huntress, her namesake.

"How are you, Spartan?" Livy returned the formality. "Look what I brought for dinner." He held up the roasted bird. "You don't look so happy. What happened?"

"You realise that this might be our last night together?" she said.

"What makes you think that you would be the one sent back to Servilia?"

"Look, Centurion, I am a Spartan, so I don't like to play games. What I tell you will be the honest truth, and you can act on it as you will." Livy was a little taken aback by her outburst.

"Please, by all means speak your mind," Livy urged her.

"You are a good man, Gaius Livius. Both Stena and I are of the same opinion. So both of us would, of course, rather be your mistress rather than work as high-class whores. There is no controversy about this. Tonight we will have to fight hard to win your affection."

"I am flattered that both of you want to stay with me."

"Servilia cannot afford to lose both of us, so one of us must return. That too is clear. What you may not know is that Stena is totally in love with you. She is not yet a whore, and she would make you a wonderful wife. She will be totally dedicated and faithful and will serve you like a king. Knowing this, if I were you, the choice would be obvious. You should take Stena."

"You mean you'd rather I choose Stena. Don't you want to be the one chosen?"

"I'd kill to stay with you. The life of an officer's woman has certainly more dignity than a whore, whatever her class. Besides, a Spartan woman's traditional role is to serve a warrior."

"I don't see the problem then," Livy said.

"I want you to know that I am certainly not the wifely sort. I can't cook, sew, or keep house. Spartan cuisine is so bad, it is practically inedible except by Spartans. Have you heard of our black broth, for instance? Besides, I am a veteran whore. Countless men have had me. So if you are looking for a good wife, I may not be the best candidate."

"You judge yourself too harshly, Artemisia. You are a beautiful girl with strong principles and a sense of dignity despite your low station. Besides, you fight like a demon, and your sexual skills are unsurpassed." Livy laughed. "What makes you think I am looking for a sweet little wife, anyway? I am far from ready to marry or settle down. Roman Army regulations forbid marriage except for senior officers," Livy said.

"So what are you looking for?" she said.

"I would be happy with a companion in arms and someone to sleep with at night."

"I don't love you, you must know this. I really like you, but it doesn't amount to love. I don't know if I will ever love any man after my experience with them."

"Well, I don't love you either. I like you and I lust for you, but it doesn't amount to love," Livy replied frankly. "Perhaps it's better this way. We will be best friends with privileges."

Artemisia looked a little startled. "Does that mean you choose me?"

"You will have to wait till morning to find out, same as Stena."

She wrinkled her nose in annoyance and pouted very briefly. She quickly regained her dignity and put on a nonchalant look. "So be it then."

At this point, Stena came in with two wineskins, looking decidedly happy. "Hello, dear Gaius Livius. I have managed to get two wineskins of

Caesar's best Pompeiian wine. I managed to make friends with a strange girl from the Far East called Jasmine."

"Small world," Livy thought. "So I guess the three of us are going to get well and truly sloshed tonight," Livy declared.

"Let's have dinner first. The centurion has brought us this nice big roast chicken. I hope it isn't too tough as it looks like an old bird," Artemisia said.

Livy sat down to eat with the two girls, who both seemed ravenously hungry. Livy himself ate little because he had already had one round of dinner with his men; also, the decision he had to make still troubled him. "How does one choose between two women who were both so different yet would both make excellent partners in totally different ways?" He sipped the sweet white wine which, he noted, was unusually strong.

In the end, he decided to make up his mind in the morning.

Murato woke up at dawn. There was a chill in the air. He wrapped a bearskin around himself. This was not the weather to go around nude. He also pulled on his leather pants as there would be much riding this day. He went to look for Leuce and found her huddled under a sheepskin, still sleeping. The campfires had burnt down to embers, and the smell of breakfast cooking polluted the crisp air.

"Get up, lazybones." He shook her. "We are riding out in an hour."

"Fuck off, Murato," she growled sleepily and buried her head in the skin.

"I mean it. Get up," he shouted angrily.

"I'm not going on your stupid mission. I'm sick," she said. The real reason was that she wanted to stay back and look after the Roman prisoner.

"You are faking it, bitch. I ought to give you a good trashing. I need every experienced warrior on this mission. We are bound to run into Roman *exploratores* or cavalry, and they are formidable troops."

"You can do to me what you like. I am sick and will be doing no fighting." She turned around and buried her head once more.

Murato was frustrated but couldn't do much. If he forcefully took her along, she wouldn't fight and would just be a burden. He gave her a hard kick in the side. She moaned, then started to sob.

He gave up and left to join his men. Ambiorix was conducting the meeting. Murato was impressed by his build, which was almost as good as his own. Ambiorix was bare-chested and didn't even need a cloak or skin against the cold. He introduced himself. "Murato, leader of the Gaesatae," he said.

"I am Ambiorix, king of the Eburones, and these are my bodyguards. Each is a skilled warrior and veteran of many battles. Our mission is to ride south. We will scout out the enemy and harass them. We will destroy their scouting parties. We will be the early-warning-system for the army of the confederation. Finally, we will lead them to the battlefield of our choice, where they will be annihilated." Ambiorix looked around at the impassive faces of his warriors, both Eburone and Gaesatae.

"Murato, you are to divide your men into teams of twenty men. We will reinforce each team with ten of my armoured knights. They will lend a stiff backbone to your teams. The rest of my knights, 100 of them, will form a central core that will go to the aid of any team that encounters the enemy."

"From which direction will the enemy come?" Murato asked, studying the crude map drawn on the sand.

"They will come either from the south or from the west. I intend to spread the five teams in a wide arc, covering these directions. The core cavalry will try to stay within striking distance of all the five groups. We will remain in a central position. If any team finds the enemy, it will send a messenger to alert the core group and we will come to its aid," Ambiorix added.

"What if we spot the main Roman Army?" Murato asked.

"Then you will merely screen and observe. You will alert me nevertheless. We can then put together some hit-and-run attacks or take out their scouts."

"Some of my warriors are women," Murato advised.

"I think we can put them in the southernmost team. The enemy are most unlikely to come from that direction," Ambiorix said. "Good hunting, fellow warriors!" he concluded.

Servilia came early to Livy's tent, accompanied by two male slaves who drove her cart. Livy met her outside the tent. The weather was bracing, but he was still nude after his morning toilet. Servilia gave him the once-over before she greeted him. Livy knew his body was not the standard of a classical statue, but at least he was not lacking where it counted. He stood unabashed.

"Good morning, Centurion Livius. I trust you had an enjoyable night"

"Your girls never fail to please, *domina*," he said.

"You have no doubt made your choice. Was it difficult to choose?" She teased.

"It was a dilemma, but I have nevertheless chosen," he said.

"Whom will you keep?"

"The Spartan Artemesia," Livy replied.

"Ah, how interesting! You pick a warrior's woman rather than a woman for the home."

"A soldier has no home," Livy answered.

"How true! So be it then," Servilia said with finality.

"I have another offer for you and a favour to ask in return." She suddenly looked serious. "Caesar is important to me, not only as a lover but more so politically. He is destined for great things. The only trouble is he takes such terrible risks with himself. I want you to protect him in battle as much as you can."

"Of course, I will willingly give my life to protect Caesar, *domina*. Sometimes in battle we may not be in the same vicinity, though."

"I understand that, but I want you to promise to look out for him and try to be near him in battle," Servilia asked earnestly.

"That is possible, *domina*. I will certainly try my best."

"I trust you because you have no political agenda. Some of the Romans wouldn't mind if he got accidentally killed in battle. Others might even lend a hand themselves. He has so many enemies."

"I promise to look out for Caesar. I do it not only for you but because I feel he is destined to lead Rome to greatness, and I admire him greatly too."

"I have great faith that you will carry out your promise. Do you swear by Venus, Caesar's patron goddess?"

"I swear." Livy put a fist to his heart.

"In that case, Artemisia is yours. I will sell her to you for the small sum of ten dinari. She is worth at least a hundred times that. Here, I have the bill of sale prepared. I had one for Stena too, in case you chose her." She smiled wryly.

"Your gift is beyond generosity, madam. I don't know what to say." Livy was amazed.

"Just say, I accept, you idiot." She put on a playful frown.

"I graciously accept." Livy smiled.

"Stena, are you awake? It's time to go, Stena." Servilia called out. Stena emerged, head bowed and red-eyed. She had obviously been crying.

Livy went to her and held her close. He gave her a kiss on her forehead and a warm hug. She didn't look him in the eye.

"Don't worry, Centurion, I will be all right. I hope you and Artemisia find happiness together."

Livy felt a pain in his chest he did not expect. Stena was indeed a gem. Was he making the wrong choice? It was too late now. There was nothing he could say to reduce the hurt.

"Please come to see me once a while," Stena said softly.

"I will," Livy said softly.

Servilia came and took Stena by the shoulder. "Come, dear. Come home. I won't bother you with clients for a while. Take your time till you are ready," Servilia said kindly.

"Centurion Livius. Do come and visit Stena as often as you want. There will be no charge for your visits. Just remember your promise."

Livy felt sad. "Goodbye, Stena. Keep well."

"Keep well, Centurion, and be safe," Stena said. She got on to the cart, and Servilia set off for Caesar's camp. Servilia had decided to set up her business within range of the general staff, who were her chief customers.

Livy returned to his tent. Artemisia was still nude, but she was getting Livy's uniform ready. There was to be a parade later, and she was starting to enjoy her new role as a centurion's woman.

Livy stood and admired her anatomy for a moment and then said, "Look what I have in my hand."

Artemisia turned and saw a scroll. "What's that?"

"These are your ownership papers. Servilia sold you to me."

Artemesia was surprised. "So I am your slave now?"

"Yes, mine and mine alone."

She jumped for joy and ran to hug him. Her eyes were bright with joy. "Does that mean I never have to go back to the brothel?"

"Not while I live," Livy said.

As he stepped out between his tent flaps, he bounced into a pair of legionaries in full armour. They were as startled as he was. "Excuse me, sir," the older man said. "We have come to fetch you to the legate's tent. You have a visitor from Bibrax."

Livy's heart skipped a beat. "Could it be . . ." He had mixed feelings. If it was Brigita, this was far from an opportune moment as he had just taken Artemisia as mistress. On the other hand, he was not unhappy to see her again. "Is it a lady?" he asked.

"We don't know. We were just ordered to fetch you," the soldier said. "I believe one of your visitors is the Prefect Iccius."

"Give me a minute." He dressed hurriedly, putting on his leather *subarmalis,* then followed the soldiers hurriedly to the *praetorium* where Crassus was quartered. Crassus and Iccius were waiting for him outside. Both looked distraught. Iccius came to Livy and hugged him warmly; then Crassus hugged him in turn. Livy was surprised by the show of emotion. Nearby was a wooden cart pulled by a chestnut mare. He recognised the horse at once.

Nobody spoke a word. He was led to the cart, where he noticed a human form under a white sheet. Iccius was lost for words. There were tears in his eyes, which looked swollen. He pulled away the sheet.

Livy was devastated. The naked body of Brigita lay unadorned under the sheet. She was lifeless and grey. He held her hand and stroked her cheek. Her body was stiff with rigor mortis. Her face was swollen, and her mouth was open, baring her teeth. It was a grotesque sight. She wore only one object. There was an arm bracelet shaped like two snakes entwined.

Iccius retrieved it reverently and handed it to Livy. "She would want you to have this," he said.

Livy had seen many corpses before, but this sight he could not bear. The tears streamed down his face uncontrollably. They were tears of indescribable sadness but also tears of guilt. He had indulged himself in the arms of prostitutes while she was recovering. Was this punishment from the gods?

Finally composing himself, he asked Iccius "How did she die"

"She was found yesterday floating face down in the Axona River," Iccius said between sobs. Crassus hugged the man round his shoulders. "Suicide," he added.

Crassus read his mind. "Don't blame yourself, Gaius. Perhaps she couldn't live with the shame."

"Did she leave a note?" Livy asked.

"Yes, she did." Iccius produced a piece of leather with neat Latin handwriting on it. The words were in black ink.

"Tell Centurion Gaius Livius that the time I spent with him was the happiest in all my life. Please deliver my body to him totally naked. He likes me this way. Ask him to remember me fondly always. Love, Brigita."

Livy was speechless. He bent over her icy lifeless body and gave her a last kiss on the forehead.

They made a funeral pyre for her. Livy put two silver coins on her eyes for Charon, the ferryman. Iccius lit the pyre, which ignited briskly, giving off a sweet aroma. Even in death she brought forth a fragrance. Artemisia attended the funeral, holding Livy by the arm, giving support.

Emotions churned within Livy's breast. There was heavy guilt for his infidelity. There was hatred for the Nervii that perpetrated the gang rape. The Remi were right. The Nervii were scum, and he would now show them no mercy.

Noviodunum, Summer, 57 BC

> Just rewards for officers and men enhance an army's morale.
> Distribute rewards without undue respect for rules.

The parade was a large one. There were representative contingents from all the legions and the auxiliary cohorts. Everyone was in their best and finest.

Armour shone with polish, and red plumes and feathers were in abundance. There were very many awards to be presented.

Centurion Gallus of the Tenth was awarded the *Corona Muralis* for being first on the walls of Noviodunum. He had a broken leg though, and had to be carried to the tribunal to receive his crown.

Antony was awarded a set of nine gold *phalarae* (medals) for his role as commander of the force which stopped the Suessiones at the river.

The Thirteenth and Fourteenth Legions got their battle honours for the battle at the Axona River. They were happy to have something to hang below their eagles at last.

The German bodyguards won battle honours for their role at the river battle with Antony and the raiders.

Four gladiators caused quite a stir as they came up for a Golden Torque each. Caesar had them dressed in the uniform of the German bodyguards.

Both the Cretan archers, Balearic slingers, and Numidian light infantry got several medals to stick on their *signum* (battle standard). They had all been involved in multiple actions over the last days.

The Seventh and Tenth Legions each got a medal to stick on their eagle for the assault on Noviodunum. Two cohorts of the Tenth got extra awards for showing up at the river battle even though they missed most of the action. There were some murmurings from the Germans when this occurred.

Finally, the raiders collected five battle honours to attach to their standard. In addition, they got a new standard with a silver Pegasus mounted on top and a long pink streamer just below it. Now the standard had five golden medallions below.

The medals were for the Battle of Bibrax, the raid on the Belgic camp which netted nearly 2,000 horses, the action at the River Axona, the brave stands against the whole Suessione Army, and the final battle of Noviodunum just before the Suessiones surrendered.

The raiders were extremely proud that they were now one of the most decorated units in the army. Livy, Paulus, and Biorix went up jointly to receive the award.

There were many other unit awards given, but the raiders were the star this day.

Biorix proudly carried the unit standard as Livy and Paulus marched beside him as they rejoined their unit. The men gave a loud cheer as they stood to attention in front of their formation. This was against regulation, but this time they were forgiven.

As they marched back to their camp, Livy asked Biorix, "Did the boys behave last night"

"Impeccably," Biorix answered.

"And the women? Did any resist"

"You know there is something about women and strong drink. Ply them with enough of it and you can get away with murder," Biorix said with a grin.

Paulus couldn't suppress a half-choked laugh.

"So what's the score?" Livy asked him nonchalantly, keeping his misery to himself.

"Me, personally? Went through four of our guests besides my Eala. Can hardly walk straight this morning. Thought I would get into trouble at the parade!"

"What about Paulus there."

"I'd rather not discuss it if you don't mind, sir," Paulus said defensively.

"He's afraid he'll get into trouble with Sabia. She's a jealous one, that one," Biorix sniggered.

"Very well, we'll let Paulus keep his secrets. Did you pick the four men I asked for"

"Aye, sir. I chose four sturdy Remi lads. All blond and pale as the moon. Totally Belgic-looking. They are good archers and horsemen too," Biorix said.

"Good. Have them report to Caesar's tent in an hour. I am going back to my tent to change into something more suitable for war." He galloped off elegantly on Nero.

At the tent, Artemesia was pensive as she helped him pack for the mission. She had prepared a sack of food and one of extra clothes for him. "I wish I could come along," she said.

"Not his time, Artemisia. The mission is deep within enemy lines and will be dangerous. I don't want anything to happen to you now that we are together."

"Likewise I want to come along to make sure you are safe."

"I don't intend to take any chances. I have a lot to live for." He smiled reassuringly and held her hands. He hoped he was convincing.

She passed him two filled canteens. "Spring water, very fresh and sweet," she said.

"That's really thoughtful." He kissed her on the cheek.

"I have something for you," she said. She gave him a rough iron medallion attached to a finely worked iron chain. "Wear this around your neck for good luck. It's been in my family for hundreds of years, since the time of Leonidas and the 300 Spartans at Thermopylae."

"Is that really true?" He looked at the iron disc. One side had the image of Athena carved on it. The other had a Spartan helmet and crossed spears and the Greek letter lambda.

"It belonged to one of the 300. He left it behind for his young son when he left for the fiery gates," Artemesia said. "You may keep it for now and give it back to me when we are all living a quiet safe life somewhere without wars."

Livy dressed in a brown tunic. He put the medallion around his neck and tucked it under the tunic. Over that he had the light chain mail and a simple steel helmet. He had changed his belt to a simple leather one with no markings, and likewise his scabbard. He packed a dagger and his *spatha*. He took two quivers of thirty arrows each and his trusty composite bow, which was a parting gift from his archery teacher, the Prefect of Tarraco's forester.

Artemisia had packed bread, cheese, fruit, some cured ham, and some cereal to make gruel. For flavour, she included a small pot of *garum*, the famous fish sauce—beloved of Romans—which went with everything.

Finally, as he was about to leave, she pulled him against her and kissed him. It was a long, deep kiss. The smell of her breath aroused passions which he never even realised he possessed.

Finally she broke off. "That's to remind you what you will be missing if you don't come back. Stay alive for me, Centurion Gaius Livius."

He held her close, kissed her one more time and quickly left. If he stayed, any longer he wouldn't be able to drag himself away.

An hour later, he was riding eastwards along the River Axona (Aisne). The special force was a strange mix. There were no Roman uniforms, and everyone dressed to look like Belgic cavalry. The men wore simple brown tunics with brown trousers with a blue-grey check tartan over their chain mail. They also wore simple round steel helmets with large cheek pieces. These were the colours of the Bellovaci. Hopefully, any confederate troops would mistake them for friendly forces or, at worst, neutral.

The commander of the team was Tribune Quintus Servilius Caepio; he was the son of an ex-praetor and brother to Servilia Caepionis, Caesar's mistress. Comprising the rest of the team were Livy and Biorix and four raiders—who were all Remi; six German bodyguards; six Suessione noble cavalrymen, including Lugurix who was Livy's prisoner and now a Roman hostage; and two gladiators, who were Gauls. Livy realised that they were an odd mix and hoped they could act together in a battle. He also did not quite trust their new Suessione allies.

Caepio was a rich boy who had bought his commission and probably used Servilia's connections. Caesar was giving him a chance to prove himself.

The man had never held independent command. Livy realised that he had the unenviable role of babysitter. Furthermore, he had to keep everyone alive without hurting the tribune's feelings. After all, he was the son of a praetor and the grandson of a consul.

They crossed the river at the site of the battle two days ago. The bodies of Suessiones still lay everywhere. Some were bloated corpses still floating near the banks of the river, caught in tree roots and reeds. Other lay about on both banks, swarming with flies. There was the sickly smell of rotting flesh, and Livy had to cover his nose with his scarf. Some of the bodies were propped up impaled on stakes. Bloated, fly-infested horse carcasses also lay with the men.

"Some may think battle glorious, but there was nothing glorious about the aftermath. The carnage after a battle was truly dreadful. The saying "*dulce et decorum est pro patria mori*" seemed like a big fat lie. There was nothing sweet or proper about ending up a stinking corpse. It was just a total waste," Livy noted mentally.

Livy wondered, "Is all this pursuit of glory just a scam by the rich and powerful to further their interest at the expense of the common soldiers and the poor civilians who are the main victims of any conflict. To the poor peasant boys who died here by this river, the political considerations of their masters are just so much chaff in the wind."

Livy and his raiders swam their horses across first, then, set up a security perimeter as the rest of the party crossed. Tribune Caepio rode up to him. "Centurion, I want your men to fall back from now on and let Lugurix and his Suessiones take the lead. They know the country and can choose the most advantageous route."

"Is it wise to trust them, sir? They were just two days ago sworn to destroy us," Livy pointed out politely.

"May I remind you that I am in command here? The Suessiones will be the vanguard. I shall follow them with the Germans and the gladiators. You may take the rear." Caepio reiterated, looking a little irritated.

Livy didn't want to provoke him further. The commander had the prerogative. As you command, Tribune," Livy said.

Lugurix led them for some miles along the north bank of the Axona. He then suddenly turned north. They were still in Remi territory, but as they proceeded northwards, they came into the territory of the Viromandui.

They now travelled in fairly open country and had to take pains to be inconspicuous. Livy was a little reassured by the tactical ability of the Suessione guides. They constantly went ahead to scout the route that gave the most cover, then led the party quickly from cover to cover to minimise their exposure. The Nervii confederation had taken pains to ravage the

Remi lands, but here in, Viromandui territory, the countryside was relatively intact. Farms and villages were left relatively undisturbed. They no doubt contributed necessary supplies to keep the enemy in the field.

Livy was tempted to disrupt the agriculture, but he realised that this would immediately alert the enemy to their presence. The terrain became more open as they proceeded, and everyone in the party became more alert as they realised that they could be seen from miles away. A party of twenty horsemen would attract attention. Their only hope was that they would be mistaken for friendly forces. Many of the farms and villages had smokestacks and other signs of being inhabited. Livy was sure that they were already noticed. Caepio rode confidently and seemed oblivious, relying totally on his Suessione guides. Livy marvelled at his confidence. He exuded an air of total nonchalance as if his patrician ancestry alone would ensure his protection by the Roman gods.

Finally Lugurix called a halt. He found a small clump of forest beside a stream. The location had an idyllic quality, but best of all it provided some cover and fresh water. The men were forbidden to start any fires, but at least they could hide out and rest till dark.

Two of Livy's men were assigned sentry duty, and the rest of the men spread themselves out in the small wood. Caepio called a meeting of the commanders. This included Lugurix, Livy, Biorix, and one of the leader of the Germans. Caepio started, "How far north do you think the Nervii Army is?"

"If I am not wrong, Tribune, they will concentrate somewhere along the River Sabis. The river will provide water and a natural defence when time for battle comes," Lugurix said.

"That means two more days north," Caepio estimated.

"At least," Lugurix confirmed.

"We are bound to be spotted before then," Livy said.

"We must move only at night from now on. Hopefully, no one will look too closely. After all, we look like Bellovaci," Lugurix said hopefully.

"Even if we get past all their patrols, we'll have a hell of a time breaking into their camp to rescue the decurion," Biorix chipped in.

"We'll have to sneak in," Livy said. "Maybe with only a small party of five men."

Caepio looked at him, surprised. He did not expect Livy to contribute.

"The centurion is right," Lugurix agreed. "If we storm in there all together, we don't stand a chance. We have to work by stealth."

"It seems you two have a plan?" Caepio asked imperiously.

"I don't really have a firm plan yet, sir," Livy said. "I do think, however, if we are to have any chance to succeed at all, we must get into their camp without being detected. A small party stands a better chance."

"I must remind you, Centurion, that I am the commander of this mission and I will decide the best way to complete this mission. Besides, I have a trump card up my sleeve. Until I decide how best to affect the rescue, I would prefer that you keep your own counsel."

"The rich, patrician tribune was being seriously oversensitive," Livy thought but kept his views to himself.

"I can get you to their camp, Tribune. Getting inside is a whole different game. I'll be damned if I know how you can just walk in there and just take your man. You better come up with a plan before we get there," Lugurix spoke plainly.

"Just, get us there, barbarian, and leave it to Roman ingenuity. Ask your men to get some rest. We move as soon as it is dark, and we will ride all night."

With that Caepio stalked off.

Livy went to talk to his men, who were busy getting to know the German contingent. They were an interesting bunch. All were large, well-built men with long hair tied into a knot at the top. They were also all bearded, though their beards were trimmed neatly.

"Four of us are Treveri from this side of the Rhennus. Our ancestors were German, but our tribe settled among the Gauls. We are famous for breeding and riding horses." He laughed. "Where come you from, Centurion?"

"I come from Tarraco in Hispania. We also breed horses. I hear the Treveri have some of the best horses in these parts," Livy said.

"I hear your Spanish horses are of high quality too. Spanish boys are like Treveri boys, eh? You ride from young. My name is Runo. What's yours?"

"I am Gaius Livius. Friends call me Livy. Where are your other two comrades from?" Livy asked.

"They are Cherusci. They come from the more barbaric side of the Rhennus, the right side." Runo laughed. "They eat children there and run around naked, ha ha," Runo joked.

"I hear the Cherusci are fearsome warriors," Livy said.

"That they are. Those two boys are each worth ten of those Belgic scum, especially that mother's boy, Lugurix, and his bunch of sissies," Runo said. "Aye, we taught them a thing or two down by that there river. Their bodies are still feeding the fish."

"I read that you the Germans and the Belgae and Gauls all fight each other every now and then over centuries," Livy said.

"You are right there. There are no permanent allies and no permanent enemies among the tribes," Runo said philosophically. "Come, Centurion. Let's join my lads. I will show you how we Germans catch fish. I think we need to have some fresh food for dinner," Runo said good-naturedly.

Livy watched the Germans fish. They used different techniques. Some used their cavalry javelins whilst wading in the water. Others tried hooks bated with bread. One man even had with him a net, which he was casting expertly.

There was soon result from these activities, and in a short time, the fish were roasting. As it was near dusk, Caepio had relaxed the rule about fires. Livy suspected that the decision was not so much tactical as it was motivated by hunger. He hoped that this small relaxation of discipline would not have too large a consequence.

Livy and his men were invited to eat with the Germans. The preparation was simple. The fish were salted and roasted. The flavour was wonderful, nevertheless, because of the freshness of the fish. The men made some barley gruel to eat with the fish, which proved just the right accompaniment. Livy donated his little pot of *garum* for the occasion, much to the gratitude of all.

Caepio had warmed a little after the food with a little help from a wineskin. "That's good *garum*, Centurion. How did you come by the stuff?" he asked in a bored, patrician drawl.

"It was a gift from a friend, sir. They make good *garum* in the town I come from," Livy added.

"You could make a fortune making and selling this stuff. A bit below the status of a senator to be in the business, but if it was allowed, I wouldn't mind being in this trade," Caepio said loftily.

"You would make a fortune for certain, sir, considering the amount of money people are willing to pay for it."

"What did your family do?" Caepio asked.

"My father's farm grew olives, sir."

"I bet that brings in a tidy sum as well, ha ha," he said.

"We get by, sir," Livy replied. Caepio was obviously getting bored as he considered Livy not quite his class.

"Well, get some rest, Centurion. We'll be moving out soon."

"Thank you, sir, just let us know when you are ready," Livy concluded and left to be with his men.

Some distance away, a mixed party of Gaesatae and Eburone cavalry were observing from atop a hill. "Is that smoke?" the Eburone commander asked.

"Three or four fires, over by the trees near the river. Men cooking," the female Gaesatae warrior replied. She wore only leather trousers but was otherwise naked except for her weapons. She had a fearsome appearance with her hair dyed bright red and her body painted with blue paint. The

Eburone commander noticed that she had a passable figure though, and that underneath the paint she may actually be pretty. Maybe he would try to bed her this night, he thought.

"Maybe we should investigate." The commander decided. "Take another of your Amazons and go check it out. Try not to be seen."

The girl, whose name was Arana, motioned to another girl, and they rode off towards the smoke. The commander continued to watch from the hill.

Biorix suddenly came running to Livy. "Riders coming, two Amazons, heavily armed."

"Alert everyone, inform the tribune. Everyone to take cover. Biorix, come with me." Livy jumped into action.

"On me, raiders," Biorix called and all the raiders ran after Biorix.

Livy readied his bow as he hid behind a tree. Biorix was behind the next tree, and the raiders had spread out in the path of the enemy scouts.

The two girls came cautiously. They rode very slowly and were alert, listening for any sounds. Suddenly Arana heard the whistling of arrows. Her horse was hit several times, and it collapsed. She was thrown violently, landing on her back, the wind knocked from her. The other girl turned to run. Arrows were hitting everywhere around her. Suddenly she felt a sharp pain as one of the missiles hit her in the back. The horse bolted, and she couldn't hang on, falling into a bush.

The raiders were dashing to retrieve the two fallen women and the loose horse. Biorix got to the first girl and hit her hard on the head with the pommel of his sword. The girl was immediately knocked unconscious.

The second Amazon had an arrow stuck in the back but was still moving fast as the raiders stalked her through the dark woods. They finally cornered her under a tree. She was unarmed and exhausted. Livy shouted at her in Celtic to surrender.

Suddenly Caepio charged out and ran at her with his *gladius* drawn, and before anyone could react, he ran her through the abdomen. The girl was stunned for a moment, staring at the blade stuck in her abdomen. Caepio withdrew the blade, and she dropped into a widening pool of her own blood, curled into the foetal position. She did not make a sound, though she was obviously still alive.

"She was surrendering, sir," Livy protested. "And what's more, she was unarmed."

Caepio stood up straight and looked at Livy down the length of his aquiline nose. "She is a spy, and she will give away our position."

Livy and Lugurix rushed to her side. "I know this girl. She is one of the Gaesatae warriors and used to be attached to my cavalry." They both tried to staunch the bleeding from her abdominal wound. It didn't look so good. The girl moaned softly.

"You're both wasting your time. She is dead already," Caepio said coldly. "I don't know why you two bear so soft with an enemy warrior."

They ignored him and tried their best to bind the wound tightly.

One of the Germans suddenly ran towards them. "Enemy cavalry approaching the woods, about twenty men."

"Spread out and take cover. Prepare to receive enemy cavalry," Caepio screamed.

Livy called out to his men, "On me, raiders."

They gathered quickly. "Spread out and use your bows. Try not to engage them in close combat. Let the Germans and the Suessiones do the work. If you see Amazons, take down their horses. If men, kill them."

"What if the Amazons attack us after we knock out their horses?" one of his men asked.

"Don't risk your own life. In that case, take them down. I don't like killing women, but I will if they give us no choice. I won't run them through when they are unarmed and defenceless." Livy said.

The men nodded and quickly dispersed, just in time too.

Livy was worried. The troops were the best, but he remembered the saying "An army of sheep led by a lion can defeat an army of lions led by a sheep". He had little confidence in Tribune Caepio.

The Eburones formed a skirmish line. They let the Gaesatae lead to draw fire and kept a few dozen yards back. Livy noticed that there were about eight Amazons in the front, all carrying lances.

His men's first volley downed four of the horses. The rest of the Amazons reigned their horses and did not dare advance further, intimidated by the arrows flying everywhere. The Eburone cavalry overtook them, and two of the armoured warriors were immediately hit, toppling from their horses. At the same time, the German and Suessione soldiers charged in among them on horses, and the whole forest became a melee of clanging swords.

Livy had difficulty trying to tell friend from foe in the dark. There were horsemen everywhere in individual combat. Suddenly he saw Caepio. He was being attacked by two heavily armoured Eburone horsemen and seemed in trouble. He was desperately fending them off as they swung at him with their long swords. Livy fired an arrow at one of them and saw the shaft sink into the chest armour of one of the horsemen. The arrow had penetrated but not enough to down the man, who disengaged and rode away from the fight, tugging at the arrow. The second man, however, slashed at Caepio's left arm and connected. Caepio squirmed at the pain, leaving his guard open, and the Eburone swung his sword at his head, connecting with his helmet with a load thud. Caepio collapsed off his horse.

The Eburone leant down to finish off the prostrate tribune. At that moment, Livy rushed up to him and tipped him over the horse. The Eburone fell with a loud clang as his plate armour hit the ground. Livy was on top of him in a flash, pointing his *spatha* at his neck and dimpling the skin with the tip. The man didn't dare to move. One small push would sever his spinal column.

The skirmish was petering out in favour of the Romans. All the Gaesatae girls had been unhorsed and captured, and the Eburones were almost all killed except for their commander.

Livy ordered one of the Germans to secure his prisoner, then looked for Biorix. "What's the score?" he asked.

"One Suessione killed on our side, and one of the gladiators has a flesh wound. The raiders are fine as they did not engage. On the other side, we got eight male bodies and two female. We have your prisoner here, who is likely the commander, and eight female prisoners, one of whom is seriously wounded. The one run through by the tribune," Biorix reported.

"How is the tribune?" Livy asked.

"Out cold, sir," Biorix replied.

"Did any of the enemy escape?" Livy asked.

"It's possible. In the darkness, we can't be sure we accounted for everyone."

"We don't have much time then," Livy said. "Tie up all the women. The wounded gladiator and one of the Suessiones will be the escort. They are to head for Bibrax and the prisoners handed over to Iccius. That's the nearest friendly base. The enemy commander comes with us. We need to question him. Load up Tribune Caepio as well. We got to move fast."

"You are right to move fast, sir. If the tribune wakes up, he will likely have all those poor girls killed."

"Get to it, Biorix."

Livy sought out Lugurix. "Do you have any idea which tribe these men are from?"

"They are Eburones," Lugurix replied.

"Have the Eburones joined the confederation?"

"I don't think so. Last I heard they decided to stay out of it. These must be volunteers. I know that Ambiorix wants to fight but his co-ruler doesn't," Lugurix said.

"Ambiorix must have come with his own retainers. These look like noble cavalry. They are well armed and armoured."

"Looks like it, Centurion. I want to thank you for sparing the women. I know most of them. They are good warriors and don't deserve to be executed out of hand."

"I'm definitely going to get into trouble when Caepio wakes up. He will likely put me on a charge. I hope you speak up for me when the time comes."

"You spared me, and I am a free man and a noble again today. I owe you, Centurion. Don't worry. I think the tribune is a fool as well. Let's hope he sleeps longer. The girls will be out of range by the time he wakes up. We have to move now."

"You are right," Livy said. He gave orders to move out. A litter had been fashioned for the wounded girl and attached to be pulled by one of the Eburone horses. The other fit girls were tied together and made to walk with the two soldiers as escort. Livy saw them off and then mounted and rode north with the rest of the party. The tribune was unceremoniously slung over his horse. He would be aching all over by the time they reached their destination.

They rode north very quickly while it was still night. The full moon lighted their way. Near morning, Lugurix took them into forest, and Livy was relieved that they had cover at last. As the sun came up, they made camp. They had made good time as they were already halfway to the Sabis River, according to Lugurix. The made camp, and this time Livy insisted there be no fires. The tribune was still knocked out. They dressed the wound on his arm, cleaned it, and bandaged it.

Livy and Lugurix got down to interrogating their prisoner.

"You must be thirsty," Lugurix said. "You want water?" He shook the canteen in front of his face. The prisoner looked at the canteen longingly. His hands were tied. "Tell us who you are," Lugurix demanded.

"My name is Drogo. I am Eburone and retainer to King Ambiorix."

"Ah, dragon," Lugurix said. "I have heard of you. You have a reputation for raiding and raping in our territory. I am glad to meet your acquaintance at last. I am Lugurix, retainer to King Galba of the Suessiones. I have always wanted to catch you and cut your balls off. Finally I will have the opportunity." Lugurix smiled malevolently.

"Fuck you, Suessione pig. I hear you cowards surrendered and then joined the Romans against your own countrymen. I didn't believe it at first, but I see for myself now it is true." He spat.

"You animal, I don't have time to trade insults with you." He took out a sharp knife and cut his trousers open, revealing his genitals.

"How many men are with Ambiorix, and where is he located?" Lugurix asked.

"Go fuck yourself," Drago replied, then he screamed loudly.

Lugurix had cut open his scrotum, revealing one white testicle. "I will ask you one more time, and if you ask me to fuck off, this nice white ball comes off. I will then move to the other side. Then I will start slicing your dick off and inch at the time, starting at the top."

Drago looked horrified. "You bastard! I'll kill you." Lugurix immediately detached one testicle and hung it before his eyes. Drago screamed.

"When I finish with you, you will be even less than a woman. You will have nothing left, and my men will then fuck your arse."

"All right." He gave up. "What do you want to know?" Drago conceded. He was reduced to hysteria.

"How many men has Ambiorix got"

"He has 150 noble cavalry."

"What about allies? How many allies"

"About 100 Gaesatae, split into five teams."

"Disposition?" Lugurix demanded.

Drago spat at him again. "I will kill you someday and somehow."

Lugurix slit open his other scrotum, revealing his remaining white testicle. Livy noted that the man could cut as precisely as a surgeon. Drago screamed loudly once more.

"I hope you have already borne children," Lugurix said. "Now once more, what is the disposition of your party?" he repeated.

"Ambiorix has 100 riders at the centre. The rest are spread out in groups of thirty in a wide arc," Drago whimpered.

"And what is your position in this arc"

Drago turned away and refused to answer further.

"Your raiding parties have attacked our villages and farms, killed our men, and raped our women. I have every reason to make it really bad for you so don't try my patience." Lugurix hit him hard in the face until he bled from nose and lips.

"All right, all right. I will tell you all you want to know. Just don't cut any more pieces off. Give me a quick death after."

"I offer you your life if you cooperate, Commander," Livy interjected.

Lugurix gave him an annoyed look but did not contradict him.

The prisoner gave the entire Eburone plan after that.

The surviving Eburone scout was happy to escape with his life. He didn't even bother to try and find the party of Gaesatae that Drago had left to guard their camp. He rode north as fast as he could to find Ambiorix.

Ambiorix and his 100-heavy cavalry were camped at a farmhouse which they had commandeered. The farmer was Viromandui and hence allies, so Ambiorix was obliged to be civil. He nevertheless took over the farmhouse, and the family was relegated to being service staff for the men. They also helped themselves to whatever food they could find, and the men helped themselves to his daughters as well.

The scout rode into the camp, exhausted. His horse was blown and collapsed after he arrived. "I need to speak to the king at once." The guards let him through.

Ambiorix was tucking in to some roast chicken. It was being served by the farmer's wife, and the king had his hand up the back of her skirt as she carved the bird. The farmer had two wives, and this was the younger, prettier one. The farmer sat in a corner, drinking to escape his woes.

"What have you to report?" Ambiorix asked the breathless scout.

"The Romans. They are approaching. They come from the south. I come from Drago's team. They ambushed us maybe half-a-day's ride south."

"Are you the only one left?"

"There are some Gaesatae, about ten. Drago sent them off in another direction, and they were not with us. Of the twenty with Drago, only I got away."

"And Drago?" Ambiorix asked.

"Killed or captured, My King."

"How big was the enemy force?"

"Difficult to tell in the dark, but they were substantial. I think several hundred. They had cavalry and were supported by archers."

"Do you think they are the vanguard of the Roman Army?" Ambiorix looked thoughtful.

"I couldn't tell for sure. It was in the woods, and it was getting dark. Many of them were Bellovaci, though."

"I don't believe it! The Bellovaci are firmly on our side."

"They may have surrendered like the Suessiones."

"I can't believe that the Bellovaci would turn against us."

"Aren't they friends of the Aedui? The Aedui are firm Roman allies."

"Did you notice anything else?" Ambiorix fixed the scout with a probing gaze.

"Yes. Some of the cavalry were definitely Suessiones. I heard them shout to each other in their dialect. Others look like Germans for sure," the scout said.

"This is all very bad news. The confederation is falling apart, and the Romans are gaining more and more allies." Ambiorix looked troubled. He turned to his officers. "We need to ride south at once and track this Roman Army."

He turned to the scout. "Get some food and drink and then ride north to the Nervii and let Bodougnatus know Caesar is coming from the south. Tell him he may have the Bellovaci and the Suessiones on his side. Meanwhile, we go to observe his movements and slow him down. I hope Bodougnatus has his trap prepared."

CHAPTER 19

Caepio woke up with a terrible headache. Actually, he ached all over. It was already morning, and the men were having a meagre breakfast of bread and cheese. No fires were lit. The surrounding trees cast long shadows. A confused babble of German, Latin, and Belgic sound assailed his ears, each syllable another needle piercing his sore brain.

"Centurion!" he yelled. "Centurion Livius!"

Livy came quickly. "Good morning, Tribune. I am glad to see you recovered from your injuries."

"I am far from recovered. I have the most horrible headache and what's been happening? I want a full report."

"Of course, sir," Livy was soon joined by Lugurix, Biorix, and the leader of the Germans.

Livy gave a full account, keeping nothing back. "So we now have the disposition of the enemy scouts. With some luck, they should be all west of us, and the Nervii main army lies a day away to the north. We should be able to ride in daylight now that we have some forest cover," Livy concluded.

Caepio looked unusually peeved. "You are an arrogant and impertinent young pup. You specifically disobeyed my orders that we are to take no prisoners."

Livy was flabbergasted. "Sir, all the prisoners were female and surrendered except the one we hold now, who has given us really valuable intelligence. We know exactly where the enemy camp is," he protested.

"I don't care about that. You deliberately flouted my authority while I was incapacitated. If any of your prisoners had escaped, they would have given our strength and position away and jeopardised our entire mission."

"Tribune, I think the actions of the centurion are not incorrect," Lugurix defended.

"I didn't ask for your opinion," Caepio rounded on him angrily.

"There was no reason to murder helpless women," Biorix exclaimed.

"That's the kind of soft thinking that will lead to the loss of this war," Caepio sneered. "You are all insubordinate, and you will all consider yourselves on a charge. I will take disciplinary action against all of you when we get back."

The four men were too stunned for words.

"Meanwhile, get the men ready. We have rested enough. We ride out in fifteen minutes. Lugurix, finish off that Eburone pig."

Caepio stormed off.

"Now we are for it," Biorix lamented.

"Don't worry. Let's just get this mission over with. I just hope our legate Crassus and Caesar himself will see through this patrician pig. I don't know how he can be related to Servilia. She is so sensible by contrast," Livy said.

Lugurix was the last to leave. He had the unenviable task of finishing off the Eburone. "You've come to finish me off, haven't you?" Drago concluded as Lugurix approached him, sword drawn.

He closed his eyes and turned his head to one side, anticipating the blow. There was a swish, and he felt his legs free. Then he was roughly turned round, and his hands were also cut free.

"I'm going to let you live because I don't kill unarmed men. Now, I want you to scream as if you were being slaughtered." Drago gave a blood-curdling scream, and Lugurix hit him hard over the head with the pommel of his sword. As far as Drago was concerned, everything just suddenly went black.

Caesar had not even reached the capital Bratuspantium when a large delegation of Bellovaci nobles came to him in supplication. They had heard of his artillery and siege machines and were sure that their town would not hold against Roman superior technology.

They begged Caesar for terms. At fist Caesar was not inclined to give quarter as the Bellovaci were a really militant lot and he was sure they would give trouble in future. (In this he was to be proven right several years hence.)

He was, however, swayed by two factors. Firstly, his Aedui allies had begged him to be lenient to their kinsmen. The Bellovaci and Aedui were previously allies. Secondly, Caesar was reluctant to commit to major military action if he could win bloodless victories. He didn't have the troops to lose, and if he could neutralise the Belgae one tribe at a time, this was strategically very convenient.

The Bellovaci opened the gates to Bratuspantium. Caesar exacted the usual tribute and hostages. The Bellovaci also had to help supply his army and were disarmed. Generously, he spared their women the indignity of having to entertain his men. Though the episode with the Suessiones had been perpetrated with a minimum of violence, Caesar sensed that the ill feeling from such action ran deep. From now on, he would only allow the women to be used if the town fell to siege or assault and not when it surrendered.

He deduced correctly that humane and generous terms would encourage more of the tribes to join the Roman cause.

Caesar did not stay long in Bratuspantium, just a day or two to collect supplies and tribute. His next target was Samarobriva, the capital of the Ambiani. His cavalry and scouts were already reconnoitring in that direction.

Caesar was in his tent, which was located in the Roman camp constructed just outside the town. He had decided not to let his legions loose inside the town except for the necessary staff required to collect supplies and tribute. There was no point to unnecessarily aggravate the inhabitants.

He was speaking to Crassus, Antony, and several of his legates. They had stripped down to tunics and were in a relaxed mood. "Any word from our scouts?" Caesar asked as he washed his face in a basin of water held by a slave.

"Caepio's patrol ran into some Eburones and Gaesatae. They have sent back two messengers so far," Crassus replied.

"So where is their main army?" Caesar asked, drying himself with a clean white towel handed to him by a jet-black Numidian in a pristinely white tunic.

"The last messenger put them here at the River Sabis," Crassus said. "We are not sure how many and which tribes. The Nervii certainly and perhaps the Viromandui and the gods only know how many others," Crassus commented, pointing to a spot on the Sabis River on the large cloth map pinned against the side of the tent.

"What about the first messenger?" Caesar asked as he took water from a silver goblet.

"Very strange, that one. Came back with one of your gladiators, who had received a flesh wound, and seven naked girls. Eight actually. One was seriously wounded. Apparently, Caepio had run her through even though she had surrendered."

"Where are the girls now?" Caesar asked.

"Iccius in Bibrax is taking care of them. Apparently, the wounded one might survive. The sword thrust apparently failed to hit any vital organs. Seems that's the only barbarian Caepio managed to try and kill, and even then he didn't manage to do a proper job of it. Apparently, she was unarmed and had already surrendered," Crassus added.

Servilia blushed with embarrassment. She knew her brother was no military man, but she hadn't realised how unfit he actually was. "I don't think you should have sent him on this mission. It's far too dangerous," she said.

"I may have made a mistake sending him behind enemy lines. If he survives, I think, I'll just have him potter around here in headquarters as one of my general staff." Caesar frowned. "The team has, however, managed to achieve my goals. We know where their army is, and I think they were a suitable diversion which may make them look southwards. They will be looking the wrong way when I come for them."

"I thought they were supposed to rescue Decurion Decius?" Antony said.

"That's what I wanted them to think," Caesar said. "Do you think I did all this just to save one insignificant decurion?"

The rescue party made good progress, riding most of the day. Livy was close to exhaustion but tried to draw energy from the beauty of the passing scenery. They rode through idyllic forest paths bordered by summer flowers. He saw deer and hares, even the occasional wild boar. Squirrels played in the trees. The songs of birds filled the air. The men rode on and on till nightfall. They did not meet any enemy patrols.

Finally Caepio called a halt and ordered camp to be made in a clearing. He had learnt his lesson and ordered that no fires be built. The man collapsed in exhaustion. A meeting of the officers was called.

"We should be nearly at the Sabis River. I estimate not more than two hours' riding." Caepio began.

"I am surprised we haven't run into any of their patrols," Biorix said.

"It's possible we bypassed them in the forest. Fortuna was on our side," Livy added.

"Nothing to do with luck," Caepio declared. "I planned it all. I knew if we pushed fast and hard, they will have little chance of catching us. The dangerous part comes now. Tonight we will go up to the river. There is a little watermill, which we must look out for. There we will meet our local contact. He will lead us into the camp past the guards, right to our precious decurion," Caepio said triumphantly.

"Are you sure we can trust this traitor? He may lead us all into a trap," Livy cautioned.

"Caesar himself assures me that the man is dependable. I am merely to show him this gold coin. Once he has done the job, we give him a bagful." Caepio smiled confidently.

Livy and the rest felt uneasy. The plan sounded too good to be true, and it totally depended on the veracity of this one traitor. Not having any better ideas, the officers decided to go along.

Two hours later, they had silently approached the Sabis River. They left their horses hidden in the trees and carefully crept up to a decrepit old mill perched by the river bank. The place looked deserted, and there was no sound except for the croaking of frogs.

"Go forward and check it out," Caepio ordered Biorix. "Wave to us if it is safe to approach."

Biorix scuttled forward, moving from cover to cover till he came to one window. There was a dim light coming from it. Biorix peeped in. He then went to the door, knocked, and went inside. In a moment he came out again and waved.

"Right, it seems to be safe," Caepio declared. "Livius, you and Lugurix come with me. The rest of you keep a lookout."

The three men ran to the mill and hurried inside. Biorix kept the door open. Inside was a man with long hair and a beard in the cape and hood of a Druid. He was making a stew on a stove, which gave off a delicious aroma, instigating stomach contractions in the hungry men.

"Greetings, Tribune. My name is Bratronos, formerly high priest to King Galba, now in the service of King Bodougnatus." He gave a sly smile. "You have come a long way and must be hungry. Join me for a small bite before you embark on our mission."

"How can we be sure you are who you are?" Caepio challenged.

"Well, I know exactly who you are, Tribune Quintus Servilius Caepio, son of a praetor and grandson of a Roman consul. Your sister Servilia is Caesar's whore," Bratranos said.

"Why, you pig, how dare you insult my sister!" Caepio went for his sword. "I'll gut you like the pig you are."

Bratranos leapt back in fright.

Lugurix held him back. "We need him."

CHAPTER 20

Liqian Summer, 36 BC

Biao Li was certainly in his element. He was a born drill master. He enjoyed yelling at recruits and turning them into hardened trained soldiers.

I had recruited 800 young farm boys between the ages of seventeen and twenty-two. They were tough lads, physically fit, and used to physical labour. A few could ride and some could even use the bow. Most were only adept at wielding the spade and the plough.

Biao Li had woken them up at dawn and made them run ten li (about five kilometres). Immediately after that came very rigorous riding practice. I purchased 1000 horses from all the horse breeders around the region, and they were now being trained as cavalry steeds. Tingmei had come to visit and to start the recruits on their sword-fighting training. We sat together on a small rise, watching the recruits train. It was a windy day, and her long brown tresses were softly fluttering. I was atop my black Arabian, and Tingmei rode a smaller but very elegant white Han mare.

The recruits rode at a canter along a runway, then loosed an arrow at a straw target. Most of the lads managed to hit the target, and about at least a third missed, some widely. Tingmei was dressed for fighting in a leather coat and breeches and a pair of fine riding boots. Her hair was tied with a red silk scarf into a top knot and a long ponytail.

"They are improving, but I do not think they will survive a head-to-head encounter with Xiongnu horse archers," she said, sounding concerned.

"I do not intend for our green troops to outshoot the Xiongnu. We will have to rely on cunning, dear," I said.

"I guess an old dog like you will have a whole gamut of tricks up your sleeve." She smirked.

One of the recruits started his run on a large grey mare. I noticed that the pace was a little too quick, and he loosed his arrow late, turning backwards uncomfortably to shoot. The arrow went wide.

"You can't be serious about taking your green unit against hardened Xiongnu cavalry," she said.

"Unfortunately, I am committed. I gave my word to Gan Yanshaou."

"You're going to get them all killed and perhaps yourself as well." She didn't mince her words.

"Perhaps after you teach them some of your fantastic sword skills, we could try to cut them down at close quarters," I said hopefully.

"They wouldn't let you get close enough to settle the issue with swords. Most of your men will be picked off before then. Both the Kangju and Xiongnu are expert bowmen," she said.

"I'll have to catch them by surprise," I said.

"There isn't much place to hide out there," she pointed out.

They watched two more recruits make the run and miss their targets. I was starting to feel depressed.

"Come, Master, let's go for tea. I might have some hardware that will even the odds. Let's go back to my place." She turned her horse around and trotted off. I followed, looking forward to whatever Tingmei had up her sleeve.

An hour later, we were relaxing at the inn. Her room overlooked an artificial lake, which reflected the setting sun, making the surface look suffused with gold. Here and there, lotus leaves and flowers floated on the surface in lazy groups. The air was beginning to cool, and the faint smell of fried dumplings tickled my nostrils. We were both reclining on couches. I was bare-chested, wearing only my trousers. She wore only a thin silk wrap-around gown—which left little to the imagination—and her breasts peeped out sporadically as she leaned over to reach for her cup of tea.

"I have here a weapon from the Southern Provinces. They have innovative weapon smiths in this region." She held up a wooden device which looked like a wooden box attached to a bow. "This is a repeating crossbow. It can fire up to ten arrows before it needs reloading," she explained. "You merely have to push this lever here back and forth." She demonstrated. "Pushing the lever forward drops a bolt into firing position, pulling it back draws the string. One final pull of the lever releases the bolt. Here, try it." She passed the weapon to me.

I looked inside the magazine box. There were stack of bamboo bolts with deadly looking steel tips. The arrows were shorter than those for a bow and had miniscule feathers arranged in a spiral. I went to the window and chose a nearby tree about fifty yards away. Raising the clumsy weapon, I sighted the tree and released the first bolt. It thudded into the middle of the trunk, sinking half its length into the wood. It was easy to use, and the penetrating power was formidable. Drawing the lever back and forth, I released a half-dozen more bolts. At this range, the weapon was accurate. I only missed once. I sauntered back to my couch with a smile.

"Amazing, isn't it?" Tingmei said.

"This could certainly level the playing field," I said happily. She was helping herself to the dumplings, and her gown had slipped, revealing a shapely white leg.

"I ordered 1,000 pieces for you and 200,000 bolts. That should be enough for training purposes. You can pay me when they arrive." She gave me a satisfied smile.

"You may have saved this campaign, me dear," I said gratefully. "What can I do for you in return?" I said.

"I haven't decided as yet. Don't worry, there will be an accounting at some point. You may start right away by pleasuring me in bed again." She slipped off her robe.

Belgica, 57 BC, Beside the River Sabis

Caepio decided to bring along Lugurix and one of his men as they stood the best chance of passing as Belgic. He brought also one of the Germans as his personal bodyguard. The four of them were dressed as Atrebate warriors because the Druid had said that it was the safest disguise as the Atrebates were still on the way and they were not likely to run into any Atrebate warriors who would immediately spot them as fake. Bratranos had provided the appropriate clothes, and he possessed a gold coin which was identical to the one that Caepio had. This confirmed his identity as the intended contact.

Livy was left behind. Caepio had decided he would claim all the credit for himself. Certainly the young centurion had already got far too many honours recently. More than he rightly deserved.

The Belgae had made a huge camp in a wooded area just south of the Sabis River. The Nervii were camped on the western side and the Viromandui on the eastern. The Druid led them to the western camp.

The five men passed several checkpoints, and the sentries did not look particularly alert. They were scrutinised occasionally because they looked different, but the Druid always managed to pass them off as envoys from the Atrebate Army. The German always drew more attention because of his huge size, trimmed beard, and top knot. Many of the Belgic tribes had German immigrants, so a Germanic-looking warrior was not that unusual. The ruse seemed to be working, and Caepio was getting more confident.

How were they going to pull off taking the Roman prisoner into custody though? The Druid told him to simply say that Commius, their king, wanted to interview the Roman personally. Of course, Caepio couldn't speak a word of Celtic and had to rely totally on the Druid to do the talking.

Finally they reached the middle of the Nervii camp. The warriors were cooking dinner over open fires. Some groups were singing dissonantly, already half drunk on beer. There were women camp followers everywhere, cooking or serving food. Once in a while there was a scream when one of the warriors became amorous.

The prisoner was in decrepit condition. He was naked and filthy, and his body bore the mark of severe beatings and flogging. He was clearly at the end of his resistance. The party walked up to the solitary guard as nonchalantly as possible. Bratranos spoke to him. "We have come for the prisoner. Commius, king of the Atrebates would like to have a word with him. You are to release him to the care of these Atrebate warriors."

"Nobody told me this man is to be released to anyone. He is to be sacrificed to the gods in a day or two," the guard protested. The exchange went back and forth as Bratranos and the guard argued. Caepio became uncomfortable. Firstly, he didn't understand a word. Secondly, they were beginning to attract the attention of the nearby Nervii groups who were at dinner.

"I need to see a more senior officer of the Nervii. I can't take the authority of a Suessione Druid. They will have my head." The guard remained adamant.

Caepio wanted to just run him through and break Decius out right this moment. He was weighing their chances amidst so many Nervii.

"What's going on here?" A loud authoritative voice broke in. The party turned to see a tough-looking man dressed in a green cape with beautifully decorated armour and carrying an elaborate helmet topped with a hawk with spread wings.

"This Atrebate party wants to take this man to be interrogated by King Commius. I told them I haven't received any such instruction, My Lord," the guard reported.

"You have orders from King Commius, have you?" The noble seemed sceptical.

"Yes, My Lord," Lugurix replied. "King Commius would like to have a word with this man."

"Your accent is strange. You don't sound like Atrebates, more like a Suessione. Your man there looks like a German, and this one here . . ." He looked more closely at Caepio. "He looks like he just arrived from the Capitol in Rome."

Caepio didn't understand a word, but even he realised that the game was up. He drew his sword, and his men did likewise. Bratranos stepped conveniently to one side as battle became imminent. The noble's guards also drew their arms.

"Besides, I am King Commius!"

There was a brief and frantic struggle. Lugurix charged at two of the guards but was overpowered by two more. The German bodyguard slew two Nervii in quick order but was himself run through by a spear and collapsed in a pool of blood. Commius quickly slew the remaining Suessione and then turned on Caepio. Caepio had managed to hold off two of the Nervii guards but was soon surrounded. He looked around frantically, but there was no help to be had.

"Put down your sword, Tribune Caepio," Bratranos spoke in Latin. "You haven't a chance. They may spare your life and ransom you since you are obviously a rich Roman patrician."

"You are a traitor, Druid. I should have run you through when I first saw you," Caepio cried out in frustration.

One of the guards moved in from behind and held him while two others quickly moved in and disarmed him. He was then stripped naked and tied up. The guards took turns to kick him a few times each, and then they threw him in the cell with Decius. To Caepio's credit, he took the punishment with no more than a murmur.

"Good work, Bratronos," Commius said. "You delivered on your promise. Now in addition to this half-dead decurion, we have a Roman tribune and senator and also this Suessione traitor. Bodougnatus will be pleased. I am sure they have useful information to divulge once the torturers get through with them."

"I'll see you all crucified," Caepio spat defiantly. "Caesar will come soon, and you will all pay for this outrage."

Commius shook his head. "It never fails to amaze me. The arrogance of these Romans."

"They will make a fine sacrifice to Esus, Taranis, and Teutates. These are the gods which demand blood sacrifices. They will be pleased to drink the blood of a Roman noble and one of King Galba's retainers," Bratronos said smugly.

"You are a dead man, Bratronos," Lugurix promised.

"We all die eventually," Bratranos replied. "Unfortunately, you will die first."

Leuce had been suspicious of the Suessione Druid ever since he had appeared around the camp. His face reminded her of a rat, and his movements were reminiscent of the animal too. Leuce was sure he was a spy. The only question was which side he was on. She decided to keep an eye on him.

When he left his tent just before dinner time and made his way suspiciously out of the camp, she followed him unobserved. He made his way along the river till he came to an old mill just perched precariously overhanging the water. The Druid went inside and soon lit a fire. She could see a glow from the window. She waited in the bushes to see who would come to meet him.

Soon a group of men came who looked like Bellovaci warriors. They moved cautiously. First one, then two more men went into the mill house. After a while, more men rose from the bushes and hurried into the building. She was close enough to recognise two of the men.

At one time, her heart leapt into her mouth with excitement. She was sure one of the men was the Roman centurion she had met several times. The other man was a Suessione nobleman named Lugurix, who was one of King Galba's retainers.

There was something about the Roman that intrigued her. He was not like the others. Sure, he was a soldier. Yet he was more. He had a gentle and merciful side. He seemed learned and civilised. He was not like the barbarians whom she daily associated with in the Gaesatae community. They were only interested in fighting, eating, sleeping, and sex, in that order.

When the small infiltration party left the mill dressed in Atrebate uniforms, she continued to tail them. She noticed that the young centurion was not with them and that they had another commander who looked Roman in his bearing and appearance.

She tailed them through the Nervii camp until they came to the cage where the Roman Decius was kept. She had been helping to keep Decius alive all this time. When the small party of "Atrebates" was ambushed by King Commius and his men, she witnessed the entire episode. She now knew that Bratranos was a double agent. He was pretending to be a Roman spy but was actually working for King Commius. She now knew what she had to do.

Leuce ran all the way to the mill. She was well conditioned and was hardly even breathless when she reached the mill. She knew that there would be sentries so she calmly and unhurriedly walked towards the building in full view. She was dressed in a plain brown tunic and her two swords were sheathed. Just 200 yards from the mill, she was stopped by two men in Bellovaci uniform.

"Where do you think you are going, miss?" one man asked politely. He had a Remi accent.

"I am here to see your centurion. I know you are Romans. Please let me through. I have important information concerning your tribune."

The young Remi considered for just a moment and then said, "Keep watch here. I will bring her to see the centurion."

"Please hurry," she said. "There may be a Nervii war party coming this way even now."

They both hurried to the mill. The Remi knocked and was admitted.

Livy looked up and couldn't believe his eyes. "By the gods, I was wondering when we would meet again." He was pleasantly surprised.

"No time for introductions, Centurion. Your Druid is a traitor two times over. He has turned your people over to King Commius of the Atrebates. Two are already dead. The stuck-up Roman and the Suessione noble yet live, though not for long."

"So, you have been observing us all along."

"That I have. If you want to save your people and your own lives you had better follow me and quickly. Even now, a Nervii patrol is on the way here. I ran here as fast as I could."

"I suppose questions can wait. Let's move out to somewhere safe. Can you lead us"

Livy took hold of her arm and hurried outside. He gave a low whistle, and all the men gathered. "Mount up and follow me," he ordered.

Livy pulled Leuce on to his horse, letting her sit in front. She took the reins and galloped off. The rest followed closely. She rode along the river for about two miles, then suddenly turned towards the river and rode across. There was a ford at this point. The water came up to the horses' chest, and everyone was drenched getting across. As they swam, Leuce explained that the patrols seldom crossed the river and this ford was usually impassable except in the night. Not many of the Nervii knew this.

As soon as they got to the other side, they looked for cover. Most of the men stripped off their tunics to dry. They didn't dare make a fire. Biorix came over to Livy and asked him to look at the other bank. There were horse patrols searching the bank.

"You were right, Amazon. They are searching for us," Livy said.

"I am not an Amazon. I am an officer of the Gaesatae," she said proudly.

"Yes, I know. Men and women with no tribe and no home who sell their swords for gold. Rome fought your kind more than a hundred years ago."

"You know a lot, Centurion."

"I also know your name is Lus."

"Lee-us-se," she pronounced. "You have a good memory. You must have remembered it when Murato called to me," she said.

"I am Gaius Livius Drusus. Most of my friends call me Livy. I've been hoping to meet up with you off the battlefield." He smiled warmly. "So why have you come to warn us"

"I got to know your friend, Decurion Decius. I had pity for him because he was tortured and stood up bravely. He showed a lot of dignity. I looked after his wounds and kept him alive. He told me about you, and he believed you would come to save him. After a while, I believed too. Also, I also wanted to see you again," Leuce spoke in good Latin.

"Why did you want to see me again."

"I don't quite know myself. By right, one of us should already be in Hades. We met twice in battle and once in the Belgic camp. I just had the feeling within me that we were meant to discover each other in another way," she said.

"I somehow always knew we would meet again, though logic dictated otherwise. I mean in a war as large as this, what are the chances that two individuals from opposite sides would meet four times."

They both then sat silently just looking at one another. Both were still wet after the river crossing. Livy had taken off his tunic to dry and sat there just in his loincloth. Leuce had her brown tunic on. Her blonde hair was straggly and wet, and her soaking wet tunic clung to every curve. Livy noticed her splendid bare legs.

"You are even more beautiful now than when I saw you last on the battlefield. I guess I was somewhat distracted then by life-and-death issues," Livy tried to jest.

"Well, I have certainly seen handsomer specimens by far. On the other hand, you have a certain dignity, grace, and intelligence. I couldn't bring myself to kill you. You have the qualities one admires most in a Roman with none of the insufferable arrogance common in your race," Leuce concluded.

Livy was stunned by her eloquence. "You speak really well for a barbarian."

"Your Celtic is inferior by far," she countered.

"Now I have seen everything. An educated, female, barbarian Amazon. Will wonders never cease."

"Stop insulting me, you beast." she laughed.

Livy laughed as well. They both realised what a connection they had. They bantered light-heartedly for a while. Finally the flirting subsided, and Leuce told Livy the fate of Caepio and Lugurix and the other two men. She also left no doubt that Bratranos was playing both sides.

"On a more serious note, we have one chance to rescue your men."

"I know we must get them out tonight. Bratranos will probably sacrifice them to his gods tomorrow. Once it is light, we won't have a chance. We still have a few hours to try. Do you have any ideas? We certainly can't get in dressed as Bellovaci or Atrebates, and we haven't got any Nervii gear."

"You can get in without any special dress," Leuce said.

"Of course, I should have thought of that."

"Smart boy, Centurion. Tell all your men to strip naked except for weapons, helmets, and shields. We will look like a Gaesatae mounted patrol. Most of the Gaesatae riders are out patrolling with Murato and the Eburones. They will think we are a returning patrol. We can ride thus confidently into camp. They know me, so I will be the leader."

"You know of course that if we trust you, you can easily lead us all into captivity just as Bratranos did the other lot," Livy expressed his fears openly.

"Well you haven't much of a choice. You can, of course, ride home empty-handed." She smiled sweetly.

"You are a real she-devil. Somehow I trust you. If it's a bad decision, it could well be my last," Livy said.

"Let me convince you." She pulled him close and gave him a very wet kiss on his lips.

"Now you have made me even more suspicious," Livy said in alarm.

She pinched his cheeks playfully. "You worry too much for a hero. Trust to your gods. Who do you worship, Venus?"

He showed her Caesar's ring with the image of Venus.

"You are a little predictable. Just like Paris in the Iliad. You choose Venus over more worthy goddesses like Juno and Minerva."

"You have read Homer? I am impressed. The goddesses were Aphrodite, Hera, and Athena."

"Greek versions of the same," Leuce remarked. "So, are we going or not? Time and tide wait for no one."

Livy went to Biorix and got his men to strip naked. There was lot of embarrassed laughter and lewd remarks. Rude comments about each other's reproductive equipment were bandied around freely. Leuce then applied blue warpaint to their faces. It would be expected that body paint would be washed off in the swim across the river.

When Leuce herself undressed, there was a strange silence as the men admired her stunning figure. Although usually comfortable wearing just skin, Leuce managed a blush at all the attention. Livy suddenly realised how young she must be. Only fifteen or sixteen seasons at most. Her body, however, was that of a fully matured woman. "These barbarian girls develop early," Livy thought to himself. She was also taller and heavier than the average Mediterranean lass. In her bare feet, she was as tall as Livy.

As soon as everyone was kitted up, or rather kitted down, the party mounted and started across the River Sabis. The water had started to rise, and the horses had only their necks and heads above the water. Livy hoped that they could get back across before it was too deep to cross.

Once over, Leuce took the lead. She rode quickly, and as she got to the outskirts of the camp and was challenged, she just shouted, "Recon patrol with important message for the commander," and rode through. They passed several checkpoints in this way. One or two guards even called out her name and made cheeky remarks.

"Hey, Leuce, whose cock are you sucking tonight?" one Nervii officer yelled as she passed. She just ignored him and rode past with her naked entourage in tow.

Finally they came to the area where the prisoners were held. There were about six guards around the cage holding the three prisoners. Leuce did not stop to parley with them. She whipped out her sword and slashed one of the guards across the throat, killing him. The raiders and the Germans made short work of the other guards. They were first taken down by arrows and then dispatched quickly by the Germans. Livy didn't even need to lift a finger. Biorix very quickly broke the lock, using a javelin.

Caepio and Lugurix were quick to grasp the situation and quickly emerged from the cage and mounted the spare horses. "Well, it's about time you showed up," Caepio ranted at Livy. "They were going to roast us in a few hours. I almost ended up a sacrifice to some barbaric God!" Caepio grumbled.

Lugurix shook Livy's hand warmly. He at least was grateful. He also gave a quick kiss to Leuce, with whom he seemed to be more than acquainted. Decius had to be carried. Leuce got him on to a horse with the help of one of the raiders. She mounted behind him, holding on to him tightly.

"You sure are a sight for sore eyes," Decius said to Livy.

"I am happy to be of service and to be in time," Livy replied. "Let's get out of here. We are noticed."

There was shouting as the Nervii woke up to what had happened. Livy overturned a few lamps and set a few tents afire as a distraction. A spear was thrown at him, narrowly missing his head as he ducked. Warriors were already rushing towards the small clearing from all sides.

"Keep close together," he yelled. "Leuce, lead the way."

Leuce galloped towards a group of startled Nervii, and the whole troop followed after her. The raiders were shooting arrows left and right to try and keep the gathering opposition at bay. Everyone felt really exposed, being without armour and not even wearing clothes.

"You lot look totally obscene. Where are your clothes and armour?" Caepio fumed.

"It's a long story, Tribune. Let's concentrate on getting out of here first." As he said that, he took a swing at a Nervii warrior, striking him hard on his helmet. The blow was enough to knock him down. The troop moved fast, galloping at full speed trough the Nervii camp. Most of the warriors were passed even before they realised what was happening, and they could not react in time.

Turning around, Livy could see a group of Nervii on foot running fast after them and shouting to their comrades, but the Roman party was outdistancing them easily. He rode up level with Leuce and yelled at her, "Where are you heading?"

"First we must get out of this camp. Then we head south and then west again. No chance to cross the river. Just ride fast," she yelled.

They were approaching the exit to the camp when a whole troop of Nervii spearmen suddenly moved quickly to form a line to block their way out. Leuce swerved sharply left and the rest followed. She galloped fast, looking for the next exit. The men coming from behind sprinted to catch up and cut them off. Several teams of warriors were now desperately chasing them. The net was closing.

Looking behind, Livy could see some enemy cavalry coming up. They were still far to the rear but were already closing. Suddenly there was a forest path ahead, and Leuce made for it at top speed. The Nervii ran as fast as possible to close off the escape route. Livy saw that a few would make it but not enough to stop them.

The half-dozen Nervii knew they would not stop the raiders, but they were determined to take down as many as they could. They formed a thin line and charged, yelling a shrill war cry. Leuce ran full speed at one of them, who was knocked off his feet by her horse; she got past and sped away. Livy slashed at the next one with his *spatha* but missed. The man tried to grab him and pull him down, but he could not get a firm grip and Livy got past. Biorix, coming from behind, beheaded the man with his *spatha*. Two red streams pulsated into the air from the severed neck. Blood droplets fell like rain.

Two of the Nervii attacked Caepio simultaneously. He was unarmed and seemed an easy kill. One man stood in front of his horse, spear raised. The horse stopped and reared, nearly unseating Caepio. The second man ran beside him and tried to pull him off the horse.

Livy turned and noticed his commander's predicament. For an instant, he was tempted to leave him to his fate; then duty got the better of him, and he put an arrow into the back of the neck of the first assailant. Biorix came to Caepio's aid and dealt the second Nervii warrior a hard blow on the helmet. There was loud clang, and the helmet caved in partially. The warrior collapsed.

"I really like your new outfit, Tribune," Biorix said with a grin. Caepio was naked and his genitalia was embarrassingly displayed. The tribune blushed and looked furious.

"We'll see how much you enjoy your joke when I have the lot of you flogged," Caepio retorted.

"Bloody ungrateful," Biorix thought to himself.

Livy rode up to them. "Get a move on. They're closing on us," Livy yelled. The three of them sprang into a gallop. The rest of the party were already far ahead.

As they moved deeper into the forest the mist seemed to thicken. Unfortunately, it was not yet thick enough for them to lose their pursuers, who were gaining on them relentlessly. Livy had caught up with his raiders and yelled for them to form up on him.

"They are not giving up the chase. Looks like they want us badly. The rest of you move along," he yelled at the German commander. "The raiders and I will try and slow them down. We meet at the river crossing."

The German saluted and ran on ahead with Leuce and the rest of the party. Livy and the raiders formed a small skirmish line. As the pursuers came out of the mist, they were met by accurate fire. The first five warriors were hit and went down. The next riders hesitated and were hit by a second volley. Three more went down. The whole mass of enemy riders came to a stop and some retreated. Livy's men kept up a sporadic fire.

"Right, let's go. Ride hard and fast." They all turned and ran. "Be ready to stop in another couple of miles and do that again." The enemy were in confusion for a few minutes, which allowed them to lengthen their lead. They finally regrouped and resumed the chase.

The mist was thickening now. Very soon, they would be at a disadvantage. The archers needed reasonable visibility to make their shots, and the visibility had fallen to less than 100 yards. They would not survive if they made another holding action. The enemy cavalry would overwhelm them in the fog. Livy decided to press ahead.

The enemy had fallen about a mile behind but were still coming. He came to the crossing and saw that the party had not crossed. He was shocked and disappointed. "Start crossing. The enemy are just behind." Livy shouted.

"The river has risen. It won't be easy to get across," the German commander yelled back. "Your archers are useless in this fog. My men and the Suessiones will cover your backs. Take the Tribune, Decius, and the girl and get over."

Livy was hesitant. The Germans were volunteering to give their lives. He felt he should stay and help them.

"I know what you are thinking. You have to get them back. They will be leaderless if you don't join them. Go!" Runo said with grim determination.

Livy decided he was right and indicated for the raiders and the rest to get into the river. Caepio went ahead. He wasn't going to risk being killed or taken prisoner again. Leuce followed with Decius. She got off to swim beside the horse, leaving Decius on the horse's back. This way the horse had a better chance of getting across.

Biorix came up to him. "Permission to stay, Centurion, my bow will make a small difference."

Livy looked at him sadly. "Try and make it back."

"Get going, Centurion. They are nearly here," Lugurix ordered, swinging a long sword he had picked up from one of the Nervii guards. Livy hesitated, then turned and plunged his black horse into the swirling river. The rearguard turned to face the enemy.

Caepio was nearly across to the other side. Suddenly Leuce's horse lurched as it lost its footing in the deep water. The horses were up to their necks in midstream. Decius lost his balance and splashed into the water. The horse recovered and started for the far bank by itself, leaving Leuce struggling with the incapacitated Decius. Livy swam frantically with his charger to their rescue.

Meanwhile on the other bank, the two forces met violently. The Belgic cavalry did not expect the ambush. The Germans and Suessiones attacked suddenly on foot while Biorix shot his arrows as quickly as possible at whatever targets presented. The fighting was savage and desperate. Both sides hacked each other to pieces in the gloom. It was a hellish battle. In the end the two sides resorted to bare hands and teeth.

Leuce was struggling to keep Decius afloat and not really succeeding. Livy swam his horse quickly towards the drowning couple and slid one arm under Decius. Decius had swallowed water and was coughing violently. Livy pulled him across his horse Nero and then slid off himself. Leuce's horse was already near the far bank.

"Here, take my horse and make towards the far bank," Livy ordered. Leuce was gasping for breath. She swam towards the horse and held on tightly to its mane. The horse being taller and larger than the average horse was able to find a footing and started to wade towards the far bank.

Suddenly Livy heard some splashes behind. A group of five enemy horsemen had waded into the water and were moving fast towards them. Livy motioned Leuce to move on. She looked alarmed and hesitated to comply.

"Get moving, girl. I can handle this lot," Livy yelled.

"Don't get yourself killed, hero," she cautioned. "We have unfinished business." She stuck out her tongue at him and started to move quickly to the far bank.

Livy turned towards the five horsemen which were struggling with the currents in the ever-deepening river. Suddenly the leftmost horse lost its footing and was swept away by the current, spilling its rider. A moment later, a second rider also went the same way.

"Well, the odds seem to be improving," Livy thought to himself. "Still, three to one seems reasonable." He was surprised at his own optimism. His confidence had grown of late.

He held his *spatha* in his teeth and dived underwater. "Thank the gods for all those days swimming in the sea with Aurora," he thought to himself. Livy could swim like a fish. He surfaced just behind one of the riders and, grabbing hold of his belt, pulled him into the water. The man sank rapidly because of his armour. Livy clung on to him as he sank and stabbed him in his unprotected groin, then let him go. The man continued to sink, trailing a stream of blood.

He was out of breath now and had to surface. He came up just beside the rider-less horse. He sensed a movement above and ducked just in time as a heavy long sword came swishing down just a hair's breadth from his head, thumping into the empty saddle of the horse. The horse was startled, and Livy did not hesitate to riposte. He stabbed the man just under the right arm, his sword penetrating deep into the chest cavity. The man screamed and withdrew, dripping blood into the water.

Livy took a deep breath and dived again, swimming for the last of the Belgic horsemen. The warrior was losing confidence as he noted the fate of his comrades. Death seemed to emerge suddenly from the dark waters. He peered around anxiously, half wanting to withdraw. He turned his horse around to swim back to the south bank, and at that moment, Livy struck.

The man screamed as he felt a sharp pain in his leg. Livy had stabbed him through the calf, the blade going right through and into the side of his horse. The water on his left side was already swirling in blood, both the horse's and his own. The horse panicked in pain and surprise, running amok. The warrior could not keep his balance and fell into the water, his armour dragging him down.

Livy was already striking out for the far shore. Along the way, he came across one of the rider-less horses and pulled himself up on its back. Looking back, he saw three riders coming at him through the mist. He sighed. "Here we go again," he said to himself.

One of the riders suddenly started to wave to him. "Is that you, Centurion?" It was the voice of Biorix. Livy waved back, and the three riders drew up next to him. Livy was relieved to see the face of Biorix, who was grinning. The other two riders were Runo, the commander of the Germans, and the remaining gladiator, Crixus.

"Are you the only survivors?" Livy asked, alarmed.

"It was a hell of a fight, but we killed most of them and the rest ran for it. I am afraid we paid quite a price, sir," Biorix answered. "Our men fought to the death, but many more of them died than us," Biorix said grimly.

"Where's Lugurix?" Livy asked.

"Runo here says he went down. We couldn't find him after the battle though. Most likely dead or captured once more," Biorix answered.

Livy felt a pang of sadness. He was beginning to like the Suessione nobleman. He had learnt what happened to Draco and was glad about it. The man was civilised and merciful. These were rare values in this war.

"Right, let's get going and catch up with the rest."

The four men waded their horses to shore and rode after the raiders and Leuce.

Nervii Camp: Bodougnatus's Headquarters

"I can't believe it. I ought to have the lot of you impaled. What kind of security have we got when a small bunch of Romans can come in here and dance off with our most valuable prisoners?" Bodougnatus yelled at his subordinates.

"They were naked. Our men thought they were a returning Gaesatae patrol," the captain of the guard explained desperately. He was a veteran member of the chief's household guard.

"Your men are idiots. We should execute all the guards involved."

"I don't recommend that, Bodougnatus." The voice came from a newcomer to the meeting. It was King Commius of the Atrebates.

"Well, well, Commius. Looks like your little game fell flat. Your little trap managed to net us a couple of fish, but the fish escaped within hours. So much for that stupid Suessione Druid. That's one traitor we should sacrifice to his gods," Bodougnatus sneered.

"We will need every warrior in the next few days." Commius ignored the bluster. "I just heard from Ambiorix and his Eburone scouts. Caesar has taken Samarobriva without a fight. The Ambiani capitulated and submitted to Rome."

"Damned cowards. Bastards. I always knew the damned Ambiani hadn't the stomach to fight," Bodougnatus growled.

"They didn't have much choice. Caesar has siege equipment and would have levelled Samarobriva and killed everyone in it."

"They should have fought to the death and taken as many Romans with them as they could to Thanatos," Bodougnatus screamed.

"That, of course, is a matter of opinion. What is important now is that Caesar will be marching here in a few days, and he will come from the west.

I suggest we prepare. You are finally going to get the decisive battle you have been wishing for."

"I can't wait to send the whole Roman Army to hell." Bodougnatus slammed a fist into his other palm for emphasis.

"Do you have a plan?" Commius asked.

"I don't need a plan. Man for man, my Nervii are bigger, stronger, and fiercer than those puny Roman dwarfs. We will slaughter them."

"You underestimate Caesar. His legions fight like machines. They are coordinated and drilled. They fight as teams. You may find that trying to overwhelm them with brute force may not be the answer."

"It is you who underestimate the fighting ability of the Nervii. We live to fight, and we are the best army in the Belgic confederation. You Atrebates do your part, and I have no doubt of a great victory," Bodougnatus boasted.

Commius rolled his eyes and gave up. "There is only one chance, the way I see it," Commius tried one last time.

"You have a plan, no doubt."

"We have to strike when they are weak and unprepared."

"And how do we catch them thus?"

"When they are building their camp, of course," Commius said. "It all has to do with the order of march of the Roman Army."

"What does the order of march have to do with anything?" Bodougnatus was sceptical.

"The Romans march with half the army in front, then a huge baggage train, and the other half of the army behind. If we hit them before they deploy, we will only be facing four legions instead of eight."

"That would be only 20,000 men to our 100,000. We will have a five to one advantage."

"Yes. No amount of fine parade ground drilling would be able to stand up to such numbers. We will overwhelm the front half, then turn on the back half after that," Commius said.

"That sounds good. Now we have to find a good place to take them by surprise. I know just the spot." Bodougnatus winked and gave a self-satisfied smile.

CHAPTER 21

Lugurix woke up with a start. There was a pain in his head that defied description. He was stark naked and covered in mud and blood. His hair was matted with blood, and he discovered a sizable scalp laceration that had fortunately stopped bleeding. All around him was evidence of a desperate struggle. There were naked men, whom he recognised as his own Suessione comrades and also a few Germans. The rest were in chain mail and were now recognisable as Atrebate noble cavalry. His side had done well as there seemed to be far more of the enemy dead.

He looked around for any left alive, but there were none. His throat was parched, and his vision swam around. He couldn't focus. He stumbled around and found his sword. It was not a great sword. His best sword had been looted during his last capture. Yes, he remembered. That damned centurion had taken it. He would have to buy it back one day. What could he possibly offer? His mind was swimming to irrelevancy. "Got to get out of here." Something rang in his brain.

He headed towards the river. He quenched his thirst in the bloodstained water. The taste was obnoxious. He spat it out. "Might catch something drinking that." He walked deeper into the water then started swimming to the other bank. The cold water woke him up and cleared his head.

Livy's party were camped in a deserted barn somewhere further west in Atrebate territory. The peasants were assumed to be hostile, and the raiders had locked up the family in the farmhouse with one raider and the gladiator keeping guard. "They would have to be tied up before we leave," Livy thought.

The farmer had a pretty teenage daughter who aroused the carnal desires of his men, but Livy gave strict instructions for the family not to be touched. He knew that the bloodthirsty Caepio would have had the women raped and the men killed without hesitation. He ignored his superior's sentiments and quickly put in strict instructions to the men before he could be countermanded.

Caepio seemed too exhausted and self-absorbed to make an issue of it. He would, no doubt, take up the issue of insubordination back in Caesar's camp. Livy doubted that Caepio was the type to let anybody off. What he expected was demotion to the ranks. What a waste that would be after all he had done.

It was dusk, and Livy decided to rest a few hours and have some dinner before continuing the journey to rejoin the Roman Army. The problem was, where was the Roman Army?

Livy called a meeting of Biorix, Runo, and Caepio. "I don't suppose you have any idea where Caesar might be at this moment?" Livy began.

The tribune had found a rough woollen tunic which was a little too small for his pudgy frame, and he looked a little ridiculous. "Actually, I do," he said pompously. "Caesar was going after the Bellovaci first and then the Ambiani next. Assuming he has already dealt with the Bellovaci he would then be headed for Samarobriva, capital of the Ambiani."

"That means we head west," Biorix said.

"I guess that's as good a direction to go as any," Livy said finally. "Nematocenna, the Atrebate capital is just a few miles north of here, so we are really exposed if we hang around here."

"If we don't find Caesar at Samarobriva, we should turn south to Bratuspantium, the capital of the Bellovaci. That will mean it hasn't fallen yet, and Caesar will be busy reducing it," Caepio said.

"It's decided then," Livy said.

"We move in four hours. Everybody is to rest till then," Caepio said. Livy could see that the tribune was on the point of collapse himself. There was one consolation. Livy had managed to retrieve his horse Nero and in the saddlebag was the light chain mail which was a possession he would have been devastated to lose. His extra grey tunic was also in the saddlebag.

Livy went to look for Leuce. She had found herself a plain brown tunic and was roasting a chicken on an open fire. "That smells delicious," Livy said.

"Sit down here. Dinner will be ready shortly," Leuce said. Livy lay down to rest beside Leuce and just looked up at the stars. He suddenly felt totally exhausted. "Go ahead and take a nap. I will wake you when dinner is ready," she said.

The next thing he remembered was being shaken awake. "Dinner time," Leuce announced. Runo and Biorix had joined them and were already tucking in. "Here, I saved you a leg and some fresh bread which we have liberated from the farmer."

Livy took the food gratefully as he was famished. He immediately started on the food while Leuce sat there looking at him. She seemed to have something in mind. She waited patiently till he finished every morsel. She then stood up, took his hand, and pulled him up. "Follow me," she said.

The others were not really paying attention as he followed after her. She took him to the barn. There were a few cows and a horse inside, but otherwise it was warm and hospitable. At the end of the barn, there was a private cubicle, which was relatively clean and covered with straw. It was lit by one candle. Leuce pulled him into the cubicle. She pulled him close and kissed him fully on the lips. Without another word, she pulled her simple brown tunic of coarse wool over her head. She stood naked, looking at him defiantly, challenging him. Her body was like that of Aphrodite. It was fully developed, perfectly proportioned, and unmarked. She was very fair. Her skin was almost translucent, marked only by the pale pink of her nipples and her *cunnus*. She had no body hair at all.

"I told you I would fuck you if you survived, and I always keep my promises," she declared with the sauciest smile. Livy did not need further prompting. He stepped forward took her in his arms, engulfed her with kisses, and lowered her into the straw. They made good use of the remaining hours.

Some hours later, they were interrupted by Biorix. He was very discreet and stopped outside the cubicle, not looking in. "Time to get moving, Centurion," he said in a low voice. Livy stood up, already dressed in his tunic. He slipped on the chain mail and started to secure the ties.

"Are the men ready?" Livy asked.

"Yes, sir. We ride in ten minutes," Biorix answered. They both had a glimpse of Leuce in the nude as she got up to put on her tunic.

"How is Decius?" Livy asked.

"He will survive but will probably be out of action for a while. He was really badly beaten up. He better ride with someone," Biorix said.

"I'll ride with him," Leuce volunteered.

Livy went to release the Atrebate family who owned the farm. He gave them ten silver denarii to pay for the food and the clothes which they took. He worked out that it was fair value.

Just as they were about to mount up, one of the raiders called out, "There is a naked man coming down the road." As the man stumbled closer, two of the men ran to help him. "It's Lugurix," they proclaimed.

Livy and Biorix ran up to him. "Welcome, comrade, you are certainly a joyful sight. We thought you were sent over the *Styx*," Livy remarked.

"I am not that easy to kill," Lugurix groaned wearily. They sat him down and gave him a canteen to drink. Runo produced a piece of bread. He was excitedly telling his story when Caepio came running.

"All right. Enough already. We are in enemy territory and the night is passing. Get on your horses. We move out now!" Caepio yelled.

The men mounted up. Lugurix had his head quickly bandaged and a blanket was found to serve as a wrap. One of the spare horses liberated from the Belgian cavalry was saddled, and Lugurix got on to it. Fortunately, he could still ride.

The dozen horsemen rode off into the night.

The next morning found them still in Atrebate territory, and instead of hiding out for the day, they decided to chance it and ride on westwards into Ambiani lands. The passed through fertile farmland and orchards, and now and then peasants could be seen working the field or orchards. They were definitely being observed.

Caepio banked on the hope that all the Atrebate warriors had gone to join the Nervii and that the whole countryside would be undefended. Livy realised that this was taking a big risk because the horses were getting tired and if they did meet a mounted patrol, they would have to fight rather than run. He could feel the perspiration on his horse and sense the animal tiring under the continuous pace.

Caepio suddenly called a halt. He called Livy and Lugurix for a conference. "Are we out of Atrebate territory yet?" he asked.

"Hard to tell," Lugurix said. "There is no clear line. We need to ride at least another hour to be firmly in Ambiani territory."

"Our horses are tired," Caepio said. "We need to give them a rest."

"It's broad daylight, sir," Livy said. "We should at least get off this hill. We can be seen from miles around."

"Too late," Lugurix said. "We have company. Look over there on the right. I make out about thirty riders. Some of them are naked Gaesatae warriors."

Livy squinted and looked intently. "I think I recognise one of them." It was Murato. Caepio looked ashen. They were outnumbered three to one, and already the enemy cavalry were turning in their direction. It was obvious that they had few options. The horses were tired, and they stood little chance of outrunning them. Making a stand was risky at these odds.

"Let's get going and make some distance," Livy said.

Caepio was at a loss and too frightened to object. The party got off the hill and urged their tired mounts to make as much speed as possible. "Leuce, take the lead. Get Decius and the tribune away. Biorix, you accompany them," Livy ordered. "The rest of the raiders, on me. We will try and delay them if possible."

"I stay with you," Runo said. "I feel like killing a few Gaesatae scum for sport."

"I am with you as well," Lugurix said. "Suessione nobles don't run from a fight. We will lose too much face." He laughed.

"I stay too," gladiator Crixus said.

Livy was grateful to them all. If he had to die, he had good company. His only regret would be not seeing Leuce or Artemisia again. "It's a good day to die," Livy yelled.

"It's a good day to die," the rest echoed.

Leuce and the tribune had already gone a couple of miles in front. The enemy was about 5 miles away and closing. It was open country, and both sides were totally exposed. A few miles later, they came to a group of farmhouses on a hill. Livy led his men towards them. As soon as they reached the buildings, he ordered everyone to dismount.

The main farmhouse was typical Gaulish construction with a stone base, wooden walls, and steep thatched roof. This particular building had two storeys, the second level enclosed by the roof.

"Gather all the horses and lock them in the barn. The rest of you, get into the farmhouse. raiders climb up on to the roof," Livy yelled. He knew that his men didn't have too many arrows, less than ten each. They would have to make every shaft count.

The men streamed into the farmhouse and bolted the door and every window. The four raiders quickly scrambled into the attic and emerged on the rooftop. Runo, Lugurix, and the gladiator would try to keep them out of the ground floor while the raiders would pepper them with arrows from the attic and roof. Lugurix moved a table and some chairs against the main door. The farmer and his family were caught by surprise as the men barged in, but Lugurix assured them that they meant them no harm and that they should just keep out of the way.

"What tribe are you from?" Livy asked the farmer, a middle-aged man, who looked frightened to death.

"We are Ambiani, sir," he answered.

"Are the Ambiani still part of the confederation against the Romans?" Livy asked.

"No, sir. Samarobriva surrendered without a fight. Our leaders decided to accept Roman rule."

"You have wise leaders," Livy observed. "Now you must help us defend against some hostile Belgic warriors. Are you with us?"

The man nodded furiously. He didn't have much choice.

"Do you have another way out of this house?"

"I'm afraid not, sir."

"Too bad," Livy thought. "Nowhere to run, so it's victory or death." He was resigned.

Suddenly there was a loud rapping on one of the windows. "Let me in," a female voice cried. Runo opened the window. Leuce clambered in through the window, then turned and bolted it tight.

"I told you to go with Decius and the tribune." Livy was livid.

"Biorix is looking after the decurion and is more than capable of getting them back to Samarobriva," she countered. "You need every fighter."

"I don't need a teenage girl. This is a desperate situation. We might all die here," Livy yelled.

"Then we die together," she said. They stared at each other angrily for a while.

"They're here!" one of the raiders shouted.

"Well, it's too late to do anything now." Livy gave up.

"I'm coming. Make every arrow count," Livy yelled and clambered up the ladder to the attic at top speed. The attic had two windows facing back and front. They were guarded by a raider each, and the other two were on the roof. The first few riders were Gaesatae, and they made easy targets for the archers. Two of the riders went down as soon as they came within range. The other horsemen spread out and quickly dismounted as soon as they were within range, taking cover wherever they could find it.

Livy fired and saw one of the armoured warriors go down with an arrow through the neck. The other raiders took down two more. The enemy were now much more wary. They dashed from cover to cover and used their shields to good effect.

Suddenly a group of about eight men rushed for the door of the farmhouse. Once under the eaves of the roof, they were no longer in the line of fire from the raiders on the roof. They immediately started to hack at the door with axes, making a huge din. The team in the house piled more and more furniture against the door, desperately trying to hold back the determined assault. Murato threw his javelin and impaled one of the raiders on the roof, who dropped off dead. Another Gaesatae archer managed to hit the other raider in the calf. The man yelled but managed to keep his balance.

Livy rushed out on to the roof to assist him, trying his best not to fall off. The Gaesatae fired an arrow at him but narrowly missed his head. Livy grabbed hold of the wounded raider and helped him into the window while the raider stationed at the window took out the enemy archer.

On the ground floor, things were getting desperate. The door had been smashed, and two heavily armed Eburone warriors barged in. They were still struggling to get past the furniture when Runo and the gladiator ran them through with spears. Four more Eburones immediately took their place, and the three defenders were now locked in combat. Just beyond them another two enemy warriors were trying to squeeze through the door. Leuce drew her two swords and charged into the fray. One of the Eburones went down, slashed in the neck, his carotids spraying blood into the air. There were now four defenders holding back the horde of Gaesatae and Eburones at the door. The situation was still desperate.

Two of the Eburones began hacking at the accumulated furniture with axes, clearing the way. Meanwhile, two Gaesatae warriors had managed to climb up on the roof and were making their way to one of the windows behind the house. At the same time, five more Gaesatae made a run for the broken door to reinforce the remaining men trying to break into the house. Livy managed to hit one in the thigh with an arrow, disabling him.

The two rooftop assailants suddenly appeared at the back window, surprising the lone raider defending it. They overwhelmed him and one of them fell on top of him. Livy turned instinctively and shot the remaining one with an arrow right through the chest. He stopped with a surprised look on his face, then spun round and dropped. Livy drew his *spatha* and immediately attacked the second assailant. The raider on the floor was holding him by both wrists one of which held an axe and the other, a dagger. He had no defence, and Livy stabbed him hard between the collarbone and the neck, plunging his *spatha* deep into his chest. As he withdrew the sword, another two Gaesatae appeared at the window. The downed raider was stunned but largely unhurt. He drew his sword to help Livy hold back the two Gaesatae.

Livy parried an overhand sword stroke from the first with his *spatha*. As he recovered from the blow, he charged and barrelled into the first man, toppling him on to the second. The man behind fell back from the window and toppled off the roof. Livy stabbed the first man through the base of the neck. As he turned around, he saw two more Gaesatae climbing on to the roof and a third halfway up. The raider whom he had rescued had recovered somewhat and immediately shot one of them through the chest. He toppled over. The second man was Murato.

"Take him down but don't kill him," Livy told the raider beside him. The raider shot Murato in the right thigh, the arrow penetrating to the other side, skewering the limb. Murato groaned and fell to his knees.

Murato willed himself up and charged at Livy, his huge sword overhead. Livy just managed to parry the skull-splitting blow. The impact was numbing all the way to the shoulder. Livy recovered and thrust at his abdomen, but Murato blocked the blow. Before he could recover, Murato slashed sideways and caught him in the left flank. The blow landed heavily on his chain mail but failed to penetrate. Livy's Spanish armour had held. Livy was knocked off his feet and felt a terrible pain at the site of the blow. Murato hesitated in surprise. That blow would have easily killed any other man.

Livy grabbed on to the roof material, desperately clinging on. Murato started moving towards him, intending to finish him. As he closed, Livy suddenly kicked his wounded leg with all his remaining strength. Murato fell with a groan as the leg buckled.

Livy was on him in a flash, *spatha* at his throat. "Drop your sword," he ordered. Murato obeyed. The third man let himself drop down to the ground again. "Tell your men to drop their weapons and surrender," Livy told him fiercely.

"I am Gaesatae. I don't surrender," Murato said defiantly. Livy fought against the irresistible urge to run him through.

"I promise quarter to your men and freedom," Livy said.

Murato looked at him sceptically. "How can I trust you?"

"Trust me or die. I don't care either way. Make an exception and surrender. I give you my word." Livy tried one last time.

Murato shouted at his men, "Down arms." They hesitated. "Down arms, I said," Murato commanded. All the remaining Gaesatae put down their weapons.

"We don't take orders from you," one Eburone said. Livy signalled, and one of the raiders put an arrow through his neck.

"Anybody else want to make an issue of it?" Livy asked in a loud voice. The remaining Eburones lowered their weapons. Runo, Lugurix, and the gladiator ran out and disarmed everyone. The raiders joined them to tie up all the uninjured men. Leuce tended to the wounded as best as she could. The farmer's wife and daughter helped her.

One of the raiders tied Murato's hands behind him. Murato looked at him wonderingly. "Well, now we see if you are a man of your word, Centurion. You don't look much like a centurion today," he commented.

"Your men will be bound and left here. The farmer and his family will tend to your wounded. We take all your horses and weapons with us. You are my prisoner. I never promised you your freedom," Livy said.

"What will happen to me?" Murato asked. He looked betrayed.

"You are a brave and skilled warrior. Have you ever thought about hiring your skills out to our side?" He helped him up and guided him in through the window in the attic.

Lugurix supervised the disposal of the prisoners. They were all tied up and locked in the barn. Livy borrowed a cart from the farmer and loaded Decius, Murato, and the wounded raider on it. Two of the horses liberated from the enemy war party served to pull the cart. They left the farmer one of the captured horses as compensation for the trouble they brought him. He was also left with some of the captured weapons.

The men then saddled up and headed west in the direction of Samarobriva.

The party reached their destination in the mid-afternoon without further interruption. The whole Roman Army was encamped around the city in several fortified camps. As they approached, they were challenged by cavalry pickets. Livy identified himself, but the pickets were not convinced. They were dressed like peasants and so had to do quite a lot of explaining. Finally Livy was able to convince the commander that he was a Roman centurion. The ring given by Julius Caesar was used as a last resort to prove their identity.

A few moments later, Biorix and Paulus came to meet them. "We were really worried about you," Paulus said.

"Actually, I knew you could handle that lot," Biorix grinned. "Still, I am glad to see you back safe and sound. Did we lose anyone?"

"One of our raiders got killed, and the one in the cart got an arrow in the leg. Lugurix, Runo, and the gladiator have all got wounds. Only our new Amazon friend and I are unhurt," Livy reported. He didn't want to complain that he had a huge bruise on one side and probably a pair of broken ribs.

"Blessed by the gods, the pair of you." Biorix laughed. "You ought to marry her!" he joked.

"We also have a prisoner. May I present Murato, leader of the Gaesatae." Livy waved towards Murato.

Biorix gave him an evil look.

"What are you going to do with him?" Paulus asked.

"Caesar will decide, but I have something up my sleeve." Livy smiled.

"Well, we have news for you," Biorix said. "Caepio went crying to Caesar and put us all on charge, you, Lugurix, Runo, and me. The charge is insubordination and not obeying orders. I gave my defence already. Told 'em everything that happened. Obviously, Caepio had a different view of the whole thing. Anyway, you three are to report to Caesar right away. He is quartered in Samarobriva. Paulus will look after things here, and I will take you there now. I think we better bring the prisoner and the young lady along and see what Caesar wants to do with them."

Caesar had convened a board of inquiry to look into what had happened during Caepio's daring long-distance raid behind enemy lines. The board consisted of Crassus, Antony, Sabinus, Quintus Pedius, and Cotta. Caesar sat in himself. All the officers were interviewed, including Biorix, Runo, Lugurix, and Livy.

Caepio had made a long report full of complains about the behaviour of everyone. He wanted the four officers charged for insubordination and failure to obey legitimate orders from a superior. Caesar conferred privately with his senior officers before deciding on the case.

"Caepio is an idiot," Antony began. "Livy and his lot are fine soldiers. I've never met better."

"I agree. It is Caepio who should be demoted for incompetence," Crassus added.

"We must be careful. What we decide today will have repercussions in Rome. Caepio is the son of a praetor and grandson of a consul. He is a member of the Senate. You already have too many enemies there," Sabinus warned.

"Sabinus is right. While I would very much like to send Caepio packing, he would no doubt complain to the Senate and cause no end of trouble."

"What are you proposing then?" Antony asked.

"The four officers will have to be seen to be punished . . . a little," Caesar said. There was a cunning smile decorating his austere face.

"And what about Caepio?" Crassus asked.

"I am going to promote him up to general staff so he can fetch and carry for me and not cause any further trouble."

"He's an ungrateful bitch. Livy and his men saved his skin several times," Antony said.

"Enough. I have decided. After all, he is Servilia's brother. Call all the men in," Caesar commanded.

The four men stood in full uniform and armour and at attention. They were escorted by provosts in black uniforms and black plumes on their helmets. Caepio was there to witness the proceedings. Caesar put on a stern demeanour as he addressed them.

"An army cannot function when orders of superior officers are not respected. Disobedience merits severe punishment. The command prerogative of my senior officer cannot be disregarded. You men have deliberately disobeyed your commanding officer. I don't care what your motives may be. The tribunal finds the four of you guilty of insubordination and wilfully disobeying orders. Your legate, Publius Crassus, will read out the sentence."

Publius Crassus stood up and cleared his throat. He tried to look serious but had a slight smirk as he read out the sentence.

"Decurion Biorix of the Remi, you are sentenced to latrine duty for one week. You will be deprived of leave pass to Samarobriva for the duration the army is stationed here. Your rations will also be reduced to barley gruel for one week. Do you accept your punishment?"

Biorix gave a little smile. "I do, My Lords." He was really relieved at the lightness of the punishment.

"Decurion Runo of the Treveri, you are sentenced to trench-digging duties for one week and deprivation of leave pass to Samarobriva for one week. You will also have your rations cut to barley gruel."

"I accept, My Lords," Runo said quickly.

"Nobleman Lugurix of the Suessiones, you are sentenced to a fine equivalent to 500 denarii. As you are nobility, you will not be required to do hard labour. Can you afford this amount?"

"I can, My Lords, and I accept my punishment."

"As you are a new ally, we would also like to extend our appreciation to you for your help on this mission. We recognise that you have been wounded fighting for our cause."

"Finally, Centurion Gaius Livius Drusus, you are hereby stripped of your command of the raider unit. The unit will pass to the temporary command of Decurion Paulus. You are to return to the command of the Sixth Century of the Eighth Cohort of Legio VII. You are to perform the duties of officer of the day to Legio VII for the next two weeks. Your main duties will be to supervise trench-digging and latrines," Crassus couldn't keep down a giggle.

"As you are of senatorial rank now, we can't deprive you of rations, so you will be fined the sum of 100 denarii. Do you accept?"

"I accept," Livy said dispassionately. He was somewhat sore that he had to accept a punishment at all as the mission was largely successful. On the other hand, he understood the need for discipline in the army.

Crassus sat down. "Well, are you satisfied, Quintus Servilius? I have taken your complaints seriously." Caesar looked at him.

Caepio looked uncomfortable. He had hoped for harsher punishment, but Caesar had done things somewhat by the book. "Well, I suppose everything is in order," he mumbled.

"I have good news for you," Caesar added. "As you have successfully completed your mission, I have decided to award you a set of *phalarae* for bravery and promote you to tribune on the general staff." Caesar beamed at him.

Caepio looked shocked. "Words escape me. I don't know what to say," he stuttered.

"You can say 'thank you'," Caesar replied.

"Thank you, My Lord Caesar." Caepio bowed low.

"Well, then that's it. You are all dismissed. I would like Antony, Crassus, and Centurion Livius to stay. The rest of you may leave."

When they were alone, Caesar offered a goblet of wine to each of the three men. For a few minutes, everyone was silent. Caesar began, "Good job on the mission, Livius. I know you are the one responsible for the success of the mission. You realise, of course, my hands are tied on this matter. Next time, I hope you will pay some consideration to the political implications of a situation. I recognise you as an exceptional soldier and that you will be a credit to the army, but right now I need you to lie low and take your punishment with equanimity."

"I will, My Lord," Livy said, looking downcast.

"I will return you to the raiders in good time, but I think a stint in the line will be good for you. Your century needs your leadership too."

Both Crassus and Antony patted him on the back in sympathy.

Caesar was aware of the unfairness of the situation. "If there is a small favour I can grant?"

"There is the question of the two Gaesatae." Livy jumped at the opportunity.

"They are fine specimens, both of them. What do you have in mind? Technically, the male warrior is a prisoner of war and therefore, my slave. The girl joined our side willingly and facilitated your mission. She is therefore a defector, and I am willingly to be more generous with her. She is beautiful. Perhaps she would like to join Servilia and her girls. She would do well there."

"Murato is an exceptional warrior. I would like to have the chance to persuade him to join our side. He would be a wonderful addition to the raiders. I even think he has command potential."

"I don't doubt what you say. The question is will he remain loyal and not switch sides at a crucial moment," Caesar cautioned.

"I cannot deny that possibility, but I would beg for the opportunity to convert him."

"All right, he remains my slave, but he will be attached to the raiders under Paulus. You have to get him to agree freely and give his word. Otherwise, I will keep him as one of my slaves and send him to the *ludus* for training as a gladiator," Caesar said decisively. "You can put it to him."

"Thank you, sir," Livy said.

"As for the girl, you seem interested in her?" Caesar looked at him questioningly.

"I can't deny it, sir," Livy said honestly.

"You already have a woman. Servilia told me she sold you one of her girls," Caesar said.

"She is also a formidable fighter," Livy said.

"So I heard. Are you proposing that we enrol her in the raiders as well?"

"Yes, My Lord," Livy said.

"The Roman Army doesn't admit women into combat units."

"The raiders are an auxiliary unit, sir," Livy argued.

"Hum. I am the sort of commander that is not averse to trying new things. All right, offer her the option. Offer her a position with Servilia as well. The third option will be for her to become one of my bath slaves. I will spare her the indignity of being sold as a common slave since she helped us."

Livy noticed that freedom for Leuce was not an option.

"I will put it to both of them," Livy said.

Caesar took him aside. "Don't make too much of the punishment I imposed on you. I have to watch my back in the Roman Senate. Caepio is close to my most relentless enemy, Cato. I will restore you to command of the raiders in a short time. I think that unit has surpassed all my expectations and has great potential. Meanwhile, if you can persuade the Amazon girl to join the raiders, I will make her my personal slave and loan her to you," Caesar whispered to him.

"Thank you, Lord Caesar," Livy said.

"Tonight, I have a small party put together. Send me the girl. She will serve us at the party. After tonight, you may have her."

Livy went to the tent where Murato and Leuce were held. They were guarded by two legionaries of the Tenth Legion. The men recognised him and saluted, admitting him into the tent. Livy took off his crested helmet and entered.

"So, the centurion returns to tell us our fate. What has the great Caesar ordained?" Murato asked, somewhat anxiously.

"You are to be one his personal slaves. You have a choice of occupation though," Livy began.

"Bath attendant to some Roman matron perhaps?" Murato quipped.

"You can go train in a *ludus* and become one of his gladiators. Caesar has a big collection," Livy said.

"I hear the lifespan of a gladiator is rather brief," Murato commented. "What are the other choices?"

"You can swear allegiance to Romans and join my unit of mounted archers."

Murato looked up surprised. This was not so bad. "I can't shoot a bow, even if my manhood depended on it."

"You will learn. We will teach you," Livy said.

"Then the choice is obvious. When do I begin?" Murato asked.

"Not so fast. Do I have your word you will not try to escape or switch sides?"

"You have my word," Murato said emphatically.

"I hope your word is good," Livy said.

"Good as yours," Murato retorted.

Livy realised that Murato had expected to be set free when he ordered his men to surrender. "It will do for now."

"What about me," Leuce asked in Latin.

"I had hoped to offer you freedom because you came over willingly and helped us. Unfortunately, that is not an option offered by Caesar."

"What are my choices, if any?" she said. She looked disappointed.

"In recognition of your services, Caesar has assured me you will not be sold like a common slave," Livy said.

"How generous," Leuce said sarcastically.

"You can become one of Caesar's slaves. He will likely assign you to be a bath slave."

"Sex slave you mean," Leuce said, disappointed.

"The second choice is to become a hetaerae, or high-class courtesan. Servilia, who is Caesar's mistress, runs such an establishment here. The work is light, and there is the prospect of freedom after a few years."

"Working on my back doesn't have much appeal for me," she said scornfully. "Isn't there any other better option?"

"You can go back to becoming an Amazon warrior like Murato here. That is, if you agree to fight for our side."

"Will I be freed?" Leuce asked. There was a glimmer of hope.

"No, you will remain a slave, but if you serve well, there is the prospect of earning your freedom."

"Well, it looks like I am enslaved one way or other. I only have the choice of which type of slave—bath slave, sex slave, or warrior slave."

"That about sums it up."

"Maybe I should have stayed with the Nervii," she said.

"I'll look after you," Livy said as kindly as possible.

"Then I choose to go with Murato to be a soldier again."

"Will you swear allegiance to Rome?"

"I don't see why not," Leuce said.

"There is one more thing," Livy added. "You have to entertain Caesar and his guests at a private party tonight."

"Hum. I guess that means I have to open my legs for some rich Romans, Caesar himself perhaps."

"It'll be only for tonight. After that, you come under my care and no one will touch you unless you consent. You won't be forced to give yourself more."

"I guess I am treated no worse than by my own kind." She gave Murato a scathing glance. "Don't worry, the Gaesatae men take me whenever they wish. There is free sex in our community, and the women are all common user facilities," she said a little bitterly.

"I promise it will be different after tonight," Livy said sadly.

"We shall see," Leuce replied. She sounded unconvinced.

Livy untied Murato. He offered his hand. "Welcome to the Roman Army and our elite raider unit. Someone outside will take you to their camp. Report to Biorix, the Remi. You know him. He speaks your language." He took away his gold torque which was Murato's last worldly possession. "You won't be needing this," Livy said.

Murato limped out of the tent and was escorted away. The bleeding from his wound seemed to have stopped.

Suddenly Leuce and Livy were alone in the tent. "I thought we could be together," she said bitterly. Livy held her close and hugged her gently. He kissed her on her forehead.

"Our separation is only for the moment," he assured her. "I am being punished for disobeying the orders of my tribune, Caepio. He wanted to kill some of your sisters, but I managed to send them away to safety."

"Do you remember any of their names?" She was suddenly anxious.

"Their leader was called Arana. She had red hair and looked fearsome but had an awesome body," Livy replied.

"I know her. Is she all right?"

"I sent her to Bibrax. I am not sure of her fate after that."

"Were any of her friends hurt?"

"Yes, two were killed in the battle. Another girl was wounded by my tribune, Caepio, but I heard that she will survive. The others were brought to safety in Bibrax under Prefect Iccius. I think he will care for them and not harm them. I helped to save his town, and he owes me a favour for that."

"I took a big chance coming over to you, and you do owe me for helping you complete your mission and rescuing the decurion. I did it partly because I felt sorry for him and didn't want to see Bratronos sacrifice him to our gods. The main reason I did it is because I wanted to be with you. I just want to be sure you know that," Leuce explained.

Livy felt saddened by her remarks. He really wished he had more power to decide her fate. Unfortunately, he was now just a junior centurion, and only Caesar could decide what would happen to her.

"Please be patient. Our fates are in the hands of Caesar, but I think he is partial to me. I will do everything in my power to bring us together soon." he kissed her again, this time on the lips.

At the back of Livy's mind was also Artemisia. She was his slave, but he cared about her feelings as well. How was he going to resolve the problem of having two women in his life? One woman was already difficult enough. Livy sighed.

At that moment the guard popped in his head. "There is a visitor for you."

Jasmine came through the tent flaps into the tent. "I bring greetings from My Lord Caesar," she said. "I am to prepare the young lady for the party tonight. Greetings, Centurion Livius, it is a great pleasure to see you again." She bowed low to Livy and gave him a warm smile.

Leuce gave him a suspicious look. "There are certainly too many strange beautiful women in this Roman camp," she thought o herself.

Livy gave a small bow. "It's nice to see you again as well."

"Lady, please follow me. I have to bathe you and get you ready for the dinner tonight. My Lord Caesar would like the pleasure of your company," she said very politely in Latin, bowing to Leuce.

As she was led out, she turned around and looked at Livy. "Will you be at the party tonight?"

"Sadly not, I have other duties. I am duty officer for my camp for the next two weeks," Livy said morosely.

"I'll see you when I see you then," Leuce said sadly.

Livy bowed to her, and Jasmine gently prodded her outside and away.

Livy reported to the *prefectus castrorum* or camp prefect and was given a briefing on his duties as officer of the watch. The camp prefect was third in command of a legion. These duties included setting up the sentries, digging the ditches around the camp walls for defence, digging latrines, supervising the distribution of rations, and other such mundane tasks. These duties would keep him fully occupied for the next two weeks. He now realised that to run an army involved many unpleasant routine details which if not done properly would seriously jeopardise a unit's combat effectiveness.

After the briefing, he sought out his century and found his tent. The clerk was anxious to see him and reminded him that he had a stack of paperwork to perform. He promised the clerk that he would get on to it as he was now going to be around for the next two weeks. Most of his century had been granted leave passes to go down to Samarobriva for some rest and recreation. He spent several hours dealing with administration.

Livy was now dead tired. He hadn't had a moment's rest since he rode back into camp. It was now already near midnight. He opened the tent flaps and strode into his tent. It felt strange, as if he hadn't seen it for a long time although he only left it some days ago. It was dimly lit by several candles. Artemisia was asleep on his sleeping couch, and she had laid out food on the table with a flagon of wine. There was a wooden tub filled with water prepared, but the water had lost some of its warmth and was tepid. Still it looked inviting enough.

Livy poured himself a goblet of wine and then took off his armour and tunic and slipped into the tub. He lay his head back on the rim and closed his eyes. In a moment, he was asleep. When he awoke, Artemisia was in the tub, gently sponging him down, removing the accumulated dirt and grease from his mission. She smiled at him sweetly as he opened his eyes, and he sat quietly, just admiring her beauty. Her long brown hair was let down, covering part of her face and flowing over her shoulders, the tips just caressing her succulent pink nipples.

"Welcome to Elysium," she said softly.

"I dozed off. It was too comfortable. How have you been?" Livy asked.

"I like my new life. I sleep late, then, go down to the camp of the raiders to practise sword-fighting with them. I stay with them till evening and join them for dinner. Then I come back, take a bath, have some wine and go to sleep. I feel like I am home in Sparta," she said cheerily. "One of your boys, Cleander, is even teaching me to use the bow. I am getting quite good at it. He says I am a natural."

"Caesar relieved me of my command of the raiders. I am now back to commanding infantry. What's more, I have to be camp duty officer for the next two weeks."

"Did you do something wrong?"

"I saved the lives of some prisoners. Caepio wanted all enemy prisoners put to death," Livy said.

"Then you did the right thing, and the gods will smile on you. Your punishment is then a mere trifle. I will do everything to make the time pass faster." She gave his member a light squeeze, which woke it up instantly.

"I feel better already," Livy said.

"Turn around. I need to scrub you back."

Livy made a face, then reluctantly complied. He was hoping for a different kind of scrub.

Artemesia gently cleaned the badly bruised and swollen area where Murato had hit him. "This must hurt," she commented.

"I got into an altercation with a naked giant. He damned near cut me in half," Livy said.

"I would like to ask you favour, Master."

"Ask. What would you like me to do for you?" Livy said. His curiosity was aroused.

"I would like to ride with the raiders when you move against the Nervii."

"You jest. You want to ride into battle with them?" Livy was surprised. "I thought you didn't like to fight for real and kill people."

"It's different now. This is war. The killing is for our country and for the cause of civilisation. We are not killing for sport."

"Believe me, it is no less horrible even if it is for a cause. I have never gotten used to ending a man's life. I hope I never do. I also never kill unless absolutely necessary."

"So all you want is for me to keep house for you?" She pouted slightly.

"You can train with them and even ride with them on the march, but you are not allowed to go into battle. I will clear this with their new commander, Paulus."

She did a mock military salute. "By your command, Centurion," she said stiffly.

"If there is any fighting, you are to withdraw to the baggage train. After all, you are supposed to take care of my things."

"You may turn around now. Your back is done." She poked him playfully in the sides. He jerked in surprise. Turning around, he suddenly ducked her playfully in the water. As she emerged gasping from the water, he came down hard on her lips, kissing her violently. She mumbled some incoherent protest and struggled a moment, then gave in.

Jasmine was shocked. She had been instructed to bathe, perfume, and dress Leuce for Caesar's party, but after the bath, Leuce had decided that she wanted to attend stark naked and had further painted herself with swirling blue patterns. Jasmine could not understand this strange behaviour and was appalled but in the end gave in to Leuce's insistence.

When she appeared in Caesar's tent, she caused a sensation. Everyone seemed to be staring at her. Even the musicians went somewhat off tune. Caesar was celebrating his suppression of the Belgae prematurely. With three of their main cities under his control, he wanted to give his senior officers a treat as well as entertain the senatorial representatives that were visiting him.

The party was being held in the council hall in the city of Samarobriva. The interior decor was in Roman style for the occasion with lots of drapery and a large number of divans arranged in a large horseshoe. There was incense and perfume in the air. There was also the smell of much delicious food. Belgic and Roman cooks had competed for supremacy as to who had superior culinary skills. The music of flute and lyre permeated the hall.

An elegant middle-aged lady in a fine silk *stola* came up to greet her. "Greetings, Leuce. You are truly an Amazonian beauty. You will drive the men crazy with desire," Servilia said with a slight smile. "My name is Servilia. I am the person in charge of the ceremonies tonight. You are here to entertain Caesar's guest, but we want you to have an agreeable evening as well and I am here to see to that."

Leuce raised one eyebrow at these strange comments. "As you can see, I am all ready to 'entertain'," Leuce said with a hint of sarcasm.

Servilia did not miss a beat. "I have a simple programme lined up for you. Your first encounter would be with someone you already know. Please follow me." Servilia led her through the throng of partying guests. Most of the men were mature. They were legates and tribunes and some visiting senators from Rome or the nearby provinces. The women were selected for their youth and beauty. They had a variety of skin tones and hair colour and obviously came from many lands. They were all clad to seduce with short tunics, transparent material, and off-shoulder outfits or long chitons with slits which went all the way up to the waist. Many of the women were stunning, Leuce noted.

"We have many, very beautiful women here tonight, but I must say you are the most stunningly provocative. You will enthral many men tonight. Your idea about the body paint is certainly innovative. I will adopt the idea in future." She laughed a tinkling laugh.

They came to a plump gentleman with curly hair, wearing a rather overly short off-shoulder tunic. Leuce recognised him at once. "I think you have already met. This is my beloved brother, Quintus Servilius Caepio, tribune and just recently promoted to Caesar's general staff," Servilia introduced formally.

Leuce was shocked. Did she have to sleep with this man? He looked like a catamite. She could swear that it was rouge that tinted his lips. She was prepared to entertain almost any man tonight so as to get a favour from Caesar but certainly not this one.

"I'll leave you two to get better acquainted. I have other guests to attend to." She bent down to kiss her brother on the cheek and then gave Leuce a warm hug and a very light brush of her lips against her blue-stained cheeks.

"Sit down, young lady. Don't look so frightened. I don't intend to have sex with you," Caepio said very directly. "As you can probably guess, I have another persuasion," he said somewhat pompously. "I merely want to thank you for saving my worthless life. I would not be here tonight if you hadn't crossed to our side and led the rescue party." He put a chubby hand on top of hers.

Leuce was relieved. "I did it because I felt pity for the poor decurion whom they tortured mercilessly and also I feared that you would suffer the same fate."

"They had already given me quite a beating, and I dread what was to come if I had stayed to enjoy their hospitality further." Caepio shuddered just remembering that nightmarish experience.

"You see, my dear, I am from a great and noble family. My grandfather was a consul and my father a praetor. Great things are expected of me. Unfortunately, I am who I am—not a great hero as you can see. Still, I am obliged to seek political office in Rome and climb the cursed *cursus honorum*, the path to high office as we call it. This obliges me to have a term in the military and to win an honour or two. Thanks to you, I have survived and achieved my goals. I will be decorated tomorrow," Caepio said proudly.

"Congratulations, Tribune." Leuce smiled.

"So now I can relax and just serve out my remaining time and head on back to Rome to run for office. I have proven myself," he said, sounding more relieved that proud.

"I can tell that you would rather stay at home and enjoy your private life," Leuce said.

"You are astute, young lady. Is there anything I can do for you?" Caepio waved a hand grandly as if a monarch offering a boon.

"I want my freedom and to live in a Roman-controlled city which is free from war," Leuce said hopefully.

"Your freedom is up to Caesar, I am afraid, though I can put in a good word for you to my sister Servilia, who is Caesar's mistress. Perhaps you can receive manumission after a short time. Your Latin is amazing, by the way," Caepio said, popping a grape between his decorated lips.

"If I can't have freedom, then at least let me choose my master," Leuce begged.

"Hum, I can guess. You want to belong to that insufferable young centurion," Caepio sneered.

"Yes, if you mean Gaius Livius Drusus."

"Don't know what you see in him. He's just an arrogant young pup."

"He did save your life. More than once," Leuce reminded him.

"Why not join my sister's merry bunch of hetaerae? They always have fun," he said.

"I don't fancy making a living on my back," Leuce replied.

"I don't see why not? I wouldn't mind." He giggled. She was beginning to like him. He was not self-deluded.

"I want to entertain one man, not a different few every night," she said emphatically.

"Oh, all right. I will speak for you. I don't guarantee anything though," he said with a pout.

Suddenly she could see sunlight through the clouds. She smiled cheerily and gave him a hug and a very warm kiss on his mouth.

"I almost liked that," Caepio said. "Must be careful." He gave her a wry smile, then signalled to Servilia.

Servilia sauntered over with a very handsome young man in tow. "Let me introduce you to Ganymede. This young man is an actor and the current toast of the artistic world back in Rome. I think you two should get together."

Caepio smiled broadly. He suddenly lighted up. Leuce noticed that the young man had eye make-up. "By all means, have a seat right here." Caepio motioned to the young man.

"Come with me." Servilia took hold of Leuce by the arm. "I think we should leave the tribune to his pleasures, I have other gentlemen for you to meet." She guided her away.

They came to a young man with dark curly hair who had the look of a Roman aristocrat with his fine nose and handsome features. He wore a red military tunic, but the material was the finest wool. He had two beautiful young women with him, both in skimpy off-shoulder short tunics. Both were giggling as he teased and flirted with them.

Servilia floated by with Leuce in tow. Leuce was acutely aware that she lacked the poise, grace, and sophistication of any of the girls at the party. She did literally stand out like a sore thumb. "Legate Publius Crassus, let me present you a remarkable young lady, Leuce of the Gaesatae or Amazons or whatever," she said flippantly. Leuce, this is Publius Crassus, son of the richest man in Rome."

Leuce tried her best to appear civilised. She bowed her head just as Jasmine did. "I am honoured to meet such a famous Roman gentleman," she said in perfect Latin.

"Your Latin is perfect. Come and sit beside us." He motioned to her to share his divan. "You two go play somewhere else for a while." He waved them away. They both pouted and looked disappointed, but Servilia whisked them away.

"I heard about your exploit," he began. "You saved Caepio and our Decurion Decius. I thank you on behalf of Rome," he said smoothly.

"I accept your thanks. However, Rome's gratitude in my case comes with enslavement," Leuce said.

"Sometimes for a woman, enslavement is a safer state than being free. Imagine if you were set free now. You will have no means of support. What will you do then? Your options may be few and unpleasant. Most likely you will have to sell your body," Crassus explained.

"I am sure I can find more respectable alternative professions," Leuce said emphatically.

"Not as easy as you think. Very few professions are open to free women—perhaps barmaid, actress, or musician. They are all not entirely respectable, and many in these professions also entertain their clients in a supine position." Crassus laughed. "I guess you could get married, of course. That would be the only respectable profession for a free woman in our society."

"That's the same as making a living in the supine position. The only difference is there is only one customer," Leuce riposted.

Crassus laughed. "I see you also have wit!" As they talked, Crassus began to caress her breasts and her thighs. "I hear you Gaesatae copulate freely with each other." His hands moved higher up her thigh and finally rested just over her labia. She did not resist.

"Yes. Gaesatae women are obliged to provide sexual services to any of our men who want us," Leuce replied. Crassus started to move his fingers, stimulating her. Her juices quickly began to flow.

"Do you have any choice about this?"

"We can refuse if the man is especially unpleasant or if we are ill or have our monthly flow. On the whole, we usually oblige. One gets used to it after a while." She was unexpectedly pleasured by his movements. He was skilled. The stimulation proved irresistible, and she felt herself losing control as the waves of pleasure swept through her body. "You play me expertly like a musical instrument," she gasped.

"I am sure you are equally adept yourself," he said.

"Very!" she gasped just as she climaxed. Her whole body jerked uncontrollably, leaving her exhausted. She took a few moments to recover, then reached under his tunic to caress his erect member. "Now it's my turn."

Leuce performed a very erotic and public fellatio, which caught everyone's attention. The whole room came to a standstill. Everyone was enthralled by her performance, most of all Servilia. "I must get that one to join my company," she said to Caesar. "She will be sensational!"

Finally pleasured almost to the point of no return, Crassus stopped her and turned her around to finish himself off inside her from the rear. Servilia ordered the lights to be dimmed to preserve some semblance of propriety as Crassus climaxed with a moan and then collapsed on to Leuce's back in exhaustion.

Antony signalled to Servilia. She went to him, and he leaned over to whisper in her ear. "I want her next."

"Of course, My Lord Antonius," she replied formally.

Leuce was brought over. Marc Antony was not into talking much, being already inebriated. He was playful though a little rough, but not unpleasant. Leuce tried hard to please and succeeded. The sex was physical and vigorous. Antony had equipment like a horse and stamina to match. He did her in half a dozen positions and managed to come several times. In the end, they both collapsed exhausted. The room lights had been dimmed now to almost total darkness. One could only see shadows and silhouettes.

"You're a great fuck," Antony finally managed to say. "You should definitely do this professionally." He was out of breath.

"Thank you, My Lord," she gasped, also quite out of breath.

"I haven't had such a vigorous session since I arrived in this primitive hole." He laughed.

"Since you are satisfied with my service, may I ask a favour from you?" Leuce ventured.

"Anything, my dear." He held her hand and gave it a squeeze.

"Please put in a good word for me with Servilia and Caesar. I was promised freedom, and the promise was not kept," Leuce asked.

"Consider it done. I certainly think Rome should keep her promises to exotic and delectable goddesses," Anthony said, scanning her luscious body once again.

Servilia came by in a moment to collect Leuce. "Servilia," Antony called out to her.

"Yes, My Lord Antony," Servilia replied.

"She served me well. Better than any of your girls. She is the best," Antony said. "Please grant her whatever favour she asks, for my sake."

"I shall try, but it is up to Caesar. Personally, I would like her to join my wicked little company," she said playfully. "I promise I won't force her. I want her to come willingly."

"I think she has something else in mind. Try and grant it if you can. The girl deserves it after rescuing your brother, don't you think?"

"I'll see what I can do, my dear. I have to pull you away from this bull of a man now. Caesar wants you for the rest of the evening." Servilia divulged.

"There you go, girl. Suck him well and you might get your heart's desire." Antony laughed drunkenly. "Servilia, send me a couple more of your girls. I think I have a few more rounds left in me! I'd like to try some of your German bitches. I hear they can go at it for a long time."

Servilia took her by the hand and led her out to an adjoining hut. There was a large wooden tub filled with warm water. Jasmine was in attendance. "Wash her and scrub off all that horrid blue paint. Perfume her lightly after that. I don't think she will be needing any clothes."

When Servilia came back to fetch her later, she had been scrubbed clean and she smelt like a rose. Not one fragment of warpaint was left on her body. It was already getting cold, and Jasmine wrapped a woollen cloak around her body. They did not return to the main hall but went instead to a large house, not far from the hall. The house was obviously one belonging to someone important in the town, a nobleman perhaps. There were guards with black plumes on their helmets by the door. Their silver cuirasses shone brightly in the light of the torches.

The two women were admitted without question. Inside the house, Caesar lay on a large bed, looking tired and somewhat flushed from alcohol. Two of Servilia's girls were attending to him. Caesar waved them away as soon as Leuce and Servilia came into the room.

"Come closer, my dear." Caesar beckoned. "Let me have a closer look at the young lady that has enthralled all my guests." Leuce came to him and bowed low. She realised that she was in the presence of a remarkable man. The man she saw sprawled on the bed was balding and middle-aged, but he had an aristocratic face with an eagle nose and an intelligent high forehead. His body was still well preserved for his age with good muscular definition. Some fat had accumulated around the middle, but it had not grown to offensive proportions. He was still a handsome man.

Caesar eyed her professionally. "She is certainly a magnificent specimen," Caesar said to Servilia. "A veritable Antiope, the Amazon queen who married Theseus of Athens."

"Killed by Hercules, I believe," Leuce spoke in almost perfect Latin. She had a slight Belgic accent, which softened her tone.

"Ah, an educated Amazon. Do you know Greek as well?"

"I know some but not enough to converse on intellectual matters," Leuce replied in Greek.

"Amazing! What a remarkable young lady," Caesar said, delighted.

Leuce bowed low. "I thank you for your kind compliment."

"So I hear I owe you a few favours. Firstly, you were instrumental in the success of the Roman mission to save Decurion Decius, and your help probably saved many lives. Secondly, you provided unmatched entertainment for my guests tonight, which I believe will contribute much to morale."

"Crassus, Anthony, and Caepio, all three commended her highly, My Lord. They asked me to speak to you on their behalf," Servilia added.

"Considering her abundant sexual skills, I should give her to you, Servilia."

"No doubt she would be excellent in the role of a hetaerae, but that is not her inclination. I believe she has other plans. Besides, I now have my own interests to think of. She is too pretty and skilled." She spoke to Leuce with a half-smile. "Caesar may become overly charmed by this vixen."

"Jealousy, my dear? I thought you had long risen above such base emotions. Besides, you are the only girl for me." Caesar grinned.

"Liar!" Servilia said with mock outrage.

"Maybe we better ask the young lady here. So, what do you want us to do with you?"

"I would like my freedom," Leuce replied emphatically. "I am not a prisoner of war as I came over to your side willingly. I should be treated as an ally like you treat the Suessiones. I should have the same status as the nobleman Lugurix."

"And what would you do once free?" Caesar was curious.

"I want to join the raiders, and I want to become the woman of Centurion Gaius Livius Drusus."

"We do owe you a favour, but those two requests are both difficult. Firstly, Rome has never made use of women in the army except as camp followers or, rarely, as spies. Secondly, Servilia here has just given Livius a very beautiful Greek slave. He already has a woman. However, as he is headed for the senate, perhaps it is not inappropriate for him to have more than one, eh, Servilia?"

"Almost all senators have more than one female slave," Servilia said.

"I don't want to be his slave. I want to come to him as a free woman."

"Well, that poses other problems then. You see, Romans are allowed to have any number of female slaves and to have sex with them whenever they want. Association with a free woman is a different story. He can only have one wife, officially. Of course, he may have any number of mistresses, but the wife then has the usual prerogative of any wife to object or even divorce him," Caesar informed her.

"You are saying then that it would be easier for me to become another slave of the centurion but more difficult to be his woman if I were free?"

"That is basically the issue," Caesar said.

"So I guess I cannot have any of my requests granted." She looked thoroughly disappointed.

"I am Caesar, and all things are possible with Caesar. Your desires may take time to fulfil. I do see it as somewhat a challenge to grant you your wishes, though. If you are a little patient, we will see what can be done."

"This was a somewhat weak promise," Leuce thought to herself.

"Tonight you will entertain us. You are hereby appointed my personal secretary for the time being. In a day or two, we will allow you to join the raiders, perhaps in disguise as a man. For the moment, you will train with them when I don't need you. At nights, you will join Servilia and me in bed," Caesar commanded.

Leuce bowed. At least she got half of what she wanted.

"This, of course, is all contingent on your serving me well tonight and subsequently. After some time, I may see fit to give you your freedom. Meanwhile, it is up to you to charm your lover, Livius."

Leuce saw some hope. There was a silver lining to the grey cloud. She decided to give Caesar a night to remember.

"I have a problem tonight, ladies. There is a part of me that refuses to rise to the occasion," Caesar said, looking disappointed.

Leuce and Servilia looked at each other knowingly and smiled. "After you," Servilia said with a wink.

Leuce didn't need a second invitation. She bent down and attended to Caesar with alacrity.

Livy and Artemisia were luxuriating outside their tent where a fire burnt briskly and the delicious aroma of a hot stew permeated the air. Livy was lying prone, and Artemesia was giving him a back massage.

The stew smelt good but tasted awful. Artemesia still had a lot to learn about cooking, and Livy was planning on getting her to take a few lessons from master chef, Biorix. The stew was only edible when one was famished, which was the only reason Livy could eat it.

"Where is Caesar going to take the army now?" Artemisia asked.

"I think he will turn east into Atrebate and Viromandui territory and into the Nervii lands. If I were him, I would head towards that camp we encountered on the Sabis River and try to bring the whole lot to battle before they move again," Livy said.

"Will we be moving soon?" Artemisia asked.

"Maybe as early as tomorrow, but I think the day after. I doubt Caesar will be able to get his legates up in time to make a move after tonight's party." He suddenly became pensive as he remembered that Leuce would be at the party.

"What do you want me to do when the army moves?" Artemisia asked.

"You'd actually be safer back with Servilia. She would be with the baggage train and well escorted by Caesar."

"I want to be with the raiders," she said.

"I am no longer in command, and that would be up to Paulus," Livy said. "It might be dangerous as they could get a mission at any moment and be off into combat."

"I could detach at that point and return to the baggage train to rejoin Servilia's party if that should happen."

"You must promise to do that. I don't want you going into battle, no matter how good your combat skills," Livy said very seriously.

"I will follow your instructions, *Dominus*." She saluted playfully.

"You'd better. Otherwise, I won't hesitate to spank you."

"I might like it," she said coyly.

"I was afraid you might," he said.

"Shall we have another round of sex?" she asked.

"I think two times is adequate for tonight. I am a little exhausted after the tiring mission," Livy said. "Besides, I have to go check on the sentries about now." He got up and went into the tent to put on his kit.

"All right, be careful. You never know what you might encounter on a night like this," she warned. "I'll be here when you return."

"I shall be back before morning. I hope you have something edible for breakfast."

She made a face at him and stuck out her tongue rudely.

Livy checked on all the sentries on horseback. It was a long ride as there were inner perimeter guards and outer perimeter guards. The Roman Army did not take any chances about being surprised. Finally he finished his task and decided to pay a visit to the raider's camp.

He was challenged by a sentry who let him by even though he didn't know the password. The man recognised him and saluted. Livy decided that he would report the man to Paulus. There should be no exceptions.

He found Paulus and Biorix sitting by a fire, having a late-night drink. Murato was with them, dressed only in leather trousers. The two regular Remi girls were asleep nearby. They waved to Livy to join them.

"So, 'officer of the watch', are we?" Biorix chuckled.

"Well, at least I am not confined to barley gruel," Livy riposted. "Here, I've got some bread and cheese for you. Don't let anybody catch you eating it," Livy warned.

Biorix quickly hid the contraband under his cloak. "Much obliged, ex-commander," he said.

"I am really sorry for what happened," Paulus said. "We'll figure a way to get back at the pompous ass."

"I don't think we should bother. Caesar knows the truth, and he is only punishing us to avoid problems with his political enemies. The whole thing will blow over. Meanwhile, I intend to take my punishment like a good Roman soldier."

"That's the trouble with you. Far too law-abiding," Biorix commented. "Sometimes you need to be able to tread the hidden paths."

"Spoken like a true *exploratores*." Livy laughed.

"Any idea what the army is doing next?" Paulus asked.

"I am sure Caesar is going after the Nervii and their allies next."

"Any idea when?" Paulus asked.

"Next two days, I think. He can't afford to wait longer. The whole lot may disperse, and then we will have a hell of a problem. He needs a decisive battle to end this campaign."

"I guess as we know where they are, we should quickly go over there and get them." Paulus said.

"So how are you keeping, Murato of the Gaesatae?" Livy addressed his erstwhile enemy. He offered him a cup of wine.

Murato took the cup gratefully. Livy notice that his hands were chained together, but his legs were free. "I've been better," Murato replied. "My wound feels better at least."

"I hope my comrades here have been treating you well," Livy said.

"I guess for a prisoner of war and a slave, things aren't too bad," Murato said sadly.

"You'll be grateful that you are on the winning side," Livy said. "After the campaign is over, there won't be much of a future in the Nervii Army."

"Provided you win," Murato said.

"We will win," Livy said firmly. "Your position and treatment in this unit will improve as you win the confidence of these officers. In time, you will function just like any other member of this unit, and I even think you will soon be promoted to officer status. I urge you to serve well and loyally."

Murato was silent. He liked this centurion who was more human than most Romans of rank. "We shall see," he thought to himself. He took a deep draught of the wine.

"May I rest here a while?" Livy requested to Paulus. "I have to make the rounds of the sentries in an hour and it's too far to return to my tent."

"Of course, Commander, you are welcome to take a nap in my tent. I will wake you in an hour."

Caesar lay exhausted. Leuce had aroused him skilfully. He had copulated with her and then with Servilia after Leuce aroused him a second time. The two women then went at each other, each taking turns to pleasure the other. The performance was so erotic that he was aroused a third time and spent himself in Servilia once more. He then fell asleep exhausted as the women went back to pleasuring each other.

The sleep was disturbed by terrible dreams. In the first dream, he saw the whole of Gaul in flames and every tribe rising against him. He glimpsed their leader, a young handsome Gaul in shining armour and wings on his helmet. Then he dreamt a second time. This time, Romans fought Romans in a terrible civil war. He saw Pompey at the head of a great army. He shuddered and awoke in shock.

It was dark, and the two women had fallen asleep in each other's arms. Their faces were calm and peaceful. They look satiated. It was too early to wake. He felt the need to sleep more. He relieved himself into a pot beside the bed, then lay down again. He took in the aroma of the two women. They both smelt deliciously of sex. It was the smell women exude when they are in heat.

Caesar fell asleep again. He dreamt of his patron goddess, Venus. She transformed into an exotic-looking dark-haired girl with mysterious eye make-up. She was in Egyptian dress with her breasts exposed. There was a shining city behind her with a tall lighthouse. Caesar didn't know who she was. She was like no other woman he had met, and she excited him.

He awoke with a start. Trumpets were sounding the reveille. Sunlight sliced through the cracks in the windows. He got up and washed himself. The women were still sleeping peacefully, and he did not want to wake them. He left the room to get dressed. His secretary was waiting for him outside.

"Good morning, My Lord. I trust you slept well?" he said with a sly smile. Caesar was a little annoyed that he took such liberties. "Call a meeting of all my senior staff at noon in the big hall. Get me some breakfast and ask Crassus, Antony, Labienus, Sabinus, and Cotta to join me."

He put on a new red tunic and started strapping on his leather skirt and silver muscled cuirass. "One more thing. The girl in there, her name is Leuce—what a barbaric name—she is to be kept here on my staff. See if she can cope with some of your secretarial work. Send her to me in the evenings."

Jasmine came in. "Good morning, *Dominus*." She smiled sweetly. "I brought you your morning tea."

"Just what I need." He smiled. "Leave it on the table." "She looks especially pretty and delicate this morning," Caesar thought to himself. "Time to change my mind about sleeping with her," he thought.

He pondered the dreams he had. The gods had spoken to him. He was a man of destiny. He would conquer all of Gaul, and then he would have to deal with his enemies in Rome eventually. After that, there was someone wonderful waiting in Egypt. It was all good. He felt his energy renewed. No time to waste. He had to finish off the Nervii as soon as possible. This Belgic campaign had to come to an end.

Caesar gathered all his senior officers for a briefing in the big hall in Samarobriva. The army was well rested and ready to move. He had all his legates, prefects, tribunes, and senior centurions assembled. A large map of the area of operations hung on one wall. It was made of cloth and painted meticulously by his secretaries.

"Gentlemen, it is time to bring this Belgian campaign to a close. Only one army stands between us and the conquest of this whole area." He pointed to Belgica on the map. "There are four tribes left against us. Chief and most belligerent of them are the Nervii. The other three are the Atrebates, the Viromandui, and the Atuatuci. We know where they are gathering." He pointed to a spot on the River Sabis which Livy had indicated in his debriefing.

"Bodougnatus, King of the Nervii, has chosen this site to give battle." He paused for effect. "We shall oblige him!" There was a loud cheer from the officers. "Till now, they have avoided a set-piece battle with us. They are afraid of us. We've beaten them in every small action, and they know we are their masters." Another loud cheer erupted.

"They are a mere three days' march away. I say we break camp today and march there and finish this."

"Hail Caesar! Hail Caesar!" the officers called out enthusiastically.

"We break camp today and march out before dawn tomorrow. I expect us to make twenty-five miles a day. Crassus, the Seventh will lead today. The Twelfth, Eighth, Eleventh, Tenth and Ninth will follow. The Thirteenth and Fourteenth will take the rear. Each legion will march with its own baggage train behind it. At the end of each day, we will make one large encampment to house everyone."

"What about the artillery, sir, and the camp followers?" the artillery prefect asked.

"We'll insert the artillery behind the Tenth, and the camp followers can follow the artillery. You can use them to help if the pieces get stuck," said Caesar decisively.

"I hate to disrupt a good plan, but I have a concern, Caesar," Cotta interjected. "Your order of march may put us in danger of sudden attack. If the front of the column is ambushed, the next legion will find it difficult to come to its aid in time because it will have to get past the first legion's baggage train."

"Your concern is noted, Legate Cotta. Nevertheless, we will stick to this order of march for the time being," Caesar said. He had his reasons, and he was not going to reveal them to anyone just yet.

"What about the recent Belgic levies from the Suessiones, the Bellovaci, and the Ambiani?" Sabinus asked.

"Detail half of them to protect the artillery and the party of camp followers. Break up the rest into squadrons of thirty men. Detail them to act as a cavalry screens to front and flanks," Caesar ordered.

The officers were then dismissed to prepare their respective legions for the move.

CHAPTER 22

The Roman Army moved out at dawn. Livy was uncomfortable on foot and carrying sixty pounds of gear just like any common legionary. He had been spoilt by having had the luxury of being on horseback since the beginning of the Belgian campaign. Nevertheless, he trudged along as cheerily as he could manage. He now had the chance to get to know his century better and found that they were, on the whole, fine soldiers. Most of them were Iberian or Celt-Iberian with a smattering of Roman colonist.

Poor Galienus had been demoted back to *optio* but seemed none too unhappy about it. Livy spent the time on the march exchanging stories and rather bawdy jokes with a Roman boy called Crispus, who incidentally also came from Tarraco. The weather had turned hot again, and parched throats and sore feet added to their discomfort. The army also kicked up a cloud of dust, which made the scarves round their necks a useful accessory.

Livy envied the allied cavalrymen, who seemed to be riding up and down, screening the column. Livy recognised them as Bellovaci warriors by the pattern on their clothes.

Twice during the long march, Artemisia came by, riding his horse, Nero. She was always escorted by one or two of his young raiders. She distributed water canteens to his men and fruit and bread, which they could munch as they marched. There was always loud cheering when she made an appearance. Once she offered to take on some of his load, but Livy refused. He would suffer with the men.

That evening they reached a stream, and Crassus decided that it was a good site to make camp. The column was called to a halt, and the men allowed a brief rest before they had to start constructing the stockade and digging trenches for defence. The Roman Army never left security to chance. They would take the trouble to build a marching camp every night when they were on the road. They would never camp in the open where they could be surprised. This was one of the hallmarks of Roman discipline.

There would be no rest for Livy. As duty centurion, he had to supervise the laying out of the camp by marking the perimeter. He had a brief ten minutes to soak his sore feet in the stream before he was on the go again.

Artemisia brought both his horses and returned Nero to him so that at least he could do his survey on horseback. Livy was equipped with a collection of flags, which he used to mark the perimeter, the main thoroughfares, the gates, and the watch towers. Very soon, the construction teams would start putting up the palisade which would ring the perimeter of the camp. Livy then had to make sure that there were latrines dug and defensive ditches. Finally, he had to see to the pickets.

By the time he had finished all his tasks, it was near midnight. He was both dehydrated and famished. He staggered into his tent and collapsed on to his sleeping couch. He didn't even notice Artemisia taking off his clothes. He woke up about an hour later with a start. Artemisia was shaking him.

"Wake up, Master," she said. "I have a basin of water for you to drink and wash and then you had better go check on your sentries." Livy groaned and forced himself to get up. He was naked.

"I don't know how long I can keep this up. I feel like the walking dead," Livy moaned. Artemisia helped him to wash. Then she gave him some cool water to drink and followed this with some emmer wheat gruel which she had flavoured with a few strips of bacon. She had made the gruel by boiling the army hard tack in water with the bacon. Livy was ravenous and ate the plain but nourishing food. Thankfully, Artemisia managed to find a little wine to go with it, and they shared a drink together.

"I have to go," Livy said reluctantly.

"Finish your rounds quickly and come back," she said. "How long more to the Nervi camp?"

"Another two days," Livy said.

"We'll manage," Artemisia reassured him.

Livy put on his armour and gave her a wet kiss. Artemisia responded warmly. "How quickly men and women start to behave like man and wife when they live together," Livy thought.

He hurried off into the darkness.

Segomaros was a Bellovaci warrior attached to the Roman column as auxiliary cavalry. He had never agreed with the elders surrendering to Caesar so easily. The Bellovaci were a proud warrior race, and he felt that the easy capitulation was a total disgrace. When his company was fast asleep he got up, put on his gear, retrieved his weapons and horse, and slipped off into the night.

The auxiliary cavalry was stationed outside the Roman encampment, so it was easy to elude the sentries. He hid in a covered place till he saw the sentry walk by. Just at that moment, the officer of the watch rode up. He recognised the young centurion who led the feared raider unit. Segomaros hid himself in the shadows.

"See anything in this sector?" Livy asked the sentry.

"It has been quiet, sir. Two hours ago some cavalry came by, but we identified them as Remi scouts."

"Who was commanding?" Livy asked.

"A decurion. I believe his name was Licinius," the sentry replied.

"They are the perimeter patrol," Livy said. "I haven't seen them for a while. Maybe I will run into them tonight. Take care and sound the alert if you see or hear anything."

"Yes sir, Centurion," The man said. Livy rode off to check the next sentry.

Segomaros waited till he was out of hearing range. He then rode out suddenly. "Halt! Who goes there!" the sentry challenged. Segomaros whipped his horse into a canter, then slashed the sentry through the neck with his long sword. The man crumpled without a sound, dark blood spreading into a pool.

Segomaros rode about five miles into the forest and came upon a thick grove of trees. He approached cautiously and saw a number of lighted torches set around an old oak tree. There was no one in the small clearing. Segomaros realised that he was in a holy place. He unsheathed his sword and slowly walked into the clearing.

Suddenly he was surrounded by men in armour. None of the men had weapons at the ready. "Sheath your sword, Segomaros of the Bellovaci," a commanding voice ordered.

Segomaros looked around in surprise and quickly obeyed. The man who gave the order was a well-built man wearing expensive silver armour with a traditional downturned Gaulish moustache sans beard. He wore a shiny helmet topped by a hawk with outstretched wings. "I am King Commius of the Atrebates, and this, my companion, is King Ambiorix of the Eburones." The man next to him was also impressively built and naked to the waist. He had on an elaborate gold torque.

"Sit down and share a libation with us," Ambiorix said. The men sat around the fire in the middle of the clearing. Two guards stood behind Segomaros. "Tell us what the Romans are doing," Commius ordered.

"They march eastwards, making good speed. They travelled twenty-eight miles today. The troops are well rested and in high spirits."

"What is their order of march?" Ambiorix queried.

"The Seventh legion leads and then baggage, and then the Twelfth and then baggage, and so on."

"Where is Caesar?"

"He is somewhere in the middle. He travels with the Tenth. The artillery and camp followers march after the Tenth as well."

There was silence. Commius broke it. "They are vulnerable. Is there anywhere we can ambush them on the march?" he asked Ambiorix.

"I have surveyed the whole route to the Sabis. Mostly open ground with some small covered areas. Not big enough to ambush such a big army," Ambiorix said.

"It's a pity. We could take them one legion at a time. The following legions would take time to be brought up."

"Let's stick to the original plan," Commius decided. "With this order of march, we will have an even easier time of it."

"Eat and drink and then you'd best be on your way," Ambiorix said to Segomaros. "Did anyone see you leave?"

"One sentry, but I sent him to Thanatos." The man smiled.

"Good. Be careful when you return. Walk like a ghost," Commius warned.

A short time later, Segomaros was back in camp. He had dismounted to sneak back into the auxiliary encampment. He felt lucky. There were no sentries to be seen. No one would know he had even left. Segomaros smiled confidently to himself.

The Roman Army started packing up early. Livy managed to catch an hour of sleep in his tent after which he was suddenly woken up by the guard commander. He put on his armour and hurried after the man. It was still dark, and mist lay on the ground. When he neared the Bellovaci encampment, there were a group of soldiers gathered just outside the camp. Livy hurried to the scene.

"We found him a short while ago. His head is half cut off. Sabre slash to the throat looks like," the guard commander explained. The dead sentry looked very pale, and his blood had soaked into the ground all around him. Livy recognised him as the man he had spoken to just hours before.

"Anyone see anything?" Livy asked.

"One of my men saw one of the Bellovaci sneak into camp." It was Licinius who spoke.

"It's a pleasure to see you again." Livy grasped his hand. "I hope he can identify the man."

"Don't worry, sir. We will sort it out shortly. My man is going around with the Bellovaci commander right now. We shall have our man before the sun rises. I'll hand him to you as soon as we catch him."

"I thank you," Livy said. "I leave the matter in your good hands. I have a lot to do before we get under way," Livy saluted and rode off.

He went to report to the camp prefect of the Seventh Legion. Crassus was already there. "I heard we had a little excitement in the night?" The legate was impeccably attired in full armour and an expensive red cloak.

"Yes, sir. Someone from the Bellovaci camp sneaked out and killed a sentry along the way. We are investigating," Livy answered. He was in *subarmalis* and chain mail with his helmet tucked under his arm. Still he felt shoddy in comparison to his commander.

"I knew we shouldn't trust our erstwhile enemies so quickly. Catch the traitor quickly."

"I'll try my best, sir," Livy replied.

"The order of march is the same as yesterday," the camp prefect said. "Get under way immediately. Caesar wants to make thirty miles today, so everyone is to march on the double."

"Why the hurry, sir?" Livy asked.

"Caesar wants to surprise the enemy before he gets away again. We want to finish this campaign, don't we?" Crassus said.

"You are dismissed, Centurion. I am sure you have much to do," the prefect said.

Livy saluted and left.

The Bellovaci cavalry contingent was paraded and every man was made to fall in. The Remi scout was escorted by Licinius and the Bellovaci commander down the ranks and files. They looked closely at every man. A small team of Caesar's provosts watched the proceedings on horseback. They were distinct in their black tunics and black plumes.

Segomaros was nervous. He worked out that he must have been spotted. His only hope was that whoever saw him did not have a good enough look to identify him. After all, every Bellovaci warrior looked very much like another to the Romans, or so he hoped. The inspection team was nearing him now. He could not help perspiring copiously. The team stopped in front of him.

"Why are you sweating like a pig?" the commander asked.

"I don't feel well, sir. I feel very hot. Maybe coming down with a fever," he mumbled.

"Step forward," Licinius ordered in Belgic.

This was too much to bear. His courage gave out. Segomaros ran for it. He didn't get far. One of the provosts rode after him and hit him on the head with a club. The last thing Segomaros remembered was a sharp pain and everything going black.

"I think we have our man," Licinius said. "What do you think?" He addressed the Remi scout.

"Looks like him. I recognise the long red moustache. Not many men have red hair like that."

The provost officer rode up. "We'll bring him in for questioning. Keep a close eye on the rest of this lot. Make sure none of them desert," the officer said.

Licinius and the Bellovaci officer saluted.

Caesar had got up early to do some planning. The Belgae were damnably difficult and unpredictable. They were fickle and acted on whim. One day they would be raring to fight. The next, they would be slinking away as fast as they could. Caesar needed one big decisive battle. He needed to destroy their army, and then the whole nation would capitulate and accept Roman rule. He pondered the problem in his darkened tent lit only by candlelight. In his left hand he held a miniature statue of Venus carved from ivory. There was a chill in the air despite the smouldering brazier nearby.

The trouble was how to bring them to battle. If he appeared strong, they would avoid battle. If he had a good position, they would avoid battle. He had to appear weak and vulnerable. The question was how to make them think that they had the advantage.

He was pondering these problems when Servilia came behind him and put her hands on his shoulders from behind. She leaned over and gave him a kiss on the cheeks. "You work too hard," she said. She had wrapped herself in a crimson woollen campaign cloak but was otherwise nude.

"I have a war to run, my dear," Caesar said pensively. "I'm working out how to bring Bodougnatus to battle."

"He is impulsive and vain but also somewhat a coward. He'll fight if he thinks he can win easily," Servilia said.

"Since when have you become a general?" He teased her.

"I know men," she said.

Caesar was happy to have Servilia around on the campaign. His relationship with her transcended sex. She was a soul mate, and, best of all, she didn't care who he had sex with.

"Did you enjoy the young barbarian last night?" Servilia asked.

"She tried hard to please. Yes, I did actually," Caesar said. "I understand you yourself used her services after I slept."

"Yes, I did," Servilia answered, unabashed.

"Did she please you?"

"Very much," Servilia said.

"I wish we could keep her, but I know she is cooperative only because she hopes I will keep my promise to free her."

"Will you?"

"I think so. It would set a bad precedent if I enslaved enemy military personnel who willingly came over to our side," Caesar said officiously.

"Couldn't we make an exception? She is exceptional in bed," Servilia explored.

"No exceptions. It could derail my very carefully thought-out policy to encourage defection to the Roman cause. No, we must free her soon," Caesar said firmly.

"You are not just going to let her go?" Servilia protested. "Her own side would probably kill her at best or, worse, sacrifice her to their gods."

"I haven't decided. She expressed a wish to join the army," Caesar mused.

"Are you going to break our ancient tradition?" Servilia asked.

"I might be able to slip her into service without causing too much of a furore, especially if she doesn't dress too conspicuously. In military gear, she might just pass off as any male soldier."

"You must be insane. She is far too pretty. Someone is bound to notice," Servilia argued.

"We shall see." Caesar's tone of voice did not encourage further discussion on this matter. "Let's just enjoy her while we can, eh, sweetheart?" Caesar kissed her on the cheek.

The Roman Army marched out at a brisk pace led by the *primus pilus* of the Seventh Legion, the grizzled veteran Centurion Priscus. Each legion was led by a colour party led by the *aquilifer* carrying a silver eagle, then a band of *signifers* carrying the vexillum of the various subunits replete with unit decorations. Then followed the *cornicens* with their horns and trumpets. As they turned on to the road east, the men passed a lone wooden cross. There was a man nailed to it. He hung silently as a reminder to the army about the price of betrayal.

Caesar did not change the order of march. Each legion was followed by its own baggage train. Livy resigned himself to another long, tiring day. He marched near the end of the Seventh Legion column with his own century. Each man carried on his shoulder a T-shaped pole called a *furca* with all their belongings attached to it. Each century marched led by a centurion, a *signifer* draped in animal skins carrying a vexillum and a *cornicen* equipped with a *cornu*. They sang bawdy songs to pass the time and lighten their exertions.

On a hill overlooking the line of the march a small band of Eburone scouts watched. They saw a single legion march by followed by a clumsy wagon train. Behind them came another legion, then another wagon train. This was important news. The commander sent one of his men to report back to King Ambiorix and subsequently to Bodougnatus.

As they trudged along, the soldiers raised a large column of dust, which marked their passage. They made thirty miles that day and arrived at their evening camping site entirely exhausted. As was their usual practice, they rested a short while, then started constructing the barricades which would secure their marching camp. Livy had his usual duties and went about them promptly. He was more familiar now with what he had to do and did it with greater speed and efficiency. Thus he bought some time to relax and rest in his tent with Artemisia. She had a treat for him this evening. There was a chicken roasting on a spit outside his tent when he returned.

"That smells wonderful to a hungry man." He brightened.

"Let me help you off with your armour, and you can rest a while," she offered. Livy gave himself up to her ministrations. He was utterly exhausted. She offered him cool water in a cup. He remembered now that he hadn't had time to eat all day, and his throat was parched as he had not drunk a drop since noon. The water tasted like ambrosia, the drink of the gods in Olympus.

He rested awhile then joined her for dinner. He was ravenous, and the chicken was delicious. "You seasoned the chicken. I taste rosemary and other herbs," Livy said, pleasantly surprised.

"Biorix came by to ride with me during the march. He gave me instructions and some herbs. I am determined to improve my kitchen skills, *Dominus*."

Livy was impressed. She was really trying to be a good personal slave. In fact, she was being more than this. She was starting to treat him like her husband. "Are you happy in your new life?" Livy asked with a smile.

"More happy than you can imagine. I feel like a real Spartan woman again. We are meant to look after our men and our home," she said proudly.

He took her hand and caressed it. "Perhaps I should set you free to go back to Sparta."

"Oh, please don't do that, Master. There is nothing left for me there. My place is here at your side, Master."

"What if I were to free you?"

"I would ask to stay as your servant. You needn't even pay me except for board and lodging," she said. "Don't do that, though. I feel more secure as a slave at the moment."

"What if I were killed in battle, my dear?"

"You can leave it in your will to set me free," she said plainly.

"What will you do then?" Livy asked.

"I will seek employment with Caesar as sword trainer in his legions." She laughed. "I have a feeling that you will survive, though. I think the gods have in mind some strange destiny for you." She snuggled close to him, and he put his arms around her, letting her head rest on his chest. She gave off a sexy, oily aroma from her hair which he inhaled pleasurably.

They ate quietly just enjoying the moment and the warmth of each other's bodies. Time seemed to slow down.

A short time later, it rained.

The legions started their march before light once more. The whole army was drenched wet, including Caesar, who was on horseback with his general staff on a hill watching his men. They marched by smartly in good order despite the rain. As each cohort passed by, it turned to the right to salute their leader. Caesar felt a deep sense of pride watching them. This was the finest army Rome had produced for a long time. The men were young, superbly trained, and had iron discipline.

He turned to Crassus. "We are almost at our destination. Camp early tonight. I want the men totally rested as we will contact the enemy tomorrow. Make sure everyone is fed well tonight," Caesar ordered.

"Don't you think we should change the order of march, My Lord?" Crassus asked. "They are obviously watching us. We are vulnerable in our present configuration."

"Keep the same order. Order the cavalry scouts to range further and engage any enemy scouts vigorously," Caesar told Labienus.

"At your command, sir." Labienus saluted and rode off.

"Do you think they will bite?" Antony said. Droplets of water detached intermittently from his helmet rim, irritating him.

"It's a little bit like fishing, Antony. I am doing everything to tempt them, but you never know," Caesar said, wiping the rain from his eyes.

The rain continued to pour, and Antony wiped the water off his face with his scarf. He worried that all those trampling feet would quickly churn the ground to mud, making it difficult to bring up the artillery and siege engines.

The rain continued till midday and then suddenly abated. Soon the sun peaked through the clouds and the temperature rose, drying out the drenched legionaries. Caesar called a halt in the late afternoon. They had got to only ten miles from the Sabis River.

Licinius and his Remi scouts reported back to headquarters.

"Where is the Nervii Army now?" Caesar wasted no time.

"They are camped just across the river, sir," Licinius replied. They have a large encampment hidden in the woods."

"How many men and which tribes?" Caesar asked.

"Mainly Nervii. We also saw Atrebates, Viromandui, and the occasional Eburone. About 100,000 men at arms," Licinius replied.

"What about the Atuatuci?" Caesar asked.

"We didn't see any. From my spies, I think they have yet to join but may appear at any moment," Licinius said.

"Thank you, Commander. Please continue to keep an eye on them. You should also send a party to check on the Atuatuci. I don't want any surprises. Will any other tribes join their confederation?"

"Most of the others are waiting to see what happens. If Bodougnatus comes off well in the coming battle, you can be sure the others will throw in their lot with him. If they lose, they will all likely come over to our side." Licinius smiled.

"Thank you. You may go." Caesar dismissed the man.

Licinius turned around and galloped off, mud spattering from his horse's hooves as he departed.

Caesar turned to Labienus and the commanders of the auxiliary cavalry and light troops. "Tomorrow we shall come in contact with the enemy. Your role is vital. When we reach the River Sabis, we will immediately construct a camp and defences on the north bank. They will be tempted to attack us," Caesar began.

"If they do, I intend for their attack to break upon our defences. Your role would be to keep them at bay till we can finish constructing our camp, digging the trenches, planting the stakes, and bringing up our artillery. Your role is not to get into an all-out melee. You are the diversion. Keep them busy till all the legions come up. If they counter-attack in force, you are to retreat back across the river. Do you understand?"

"Yes, sir," all the commanders agreed.

"Try not to close with them. Harass them with missiles. Use your bows and javelins," Caesar added.

"What if they attack in force?" Kleon asked.

Caesar noticed him. "Ah, Kleon, I am happy to see you are recovered. I doubt they will mount an all-out attack at short notice. From what I have observed of their behaviour, they tend to take their time to form up and make a demonstration first. By the time they get done with the preliminaries, we will be ready for them," Caesar said confidently.

"We will be ready to perform our role in the morning," Labienus assured him.

The Belgic camp was in a flurry of activity. The enemy was arriving on the morrow, and the army was preparing for the upcoming battle. Weapons were being sharpened. Extra javelins and arrows were being readied. War paint was applied. The unit commanders were conducting their briefings.

Bodougnatus had assured his battle-hungry horde that they would go into battle for certain the next day.

The army was issued extra rations, and the camp followers were doing their best to raise the morale of the troops with some serious pre-battle sex. Morale was high as the Belgae knew they outnumbered the Romans at least two to one. At long last, they would have their decisive battle and would destroy the accursed invaders who dared to mess with them and take their land.

As usual, Bodougnatus and his nobles were feasting with the kings and nobles of the Atrebates and the Viromandui. Bodougnatus had drunk mightily, and his red face showed the effects of the beer and wine. He had also eaten heartily, and bits of roasted meat adorned his large beard. He held a slim half-naked girl on his lap, and he was presently biting her nipples and making her scream. No one was sure if she screamed in delight or just in pain.

Commius, who sat beside him, was disgusted. He held his counsel and drank moderately. It would be good to have a clear head tomorrow morning as they went into battle. He was quietly confident that the Romans were overconfident this time and they would give them a good drubbing in the morning. He ignored the rather pretty brunette who sat next to him with a hand on his thigh.

They had taken over a large farmhouse as was their usual practice, and the house was reconfigured for the party. The whole room reeked of alcohol as the nobles frolicked with scores of young serving women. A band played loud music in the background, and some jugglers were performing, ignored by everyone.

The door suddenly opened to reveal Ambiorix, King of the Eburones. The room suddenly went quiet. Ambiorix walked slowly to the low table where Bodougnatus and the other kings were dining. He had a serious look on his face and did not smile.

"Ambiorix, friend and ally, what news do you bring? Come and join our feast for tomorrow we kill Romans, eh?" Bodougnatus said.

"The Romans camp not ten miles from here. Their scouts have come as far as the river. Be prepared for battle, Kings. The time is nigh," Ambiorix announced.

"My men thirst for blood. Tomorrow we will soak the ground with Roman blood," Bodougnatus boasted.

"Your commanders look in no shape to fight," Ambiorix said angrily. "They reek of wine and beer. How will they lead the men tomorrow?"

"We Nervi can fight, drunk or not. You will see, Eburone. You will see how we do battle."

"I hope you live up to your boast, King. If you don't, you will be hanging on a cross by evening," he warned. Ambiorix turned and walked out peremptorily. Commius toasted his host, then made an excuse to leave. He ran after Ambiorix.

Ambiorix turned as he heard footsteps coming from behind. "The man is a fool, Commius. The Romans won't be beaten easily even if outnumbered."

"I know, Ambiorix," Commius said. "I have a little surprise for them, though," Commius said. "Come to my tent, and I will explain. I have a little entertainment just for you, and we won't drink anymore." He put an arm around his shoulder.

Ambiorix liked this king. He was serious and clever. "All right," he said and followed Commius.

In the shadows, Bratronos the Druid watched the pair. Tomorrow he hoped that the Romans would be crushed and their Suessione allies with them. After that, there would be retribution on all the turncoats that went to the Roman side. This included the Bellovaci, the Suessiones, and the Ambiani. He rubbed his hands in glee. There would be many human sacrifices to the gods.

One of those he hoped most to get his hands on would be that traitorous Gaesatae bitch Leuce. He had tried to force his attention on her, but she had rejected him and called him a weasel face. She would burn for that. He would make her die slowly and painfully. She would pay. Just thinking about it made him erect.

Caesar called a meeting of his senior officers after the marching camp had been constructed and all the soldiers had been fed. There would be no revelry in the Roman camp. Things went on as usual as the Roman Army quietly prepared for battle. There were extra rations for dinner, but the soldiers were told to sleep early and get an early start. A double sentry was organised as they were now really near the enemy.

Outside the palisade of the camp, deep trenches were dug with sharp spikes at the bottom. Watchtowers and firing platforms for the artillery were hastily erected. There was a calm and quiet atmosphere in the camp. The camp followers were kept in a separate encampment away from the soldiers. Caesar did not want his soldiers disturbed at all this night. He wanted them fresh and rested in the morning.

When the legates, camp prefects, auxiliary prefects, and chief centurions of all the legions had gathered, he started his briefing.

"Gentlemen, the enemy are a mere ten miles away across a small river. They seem in no hurry to move, so tomorrow we will meet up with them. We will camp on the north bank of the river and set up defences around the camp. Let's see if they will come forth and give battle this time. We are in Nervii territory now, and they have nowhere left to run," Caesar began.

"How are we going to get them to commit to fight?" one of the senior centurions asked. "The last time, they just paraded around and wouldn't attack."

"I have ordered our light troops to cross the river and harass them. Hopefully, that would stir up the hornet's nest enough to get them to swarm over the river and try and slay us," Caesar said.

"Are you going to reveal now the order of battle?" Cotta asked.

"The order of battle will be the same as always. There will be some changes to the order of march. New orders will be issued to the legates in the morning, and they are to be disseminated just before marching out and not a moment before," Caesar said.

"Why the mystery, Caesar?" Sabinus asked.

"There are spies among us." That was all Caesar said. "You are all dismissed back to your units. Prepare for battle tomorrow." The meeting was dissolved.

Caesar spent a nervous night. He had a light meal with Crassus, Antony, and Servilia. They ate privately as Caesar had dismissed the servants. The wine was drunk sparingly and well-watered. The meal was simple consisting of bread, cheese, fruit, and some river fish, which Caesar's German guards were able to catch in a stream. The conversation was sparse. Everyone ate quietly. Finally Servilia broke the silence. "It's as silent as a tomb in here," she complained. "I've never met a more morose lot. You shouldn't be so anxious, Julius. You have an excellent plan and the best army in the known world. Tomorrow, Jupiter Optimus Maximus will grant you a great victory which will earn you a great triumph in Rome. After all, that's what it's all about isn't it?"

"You fail to understand, Servilia. Of course, you are only a woman," Caesar began.

"How condescending!" Servilia retorted.

"It's not about just a triumph in Rome. The Roman Empire needs to expand, to secure its borders and bring civilisation to these barbaric tribes who sacrifice their children to their terrible gods. I want to see this land developed and civilised. I want to grow towns here with villas and temples and baths," Caesar spoke earnestly.

"Well, you'll have to kill a lot of people to do it," Servilia said.

"Yes, it would seem the barbarians are happy to resist your very good intentions." Antony laughed.

"In a few years, they will appreciate the peace, security, and prosperity of Roman rule and Roman civilisation. The ordinary citizen of Gaul will no longer be subject to constant inter-tribal warfare and the burning, raping, and pillaging that goes with it," Caesar said.

"They like the burning, raping, and pillaging," Antony said.

"They will need to be taught respect for the law and the rights of their neighbours then."

"You will have to change a thousand years of culture," Crassus said.

"Yes, we will have to," Caesar replied.

In another simpler tent in the encampment of the Seventh Legion, Livy was finishing his simple dinner of bread, cheese, and fruit. He was better organised now, so he was able to take a few hours of private time with Artemisia. The camp prefect had been happy with his performance the last few days and given him a few hours off to rest. He had even offered to check the sentries himself this night.

"Tell me more about this famous battle at Thermopylae," he asked Artemisia, who was lying beside him outside the tent, enjoying the cool night air and watching the sparkling stars.

"Well, the first myth I want to dispel is that the Spartans fought naked. We train in the nude, but we always went to battle in full armour. A Spartan soldier doesn't go to war with his penis hanging out like those obscene Gaesatae that you regularly encounter in this cursed land," Artemisia began.

"I never ever thought that!" Livy laughed. "I think the numbers were somewhat exaggerated as well."

"Ancient sources claimed a million or even two million Persians, but I think this was exaggerated. I guess the main problem was the Persian Army was too big to count. The Greeks didn't have a very good system to gather military intelligence," she said.

"So how many Persians do you think Xerxes had in his army?" Livy asked.

"My teachers estimated about 300,000," Artemisia said. "I think the exact figure will never be known."

"I am sure there were more than 300 on the Spartan side as well."

"The three hundred were the companions of King Leonidas. That was the number of the true Spartan warriors. Then there were Perioci, Helots, other Peloponesian allies, Phocians, Thebans, and Thespians. All together, the small army numbered about 7,000," she answered.

"You know your military history well." Livy congratulated her. "Still 7,000 against 300,000 are heroic odds," Livy replied.

"I hear tomorrow we are outnumbered at least two to one," Artemesia said as she stirred the dying embers of the wood fire.

"Looks like it's going to be a walk in the park, then," Livy laughed.

"Don't underestimate the enemy. I have been speaking to your friend Biorix, and he tells me the Nervii are a pretty scary bunch. They live to fight and look down on any other activity. Besides, this is not Thermopylae, the hot gates where you have a battlefield limited to a hundred yards. They have the numbers and will try and swamp you," she warned.

"I am sure Caesar has planned for every contingency. I just need to play my part with my eighty men," Livy said confidently.

"Just take care of yourself and come back alive, Master."

"You don't subscribe to that old Spartan custom where the woman tells her son or husband to come back with his shield or on it?" Livy teased.

"No. I know better now. Just come back, with or without your stupid shield."

"I will try my best to oblige." Livy smiled and gave her a warm kiss. "I need to discuss another matter with you."

"Yes, Master?"

"You may ride with the raiders till we reach our campsite. After that, I want you to return to the baggage train and stay with Servilia and her party. I am sure Caesar would have assigned some men to guard them. I don't want you with the raiders when the battle begins," Livy said seriously.

"I will obey, Master," she said with a reassuring smile,

"I am serious, Artemisia. Go back to Servilia and stay there till the battle is over." Livy held her hand in his.

"I will," she said.

"There is one more thing. I have made up a letter of manumission for you and left it with Servilia. If anything happens to me, you are a free woman," Livy said.

Artemisia was stunned for a moment; then a tear appeared at the corner of one eye. Livy was surprised because he believed her a tough girl. He didn't know quite what to say.

"Any joy I would derive from my freedom would pale to the devastation I would feel if you didn't come back," she said with anguish. "These past days have been the happiest days for me since my childhood before my father died. You have brought the sunshine back into my miserable life."

"I will be back," Livy said plainly.

She looked into his clear blue eyes and read only quiet determination. Somehow deep within herself she believed him. "I will be waiting for you." She kissed him, a long lingering kiss.

They slept in each other's arms, too tired to do anything else except sleep.

Bodougnatus was lying in a large bed with four naked slave girls. He was happy with his chief retainer who had been supplying him regularly with fresh fodder for his bed. This night, he had exhausted himself eating and drinking large amounts and then tried his best to ravish all his bed companions. They were all very young, no more than fifteen or sixteen seasons. By the time he had finished with the fourth, he was too exhausted to move and fell asleep.

He woke up in the early hours of the morning to a darkened room lit by only a few torches. The women were lying naked around him, sound asleep, and one of them was actually snoring. He was somewhat disgusted, forgetting that he probably snored the loudest himself when he slept.

His mind was troubled. The next day would be a climactic confrontation, one which bards would sing about for centuries. He had twice the numbers, and his army was rested and well fed. They had the advantage of preparation, and they had the better position. The river had receded, so there would be no trouble charging across. How could they lose?

Yet, doubt crept like a spider into his mind. This Caesar was a very special general, and the Romans were very special people. They were well organised and tenacious. They didn't know how to give up. They always fought against larger odds and usually won. They would not surrender or run away. Bodougnatus decided that the Belgae would have to slaughter the Romans to the last man. There would be no quarter tomorrow.

He couldn't sleep any more. He pushed away one of the girl's arms which lay across his chest and got up. His head hurt from too much wine. He reached for a half-full horn and gulped the stale wine. It tasted nasty. "Better get up and prepare myself for battle," he thought to himself.

Commius slept alone. His mind was troubled. His own Atrebates had been made ready as much as he possible could. His sub-commanders were well briefed, the weapons were sharpened, and his army had been properly deployed for the assault in the morning.

The enemy would come along the road from Camaracum. It was a good road, and they would come in briskly. In their present configuration, each legion would be followed by a baggage train, which would make it difficult for the following legion to come to its aid. The whole army of the confederation would go in as soon as the first baggage train was spotted, thus taking the legions one at a time before the whole Roman Army could deploy. They would thus take full advantage of their numerical superiority.

If all things went as planned, the Romans would be given a sound drubbing. He doubted that it would degenerate into a rout as the Romans were disciplined and well trained. Still, he hoped that they would be hurt enough to quit Belgae territory and think twice about coming back. Perhaps they could then hope for an equitable peace treaty which would allow them to coexist peacefully as friends and allies of Rome.

Perhaps all this was wishful thinking because Bodougnatus would never acknowledge the Romans as overlord. Still, a defeat would affect Caesar's standing in Rome, where he had many enemies, and this would check his ambitions in Gaul.

Commius tossed and turned as all these thoughts circled in his mind. Finally, he drifted off into a fitful slumber.

Caesar was having an after-dinner bath in a huge tub of warm water. He liked to be clean and felt that bathing was one of the greatest benefits of being civilised. He had two bath slaves scrubbing him down. Leuce was in the tub with him, and Jasmine standing naked outside was scrubbing his back. When she finished, she climbed in to join them in the tub. Caesar felt relaxed, but his mind was not on sex tonight, although his two companions were stunning. Leuce, with her very pale complexion, azure eyes, golden hair, and a figure better than Aphrodite's was the perfect northern beauty. Jasmine was a total contrast with her ebony straight hair set against her ivory skin, jet-black eyes, and delicate slim figure was every man's idea of the exotic East. He felt privileged to be in the company of two such perfect creatures.

Leuce sensed that the great Caesar was not in the mood today. He seemed quiet and thoughtful and did not make any sexual advances to either girl. His mind seemed to be elsewhere. He seemed satisfied just to have them sit in the tub with him.

Finally he spoke, "Tomorrow will be a deciding day. If all goes well and victory is ours, the Belgae will be decisively beaten and all will be well. If not, I cannot even imagine the consequences. You have both been wonderful companions. Though you are technically slaves, I have not treated you as such." He held both by the hand.

"In the morning, I want you both attached to Servilia's party. I have attached a small detachment of six Germans to guard them, but I know you both have considerable fighting skills. I will see that you both are armed and armoured. You will protect Servilia and her party at all costs. Do you understand?"

They both nodded.

"If we win, you will both be richly rewarded. I will see to it personally." Caesar leaned back and closed his eyes. He stayed in the tub a few more minutes, enjoying the moment.

Suddenly he got out of the tub. The girls dried him with towels and helped him into his silk robe. When he was done, he turned to them. "I sleep alone tonight. You are both dismissed. Go get some rest." He walked off to his tent. Both girls bowed low as he exited.

Jasmine turned to Leuce. "Will you sleep with me tonight?"

"Thank you. I have nowhere else to go," Leuce replied.

"I know," Jasmine said and took her by the hand and led Leuce to her tent.

CHAPTER 23

He changes his ways and alters his plans to keep the enemy in ignorance.

The morning was bright and sunny with few clouds in a clear blue sky. Caesar looked up and saw two eagles circling, looking for prey. He interpreted this as a good omen because eagles represented Rome. The augurs had done their usual ceremony at dawn. A goat was killed, and its entrails were examined. The priest had taken a long time to come to a decision. At last he pronounced that the omens were good.

There was a loud cheer from the men, and the army had marched off in good spirits. Caesar had made a last-minute change in the order of march. As they were definitely contacting the enemy this day, he put his six veteran legions out in front with the consolidated baggage coming after. The last two newly recruited legions, the Thirteenth and Fourteenth, brought up the rear. There were only ten miles to march to get to the Sabis River, and they would reach it by mid-morning. The column had set off before first light.

Livy was riding at the head of the Seventh Legion with Crassus, his senior tribune, the camp prefect and the first spear. He was still officially the duty officer and had to be ready to take orders from the commander. The Seventh Legion was in the vanguard with the Twelfth Legion immediately behind them. At the front was a large screen of Roman cavalry, auxiliary cavalry, Balearic slingers, Numidian light infantry, and Cretan archers. These light troops would be first to contact the enemy. If pressured, they would withdraw. The legions would have been warned and formed up before that happened.

The road was wide and that made marching easy. Both sides of the road were also relatively clear. The column made good time. Livy had woken up early to supervise the disposal of the Seventh Legion's baggage to the rear. He made sure that Artemesia went along to the baggage train. She had made sure he had a good breakfast of emmer wheat gruel flavoured with a few pieces of bacon. She had also given him two canteens of fresh water drawn from a nearby well.

Livy was fortunate enough to be allowed to ride with the legate today as part of his staff. He had turned the direct command of his century back to Galienus. Nero, his horse, was in good spirits for having been rested the last few days.

The raiders, under the command of Paulus, were tasked to be a rearguard and were positioned just before the immense baggage column where the artillery pieces were stationed. They too were well rested as they had not seen actions for some days now.

At the Tenth hour, the Seventh Legion arrived at the north bank of the Sabis River. The screening light troops were already at the river bank, forming a rough skirmish line. Livy could see light troops of the enemy on the other side. Most of them were half-naked javelin troops and archers. The two sides began to exchange fire. Livy regretted that the raiders were not around. His men would have made mincemeat of the enemy skirmishers with their longer range and more accurate fire.

Crassus formed up four of his cohorts as a security screen, and the Twelfth Legion immediately did the same. The rest of the men of the two forward legions immediately started camp construction. Laying their packs, shields, and helmets aside, they began digging trenches and erecting a wooden palisade. The men worked quickly and efficiently, a result of their constant drill.

Within a half-hour, the Eighth and the Eleventh were also deployed to help in the camp construction. The Ninth and Tenth Legions were already marching quickly on to the scene.

By the river, the battle between the skirmishers was becoming more intense. The Romans had driven the Belgic light troops back and were pursuing across the river. The Cretan archers were getting the better of the exchange of missiles, knocking out many of the enemy archers. The Balearic slingers were driving back the enemy *velites* with their stones and lead pellets. Those of the enemy javelin troops which ventured closer were quickly engaged by the Numidians, who were deadly with their light javelins.

As the Roman skirmishers advanced, the Belgic troops slowly withdrew. Now they were at the edge of the forest and were slowly withdrawing into it.

Inside the forest, Commius waited with his men who remained hidden but were already in battle formation. He saw the light troops slowly withdrawing, seducing the Roman skirmishers forward yard by yard. He himself was looking keenly at the other bank. The signal for attack would be given the minute the baggage train was sighted.

He had expected only one legion to be on the scene, but there looked like several legions. He still had the hope that the Roman Army was divided and this was just merely half of their forces or less. Still he had a feeling of dread.

As soon as the Ninth and Tenth Legions came on the scene, they also gave a hand in building the camp, which was coming up rapidly and was almost complete. A short while later, the huge baggage train appeared and started moving into the camp. This was the signal which the whole Belgae Army had been waiting for.

Horns sounded from the forest. It was an eerie sound and was repeated from several directions. The trees in the forest started to tremble and shake as the huge Belgic host started moving. They burst forth from the forest like a flood of angry locusts.

The skirmishers on the far bank did not even have time to fire a volley. They turned and ran, and the Belgae sprinted after them, slaughtering the stragglers. The horde rushed towards the river like a tidal wave of berserk killers. Anyone they caught up with was brutally hacked down.

The Roman *cornicens* sounded the alert. Caesar looked across the river and immediately ordered the flag to be raised, calling the army to arms. Centurions everywhere yelled, "*Ad aciem*" (action stations). The Romans were totally caught with their guard down. This immediate attack was unexpected. It was atypical for the Belgae to mount a precipitous attack without the usual posturing.

All the legionaries dropped their tools, picked up *pila* and shields, and quickly got into line. Some soldiers didn't have time even to put on their helmets, and many of the shields still had their cloth covers on. There was no time to find one's exact cohort or century, and the men just formed under the closest standard which they saw. The soldiers, for once, were thankful that they worked with armour on and their swords slung over their bodies.

The Romans managed to form a rough defensive line just in front of their camp. The Seventh Legion was on the extreme fight followed by the Twelfth. The Eighth and Eleventh covered the middle and the Tenth and Ninth were on the left flank. Facing the Seventh and the Twelfth were the 50,000 Nervii under Bodougnatus. The Viromandui hit the centre with 25,000 men, and the 25,000 Atrebates on the Belgic right hit the Roman left, defended by the two veteran legions, the Tenth and the Ninth.

The surviving light troops managed to pass through the Roman lines before the two sides met with a thunderous crash of steel against steel. The Romans fought in deadly silence while the Belgians roared like fiends.

The battle on the left was a textbook battle. The Ninth and the Tenth were elite troops. The first was raised by Pompey, and the second was practically Caesar's Praetorian Guard. They formed up briskly and expertly and readied their *pila*. The Atrebates came to thirty yards and received the first volley of javelins. The second volley was launched at the survivors at fifteen yards. The effect was devastating. The spears either pierced men or lodged in shields. If the latter happened, the *pila* were designed so that they could not be extricated and they bent out of shape. The warrior had no choice but to drop the shield. Unprotected, he was totally vulnerable. When the *pila* hit flesh, it penetrated like a knife through butter.

Before the front line of the Atrebates could reach the Romans, the two legions charged while still maintaining formation, cutting down everyone in their path. Commius desperately tried to urge his men to hold them but was inexorably pushed back towards the river.

In the centre, the Viromandui got across the river so fast that the two defending legions had no time to throw *pila* but were fully formed when the enemy came into contact. Despite the ferocity of the assault, both legions were able to hold the line. Keeping the shield line intact, the Roman legionaries then stabbed through the gaps and decimated the assaulting warriors rank by rank as they threw themselves against the impenetrable shield wall. Casualties among the Romans were quickly evacuated backwards and fresh soldiers stepped up to maintain the line. The centre was holding.

On the Roman right, it was a different story. The Romans were clearly in trouble. Bodougnatus was leading from the front, wielding a huge double-bladed axe. The Nervii were the most numerous contingent and also the best fighters. The two Roman legions were tired from constructing the camp, a task which they had done the most and worked the longest. They were somewhat slow to assemble and could not even get a defensive line together when the Nervii struck.

The Twelfth Legion had the worst of it. Their partly formed line was immediately breached by the rampaging Nervii horde. Relatively inexperienced legionaries were being cut down by the score. Bodougnatus was in his element as he waded into the disorganised Romans, many of which did not even have helmets on. His formidable axe took off a head and then smashed another legionary's skull, spilling blood and brains. A centurion tried to rally the men and form a line, but Bodougnatus ran up to him and swung down from overhead. The centurion blocked with his shield, but the shield just crumpled with the blow. Now with the centurion defenceless, Bodougnatus chopped through his helmet, splitting his skull in half.

The tribunes and centurions of the Twelfth tried valiantly and repeatedly to form one line after another only to be have it once again disrupted. Many an officer perished, fighting desperately against the unstoppable Nervii. These were men like the Spartans who knew only one profession, warfare. Bodougnatus could smell victory as he pressed on, killing one Roman after another in a mad lust for blood. The Twelfth Legion was also now being flanked from its left as a gap opened up between itself and the Eighth. The Eighth was finally pushing the Viromandui back. The canny Nervii immediately exploited this gap and pushed against the left flank of the Twelfth turning in back.

This had an effect of opening the way to the Roman camp. A group of Nervii eager for loot immediately made for the camp, intent on pillage. To its credit, the Twelfth Legion did not route but gave way steadily as it was pushed to the right of the Roman camp and up a small hill.

On the extreme right wing, the Seventh Legion was also engaged in a life-and-death struggle. Crassus had managed to form the legion up into two lines, but the men had no time to throw their *pila* before becoming engaged. The line was holding but just barely as the Nervii pushed forward furiously.

Now and again, the determined Nervii would break through and cause a gap, but the veteran centurions would always reinforce the gap from the second line and close the gap. Time and again, the centurions would give their lives, plugging the gap.

Livy was on his horse and this gave him a good vantage point to do some firefighting where the breakthroughs were most critical. He had his bow with him and could shoot at any groups of Nervii who managed to smash through the line and help the centurions and the *optiones* plug the gaps. The units were all mixed up as men rallied behind the nearest standard they came across. Officers and men were fighting not with their usual comrades but with men from other units.

Livy got hold of a few archers who had fled into their ranks and some Numidians and used these as a reactionary force to help plug any gaps in the Roman line. Whenever a gap appeared, Livy's squad would immediately run there and pour missile fire into the Nervii who had broken through. The men from the second line would then quickly advance to seal the gap. This worked well a number of times and saved the gaps from widening and the whole front line from collapsing. Crassus too ran about on his horse accompanied by his bodyguard and tribunes, trying to seal gaps and encourage his legion.

On the right flank of the Seventh Legion, the Nervii were also trying to inundate the flank with superior numbers. The *primus pilus*, Priscus, a veteran of twenty years was with the first cohort which had double the usual strength of a normal cohort. The men of the first cohort were the most experienced soldiers of the Seventh, and they were just about holding the line. Priscus had spread out the men to contain the threat from the right. Suddenly he was set upon by three heavily armoured Nervii simultaneously. He knocked down the one to his left using his shield, but his right was unprotected and he was run through with a spear, the tip coming out through his back armour.

Gritting his teeth against the searing pain, he let go of his shield, grabbed the shaft of the spear, pulled the spear against himself so he could slide closer to his assailant, and stabbed the Nervii in the throat with his *gladius*. The third man was too stunned to move as he witnessed this act. Priscus, with the last ounce of his strength—the spear impaling his own body—moved swiftly to stab him in the chest. The two men collapsed together.

Caesar had seen the carnage to his right and rode with his general staff to support the two beleaguered legions. Caepio followed him reluctantly into the fray. Meanwhile, Caesar had sent messages to Sabinus and Cotta to bring up the Thirteenth and Fourteenth Legions as quickly as possible and also to the artillery prefect to bring up his ballistae and scorpions.

He came to the Twelfth Legion and dismounted. Grabbing a shield from one of the fleeing legionaries, he rallied the few retreating men and joined the fighting line which was now steadily retreating. His men were now so bunched up that they could hardly wield their swords. Caesar shouted at them to open up their ranks to create more space. He knew almost every centurion by name but there were not many left, so he called out instructions to those left alive to encourage them and restore order.

Caesar's red cloak and tall red plume were now distinctly visible and noticed by the men of the Twelfth, who realised that their commander was among them and morale received a tremendous boost. What was almost a rout stabilised, and Caesar organised a gradual retreat up the small hill to the right of the encampment. The legion gave ground but in good order. Caesar stood just behind the front line, but when a man went down, he immediately rushed into the gap, stabbing at the enemy. He even personally dispatched a number of the half-naked warriors. Legionaries would come up from behind and relieve him almost immediately, allowing him to step back once more.

As the Twelfth moved back, the left flank of the Seventh became exposed, so Caesar sent a messenger to ask Publius Crassus to pull back his legion in tandem so that they could maintain a line. At the top of the hill, he ordered the two legions to combine and form a large square.

The well-drilled Romans were able to do this despite the enemy pressure because of the incessant drilling during their training. The surviving skirmishers sought protection inside the square and were able to provide a hail of missile fire at the assaulting Nervii.

Bodougnatus was covered with the blood of the many men he had slain. He and his group of heavily armed retainers were almost irresistible as they broke through the Roman line again and again. He was surprised that the battered Romans could still maintain order and not rout. Then he saw Caesar and felt the resistance hardening as the soldiers rallied. The Romans had then retreated up a small hill and formed a square. Bodougnatus called his best men together and regrouped them for an assault to break through the square and kill Caesar. The Romans could no longer manoeuvre in this position. If he could just break through the flimsy square and kill their commander, he felt it would be all over for the Romans.

On the left, Labienus, commanding the Tenth and Ninth Legions, had chased the Atrebates across the river. Despite Commius's best efforts to rally his men, they were retreating headlong, pursued by the two elite legions who were slaughtering them like sheep. The Romans chased the Atrebates all the way back into the forest and right into the Belgic camp, where they started slaughtering everyone they could find. Labienus was not one to show mercy and let the troops have free reign. The non-combatants in the camp did not stand much of a chance and scattered in every direction. The soldiers then pillaged the defenceless camp, looting everything they could find.

In the centre, the Eighth and Eleventh Legions had pushed the Viromandui to the river and were slaughtering them as they were pushed back into the water. Soon, the Viromandui broke and retreated headlong, pursued by the two victorious legions. They too headed in the direction of the Belgian camp, hotly pursued by the Romans.

Meanwhile in the Roman camp, chaos reigned. A few thousand Nervii had broken into the camp and immediately started to massacre the non-combatants inside. Among the victims were slaves, porters, logistic personnel, and the camp followers. The barbarians ran amok burning, looting, and raping any women they came across.

The few auxiliary cavalry, who had taken shelter in the camp, immediately fled, thinking the battle was lost. They were mainly Bellovaci, Ambiani, and Suessiones.

Servilia's caravans attracted the attention of a Nervii warband because they were richly adorned, and a large group made for them to discover what they contained. When they saw her girls, they went mad with lust and immediately attacked the group of caravans.

Caesar had left a dozen German bodyguards to escort the girls, and these now formed a small circle to try and defend the screaming terrified girls. The Germans were fearsome fighters and cut down many a Nervii, but the numbers soon began to tell and one by one, they fell.

Servilia had gathered all her girls into one caravan, where they huddled in abject terror. She handed out daggers to everyone. They had a choice of fighting with them or turning the blades on themselves to avoid further horror. The girls seemed defenceless, and the Nervii moved in to enjoy the spoils.

Suddenly Leuce and Jasmine appeared, barring their way. Leuce was completely naked, devoid of warpaint. She wore a legionary helmet and carried two slim curved swords. The men had offered her chain mail, but she was more comfortable fighting this way.

Jasmines had on a light silk gown which came to mid-thigh, revealing bare legs. She wore calf-high boots and had a green silk scarf tying her hair into a ponytail. She carried a Han weapon called a *guang dao*. It was a pole with a broad curved sabre affixed to the end. One blade was convex and continuous; the other edge was concave and serrated. The two girls looked beautiful and formidable.

The Nervii paused in surprise and some admiration. "You are that Gaesatae bitch who betrayed us. I recognise you," one of the Nervii called out. He was a dark, handsome young man with a small moustache.

Leuce didn't bother to reply. She twirled both swords once in confidence.

"I'm going to fuck you till you die," the warrior taunted.

"Come and get me," Leuce replied, sticking her tongue out at him.

The young warrior came charging, his long sword raised over his head. Leuce parried his blow with both swords and kicked him hard in the groin. The man had a pained and shocked expression on his face, then slowly collapsed on to his knees and the fell sideways, groaning loudly.

"Let's kill the bitches," another Nervii yelled, and half a dozen men charged the two women. Jasmine moved with what seemed like lightning speed. She seemed to be in several places at once. Her *guang dao* whirled and struck like lightning. Suddenly three men were down with terrible wounds, and blood was spraying everywhere from cut arteries.

Leuce had managed to slice one assailant in the thigh and just narrowly parried the blow from another. The man was immense in size, and the blow numbed her hands. She somersaulted on the ground and avoided a second blow from the big man. As she recovered, she came up from under a third warrior, burying both blades in his abdomen. He collapsed.

She turned in time to see the large man about to cleave her in half. She was defenceless and prepared to die, when suddenly a shiny blade protruded from the man's abdomen. Jasmine had skewered him from the back with her fantastic weapon. Both women were covered in blood as they got up and positioned themselves back to back.

"Thank you for saving my life," Leuce said to Jasmine.

"Think nothing of it. You already paid me last night," Jasmine said, remembering the exquisite experience they shared the night before.

Leuce smiled and prepared to meet the assault of the now dozen men surrounding them. Half of them suddenly charged, but two of them suddenly sprouted arrows, one in the neck and the other in the back. Jasmine quickly dispatched two with her *guang dao*, and Leuce took out another, stabbing him in the side.

The remaining man retreated. Another of the Nervii was struck by an arrow to the thigh and screamed in pain. Everyone turned to see who had joined the fray. It appeared to be an Amazon riding a white horse. She had a cavalry helmet with red plume and chain armour. She carried a composite bow and was firing arrows in quick succession.

Jasmine recognised Artemisia and called out to her. Leuce had never met this apparition from Hades. The Nervii warriors hesitated, and the three women took the opportunity to attack. Caught between the Amazon on one side and the two Furies on the other, the men decided there were easier pickings elsewhere and fled in all directions.

Artemisia rode one of them down and cut him down with her *spatha*. She took out two more with arrows, sinking the shafts into their backs. Jasmine chased one down and beheaded him with a swipe of her *guang dao*. Leuce was just too tired to chase them. Her naked body was streaked with blood, and she looked like she had just returned from across the *Styx*.

Bodougnatus had regrouped his best warriors into a wedge formation with himself at the apex, and they now launched themselves at the thin Roman lines. The impetus of the charge was unstoppable. Bodougnatus smashed through two young legionaries of the Twelfth and chopped them to pieces in short order. His bodyguard swarmed around him and enlarged the breach. Romans were being butchered in every direction as the wedge drove in. Crassus immediately rode for the gap at full speed, followed by his tribunes and a few legionaries.

Bodougnatus saw the young commander coming. He could move fast despite his size, and he swung his axe at the horse's legs. The legs were amputated, and the animal crashed. Crassus flew off the animal, landing on his back, and Bodougnatus strode towards him to finish him off. The tribune accompanying him was dragged off his horse and hacked violently to death.

Bodougnatus stood over the supine Crassus, who was too stunned to react. He raised his immense axe to finish off the legate when he suddenly felt a sharp pain in his arm, which forced him to release the axe. About fifty yards away, Livy had shot an arrow into his upper arm and now charged towards him on Nero, *spatha* drawn.

Bodougnatus had barely time to raise the axe with his left hand and block the blow. Livy's *spatha*, however, had cut just under the blade and severed the axe-head from its pole. Two of his bodyguards immediately drew him back behind them. Before Livy could turn his horse for another run, the king had disappeared behind a mass of bodies.

With Crassus down, the gap could no longer be closed, and the Nervii rushed through into the square and headed up to the summit of the small rise where Caesar stood with his general staff and a few bodyguards. They immediately formed a circle to protect the commander. Livy dismounted to make sure that Crassus was safe. The legate was winded and stunned but was otherwise unhurt. "They are after Caesar," Livy said in alarm.

"Let's go join the party," Crassus said calmly. He looked down, and he saw his poor horse with two legs severed. He reminded himself to put it out of its misery later. Now they had more important things to do. Livy got on to his horse and rode towards Caesar's position. His small reactionary force of archers, slingers, and Numidians ran after him. Crassus and his small band of legionaries followed on foot.

There was a band of about fifty Nervii engaging Caesar's party. Caesar had a dozen bodyguards and maybe half a dozen tribunes on his staff. They were hard-pressed, and two of the tribunes were almost immediately killed. Livy started shooting while on the gallop. He took out a Nervii who was wielding a spear and had broken through the ring around Caesar. He was about to attack Caesar with his weapon.

Caesar and Caepio were side to side, shields raised, fending off four attackers. The situation was desperate. Livy fired another arrow, taking down one of the four. Caesar killed one of the Nervii and turned to help Caepio, who was almost overwhelmed. The Cretans and Balearic slingers then all got within range and started a deluge of missiles at the Nervii. Attacked on two fronts, the assault wavered.

The half-dozen Numidians then came up and threw their javelins at close range into the backs of the surviving Nervii. They broke and retreated. Caesar stabbed one of the remaining Nervii in the chest, and Caepio finally killed his first enemy, stabbing the last Nervii in the side. Caesar's party had been reduced to a mere half a dozen.

Crassus's men finished off the remaining Nervii within the square, and the gap was finally closed and the square re-established. Caesar sat down in exhaustion, and Livy came to him. "Are you well, My Lord?" Livy asked.

Caesar looked at him with a smile and took his hand. "Yes. I believe I am." Livy gave him a hand to get up.

The Nervii were pressing still against the square but were slowly losing energy. Over on the other side of the river, Labienus was finally informed by one of his men that the Roman camp had been invaded and that the right flank of the army was hard pressed. He immediately sounded the recall of the Tenth Legion and hurried them back towards the camp.

Meanwhile, in the Roman camp, much of the baggage had been destroyed and looted and fires were breaking out everywhere. Paulus arrived with his raiders and immediately started mopping up the scattered Nervii bands, who were too busy pillaging to put up an organised resistance. Behind them came the artillery train. The artillerymen immediately started deploying ballistae and scorpions to fire at the horde of Nervii still surrounding the Roman square.

As a final straw, the Thirteenth and the Fourteenth Legions appeared up the road, deploying into line rapidly and sweeping down towards the milling Nervii. The odds had incontrovertibly turned. There was nowhere to retreat. The artillery soon opened fire, cutting down the doomed warriors by the score. Ballista bolts flew into their ranks, skewering two or three men at a time. The carnage was terrible. The surviving archers and slingers joined in with their missiles. The corpses piled up in heaps.

Caesar shouted at them to surrender, but the Nervi refused. "Nervii never surrender," they screamed back at him. They preferred to fight to the death, taking down as many Romans as possible. The whole contingent of Nervii was gradually pushed down the slope towards the river, where the Tenth Legion now cut off any hope of escape.

As the dead piled up in their midst, the remaining Nervii soldiers stood on the mountain of corpses composed of their comrades to continue the fight. Soon they were totally surrounded by five legions with locked shields while the ballistae and scorpions continued to pour heavy fire into their midst.

Livy was reminded of the last stand of the Spartans at Thermopylae. The Nervii repeatedly launched themselves at the Romans to break out but were mercilessly cut down. If they stayed in place, then they were just target practice for the artillery and the archers.

Soon there was not a single Nervii warrior standing. They had died to a man. The battle was practically won except for the mopping up. Caesar ordered the remaining cavalry to pursue and kill or capture any of the fleeing enemy they could find. The non-combatants in the Belgic camp had already been rounded up and secured. Most of them would be sold as slaves, and the proceeds would belong to Caesar. The four legions who pillaged the camp had already stripped it of any valuables that could be found. These were spoils of war for the legionaries.

Bodougnatus had tripped and fallen at the river bank. The retainers around him were cut to pieces by scorpion bolts, and two of them had fallen over him as he lay on the ground. He decided to remain motionless and was soon covered by a few more corpses. There he remained undiscovered till dark. The Romans had been poking around looking for him, but fortunately his helmet was lost and his clothes were in tatters and they did not discover him lying in the mud covered by the bodies of his men.

When darkness came, he slipped out from under the corpses, shed his armour, and went for a swim. The current swept him downriver to safety.

Crassus and Livy surveyed the battlefield and were appalled at the terrible carnage. The whole area was littered with the dead and the dying from both sides. Blood ran on the ground like little rivers. The aftermath of battle was always a depressing sight.

> *Dulce et decorum est pro patria mori:*
> *mors et fugacem persequitur virum*
> *nec parcit inbellis iuventae*
> *poplitibus timidove tergo.*

> How sweet and fitting it is to die for one's country:
> Death pursues the man who flees,
> spares not the hamstrings or cowardly backs
> Of battle-shy youths.

Crassus vaguely remembered these lines, which some obscure poet had written in Rome recently. "Was it Horace?" he thought to himself. He couldn't quite remember. Looking at all the corpses and the moaning and screaming wounded, he could find nothing sweet or fitting about the scene that lay before him.

Livy's attention turned to Artemisia. Where was she? The Roman camp had been sacked. What had happened to Servilia's girls? He had not time to find out. Caesar rode down towards them with his small, surviving retinue. He noticed that Caepio had survived and, though looking somewhat flustered, was not injured.

Crassus and Livy gave the military salute as Caesar reigned up beside them. "I am sorry, but we can't rest yet. Livy, go find your raiders. I want you to go after the remaining Atrebates. The Nervii are finished, but large numbers of the others are on the run and we must pursue and hunt them down so they won't regroup."

"Yes, Lord Caesar." Livy saluted.

"Your men are already on the way. They will be waiting for you by the river."

Livy rode off.

"Crassus, get your men to rebuild the camp and set up the ditches and defences. We must be secure by the night."

Crassus saluted, and Caesar and his party rode off.

Livy found his 300 men at the river bank. Biorix and Paulus saluted. "Welcome, Commander. Glad to have you back with us," Paulus said. They both smiled, genuinely happy to see him.

Livy didn't recognise at first the raider beside them. He had long brown hair coming down below his helmet. A feminine voice greeted him. "Ave, Commander. I too am happy to see you well." She smiled sweetly. It was Artemisia.

Livy felt relief wash through him. He couldn't be happier. "Right, men." He became serious. "Let's catch us some Atrebates. Split into three columns, 100 men each. Biorix and Paulus take one column each. Keep no more than one mile apart. Artemisia, stay in my column. Let's go." The raiders crossed the river together, then fanned out.

Artemesia rode up beside him. She handled her horse expertly. "I see you have improved your riding skills," Livy commented.

"Wait till you see my skill with the bow," she said and winked at him.

The raiders pursued all afternoon. They came across a number of fleeing bands of Atrebate warriors. Most surrendered readily. A few resisted and were shot down. None of them had any missile weapons and thus had no answer to the raider's arrows. Those who surrendered were tied up and taken prisoners.

Towards dusk, they spotted a farmhouse. Livy and his men surrounded the place. There seemed to be no activity. At last, Livy took along two of his raiders and rode up to the front door.

"Come out now and surrender. We have you surrounded," Livy said loudly.

There was no response. "We will burn the house down if you don't come out," Livy threatened.

The door opened a crack, then wider. Finally, a figure stepped out into the half-light. He was in armour but wore no helmet. The armour was streaked with blood. Livy recognised King Commius. "Your Majesty, it is good to see you well," Livy said politely.

"The young centurion. We meet again. I wish it were under better circumstances," Commius returned the polite greeting.

"I believe it is time to end the war, Your Majesty. If you would be so good as to come with me, I am sure my Lord Caesar and yourself could agree on some equitable terms," Livy said politely, dismounting. Coming to within a few feet, he bowed low to the king.

"I don't see that I have much choice, young man. I guess that of all Romans, I would rather surrender to you than to anyone else." Commius bowed in return.

"I think you will find Caesar quite reasonable."

"I certainly hope so." Commius managed a smile.

"Is there anyone else in your party?" Livy asked.

"I have one of my wives with me and two retainers," Commius said.

"Please instruct your party to come up and get saddled so that we may be on our way," Livy said. "It is getting late and will be dark soon."

"Don't you want to seize our weapons?" Commius asked, surprised.

Livy thought about it. Actually he had forgotten entirely about taking his sword. "That won't be necessary. I think we are both men of our word," Livy reassured him. Commius was very impressed by the young man's civility.

Commius asked his party to come out of the house. The raiders brought his horses from the barn, and they all mounted up and headed back towards the Roman camp. Livy had the two heavily armed retainers disarmed. A rather comely lady, who was his wife, emerged. She was dressed in a richly embroidered dress and expensive cloak. Livy ordered the raiders to treat her with deference.

He sent messengers to the other two columns to rejoin them, and all returned to the camp together. Several batches of prisoners had already been dispatched back to camp, escorted by small parties of raiders.

When they arrived back in the Roman camp, it was already night. The smell of burning bodies permeated the air as the Romans built huge funeral pyres for their dead. The Belgic dead were just thrown into huge pits and buried unceremoniously.

Livy directed his party quickly away from the depressing scenario and headed for Caesar's headquarters. When they arrived, a long line of soldiers of various ranks were waiting to see the supreme commander. A tribune outside Caesar's tent was trying to make some order out of the chaos. Livy dismounted and spoke to the tribune. He disappeared into the tent and came out a moment later. "Caesar will see the king right away," the tribune said.

Livy escorted King Commius into the large tent. Caesar sat at his desk, flanked by several of his legates. He was in a white *subarmalis* and was bareheaded. He seemed physically fatigued but was full of nervous energy. "King Commius of the Atrebates, My Lord," Livy announced. "His Majesty surrenders and requests peace terms."

Commius bowed low.

Caesar got up from his chair. He walked over and took him by the hand. "Please come and take a seat, Your Majesty," Caesar began politely.

They sat and looked at each other for a while. Commius looked tired and beaten but still had an air of authority and dignity about him. Caesar had been cleaned up. He looked confident and genial. The servants served Commius a goblet of wine.

"I have come to surrender the Atrebates and ask for terms," Commius began. Livy translated.

"Do you accept Rome as your overlord?" Caesar asked.

"I accept," Commius said.

"Your nation will come under our protection. You will give up all your arms. I will require 500 hostages to guarantee your good behaviour. They should be your children and the children of your nobles. The hostages will be treated well and will be educated as Romans are educated," Caesar said.

"I agree," Commius said.

"There is more. You may retain your title as king, but your lands will be administered by a Roman prefect appointed by me. He will have the last say on matters of law and policy and you will consult him on all major issues. Your people may have their own council or senate to advise him, but his word is final as he is my representative." Caesar looked at him intently.

"I accept," Commius said in a resigned manner. "Will my people be enslaved?"

"Any captured before this will remain prisoners of war and will be sold as slaves. After this moment, any who are free will remain free," Caesar said.

This was a little painful to take, but Commius knew he had no bargaining power. "I agree," he said after a pause.

"Lastly, your people will pay reparations for taking up arms against Rome. My quartermaster will determine the amount after we assess your treasury. We will be taking half of your treasure."

Commius was prepared for this and half was generous, so he agreed once again.

"In return, you are now under the protection of Rome, and we will war against any that war against you. The Atrebates will, of course, be required to provide supplies for the Roman Army and some of your warriors will be required to join us as auxiliaries. I think some of your troops will make good skirmishers and scouts," Caesar added.

"Will that be all?" Commius asked.

"Yes. We now consider you a friend and ally of Rome." He rose and shook his hands. Commius took the proffered hand and looked straight into Caesar's eyes. He knew from the look that as long as he kept his word, Caesar would as well. "Please take His Majesty for some dinner and refreshments," he ordered the duty tribune.

Commius was led out of the tent. He bowed deeply to Caesar at the exit. Caesar nodded curtly in return. He had taken a liking to this strong silent leader. Maybe they could work together in the coming campaigns.

Outside the tent, Commius grasped Livy's arms. "Centurion, I want to thank you for your kindness. I have nothing left to give you except this." He unbuckled his belt and gave him the belt and the sword. The sword was beautifully crafted and inlaid with precious stones. The scabbard was silver, and the belt was of fine leather, trimmed with gold designs. Livy was stunned by the enormity of the gift. It was a king's sword and worth a king's ransom. He was reluctant to accept.

"Please take it," Commius insisted. "Otherwise, all arms will be confiscated anyway."

Livy saw the truth of the reasoning. "My deepest thanks, Your Majesty. I will always remember your kindness. Let me know if you ever need anything. I am pleased we are on the same side now," Livy said sincerely.

Commius was led away. He would be fed well and given a luxurious bath to help him forget his disastrous defeat.

"Caesar wants to talk to you more," the tribune said to him.

Livy re-entered the tent. He stood at attention before Caesar's desk.

"We won a great victory today. We have broken the back of the Belgic confederation, and it only remains to mop up the remnants. The Atuatuci Army heard of our victory and immediately turned around to go home. I think it won't be long before we see their envoys. The Viromandui have surrendered and so have the Nervii, though we have yet to find King Bodougnatus. It seems that of 600 nobles among the Nervii, only three are left alive."

"Congratulations, sir," Livy responded.

"The victory did come at a great price. The Twelfth Legion has almost lost all their officers and two thirds of the men are dead or wounded. Furthermore half of the centurions of the Seventh are either dead or wounded. I need to find new leaders very quickly to get these two legions back into action," Caesar said.

"Publius Crassus, your acting legate, has commended you highly once again. Your actions today helped to save your legion and the lives of your legate and myself. It seems that we are once more in your debt. I believe it is time to reward you to the extent which you really deserve," Caesar said. "Crassus, you may do the honours."

Crassus smiled broadly at him. "The centurion of the Second Cohort, First Century, our second spear, Centurion Trebonius, has been promoted to *primus pilus*. You, Gaius Livius Drusus, will take over as the second spear of the Seventh Legion," Crassus announced officiously with a slight grin.

Livy was stunned. To be promoted from junior centurion up so many steps to second spear was unheard of. In war, strange things happen. "Thank you, sir, Thank you, Lord Caesar," Livy gasped.

"There is more." Caesar stopped him.

"In addition, Centurion Gaius Livius Drusus is also reinstated as commander of the special operations cavalry unit commonly called 'The raiders' as permanent auxiliary prefect of cavalry," Crassus announced, this time grinning broadly. "You deserve it, my friend." He came forward and clasped Livy's arm.

Livy was lost for words. "No words can express my deep feelings about this matter," Livy stammered.

"We will celebrate with a drink tonight. You can join us after you take over your new command," Caesar said with a fatherly smile. "You have made me very proud, young Livius."

This from Caesar was worth more than any promotion or award, Livy felt.

"One last thing. I am assigning some replacements to your raiders. It seems all of them are veteran fighters. You will treat them like any other members of your team and will not discriminate against or for them because of their, ahem, differences," Caesar ordered.

Livy was surprised. "What sort of differences?" he thought to himself.

"Don't worry. Your men will get used to them, and they have already proven themselves. They protected Servilia's retinue and accounted for a fair number of Nervii assailants. I am sure you will get the full story when you see them," Caesar said.

"Of course, My Lord," Livy stammered.

"You are dismissed." Caesar waved him away. "Go get cleaned up and report back for dinner around the eighth hour."

Livy saluted, bowed deeply, and left the tent. His mind was moving in a daze. Things were happening too fast. He mounted Nero and headed back towards the Seventh Legion's lines. He heard some hoof beats behind and saw Crassus riding after him.

"Well, my good friend, congratulations."

"Thank you, Publius. I am sure you had a big part to play in all this," Livy replied.

"Of course I did. You owe me." Crassus grinned. "The promotion was high time. You were doing the job of an auxiliary prefect all this time anyway. What's more, you are still under command of the Seventh. So you are mine," Crassus smiled smugly.

They shook hands once more, grasping each other's forearm. "I will never forget your help and support, Legate Crassus," Livy said sincerely.

"Call me Publius. I'll still call you Livy." Crassus laughed.

When they reached the Seventh Legion's camp area, Livy had another surprise. Crassus had ordered the raiders and the Second Cohort to camp next to each other. Outside his tent there was a startling sight. Three cavalrymen in full armour, helmet, and leather trousers guarded his tent. They even had red horsehair plumes. One held an unusual pole arm with a curved sabre at the end. The tallest held a cavalry spear and was equipped with a *spatha*. The blonde one had two curved swords. All three saluted smartly.

"These are your new recruits." Biorix grinned. "Hope these newbies can cut it with the older boys," he sniggered.

"Hail, Prefect Livius." The three presented arms.

"Welcome to Livy's raiders." Livy returned the salute.

Three days later, the raiders moved out under the command of Prefect Gaius Livius Drusus. They had new replacements to make up their numbers back to 300. If one looked closely, a few of the new recruits' features were, well, not exactly masculine. No one seemed to notice.

Livy now had three women in his entourage, at least two of whom had feelings for him. Nothing in his learning or experience gave him any clue as to how to resolve that issue. The situation was delicate to say the least. Leuce was now a free woman. Caesar had kept his word to set her free and allowed her to join the Roman Army. The raiders were now the first Roman "equal opportunity" force.

The mission was well suited to the unit. They were to scout out the Atuatuci *Oppidum* (fort) at the confluence of the Sabis and the Mosa Rivers. It was well defended and fortified. The town lay on a hill with steep slopes on every side except a 200-yard approach which had a gentler slope. At the top of this gentler slope was a double wall and a ditch. It was going to be a tough nut to crack. The mission would be dangerous. The men were in high spirits. They were an elite force. They were Livy's raiders, and they were the best.

Liqian, Summer, 36 BC

It was late at night when I finished my book. I was satisfied that those momentous events were now recorded. One day, the people of this great empire would learn more about its sister empire at the other end of the world. In some ways, the two are so similar. In other ways, they are so different.

Rome was the greatest civilisation of the West. The Han Empire represented civilisation in the East. The two have so much to learn from each other, yet they know so little of one another. It is a great pity. What great things could result if the two empires came into contact? Then again, they may just not understand each other and fight constantly for domination like Rome and Parthia. It is my observation that when two great powers meet, they have a tendency to fight rather than coexist in peaceful harmony. We have only to look near by at the Han Empire's constant wars with the Xiongnu. I hear news that wars come as regular as the floods that inundate the Yellow River.

In a few days, General Chen Tang comes to discuss what to do about Zhizhi *Chanyu*, who is preparing to war against the Han once more. Will the killing never end? Will men never learn the futility of it all?

I walk on to my balcony to enjoy the night air and look at the starlit sky. The heavens are magnificent tonight, and the night sky reminds me of the campfires of a large army spread as far as the eye can see.

I must go back to Jinchang soon. There is too much work to do, and I have been negligent of my duties as prefect because of my obsession with my book. The governor of Gansu will not be pleased. In the summer, I will come back here and continue my story.

Meanwhile, I will get my secretary, Kwan Wei, to copy the book from silk to bamboo strips. Hopefully, that would preserve it for my descendants.

My youngest wife, Qingling, is upset with me of late. I spend so much time writing that I do not spend enough time entertaining her. I found out a long time ago that women need attention. I smile to myself.

I decide to go indoors. I order the servants to summon her. We shall have a late supper together and drink some wine. She will play the *gu zheng*. After that, I must do my duties as a husband and make love to her passionately. It is time for my jade staff to enter her lotus garden.

EPILOGUE

Early Winter 36 BC, the Tenth Month, Near Dunhuang, Gansu, China

The winds blew steadily, sending bolts of frost through my woollen cape, armour, and inner silk garments. The journey tested men's souls. My 800 men were well equipped for the frosty weather, yet each man suffered. There were icicles in my beard, and each time I spoke, puffs of mist blew from my mouth like smoke from a dragon.

As we approached Dunhuang, we saw cultivated fields once more. They were already harvested, yet the signs of civilisation were heart-warming. The men looked forward to proper shelter tonight and a hot meal. Dunhuang was a verdant oasis in the midst of sand and rock. It was the last outpost of Han civilisation in the West. It guarded the strategic Hexi Corridor, the gateway to Han China. Beyond lay the famed Silk Road.

In the distance, we could already see the town and the gaunt fortifications and the guard towers—lonely sentinels guarding civilisation against the barbarian hordes of the West. Just visible in the far north are the final segments of the Great Wall, an amazing edifice stretching thousands of li. It was started during the previous Qing Dynasty, but the Han emperors had continued the project. It protected the northern border of the empire.

As I peered out through the narrow orifice of my woollen hood, I saw movement in the hills around us. We were not alone.

Biao Li rode up. He looked impressive in his full-length grey lamellar armour over his cloudy blue uniform. He carried his trusty composite bow and red-tasselled spear. "We have company," he said.

"I've noticed." I flipped back my ermine hood to have a better view. Horsemen were approaching. "Defensive formation," I said quietly. Biao Li gave the signal, and the men responded instantly.

They immediately formed into an arrowhead formation, protecting the command element; two rows of cavalry screened each side of the road, and the front row dismounted, pointing their repeating crossbows outwards towards the approaching riders. Moli, my second in command, galloped to the centre to join us. "They are Xiongnu," she said.

"They fly the Han banner." I noticed. "I think they are on our side. Keep the guard up. We must be totally certain," I said. I had been informed before leaving in a letter from Chen Tang that *Chanyu* Huhanye, the leader of the Xiongnu faction on our side was sending a small contingent of 200 cavalry to make up our shortfall.

The visitors stopped about 300 yards away from us, and a small group of three horsemen continued forward. They had pristine snow-white uniforms, which gleamed in the golden sunlight of the late afternoon. The leader rode a white stallion and was wrapped in furs with a white fur hood. I noticed that the escorts were both women. One of them carried an emerald green banner decorated with a golden boar. They stopped twenty yards from our front line. The leader pulled back her hood revealing lustrous golden hair which cascaded down over her shoulder. My heart skipped a beat. Before I could recover, she gave me a smile as warm as the summer sun.

"Gaius Livius." Her voice tinkled like bells. "I was wondering if we would ever meet again?"

It was a voice from the past. The golden locks were unmistakable. The barbarian queen had returned to haunt me. I gave the order for the men to down arms and stand down. I trotted my black charger up to her. "Ave, Leuce," I replied in Latin because she had greeted me in that language. I took off my helmet with the blue plumes and cradled it under my arm. "How have you been? You look, well, amazing."

There was a loud snap, and I felt the sting of her whip on my face. My hand came up involuntarily and came away smeared with blood.

"That's for leaving me stranded among the Xiongnu and making no effort to rescue me all these years." She looked annoyed. Her clear azure eyes looked icy but exquisite, nevertheless. They reminded me of the colour of the sea around Tarraco. The years had been kind to her, and she looked in her late twenties though she must be in her late thirties.

I was stung, but she could not be blamed for her harsh views. "You have every right to be angry, but you don't know the whole story. Give me a chance to explain," I begged.

"I volunteered for this mission so that I could hear your explanation. It better be good," she said. "I also expect a very long and formal apology from you, after which I expect substantial recompense," she demanded.

I was relieved. Perhaps forgiveness from this remarkable creature may be possible after all. "Please give me a chance to explain." I grovelled. "You must see that my actions in this matter were curtailed by circumstances..."

"I must nothing!" She cut me short. "We will see." She turned her horse round. "The prefect of Dunhuang has quarters prepared for you and your men. You and your men are to follow my troop."

I trotted after her and waved at my men to follow. We talked as we rode.

"I see you are still with that Greek bitch of yours. Did you marry her?" she asked.

"No, she refused me," I answered.

"She is smarter than I thought," Leuce retorted. "You're nothing but a heartbreaker," she proclaimed.

"I never meant to break anyone's heart. I am always prepared to take the honourable course. Unfortunately, I am either turned down as in Artemisia's case or some tragic turn of events interfered with my plans as in yours." I tried to explain.

Leuce did not answer. She was still upset with me.

"So, may I ask, what is your relation with the present *Chanyu*?" I asked, trying to sound nonchalant.

"*Chanyu* Huhanye took a fancy to me when he beheld me at the court of Emperor Yuandi. For political reasons and totally against my will, I was given as a gift to the *Chanyu*. The intention was for me to become one of his many concubines so that good relations between the Xiongnu and the Han court would be maintained."

"So I gather you played your role well," I said.

"On the contrary. Even though I had no choice but to submit to him in the bedroom, I did not make it especially pleasurable for him, nor did he find me particularly arousing. I think he preferred petite, dark-haired, almond-eyed Han damsels," she said. "He liked them gentle and submissive."

"Not into big, blonde, busty, barbarian bitches, I guess." I couldn't resist digging at her.

"One more remark like that and I will sting your other cheek," she threatened.

"I put up my hands in a gesture of surrender. "No more rude remarks, I promise," I said with a cheeky smile. "Shall I embark on my explanation now?" I asked.

"No, I am not in the mood to listen right now. I'm tired, cold, and hungry, and if I don't like your explanation, I might just be tempted to kill you," she said. "Besides, we have arrived."

Just ahead I saw the green oasis where we were to spend the night. It looked supremely inviting after the long hard journey.

That night we had dinner in a large room at the prefect's residence. The room had several large bronze braziers burning, which provided a degree of comfort though they did not negate the chill completely. The food was simple desert fare of mutton stew and flour pancakes. We had dates for desert and fermented milk. Tingmei managed to procure some passable wine.

The prefect of Dunhuang was advanced in years and retired early, leaving us to our own devices. The atmosphere in the room was strained. Leuce and Tingmei eyed each other warily while Moli and Biao Li tried to make light conversation. They recalled the times in Belgica when they were Jasmine, the slave of Caesar, and Biorix, a *signifer* of the Seventh Legion. I remembered those scenes nostalgically through the mist of time.

Leuce came to sit beside me and began to ply me with more wine. She was dressed in a very thin and transparent white silk garment. The folds of her gown were loose, and she flaunted the ample mounds of her breasts blatantly. Occasionally, she even allowed a glimpse of a plump, pink nipple. She caressed my cheek where she had hit me before. I could see murder in Tingmei's eyes.

Tingmei sat at the table to my left. She wore a black silk gown embroidered with phoenix emblems. Her hair was styled into a topknot held with a silk ribbon and a jade hairpin. She looked regal and upset.

"So tell me, Gaius Livius, where were you when I needed you?" She deliberately ignored my Han name and title.

"The night you were sent away with *Chanyu* Huhanye, I was forcibly locked in my quarters on orders of the emperor. The next day, I was sent under escort to the south of the empire to quell an uprising in Yunnan. It was two years before I could return to the capital."

"You didn't try to find me after you came back north?" She was still upset.

"Yes, I did," I protested. I sent out half a dozen teams of spies to locate you and even went on a year's journey, scouring the northern grasslands for you."

She seemed to be struggling within herself, wondering whether to believe my story.

"I came back to the capital a broken-hearted man," I added. "The emperor sent me away again. I had to keep busy fighting one campaign after another just to keep sane,"

The ice in her eyes seemed to soften. "I guess I was also on the move constantly."

The relief I felt was almost audible. "You had disappeared without a trace," I added.

"The *chanyu* freed me from my concubine status after a year. I had demonstrated to him my martial skills, and he allowed me to become a weapons instructor in the Xiongnu Army. I followed him on a few campaigns and helped him win some battles. Later, he allowed me to form my own troop of female cavalry. You Romans would call them Amazons."

"It's not a derogatory term, my dear. Amazons are held in high regard in Greco-Roman culture. On the other hand, I am officially Han, Chinese now," I proclaimed.

"You almost pass as a Chinese with that beard of yours," she said. "That is until they notice your eyes."

I glanced over at Tingmei. She was fidgeting and fondling an iron medallion which looked familiar. It was the medallion of her ancestor who died at Thermopylae. I remembered returning it to her one day in Chang An. It was a day I thought we had seen the last of war.

"So did you never marry?" I asked Leuce.

"I was briefly married to one of the Xiongnu *donghu* or army commanders. He was a severe man, not very affectionate. I tried hard to be a good wife, but the culture was too different. They expect their women to be really subservient. He was killed in battle two years later, and I never remarried. I am happily single."

"Unfortunately, I am no longer in a position to exploit your availability," I lamented.

"Yes, too bad. Jasmine told me you have a new wife, a present from the imperial court, no less," she said.

"She is a little too young, but I cannot fault her in anyway," I said.

"You Han officials can have any number of wives," she said.

"The legal position is one thing, keeping them happy is another." I laughed. "I was married to Han women twice before the present wife, and both times proved to be more sorrow than joy. I have sent both women back to their families," I said.

"How sad," she said, not looking at all sad. "I can guess the reason," she added, sipping from her wine bowl. "You were never faithful. I bet you cheated with your Greek whore over there," she said.

"You are wrong, Leuce," I said. "I never met up with Artemisia all those years. She moved to Ganzhou only recently, and we came into contact," I said, feeling a little guilty. I had not lied when I claimed that Tingmei was not the cause of the failure of my first two marriages, but I preferred not to mention that I was currently sleeping with her once more.

"I hear you seem to have a happy marriage this time," she said.

"Jasmine must have told you. Yes, we seem to be getting along well." My tone did not invite further questions about my private life.

"Well, that's that then. We should retire. Tomorrow we should rise early and prepare to meet General Chen Tang and the rest of the Han Army. The servants will show each of you to your rooms."

We drank a final toast to the success of the expedition and got up to retire. I saw Leuce and Artemisia look at each other meaningfully. They seemed to exchange a silent message. I didn't know what thoughts flowed between them. I have long since given up trying to understand what transpired in the minds of women. There was no hostility. By that look, they seemed to have reached an understanding.

We were quartered in a large stone tower. The room was austere but comfortable. There was a small slit window out of which one could fire arrows. The bed was a four-poster with a firm mattress and a wooden pillow. There were soft cushions decorated with tribal patterns. I washed myself in the bowl of water left for my toilet and lay down to sleep. A single oil lamp gave a gloomy illumination and cast long shadows.

I could not sleep. I needed the comfort of a warm body, the feel of soft female flesh. I thought first of my wife Qingling. I could picture her unblemished face and dark eyes. I missed her. My thoughts then strayed guiltily to Leuce. I remembered her naked body in a barn deep in Atrebate territory as we fled from Nervii pursuers. I felt once more the danger, the unbridled lust, and the excitement. I have never felt such an intense combination of sensations again.

I fondled the gold ring on my right fourth finger. It was the only object left from my old life. For the thousandth time I examined the remarkable figure of Venus and the words JULIUS and CAESAR carved on it. This ring and I had seen so many adventures together. Indeed, Caesar's favour had exerted its magic long after Caesar had left this world to take his place in Olympus. His legacy had found its way to the ends of the earth.

I toyed with the idea of visiting one of the girls. Should I visit Artemisia? She would be happy to see me. I had spent most of the evening talking to Leuce, and that had made her uncomfortable. Tingmei was always someone I enjoyed sleeping with.

On the other hand, I hadn't been intimate with Leuce for a long time, and she still excited me as she did when I was a young centurion in Caesar's Army. Would she still welcome me in her bed? To seduce her again was a tempting challenge. I hadn't needed to exercise those skills for many years. Could I still do it?

Qingling's sweet smile intruded into my thoughts. I felt a very small pang of guilt. For once, I was actually happily married. Why was I incapable of ever being faithful? Do I have a character flaw? I don't think so. Perhaps it's just that I keep running into such amazing women. Perhaps I just fall in love too easily.

I loved every one of them, Leuce, Artemisia, and Qingling. How can any mortal choose between three goddesses? I felt the predicament of Paris having to choose between Hera, Athena, and Aphrodite.

There is a knock on my door. It's very soft, almost imperceptible. My heart palpitates as I get up to walk to the door. I can smell a woman's perfume. My hand trembles as I reach for the latch . . . I won't be sleeping alone after all.

To be continued

CAST

Principal Cast

Gaius Livius Drusus, Livy, Li Bi: Roman centurion, prefect, and senior general of the Han Army
Artemisia, Ai Tingmei: Spartan slave, whore, ex-gladiatrix, brothel madam, and kung fu master
Aulus Paulus: Raider decurion, Livy's second in command, and Xiongnu commander of infantry
Aurora: Slave of the family Livius and governess to the young Livy
Brigita: Remi girl from Bibrax
Biorix Biao Li: Remi warrior, raider signifier, and later Han Cavalry trainer and commander
Bodougnatus: King of the Nervii
Chanyu Zhizhi: King and warlord of the Western Xiongnu
Gaius Julius Caesar: Proconsul of Rome, later dictator and demigod
Galba: King of the Suessiones and commander of the army of the Belgic confederation
Iccius: Prefect of Bibrax
Jasmine, Moli Hwa: Han slave to Julius Caesar, brothel madam, and kung fu grand master
Leuce: Gaesatae commander, Commander of Cavalry in the Eastern Xiongnu Army
Lucius Decius: Veteran decurion and commander of Roman cavalry
Lugurix: Suessione nobleman
Marcus Antonius: Roman tribune and ally of Caesar. Subsequently tribune of the plebs and triumvir
Marcus Livius Drusus: Olive farmer in Tarraco, father of Gaius Livius
Murato: Gaesatae commander and later general in the Xiongnu Army
Publius Crassus: Son of Marcus Licinius Crassus, triumvir and richest man in Rome, legate of the Seventh Legion
Quintus Servilius Caepio: Brother of Servilia and Roman tribune

Servilia Caepionis: Mistress to Caesar and mother of Marcus Brutus, who assassinated Caesar
Titus Atius Labienus: Legate and Roman cavalry commander

Supporting Cast

Ambiorix: King of the Eburones
Arana: Female Gaesatae commander
Aristarchus: Greek teacher employed by the prefect of Tarraco
Avila: German teenager, slave of Publius Crassus
Baidu: Chief retainer to *Chanyu* Zhizhi
Bratranos: Suessione Druid, high priest to King Galba.
Chen Tang: Second in command of the Han Western Commanderie and leader of the Han expedition against the Xiongnu
Cleander: Handsome young raider from Crete
Commius: King of the Atrebates
Crixus: Gladiator bodyguard working for Julius Caesar
Dagu: Senior Xiongnu general
Drogo: Eburone cavalry commander, retainer to King Ambiorix
Eala: Remi girl, girlfriend of Biorix
Gan Yanshaou: Han governor of the Western Regions
Galienus: *Optio* and acting centurion of the Seventh Legion, Eighth Cohort, Sixth Century
Gallus: Centurion of the Tenth Legion. Awarded the *Corona Muralis*
Gunda: German teenager, slave of Publius Crassus
Kleon: Prefect of Cretan auxiliary archers in the Roman Army
Licinius: Roman decurion and commander of Scouts
Lila: Suessione girl, Resident of Noviodunum
Lucius Aurunculieus Cotta: Legate in Caesar's Army
Lucius Cornelius: Veteran Roman decurion, predecessor to Lucius Decius
Modu: Senior Xiongnu general
Mr. Ma: Chinese builder in Liqian
Quintus Pedius: Roman staff officer on Caesar's staff.
Quintus Titurius Sabinus: Roman legate in Caesar's Army
Runo: German cavalry commander of German auxiliary cavalry
Sabia: Remi girl, girlfriend of Paulus
Stena: Celt-Iberian mother of Livy
Stena: Celt-Iberian prostitute, a hetaerae in Servilia's entourage
Suren: Parthian princess and sister of The Surena
Terentia: Sister of Prefect Iccius of Bibrax

Telemachus: Veteran raider and best swordsman, Originally from Argos in Greece
Timorix: Roman scout of Remi origin
Vasco: Livy's grandfather, Celt-Iberian chieftain. Father of Stena
Vesna: Slavic prostitute working for Ting Mei and Moli Hua
Vindiacos: Retainer to Galba, king of the Suessiones
Xeno: Forester and expert archer, archery instructor to Livy

Note: Historical characters are in italic font

Glossary of Roman, Gaulish, Chinese, Greek, and Xiongnu terminology

Actuarius: Civil and military clerks. Those who do paperwork and administration.
Agoge: Military training school for Spartan males.
Amphora (pl. amphorae): A large clay vessel for wine or olive oil. It usually had a narrow neck.
Aquilifer: The bearer of the legions' Eagle. A very prestigious appointment.
Auger: A priest who could read the future by examining entrails of sacrificed animals.

Ballista: Giant crossbow which can fire a deadly iron tipped bolt powerful enough to skewer several men.
Belgica: Area occupied by Belgic Tribes in North-west Gaul. Now Belgium and The Netherlands.
Bucellatum: Hard tack. Dry biscuits issued to soldiers as combat rations.

Caligae: Roman military boot with hobnailed sole.
Casa: House or home. Casa Livius means home of the Livius family.
Cena: Dinner.
Centurion: Officer in the legion. There are sixty in each legion. Equivalent modern rank is from lieutenant to colonel.
Century: Roman military unit with eighty infantrymen. Equivalent to the modern company. Commanded by a centurion.
Chanyu: Xiongnu king of kings and son of heaven. Ultimate ruler. In 36 BC, there were two.
Cis Alpine Gaul: Roman province in northern Italy.
Clunia: Town in north-west Spain.
Cohort: Roman military unit of six centuries. Ten cohorts make a legion.
Conditum: Spicy wine flavoured with honey.

Consul: Highest political office in Rome. Similar to prime minister. There are two at any time, and they hold office for only one year.

Cornu: G-shaped horn used for signalling.

Corona Civica: State award for saving the life of a fellow citizen at great personal risk. It comes with honorary membership of the Senate of Rome.

Corona Muralis: Roman military award for the first soldier over the walls when assaulting a city.

Curile Aedile: Roman political office below consul and praetor. He is in charge of public works, grain supply, and games.

Cornicen: Trumpeter or horn player. Used to give signals to Roman forces.

Cursus Honorum: The road to political office in Rome.

Da Qin Quo: Chinese name for the Roman Empire.

Decurion: Cavalry commander of at least thirty men.

Dimachaeria: Gladiator or gladiatrix who fights unarmored with two swords.

Dominus/Domina: Lord/lady or sir/madame in Latin. Terms used to address a superior.

Donghu: Xiongnu army commander.

Druid: Gaulish or Belgic priest.

Editor: The chairman at a gladiatorial game. He makes the life-and-death decisions.

Equites: Roman knight or cavalryman. In earlier times, the cavalry consisted of rich Romans who could afford a horse. It was much more democratic by Caesar's time.

Equites Sagitarii: Mounted archers. The raiders were in this category.

Exploratores: Roman military scouts. Usually they were mounted.

Falernian: A wine from a region around Rome.

Fossa (pl. Fossae): Defensive pits dug around a Roman fortification.

Furca: T-shaped pole carried by legionaries on the march. Their belongings were attached to this device.

Gaesatae: Naked Belgic and Gaulish mercenaries. They have no tribe and hire their services for money. They fight stark naked as a matter of honor and courage.

Galla Narbonensis: Another name for Transalpine Gaul. Now Provence in France.

Garum: Sauce made from fish entrails used to give flavor to almost everything. Think of it as ancient ketchup.
Gaul: Home of the Celts, now modern France.
Gladius: Roman short sword of Hispanic origin. It is made of Spanish steel and is 30 inches long. It is sharp along both edges and has a sharp point.

Hetaerae: Greek style courtesan. A high-class prostitute with skills beyond the physical. They are usually well educated. They can play musical instruments, discuss politics, recite poetry, etc. They are much like a Mediterranean version of the geisha.
Hispania: Roman-Spanish Province.
Homoioi: An equal. A pure, born-and-bred Spartan male with full citizen rights and responsibilities.

Kung Fu: Chinese martial arts.

Lanista: Owner of a gladiatorial school or *ludus*
Legion: Roman military unit capable of independent operations. It has 4,800 infantry divided into ten cohorts. The legion has in addition cavalry, auxiliary allied troops, and artillery.
Legate: Commander of a legion. Equivalent modern rank is brigadier general.
Lilia (Lilies): Sharpened stakes lining the bottom of defensive pits.
Ludus: A training school for gladiators.
Lupanaria: Brothel

Onager: Roman artillery, stone-throwing catapult.
Oppidum: Gaulish Hill Fort, a walled settlement.
Optimates: Conservative senators opposed to Caesar's Popular Party
Optio: Second in command of a century of eighty men, equivalent to a platoon sergeant in modern terminology.

Patrician: Roman of the aristocratic class with noble lineage extending many generations.
Phalarae: Set of metal medals attached to a leather harness. Military decoration.
Pilum (Pila): Roman javelin. It had a wooden stock and a long metal point designed to deform on impact. There were light and heavy versions. It is about six feet long.

Plebian: Roman citizen with no aristocratic lineage.

Praetor: Roman magistrate and political office holder, second in rank to consul.

Praetorian Guard: The Roman Emperor's bodyguard. In Caesar's time, it had not been formally organised as yet. Later in imperial times, it would grow to comprise an entire legion.

Prefect: Commander of an auxiliary military unit or mayor of a town.

Prefectus Castrorum: Camp commandant of a legion. He is third in rank next to legate and *primus pilus*.

Primus pilus: First spear. The senior centurion of the legion. He is commander of the First Cohort, First Century. He is second in command to the legate.

Proconsul: An ex-consul with consular powers in a province. He is also usually a governor.

Pteruges: Leather straps hanging over the shoulders and the waist. It is attached to the *Subarmalis*, the leather garment worn under armour.

Scutum: Roman legionary shield. It was elliptical but truncated at top and bottom.

Scorpion: Light artillery. Portable mounted crossbow. There are rapid-firing and multiple-bolt-firing varieties.

Signifer: Standard bearer of cohort or century. They wore animal skins to distinguish them from standard legionaries.

Spatha: Roman straight-bladed cavalry sword. It was longer than the *gladius*. It ranged from 2.5 to 3 feet in length.

Subarmalis: The leather garment worn under the chain mail or metal cuirass.

Tarraco: Roman town in north-east Spain. Modern Tarragona. Livy was born here.

Testudo: Lit. Tortoise. A roman formation where a century forms into a rectangle with shields protecting all sides and overhead.

Thermopylae: The Fiery Gates, where 300 Spartans made their famous stand against the Persian Army of King Xerxes.

Transalpine Gaul: Roman province in southern Gaul. Now known as Provence in France.

Tribune: Staff officer in the Roman Army. In rank they were above a centurion and below a legate. The senior tribune was often a career soldier, but junior ones were senator incumbents doing their compulsory stint in the legions.

Tribune of the Plebs: Political office in Rome. They represented the majority plebian interest and had veto power in the Senate.

Tribunal: A raised platform where the general would give speeches, distribute awards, or accept surrender.

Valetudinarium : Field hospital

Wu Shu: Chinese martial arts. It includes unarmed combat and skill at arms.

Xiongnu: An empire to the north and west of Han China. They consisted of nomadic tribes and their armies comprised mainly of cavalry. In 36 BC, the empire had split into the Eastern Xiongnu under Huhanye, who was pro-Chinese, and the Western Xiongnu under Zhizhi, who wanted an independent empire.

HISTORICAL NOTE

Eagle in the Land of Dragons is a work of fiction. It is, however, set in the midst of real historical events. Many of the Roman, Belgic, Chinese, and Xiongnu characters are real people. In the Cast of characters in the end of this book, I have highlighted the historical characters in italic print.

Caesar's campaign in Belgium is fairly accurately portrayed. The three main battles at Bibrax, the Axona River, and the climactic action against the Nervii at the Sabis River did really take place. Noviodunum surrendered after a brief siege. I took liberties with the details as to how this came about because the historical accounts are rather sketchy about this event.

There is historical evidence for the roles of Crassus, Labienus, Cotta, Sabinus, and Quintus Pedius in this campaign. I added Marc Antony for good measure. He was not mentioned in Caesar's commentaries but could have been there. The same can be said for Servilia. She was definitely Caesar's mistress. I brought her along for added colour.

In 36 BC, there was a conflict between the Han Chinese and the Western Xiongnu led by *Chanyu* Zhizhi. Gan Yanshaou and Chen Tang were real participants in that war. Chinese history does mention a contingent of infantry who fought in a fish-scale formation. Some historians believe these to be Roman infantry. It is postulated that they were the remnants of the lost 10,000 captured by the Parthians at the Battle of Carrhae. In this battle, Marcus Licinius Crassus with seven Roman legions was defeated by The Surena, who commanded 10,000 Parthian Cavalry.

The Han Army stormed the fortress of Zhizhi at the end of 36 BC. The "Romans" who were fighting on his side, surrendered to the Han Army and were subsequently settled in the town of Liqian. The ancient city of Liqian lies in the modern village of Zhelaizhai in Gansu province in the Hexi corridor.

The modern inhabitants claim descent from the Romans. They have unusual racial characteristics. Some are fairer than the typical Han Chinese, others have blond or light-coloured hair, and still others have blue or green eyes. A recent DNA study shows that 56 per cent of the DNA of samples of individuals from the village were of Caucasian origin.

In the end, scientific and archaeological evidence offered no conclusive proof of the claim but could not disprove it either. The theory remains an enigma.

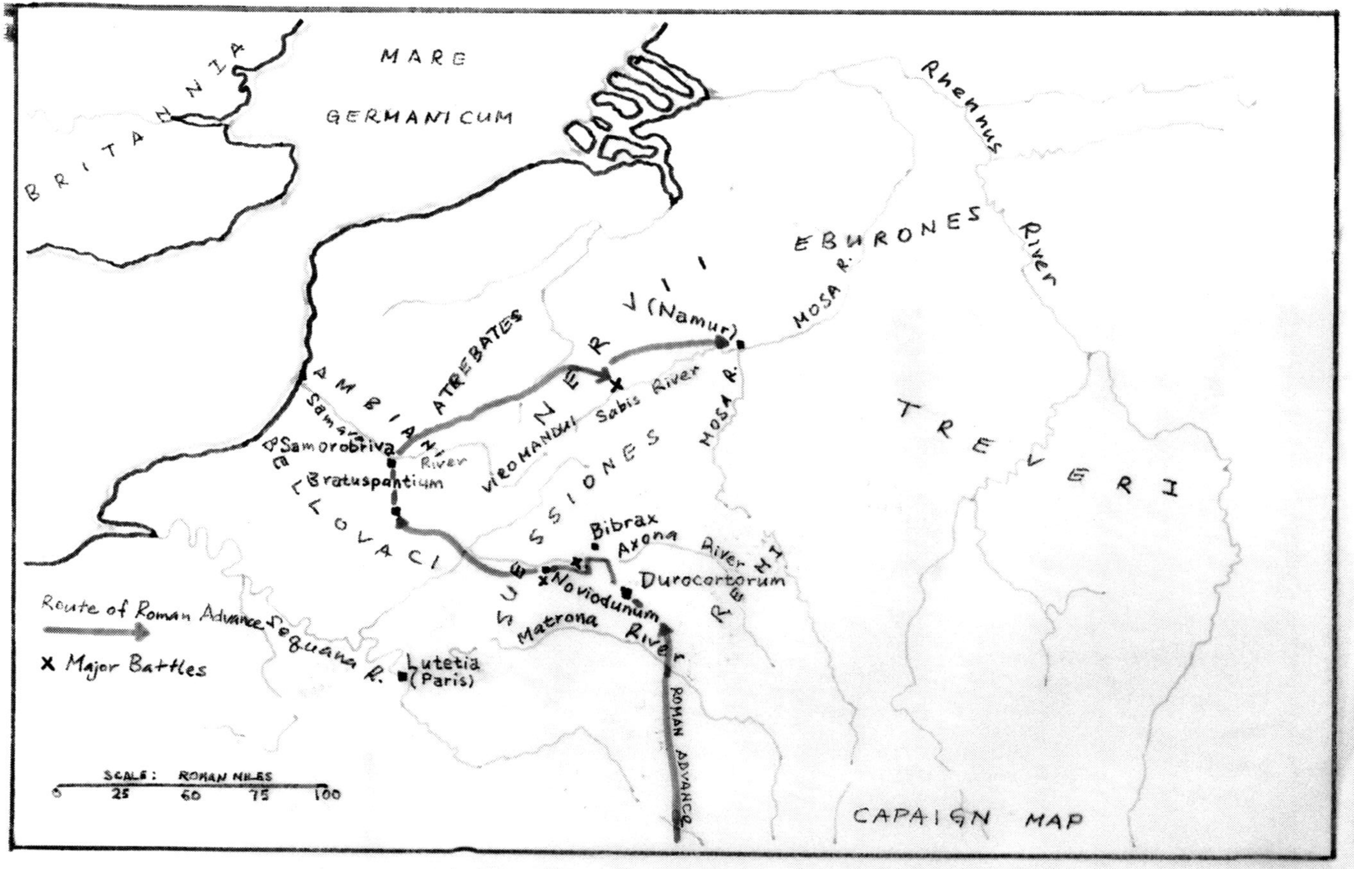
MARE
GERMANICUM
BRITANNIA
Rhennus
River
EBURONES
MOSA R.
NERVII
(Namur)
ATREBATES
AMBIANI
Samara
Samorobriva
River
Bratuspantium
BELLOVACI
VIROMANDUI
Sabis River
SUESSIONES
MOSA R.
TREVERI
Bibrax
Axona
River
REMI
Durocortorum
Noviodunum
Matrona
River
ROMAN ADVANCE
Route of Roman Advance
Sequana R.
Lutetia
(Paris)
X Major Battles
SCALE: ROMAN MILES
0
25
60
75
100
CAPAIGN MAP

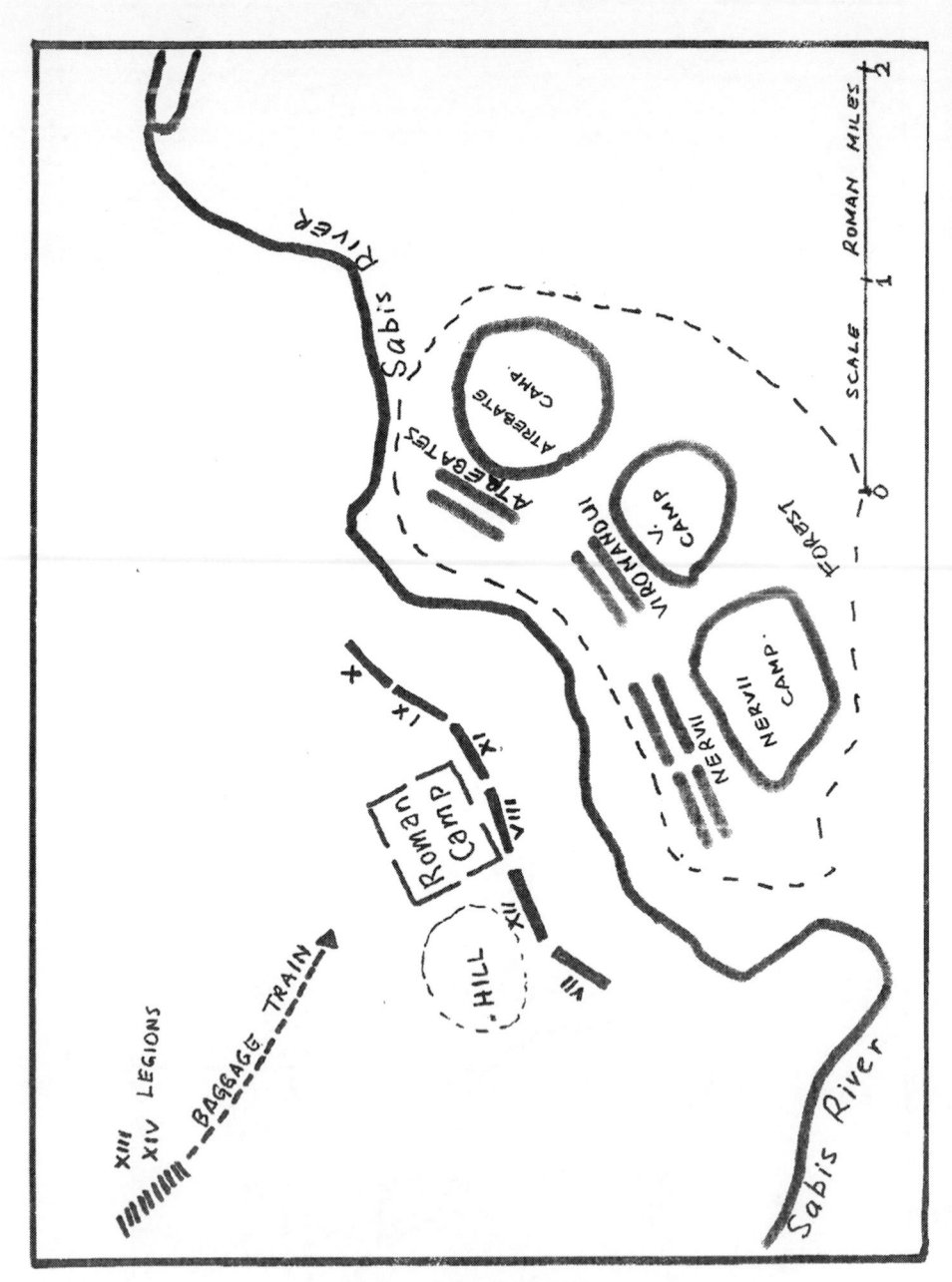

Battle of the Sabis River

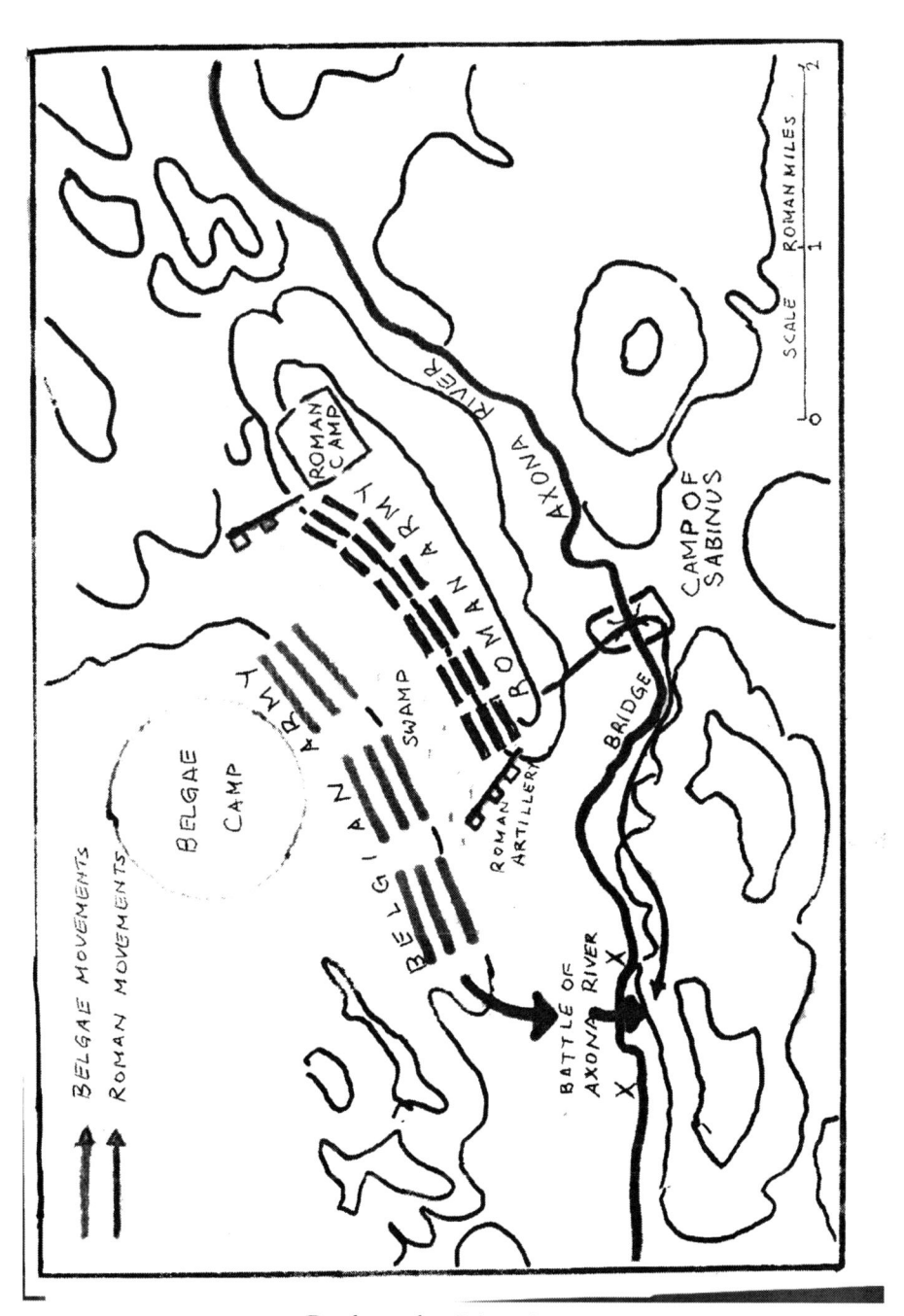

Battle at the River Axona

INDEX

A

actuarius 207
agoge 218
Ai Tingmei 238
Ambiorix (king of the Eburones) 234-6, 247-8, 261-4, 285, 319-20, 323, 327-8
Amphora 365
aquilifer 323
Arana (Gaesatae commander) 259, 301
Ariovistus 27, 30, 118, 137
Aristarchus (philosopher) 16, 18-19, 21, 23, 25
Artemesia (Spartan slave) 137, 146-9, 217-24, 245-7, 249-51, 317-18, 343, 346-7
Auger 365
Aulus Paulus 45
Aurora (slave) 19-23, 25-6
Avila (slave of Publius Crassus) 117, 119, 128-9

B

Baidu (chief retainer) 46-7
ballista 192, 345
Belgae 53
Belgica 45
Bibrax 11, 28, 30, 252
Biorix (signifer) 51-6, 94, 164-5, 178-80, 198-9, 288-9, 292

Bodougnatus (king of the Nervii) 99, 234-6, 285-6, 326-7, 332-3, 337-41
Bratranos (Suessione druid) 191, 235-6, 270, 273-6, 278-9, 328
Brigita (Remi girl) 39-42, 67-9, 81, 110-15, 129-31, 250-1
bucellatum 197

C

caldarium 15, 22
caligae 131
calligraphy 8, 242
casa 14, 20
cena 18-20, 131
centurion 69, 170
century 75, 153, 194, 297, 350, 365
Chen Tang 45, 62-3, 71-3, 240, 353, 356, 359
Cis Alpine Gaul 29, 137, 365
Cleander (Cretan raider) 228-9, 303
Clunia 138
cohort 22
Commius (king of Atrebates) 99, 273-7, 347-50
composite bow 17, 28
conditum 137
consul 25, 29, 46, 366
Cornicen 366
cornicens 170, 323, 366
cornu 170
Corona Civica 127, 153
Corona Muralis 193, 252

Crixus (gladiator) 284, 291
curile aedile 135
cursus honorum 135

D

Da Qin Guo *see* Roman Empire
Da Qin Quo 366
Dagu (Xiongnu general) 44-5, 168-9, 171
decurion 158
dimachaeria 142
domina 248-9
dominus 313, 315, 324
Donghu 366
Drogo (Eburone cavalry commander) 262
druid 167, 191, 270, 273-7, 328

E

Eala (Remi girl) 198-9, 226, 253
editor 142
equites 214, 366
equites sagitarii 28, 76
exploratores 79-80, 313

F

falernian 134, 139, 196
Fossa 366
frigidarium 15
furca 323

G

Gaesatae 52
Gaius Julius Caesar 25, 27, 29, 80, 95, 99, 105, 107, 140, 192, 295

Gaius Livius Drusus 7-8, 15-16, 31-9, 54-8, 70-3, 120, 122, 127, 131, 133, 153, 195, 198-9, 239, 250-1
Galba (Belgic commander-in-chief) 85, 89, 96, 99-100, 117-19, 203-6, 208-13
Galienus (optio) 85, 88, 93, 155, 194-5, 201, 317
Galla Narbonensis 130
Gallo Belgica 28
Gallus (centurion) 252
Gan Yanshaou 62, 71, 272
garum 254, 258
Gaul 314
gladius 22, 24, 165, 170, 259, 340, 367
Gnaeus Pompeius Magnus 27
Gunda (slave of Publius Crassus) 117, 119, 128

H

hetaerae 144, 300
Hispania 17, 24, 257, 367
homoioi 141, 367
Huhanye (brother of Chanyu Zhizhi) 45, 356-8

I

Iccius (prefect of Bibrax) 11-14, 39-41, 113-14, 250-1

J

Jasmine (Han slave) 131-3, 150-1, 342-3
Jiang Ziya 8
Jupiter Optimus Maximus 9, 16, 329

K

Kleon (prefect of Cretan auxiliary archers) 77-8, 84, 86-7, 89-92, 94-6

L

lanista 142-4
legions 323
Leuce (Gaesatae commander) 11, 124-5, 158-61, 275-81, 299-302, 304-12, 314-15, 342-3, 360-1
Li Bi *see* Gaius Livius Drusus
Li Shu 8
Lila (Suessione girl) 227-9, 364
lilia 74, 367
Liqian 7
Livia (mother of Gaius Livius Drusus) 16, 23-5, 42
Lucius Aurunculieus Cotta 29
Lucius Cornelius 9, 364
Lucius Decius 364
ludus 141, 220, 298-9
Lugurix (Suessione nobleman) 179, 255-7, 261-3, 266-7, 289-91, 294-7
Luoma *see* Roman Empire
Lupanaria 367

M

Marc Antony 156-7, 161-5, 173-5, 180-4, 186-7, 189-90, 192, 210-11
Marcus Antonius 210
Marcus Licinius Crassus 28, 46
Marcus Livius Drusus 14
Mithradates 14
Modu (Xiongnu general) 168-9, 364
Mr. Ma 364

Murato (Gaesatae commander) 45-6, 64-6, 97-100, 158-60, 167-71, 293-5, 298-301

O

Onager 367
oppidum 352, 367
Optimates 135, 367
optio 195, 317
Orodes (Parthian king) 46

P

Patrician 367
phalarae 367
pilum 16, 22, 338
Plebian 368
Pompey 16, 24, 337
praetor 135, 368
Praetorian Guard 338
prefectus castrorum 302
primus pilus 134, 323, 339, 350
pteruges 75
Publius Crassus 28-9
Publius Licinius Crassus 28

Q

Qingling 48, 59-62, 241, 353, 360-1
Quintus Pedius 91, 104
Quintus Servilius Caepio 254, 270, 305
Quintus Ti015 Sabinus 29

R

raiders 27
Roman Empire 8, 45, 329, 366
Rome 8

379

Runo (German cavalry commander) 257, 288, 291-2, 295-7

S

Sabia (Remi girl) 198-9, 226, 253, 364
scutum 170
Seres 18-19
Sertorius (rebel) 14, 16, 134
Servilia Caepionis 134, 254
Servius Galba 29
signifer 77
silk 19, 133
Spartacus 28
Stena (Celt-Iberian prostitute) 137-43, 146-50, 217, 223-4, 245-6, 249-50
Stena (wife of Marcus Livius Drusus) 15-16, 18-21, 23-5
subarmalis 75, 131, 201, 321
Suessiones 51, 98, 181
Sun Bin 8
Sun Tzu 8
Suren (Partian princess) 46-7, 364
Surena 46, 48, 364

T

Tarraco 22, 138, 356
Telemachus (raider) 218-19
tepidarium 15
Terentia (sister of Iccius) 114-15, 129-30, 364
testudo 22, 170
Thermopylae 30, 181, 200, 253, 330-1, 345, 359

Tiber 8
Timorix (Remi) 9-10, 12-14, 365
Titus Atius Labienus 29
Transalpine Gaul 11, 29
tribunal 252, 296
tribune 85, 104

V

Vasco (Celt-Iberian chieftain) 14-15, 365
Vesna (Slavic prostitute) 242, 244, 365
Vindiacos (retainer of Galba) 175-6, 181, 184-5, 188, 190-1

W

Wei Liao 8
Wu Shu 240

X

Xeno (forester) 17-18, 24-5
Xiongnu 44-5, 171

Y

Yuan Di 7

Z

Zhizhi 42-8, 72, 168-73, 240, 353